Lockdown Tales

Lockdown
Tales
Neal Asher

NewCon Press
England

First edition, published in the UK December 2020
by NewCon Press
41 Wheatsheaf Road, Alconbury Weston, Cambs, PE28 4LF, UK

NCP249 (hardback)
NCP250 (softback)

10 9 8 7 6 5 4 3 2 1

ISBN: 978-1-912950-74-4 (hardback)
978-1-912950-75-1 (softback)

Cover Art and front cover titles by Vincent Sammy
Editing and text layout by Ian Whates

Contents

LOCKDOWN TALES
An Introduction

Seven years ago as I write this I was feeling very pleased with myself. I'd got well ahead of my Macmillan publishing schedule of one book a year and written an entire trilogy to first draft well before I had to hand in the first book. This was the Transformation Trilogy consisting of *Dark Intelligence*, *War Factory* and *Infinity Engine*. Now I had time to turn my attention to other projects, like getting back to writing some short stories. As it turned out, I'd written the trilogy just in time to watch my wife die of bowel cancer, and it tided me over that hideous time and what ensued. I did write during that time: 20,000 words to start off a new Owner trilogy and the start of another Polity book, but with my mind screwed the lengthy concentration a book requires escaped me and I kept deciding the work was rubbish, constantly rewriting it and making false starts on other projects. Three years later, while I was still in this state, a project came along that pushed me to make some changes: dumping a toxic relationship, returning to the UK from Crete, and getting on with some WORK. That project was involvement in the initial stages of the *Terminator Dark Fate* film.

From then on the pieces of my mind started coming back together and work continued. The Polity book I had alternately loved and hated was near completion and definitely all over the place, but I worked it and it became *The Soldier* – first book of the Rise of the Jain trilogy. I didn't stop and had all but completed the next book – *The Warship* – by the time the first was published. I then wrote the final book *The Human* well before *The Warship* came to be published and so it continued. With these three books done my latest contract with Macmillan finished and I again turned to writing short stories. The problem here was that my mind still seemed to be in novel writing mode and after one or two longish 'short stories' one grew legs and kept running.

Talking with Bella Pagan, my editor at Macmillan, about a new contract, I made the suggestion that had long been on my mind, that maybe it was time to write some stand-alone books. These would give new readers entry points into the Polity universe, which now stood well above twenty books. She thought that a good idea and so the new contract began. The short story with legs turned into the tale of a clone delivered to the king of the prador's ship and, told in first-person, it zoomed along to become *Jack Four* – first book of the new contract. But still way ahead I again turned to writing short stories. Yeah, I did a couple, but then another grew in the telling as I filled in background. This became something quite odd with a timeline all over the place, but it worked. I completed it to first draft with the provisional title *Raptors*. Weapons development in the Polity can be a complicated and vicious exercise.

With these two books done to first draft it was time to get back to those damned short stories – this was in 2019 after my return from Crete late in the year. I got into them and though producing one for an anthology that can be classified as short, everything else just kept growing. These weren't short stories; they were novellas. What the hell. I was enjoying them so kept writing and looking forward to what next. Also on the horizon was the enjoyable prospect of my return to Crete in the spring. Then along came coronavirus. I continued writing the novellas. What else was there to do besides get some exercise and do a bit of shopping? A couple have been published. One called *Moral Biology* was taken by Analog Magazine and another called *The Bosch* is on Amazon Kindle and POD. But what to do with the rest? How about a collection? What should I call it…Well you see the answer to that here.

Neal Asher,
June 2020

In the story "The Bosch", published on Amazon, I played with the idea of the 'far future Polity'. Imagine a time when the Polity has collapsed or in some manner moved on. It has always, remember, been the aim of the AIs to get humanity to catch up. In this future the dregs and ruins of the Polity remain because, well, stuff gets abandoned, and there are always those who simply won't move on or by accident get left behind. But of course it is not the case that those past Polity citizens have moved into some ethereal realm or sublimed. They're still about, but maybe in forms most would not recognise. Here's another story set in that milieu.

THE RELICT

The sirens sounded first and black-clad Cheever grandmas made the fist sign to their God as they ran for cover. Seemingly exhausting their energy after a run of three soundings, the sirens died, and then Rune could hear the groan of the Gorst-vaankle engines of the bombers. He walked out onto his terrace and peered up at the sky, seeing nothing until the guns of Foreton lit up the clouds to show the neat array of cruciform gunships dropping their loads on the town. Supposedly he was safe out here in the village of Meeps, because the Grooger were after the warehouse and factory district lying between Foreton and the sea, but the weariness of war had begun to impinge, command structures were breaking down, and many crews now tended to drop their loads anywhere on the mainland here, before reaching the range of Foreton's guns, or while escaping them.

He grimaced. Weariness might well be impinging, but this conflict was set to run and run. Here on mainland Cheever they had taken many factories underground, and many communal dwellings too, and they had the metals, the coal and had maintained wartime production at a peak. All they seemed in danger of was running out of people, though the Church had foreseen that and made all forms of contraception illegal. Meanwhile, a similar situation existed out at the islands: the Grooger had their factory rafts, undersea facilities, and access to raw materials to keep their production up as did the Cheever. This would last for at least another twenty years. Both sides had good defences and the ability to attack the other side, but though the detestation of each for the other ran right down to the roots of religious indoctrination, neither side committed more to the war than they could sustain.

As a particularly ugly relict digger the villages had long ago labelled as mentally subnormal, there were many things Rune should not know. For example, he should not know that it would take the Cheever between ten and fifteen years to finally find the large uranium ore deposit in one of their mountain chains, then maybe five years to develop nuclear weapons which, if used, would drive the Grooger to use the biotech weapons they would be struggling to develop by that time. Based on the viruses here, with their huge genome, and being deployed in a radioactive environment, mutation was inevitable. It would be a perfect storm. Presently the war was killing hundreds of Cheevers and Groogers every day. The future scenario would result in over two billion dead.

The bombing lasted half an hour, by which time the Crudas Moon had lit up green – that same green separating horizon from sky prior to sunrise. The gunships became easily visible as they turned for home in frosted-emerald clouds. Without fear he watched them passing overhead, ready to make a second turn out over the mountains and head out to sea again – their route in to avoid the sea forts off the coast of Foreton. But then a sucking thump seemed to pass right through him, the dusk lit up with a bright orange explosion, and he hurtled back to crash into his wooden door shutters.

Rune walked down the concrete road pushing a barrow loaded with his relict hunter tools. Houses lay in ruin with fires burning in the rubble about a crater twenty feet across. Others were arriving too with shovels and picks and some helped themselves to some of his tools. He pulled on his snake hide gloves, took up a pick and, utterly in character, looked around dimly where to start.

'Over there, Rune,' said Drast the air raid warden. 'The entrance to the Loober cellar should be about two spans down.'

Rune headed where directed and began hauling out stone blocks and shattered timber, going back to fetch a shovel when what remained was too small to pick up with his hands. As he worked, and as others worked around him digging for other cellar hatches, he saw Ma Loober being hauled from rubble over to his right. The blast had rendered her undignified in death, stripping away her clothes. He eyed the body with its bald head and lip tendrils, hands with three fingers and rows of six teats down her front, her yellow-green skin and back ridge with adult scales. But she was a perfectly normal Cheever or Grooger. Rune, with his extra fingers, olive skin, a head he had to shave every day not to look too aberrant, and lack of a back ridge, was the deformity.

By mid-morning he had made good progress digging down to the hatch, especially when his apprentices Snerl and Gibbon joined him, and by lunchtime the hatch was open and the dusty surviving Loobers crawling out.

'Won't be finding any relicts here,' said Snerl.

'Well yeah,' said Gibbon. 'They carted off Ma Loober earlier.'

Rune's response of smacking him across the back of the head for that felt utterly automatic. The boy seemed to invite it. By the afternoon all the survivors were found – the eight dead piled up ready for the long composting service in the evening.

'No further digging today, boys,' he told them – a general term for them since Snerl was female. 'But up bright and early in the morning. We have a relict to find.'

In the evening Rune shaved his head again, put on his best cloak, cotton trousers and pointy boots and headed down to the church. Most of the village was in attendance since though that might not be enforced it was always healthy. Notable absence from services usually resulted in a report from the Rector to Foreton and a visit from the ecclesiastical police. Those who returned always did so with a renewal of faith, burns on their back ridge and pissing blood for a few days.

The church stood down by the road, an open structure below with the Rector's apartments supported in the upper section by arches. Rune stood meekly in the crowd with his head bowed, repeated the prayers as he should and made the responses he must, all the time trying not to catch the Rector's eye. The man did not like him – thought that one so deformed should not be a relict digger, and had been looking for excuses to report him for a long time. But only some major infraction could lose Rune his job since his papers of recommendation had come from the Foreton Divinity College itself.

The Rector stood up in a pulpit overlooking the crowd and the mulcher that had been wheeled out earlier. The first body – that of Ma Loober, now clad in paper robes – was placed on the upper trapdoor, while the Sexton Bains cranked the starting handle. At the correct juncture, when everyone was singing a song that bore a striking similarity to one called Jerusalem – sung in another time on a very different world – the trapdoor opened and dropped Ma Loober inside. With a crunching sound the machine rendered her down to slurry and the pipe leading from it expanded, a fine stinky spray from the decay within the pipe issuing from one hole as her remains made their way to the composting pits. The other bodies went in at their turns and then it was all over and the crowd moving away. Rune stuck with them, keeping ducked down, but it seemed he had been spotted and the crowd parted ahead of him to reveal the Rector.

'Rune,' said the man, stepping in and jabbing him in the chest with one solid finger.

'Your Reverance,' Rune replied.

'So what you found up there?' asked the man. 'You've only ever found us one relict in all your time here.' He scratched his chin. 'What was it? A ching glass or something?'

'It was a piece of Polity era chainglass,' Rune replied. 'Your Reverance.'

'Not much use then, was it?'

'Small items find their place in the greater good,' Rune replied.

The Rector grimaced – he did not like having scripture quoted back at him.

'What do you have up there?' the Rector asked again.

'There appears to be an item in the lava rock. I cannot know what it is till I reveal it.'

'But how do you know something is there?'

'My training at the Divinity College was most intensive.' Again the grimace and before the Rector could say anything more, Rune continued, 'My training indicated something might be there, and now I have proof.'

'Oh really?'

Rune dug in his pocket and took out an octagon of material the size of a coin. 'This is ceramal with meta-material layers throughout. It is likely a fragment of armour.'

'Armour you say?' the Rector then showed annoyance at his surprise and said, 'This has been documented?'

'I have drawn up the papers but other events this morning have prevented me from filing them with the Sexton.' He could have filed them the day before, but was deliberately giving the Rector small infractions to keep him happy – keep him thinking he was making headway in getting rid of Rune.

'This morning was no excuse. I will report your tardiness.'

'My apologies.' Rune bowed his head as if in shame, then moved away.

Dawn came with flashes of light from the ocean and rumbles like distant thunder – doubtless a sea battle occurring out there. Snerl and Gibbon were waiting for him when he exited the house carrying his packed lunch and flask. They had their packs of tools acquired during their apprenticeship and as usual did not look eager for the task ahead. Rune collected up his wheelbarrow, put his lunch inside his pack and set out with them trailing behind.

'Should be a good day today!' he said. 'We're sure to find something – I feel it in my water.'

Snerl grunted dismissively and Rune knew Gibbon was making the buffoon sign behind his back. He had said the same thing each morning for weeks now and, like the villagers they were, they had come to the conclusion that his appearance did indicate stupidity. This whole reaction he found amusing, since they were unaware that he wore the appearance of the humans who had built the Polity they unearthed – from whose fragments they sought to garner godlike knowledge. It also amused him that today really was the day they would find something.

They trudged up the path from the village, first through fields of vegetables bordered with squat walnuts and artichoke cycads, then up through a grove of tea oaks to the mountain path. Soon they were walking between boulders and stands of pine in one of the few areas of Cheever too expensive and labour-intensive to turn over to agriculture. Finally they reached the slopes of the Dombar Volcano. Here Rune paused to look back at the patchwork fields, groves and irrigation ditches. The stone buildings of Meeps showed just below him and in the distance he could see Foreton with the sea lying beyond. The flashes of gunfire were muted now the sun had risen but he could still see them, as he could see fires burning on the far side of the town. Missile strike, he suspected. The Grooger must have got one of their missile barges near enough to bombard the town. They, like the Cheever, had yet to acquire the technology for long-range ballistic missiles.

The path wound up to and then petered out alongside a sheet of old lava down the slope. High above some steam rose from the hot springs in the caldera. Rune climbed up on the lava before taking hold of the barrow the other two lifted up, and then they followed. Finally they reached a dip in the rock and moved back along it to the workings. At the back a lava tube cave speared down deep. Their excavation wasn't there, but on one side of the opening. Over the weeks they had chiselled a chunk the size of a small house out of the rock on that side, since it was highly frangible and in places filled with bubbles – almost like pumice. Rune pulled on his gloves, took up his hammer and chisels, and set to work on the section he had been working before. Snerl and Gibbon returned to their sections – Gibbon stopping her work periodically to shovel away debris.

Rune worked around and around a protrusion like a rose bud a metre long, chopping away the stuff easy to break leaving a core of rock similar to obsidian. Again he knew more than he should, because he knew precisely what lay underneath and where to deliver the correct blows. By mid-morning he was ready.

'I think there's something here,' he said, then delivered a hard blow in precisely the place he had been avoiding for some hours.

A great chunk of the brittle stone, a foot long and wide and six inches thick, fell away. He glanced down at the imprint on the rock of what he had revealed. Of course the rock had come off easily, for what lay underneath had a frictionless smooth surface even molten rock could not bind to.

'Yes, definitely found something.'

Snerl and Gibbon came over.

'Looks like a crab claw,' said Snerl. 'What is it?'

'Yes, it looks like that,' Rune replied, in no mind to correct him. If he told them it was a ceramal and meta-material facsimile of a scorpion's claw plated with nano-chain chromium, that would display far more knowledge than he could possibly have. Anyway, scorpions were something only academics in Foreton knew about from the recovered knowledge, because the creatures did not exist on this world.

He stepped back, eying the thing. A claw like that could snip a person in half with infinite ease, and he knew it had.

'Right, we'll work back from this. If it is like a crab claw as you suppose, Snerl, there may be more behind it.'

They set to with greater eagerness now. Snerl fetched a pick to work on the softer stone, his growing muscles bulging, while Rune and Gibbon worked with their chisels. By midday they had revealed the claw entire, its fat joint with a cylindrical object attached down the side with a ring of holes in one end, a section of thick limb behind it with vein-like protrusions running down it, and then the next joint. Such was their eagerness for this work that Snerl pointed out it was lunch time an hour later than usual.

They sat eating sandwiches and drinking soup, gazing in fascination at what they had revealed.

'I think you two need to set to work there.' Rune pointed at a lava bulge a little further along. 'If this is some sort of facsimile of a creature, the positioning indicates that you might find another claw there.'

'You don't want us working on this?' Gibbon pointed at the revealed claw.

Rune shook his head. 'We're getting in each other's way. Don't worry. If I'm wrong I'll let you take over from me. It seems unlikely you'll damage anything.' Already Snerl had pick-axed the thing and not even left a scratch.

Two hours later Snerl shouted victory and Gibbon laughed in delight. They had revealed the other claw. Snerl and Gibbon subsequently revealed more of the limb they had found, with all its odd attachments and protrusions, while Rune chiselled down to the base attachment point of his limb – the whole thing now standing clear of the rock.

'Okay, we're done for today,' said Rune, and it was with unusual reluctance that his two apprentices quit their work. As they returned to the village Rune knew that Snerl would, after eating a large meal, be straight round to the Rector's apartments. And tonight the Rector would be calling Foreton. His intervention here was reaching its end at last, his thumb firmly on the scales of the war.

On the second day, Rune began to reveal the clustered sensory arrays of the head and the macerating equipment below. The nightmarish thing had two glassy red eyes set within all this, over each of which he could spread his whole hand. When he did this, feeling the cool surface against his palm, and then pulled it away, he was sure he saw a glimmer of something in the eye. He felt this must be imagination, though he did know the revealed armour would already be sucking up further energy from the sunlight. This of course was only in complement to the energy it had been harvesting from temperature changes in the rock and those parts of the EMR spectrum that penetrated it.

He chiselled with a little more care here because, though the materials were all incredibly hard and tough, the thing was powered down and none of its molecular binding fields in operation. Not that he really knew that, of course.

'So what do you reckon it is?' asked Gibbon when they stopped for lunch.

'I think it must be some kind of robot,' Rune replied. 'The Divinity College has much information on them. They were used in building and suchlike.'

'It was alive?' she asked.

'No, not in the sense that you or I are for it possessed no soul – it was merely a powered mechanism just a little more complicated than a piston engine.'

'I heard that they could think,' interjected Snerl, when he finally finished inhaling his sandwich.

'Yes, things like that have been said, but they are contrary to theological thought,' Rune reprimanded him, while laughing inside. Both here and out on the islands they believed in a god and a fall. The Polity was a strange combination of the Garden of Eden and the Tower of Babel. Humankind had been ejected for the usual. Now they must live good religious lives to return to their garden, while disagreements on precisely how those lives should be lived had led to the war. All of this was a very old story.

Meanwhile both sides sought to find fragments of that lost Polity from which to learn about their sin; the fact that much of what they found also turned out to be very useful in their growing technological bases was a bonus. Fragments of materials they found turned out to be so hard and tough they worked as almost wear-proof cutting tools for the metal they were now smelting. Chainglass got used in fine optics. Some materials, when attached up to a generator in the correct way, stored ridiculous amounts of energy. The shattered crystals they found, though certainly showing vastly complex structure at the microscopic level, which was as deep as they could reach, seemed to have no purpose at all. This was both amusing and sad, since those fragments were pieces of the minds that had built the Polity.

'Okay, let's get in a good afternoon's work before sundown,' said Rune when they had finished their meal.

They revealed the first legs and further curious devices attached either side of the thing's head. Rune gazed at these and the feed tubes leading into the body behind and, even though he was what he was, felt a shiver run down his spine. Finally, when they returned to the village, the Bishop's Hand and some of his police were waiting, as expected.

The Bishop's Hand stood by Rune's house with the Rector, the Sexton and four ecclesiastical police. Rune glanced over at Snerl and saw him duck his head guiltily, confirming what he had expected. The Hand stepped forwards, touched a curled finger to his chin then pointed the flat of his hand to Rune – a gesture meaning glad to meet you and I have something to say. It was so unexpectedly polite it took a moment for Rune to give the correct response.

'I am Bishop's Hand Eller, and you are Rune the relict digger.'

Eller was a slim individual without so much of a back ridge, his skin more yellow than green and his lip tendrils short and all but useless for testing his food. He was, in fact, closer in appearance to Rune than the four bulky soldiers he had brought with him. All were dressed in black uniforms – Eller having more in the way of silver decoration and less in the way of padding and armour plates. In such things Rune felt history tended to repeat itself.

'I am that,' Rune replied.

'You have found something in the mountains, yet the Rector has no report on it yet,' said Ellor, gesturing to the Rector who was now frowning at the two of them.

'I still haven't dug it free, your Reverence,' Rune replied. 'I was going to submit a report when I've revealed it all.'

Eller nodded. 'Okay, no problem. We've taken rooms in the village and you will take us out to your find in the morning. Is that suitable?'

Rune felt a degree of wariness kick in. The man was being far too reasonable, which meant intelligence.

'Fine by me,' he replied.

Eller turned to the Rector. 'Thank you for your assistance, Rector. I'll deal with things from here. I'm sure you have important work to be getting on with.' He eyed the Sexton, Snerl and Gibbon. 'I'm sure you all have places to go and things to do.'

The Rector looked set to explode, but his gaze strayed to the four ecclesiastical police and he deflated. 'Then a good evening to you,' he said, and turned away, the others scuttling after him.

Eller turned back to Rune. 'You will, meanwhile, join me for a meal and a drink in your local hostelry. Do you need to get cleaned up first?'

'No sir – I'm hungry now.'

He was dusty and sweaty from work, but with the depredations of war, standards of cleanliness were much lower than they had once been. He dumped his wheelbarrow by the house and followed Eller and his men down into the village, entering the local tavern where old male Cheevers were downing shot glasses of plum brandy and eating toasted bread biscuits spread with nut paste. Eller waved his men to a large table in one corner then headed over to another smaller table in the tavern. Rune felt the beady eyes watching him, Eller and his men. Entertainment was severely lacking in Meeps and everything would be noted, and gossiped about at length tomorrow.

'The Rector doesn't like you much,' said Eller. 'I suspect that has something to do with your appearance.' He gestured over Ma Dourt from the kitchen door.

'Since I am not pure Cheever I am apparently too stupid to be a relict digger,' Rune replied. He knew that pretending to be stupid here would not be a good idea.

Ma Dourt came over and they ordered food and drink. She lingered at the table hoping to hear something until one of the four policemen called her over. She lingered there too.

'Your appearance is that of an extreme throwback,' said Eller. 'People in the Polity looked like you in their primary form, though they had the ability to make extreme changes to their bodies.'

18

'Yes, apparently – from what I've read in the Divinity College Library.'

'You spent four years there,' said Eller. 'And qualified with high honours as a relict hunter. It quite surprised me how few people there remember you, considering your appearance.'

Rune shrugged. 'Perhaps that is because those who look as different as me are excluded from social circles. People tend more to remember the beautiful.'

It was all utter nonsense, since Rune had never actually been in the Divinity College, but he knew that Eller would have some fellow feeling here. The man was himself at variance from the norm and had doubtless been socially excluded. Quite possibly the same exclusion had been the driver of his ambition to take him to the position of Bishop's Hand, while it seemed likely his appearance would not allow him to climb any higher.

Instead of agreeing, Eller simply said, 'So tell me about what you have found,' just as Ma Dourt arrived with a carafe of brandy, two shot glasses and plate of paste biscuits. She hung around the table again till Eller politely enquired about who was cooking their food, then she moved off resentfully. Rune detailed what they had revealed from the rock, confining his description to that and any observations another relict digger might make, and not speculating too much on the find.

'It could well be a drone, maybe even a war drone,' Eller stated. 'General robots of the time only resembled living creatures because of utility of purpose, and those objects attached to the claws might well be weapons.'

Rune nodded, pretending some surprise, then realising he had done the wrong thing as Eller watched him. Eller knew that Rune knew.

'I did not want to speculate too much on what it was,' he said. 'I find things and knowledge is required for that, but it is for those higher in the Church to judge precisely what I have found. Perhaps it will be useful... for the war?'

It wasn't enough, for as their food arrived, Eller said, 'There is something not quite right about you, Rune. But I will find it out.'

When Rune woke up in the morning he felt as if he had been in a mental battle. Throughout the meal Eller had probed him and he found himself increasingly struggling to make the responses that fitted his present persona. The man kept dropping information bombs on him that were at the cutting edge of Cheever relict research, eased into heretical territory on some subjects and continually pushed for details of Rune's past. The man was very intelligent for what he was, and Rune did not want him to divine Rune's ultimate purpose here, which seemed all too possible. It was time to upgrade.

Rune washed and dressed, then went to stand in front of his mirror and gaze at himself. Almost certainly Eller had sent messages last night and investigators were on the case called Rune. He could intervene on the wider scale and shut that down, but his intention here had been to move events with a light a touch as possible. Such intervention could reveal a larger actor here to Eller, lead to paranoia and actions and responses that might stray into the unpredictable. The most sensible thing to do now would be to disappear, but Rune simply did not want to do that. This wasn't in the end about the best way to do something to save the most lives, since that would be utterly totalitarian seizing of power here and shutting down their war. Nor was it about subtle intervention that allowed a civilisation to go its own way, learn from its own mistakes. In the end it was about Rune and the way he wanted to do things, his interaction and his choices. And he wanted to stay and greet an old friend.

While staring into the mirror, he looked internally with other senses at the switches and sliders of his mind and this body he wore. He would become more useful, take on a persona more likely to stay with developments, and for this he clicked over the switches giving him access to greater mental resources. As his mind heated up and more of his whole being became accessible to him, this had immediate visible effects. His stance straightened, his eyes looked brighter and intelligence showed in the subtle shifting of muscles in his face. But further physical changes were required, since he was moving into dangerous territory in which he needed this body to be more able to survive and act quickly. He allowed the neurochemical changes in his mind and began to make demands on his body. The long inactive nansuite kicked into motion, biological processes changed, growth in many areas ramped up as his bones began toughening and his muscles layering in stronger more reactive materials. His heart rate increased to move blood increasingly laden with new factors about more quickly – a temporary measure until his heart grew to capacity. Further alveoli budded in his lungs. His skin thickened and began to acquire new dermal layers.

Rune turned away from the mirror, making a mental effort to suppress interior changes from showing too much externally. He then went to his fridge and cupboards to feed his sudden ravenous hunger and thirst. By the time he heard the vehicle he had eaten the equivalent of four standard meals here, and been to the toilet twice. Gulping from a large bottle of sugary mandarin juice he headed out onto his terrace and looked over to the track up into the mountains.

The vehicle was military – an armoured car with pairs of caterpillar treads front and back – but the only weapon was a turret machinegun on the roof of the cab. Numerous items and supplies bulked under a canvas tarpaulin over the back of the thing, while at least twenty workers in drab olive overalls and carrying hand tools were following it. Behind them walked three of Eller's police, carrying squat heavy machineguns. For a second Rune thought the twenty were prisoners, but with his mind now functioning on a higher level, he read detail he would not have seen before. The casual way they walked and talked with each other, minutiae of movement, their physical condition and finally the fact that some of them had sidearms strapped on. These were sappers out of Foreton North – builders of defences and gun installations.

The truck stopped and Eller climbed out, looking up towards him. The man gestured peremptorily for him to come over. He raised a hand in acknowledgement and returned inside to gather up food and drink to put in his bag with his hammers and chisels. Outside he did not bother collecting up his wheelbarrow. When he saw Snerl and Gibbon hanging back looking bewildered he gestured them over as he headed for the truck.

'A little assistance in your endeavour,' said Eller, gazing at him with a slightly puzzled expression.

Rune nodded to the back of the truck. 'You have a compressor and air chisels?' Before Eller could answer he continued, 'We'll need to do some work on the way to make a road up the side of the old lava flow. I suggest you also requisition a flatbed trailer.'

Eller just stared at him for a long moment, then reached back into the cab of the lorry and took out a radio handset. It was very modern for it had its own aerial and power supply and did not need a wire to connect it to a larger set in the truck. Rune suspected a piece of power-storing Polity meta-material inside the thing, but wouldn't know without a closer look. He glanced at Snerl who was about to say something, and held a finger to his lips – a gesture that had not changed in an age. He then pointed to the men behind and made a walking motion with his fingers. They got the idea and headed over to join those men, knowing that hanging around near Eller might get them sent away.

Eller walked back alongside the truck still holding the radio. 'Get this tarpaulin off,' he instructed, and the men in overalls quickly got to work removing it. When it had finally been rolled back, Eller weighed the radio in one hand for a moment, then brought it up to his face.

'Jaston, are you receiving?'

The acknowledgement came back with a loud crackle.

'I'm handing you over to our chief relict digger. He will give you a list of the things we may need.' He next held out the radio to Rune.

Rune took it. It seemed he had now become the 'chief relict digger'. That was faster than he had expected, and he knew that was all down to Eller and something the man suspected about him. As he took the radio he analysed that: backwater relict digger, obviously intelligent, detail about his past lacking. Eller probably thought he was someone high up in the Church hierarchy – perhaps the bastard son of a Bishop – put into an ecclesiastical job out of harm's way. Either that or a spy.

Rune walked around the truck peering into the back, while Eller walked with him, hands folded behind his back. They had a large generator there, compressor, reels of hose and air chisels. Other items included hand tools of every variety, wheel barrows, scaffold boards and a large cable winch. The last two would be helpful in moving what he had been digging out of the lava, but not sufficient. He also noted tents, lights, cooking gear and food, and other things intended to set up a semi-permanent encampment. He considered whether or not to wait, then decided against it.

'Jaston?' he enquired into the radio.

'Yes, I'm Jaston. Who am I speaking to?'

'My name is Rune – the relict digger.'

'Eller tells me you have a list?'

'A provisional one to begin with,' said Rune, while watching Eller's expression. 'Once the item is dug clear we'll need a lot more things to get it out of there. One is a flatbed trailer with a rating upward of twenty tons. A tank transport may do, but it would probably be better to reinforce it. The ramps for such a trailer will be required too, also reinforced. We will also need hardened steel machine skates and rollers, a Gratlian Yard ship winch rated at thirty tons upwards and a great deal of reinforced webbing straps.'

'So a big item weighing more than a tank?' said Jaston, just a little breathlessly.

'Yes, very definitely.'

'Anything else?'

'For the present no – we first need to dig it out.'

'Pass me back to the Bishop's Hand.'

Rune did so. He had noted the changes in Eller's expression – the combination of surprise and suspicion, then the confidence that this was a puzzle he would solve as he always had.

'Yes, get them,' Eller replied briefly to Jaston's query. He then turned off the radio and eyed Rune. 'From what you told me last night I can't see how you can know what is underneath that rock…'

'The second claw was precisely where I estimated it would be should the robot be in one piece. The size of the head thus far revealed indicates the size of the body behind and what it will take to move it.'

'But your estimation on weight interests me,' said Eller. 'We have found Polity items before that are ridiculously light – composed of bubble metal.' He paused, frowning at the ground, the looked up again. 'How do you know it will be so heavy?'

Rune reached into his pocket and took out the hexagonal chunk of armour he had first shown to the Rector. 'This is the item that first indicated to me that there might be Polity tech in the vicinity, while formations in the old lava flow indicated an object that had not been shifted or ablated by it but created some strange flow patterns. Hold out your hand.'

Eller stared at him dead faced. He had given an order to a Bishop's Hand and his mode of address had not been sufficiently respectful. This had been precisely Rune's intention – the knock on psychological effects culminating in Eller estimating his usefulness upwards. After a moment the man did hold out his hand, and Rune dropped the object into it.

'Damn,' said Eller, offence immediately forgotten. The coin-sized piece of armour was heavier than lead. Heavier in fact than any substance the Cheevers had ever refined or made. But then the Cheevers did not have factory facilities on the surfaces of brown dwarf stars, gravity presses, or techniques for collapsing down matter and increasing molecular bonding forces.

'I thought this might be a piece of the item's armour,' Rune said. 'Now I'm not so sure because its armour does not seem to be formed in pieces, however I am sure that the item's armour is of a similar if not the same material. That being the case, even just one of the claws revealed may weigh in at many tons for its armour alone. God knows what lies underneath it.'

Eller grimaced at him for a moment then nodded. It had actually been an acceptable use of the Lord's name. He turned and gestured to the men nearby and they moved back to reattach the tarpaulin.

'You will ride in the cab with me,' he said, heading there.

They reached the edge of the lava flow where Rune slid easily into the role of foreman, issuing instructions the moment he climbed down from the cab. The hoses had a good reach, so he instructed that the generator and compressor run while still on the back of the truck, and the men set to work with air chisels. He meanwhile included Snerl and Gibbon, getting them moving rubble and providing drinks. It took four hours to cut a rough road the truck was more than capable of climbing with its caterpillar treads and Eller became anxious to move on.

'It would be better to make this stable while we have the equipment here.' Rune gestured to the road. 'When we come back this way with the item we don't want any accidents or you might need to requisition a new trailer, or vehicle, or face other problems depending on what has collapsed or where the item has fallen.'

Eller reluctantly conceded the point.

Rune now endeared himself with the workers by ordering a lunch break. After that they worked for another two hours cutting the road wider and using an air-driven compactor to crush down the broken stone of the slope into something a lot firmer.

'That'll do,' Rune called, and they set out again.

The tracked vehicle motored up the new road with ease and once on top of the lava, where the going was smooth, Eller accelerated ahead of the walking men.

'Go easy,' said Rune. He pointed ahead. 'You see that ridge?' Eller nodded. 'Go to the right and around the bottom of it.'

'Why? This vehicle could go over it easily.'

'Yes, it could, but such a ridge is usually indication of a lava tube underneath. It might well collapse.'

Eller nodded and did as instructed. Finally they turned into the declivity leading to the mouth of the lava tube where the workings were located. Eller parked and engaged the brakes. The light was behind them now as the sun set in a blaze of green and gold. The claws protruding from the rock cast dark shadows down into the lava tube. The scene looked quite sinister, as if some terrible monster was intent to break free from its prison of centuries. Rune acknowledged to himself that, with some provisos, this was indeed the case.

'My God,' said Eller – again acceptable usage.

'Quite,' said Rune.

They climbed out of the truck and walked up to look at the claws, the limbs and that portion of the head revealed behind. Two red eyes glinted at them, and Rune felt sure now that not all the glimmer there was due to reflection.

'This is almost certainly a Polity war drone,' said Eller.

Rune nodded. 'I've never fully admitted that to myself until now,' he lied. 'If my reading is correct, I would say it is one of those made during the monster war.'

In the Cheever and Grooger mythology a kind of Ragnorak lay in the distant past. The Polity had gone to war against monsters and it had been devastating. Humans had fought in it, spaceships too, and machines like the one buried in the rock here. In this mythology the war had come immediately prior to the Fall – the only part of it that was completely wrong.

Rune turned to watch the workers approaching – Snerl and Gibbon running ahead of them. 'We'll set up camp and get to work in the morning,' he said. 'Better to get organised in daylight and now just get set up what we can.

'Seems like a plan,' said Eller noncommittally.

'You two might as well head home,' he told his two apprentices when they breathlessly arrived. Then seeing their disappointment added, 'Return in the morning first thing.'

As they turned and headed away, Eller stepped up beside him to watch them go. 'You, however, will remain here with us,' he said.

'Of course.' Rune smiled. The Bishop's Hand now did not trust him out of sight, which in terms of his intention to stay with this was a good thing, but in other ways might be bad.

In the evening they had set up four tents, a cooking area, the lights, generator and compressor. Eller slept in a tent with his four officers while Rune managed to acquire a blanket from supplies, but not one of the foam mattresses. It didn't matter – his body now had no problem with a bed of stone and sleep had become a matter of choice. He lay flat on his back and simply switched himself off for the required hours.

One of the workers cooked a breakfast of fish and vegetable stew from dried supplies, complemented by bread obviously bought in Meeps. Rune ate as much of that as he could without being branded a glutton, then complemented it from his own supplies. He then selected two of the men to follow him to where a hole lay open in the top of a lava tube and instructed them to set up the toilet tent there, before returning.

Next he had the men chiselling and shifting the rubble they dug out, cutting a circuit around the item, but also instructed them to cut test holes in towards it, as if he didn't know its shape under the rock and had to keep checking. Snerl and Gibbon arrived tardily and he waved them over and headed to where Eller was watching the work.

'We're going to need more food and water,' he said to the man. 'These two can fetch it for you, but they'll need money.'

Eller eyed the two. 'I'll send two of my guards with them.' He marched off to issue instructions and give money to the two guards. A little while later the four set off with two of the barrows. Rune felt glad his apprentices were now included – he owed them at least that. But in the end, when they towed the war drone out of here, they would remain in the village. It would be the safest place for them.

By the evening they had cut a path all around the war drone wide enough for wheel barrows and for two people to easily pass each other. In the oval within, they had made exploratory cuts to find armour.

When they didn't find any near the back they cut in, but in doing so revealed the spiked tail high up.

'You are familiar with the bestiaries in the Divinity College,' Eller commented.

'I am indeed,' Rune replied.

'I wasn't sure until seeing that tail.'

Rune nodded, but allowed Eller to say the words.

'The thing looks like a giant metal scorpion.'

'Yes, one has to wonder what toxins that sting delivered.' Rune knew that the tail could deliver any toxin the drone decided to make in the factories inside its body, that the tail could also extrude a wide variety of boring tools, but that mostly it used it as a spiked club in close combat for punching through armour – the spike being formed of a collimated diamond material that wouldn't blunt its tip even piercing advanced ceramal.

The lights came on as the sun went down and, pretending he did not know precisely what lay underneath the stone, Rune ordered the air chisels shut down and hand chiselling to commence. After one man managed to smack his own hand with a club hammer and another dropped a rock on another's foot as if performing a comedy routine, he called a halt to the work. The cook meanwhile had been preparing an evening meal, while Eller's guards had gone off to fetch fire wood. They sat around campfires eating bread, roast vegetables and meat and drinking hot tea. Eller of course had his own personal fire and invited Rune to sit with him.

'One has to speculate what this will mean for the war,' the man said.

Rune immediately became cautious. 'Quite possibly very little at all.'

'And your reasoning on that?' The enquiry was light – just conversation, apparently.

'We have learned much from the relicts we have found,' said Rune, 'but very little we have been able to copy. We use their power storage devices and we use their hard materials, but we cannot make them.' He waved toward the drone. 'We may find weapons here we can activate, but I very much doubt that any of them will make a difference to the war. It is a matter of scale. Perhaps we will find something to kill an enemy quickly, or shoot down a gunship, or sink a missile raft, but it can only be in one place at a time. The war is large and on multiple fronts. The enemy is numerous and their gunships and rafts are many.'

'This is obviously something you've been thinking about.'

Rune shrugged. 'Of course it is.'

'But my understanding is that these drones were very powerful, and that they wielded devastating weapons…'

'The writings in the Divinity College indicate so,' Rune said noncommittally.

'Could they be wrong?' Eller enquired.

This had now become dangerous territory. If he started criticising holy writ he might well end up on a charge of heresy. He then considered how, if Eller so wished, charges of heresy were not necessary should the man want to dispense with him.

When Rune did not reply, Eller added, 'You may speak freely on this matter, here. We are just two men discussing possibilities.'

'I would not want to inadvertently slip into heresy while talking to the Bishop's Hand,' said Rune. 'That would be unhealthy.'

Eller nodded while staring into the flames, then said, 'Have you heard of the Occam Heresy?'

'I have. The heresy is that only verifiable facts can be assumed as truth, while ecclesiastical thought is only speculation. It is denial of God. It negates the idea that the Fall was due to the sin of pride.'

'Very dangerous in religious circles,' said Eller. 'We wouldn't want facts to get in the way now would we?'

Rune stared at him for a long moment realising Eller had just broadly hinted that he was in agreement with that heresy. The man had given something and expected something in return. Rune well understood that perhaps this might be a lure into a trap, but decided to take the risk.

'We have no physical proof that the war drones wielded great power,' he said. 'All we have are the writings, translated and copied down the ages. It could be that some of those who did that job exaggerated.'

'Quite,' said Eller, grimacing in disappointment.

Rune didn't feel very good about himself just then, since the writings, if anything, had downplayed the contribution of war drones in that long ago war, in preference exaggerating what the humans did. He felt this to be necessary, however, since he did not want them to be too cautious with this drone once it reached Foreton. Eller's present disappointment would then be dismissed, though whether he would like the consequences of that stayed open to question.

A little while later Eller retired to his tent and this was the signal for everyone else to do the same. Rune watched them all go while tossing twigs into the fire. Someone switched off the generator and the lights went out. He waited just a little bit longer then stood up in the moonlit night and headed over to the excavation, finally coming to stand before the now fully exposed head of the war drone.

'I wonder how much you can see now,' he said quietly. 'And I wonder if you care enough to rise out of sleep.'

The eyes flickered brief ruby fire and flakes of lava fell from one of the claws as if it had moved, just a little bit.

Over the next four days they chiselled away all the remaining stone. Rune considered ordering work to remove all the remaining stone underneath as well, but that was a subterfuge he did not need, for they all now knew that the lava had not bonded to its armour. On the second day Eller took the vehicle back to Meeps and returned with a reinforced tank trailer with a ship winch attached, the skates and rollers and the heavy webbing straps.

First they used the smaller winch – bolted down hard in the ground – levers crow bars and physical toil to pull the drone free. It did slide out on its belly off of a pedestal of stone – that being higher than the thing's feet – and as it slid off the legs hinged to the same level flaking off remaining stone. Seeing those legs were now moveable, Rune ran ropes around them and across its back, using a tourniquet bar to lift the feet from the ground. Next they backed in the trailer, put down the ramp and attached the ship winch. It then took many hours with jacks and levers to lift the thing up sufficiently to insert roller bars. As the winch hauled the drone round to face the trailer, one of the claws dropped to the ground, the points of the claw stabbing straight into stone. Despite much effort with ropes and then webbing straps they struggled to raise these up, and instead rested them on chunks of metal on top of skates, with a work crew using levers detailed to push these ahead of the thing.

The ramp bowed underneath the drone, and the trailer sank down to the bottom of its suspension, but by evening they had it as secured as they could with ropes and straps, and then covered with a tarpaulin.

Eller wanted to start the journey back to Meeps and then Foreton right then, but Rune advised against it. Eller reluctantly agreed.

Later Eller told him, 'We'll stop off at your house and you can collect some belongings. Plan on a long stay in Foreton.'

'As you command, Hand Eller,' Rune replied.

Eller snorted annoyance and walked away.

Before sunrise another air raid was in progress over Foreton. They turned off the excavation lights and waited, because it was not unknown for the gunships to hit likely targets outside of the town. Rune watched a gunship shedding pieces of itself and streaks of fire as it fell to the mountains inland of Foreton. As he was watching, Snerl and Gibbon came out to stand beside him.

'I am going with the drone to Foreton,' he told them.

'You won't be coming back, will you,' said Gibbon.

He turned and studied her. As ever the perspicacity of some people surprised him. How could she possibly know this for sure, and how had she been so right?

'I expect I will be gone a long time,' he lied. 'Doubtless they'll send another relict digger to Meeps. This find will ensure that.'

'You're not what you seem,' said Snerl.

Rune stared at him blankly. 'I am just a relict digger.'

They looked at each other, definitely annoyed, then headed away. He knew that was goodbye. He hoped they survived what was to come.

Once the gunships had departed and the sun drew an emerald line across the horizon, Rune instructed that the back of the vehicle be loaded with equipment. He hadn't intended that at first, but the weight of the load on the trail had lifted the back of the truck high on its suspension so the treads were almost loose underneath. The new load in the back brought that down again and made it stable. Once this was done, Eller climbed into the cab on the passenger side and waved Rune to the other.

'Is this a good idea?' Rune asked as he climbed inside.

'I'm assuming you know how to drive?'

Rune dipped his head in acknowledgement and started the vehicle. In first gear he motored slowly away from the excavation while the workers stowed final items into their packs. Those same men were still in sight behind on the journey to Meeps so slowly did Rune drive. Eller did not object – they were on their way now.

In Meeps, Rune returned inside his house and packed up two large bags with clothing and other items, then looked around the interior at stuff he had collected over the last three years. None of it was important to him. He headed back to the truck leaving his key in the door.

'We'll send another relict digger here.' Eller stabbed a thumb behind. 'There might be other stuff underneath that lava flow.'

Rune acknowledged that with a nod. This was confirmation of what he had told his apprentices and of what they suspected.

The road around Meeps wound down to the main road where Rune took the truck up a few gears, then slowed again when the trailer showed signs of beginning to fish tail. An hour of driving brought them down onto the agricultural plain – fields pale green with spring barley and young vegetable plants, fruit trees shedding their blossoms across the road, which slowed him down further. They reached a checkpoint where Eller unnecessarily showed papers to the guards, for it was obvious they recognised him. He then stepped out and barked orders and they brought out cans of diesel to fill the truck's tanks. When one of the guards strayed close to the trailer he drew his sidearm and fired once in the air, and barked some more orders. They then quickly raised the barrier to let them through.

Warehouses and factory units steadily displaced fields and the traffic increased. Most of it was military or ecclesiastical – there being little distinction here. Rune noted one area that had been hit, piles of rubble and broken fibre sheeting lying between monolithic presses and furnaces, some bodies yet to be removed by those in hazard gear picking through the wreckage. The air became thicker, smoky with the stink of burning coal and oil. Larger buildings began to appear: ecclesiastical bureaucracy, ministries and clean manufacturing blocks. Rune thought they might be heading straight into the centre until Eller directed him elsewhere. Eventually they pulled into a yard while the man spoke on his radio. Large doors opened in the warehouse ahead. Within, Rune eyed the men in black and kaki overalls, the beams in the roof and winches up there, and all the other equipment and work benches scattered all around. Had this been quickly prepared since he found the drone, or was it something they had prepared for a long time?

Even as he drew to a halt workers began scrambling over the trailer, pulling off the tarpaulin while the big doors closed behind. Eller climbed out and he did too, moving back to watch the work. The workers quickly wrapped heavy straps, which seemed to be a mix of metal and fibre, about the drone attached a series of winch cables from the ceiling beams. They began hoisting the thing up even as someone else climbed into the truck and drove the trailer out from underneath, taking it out again through doors that were open at the other end of the warehouse. Next they came in with heavy steel pallet jacks and began raising them as the cables lowered the done. It came down with a crunch. Someone climbed on top, cutting the ropes and stripping them away, the feet dropping down to the floor in eerie silence as if the thing were getting comfortable. They brought in further jacks and, using the hoists, again raised the claws level with the drone's eyes.

But he wondered what now? They had their X-ray machines but they were all but useless in penetrating that armour. They had many tools and machines, but nothing that could dismantle this drone. They would now measure and catalogue it, write tracts about it, break their machines on it and finally consign the drone to some hidden location and pretend it had never been found. That was, of course, if it just remained there totally inert.

Eller showed him to quarters attached to the warehouse and there he installed himself. The accommodation was modern but austere, though food had been provided in a noisy fridge in the corner, and he cooked himself a meal on the smelly coal gas stove. He then washed and changed and went back to see what was occurring. Yes, they were measuring the drone and meticulously recording detail of its shape. They even managed to obtain its weight from the jacks underneath. As he arrived they were pulling away a pedestal drilling machine, many blunt and broken drill bits lying on the floor.

'I would be interested in how you would approach this matter,' Eller said to him, as they spectated from a couple of packing crates. 'How do we learn from this thing if we cannot even penetrate its armour?'

The question was casual and loaded. Eller had understood that Rune knew more than he was letting on, and now intended to test his utility in this matter. Rune looked around the interior of the warehouse. Buss bars ran around the walls and twenty feet in from the walls into which they could plug their various machines. They carried a heavy current required by those same machines.

'I suggest feeding it,' he replied.

Eller turned and looked at him in puzzlement.

Rune shrugged. 'It must have a power source inside that is probably dead. It must also have methods of recharging that source on or about its exterior.'

'Really?'

Rune turned to him. 'You know about photo-optical cells – they made one in Foreton some years ago, but considered the technology nowhere as useful as generators and batteries.'

'Yes, I know about that.'

'I am sure I saw a claw move at one point, and luminescence from those eyes. I suspect that exposing it to the sunlight allowed its system to garner some energy. I suppose that it must have other methods of doing the same – quite possibly it has charging points like a battery.'

'But that might result in damage to things inside we have no idea about.'

'I suspect that if we do something wrong it will have numerous ways internally to prevent damage. It is a war machine and therefore all vulnerabilities are likely covered.'

'You seem quite confident about this?'

'Not confident, no, but I do know that we have to try things and take risks if we are to gain anything from this find beyond reinforcement of doctrine.'

Eller looked at him for a long moment, then said, 'What do you need?'

'The heaviest cables you have available that can reach the thing from the power here… and some big clamps to hold them in position.'

They walked over to the drone where Eller called over a man and a woman dressed in long hide coats and small narrow-brimmed black hats. Rune recognised them as researchers from the Divinity College, though of course he did not know them personally because he had never been there.

'Tell them,' said Eller.

Rune looked at the two and knew at once that they would not agree with his idea and would vehemently defend what they now considered their territory. He pointed to the nearest buss bar. 'I propose running cables from one of those. I think it unlikely to matter what current or voltage we use. Attach them up front and back on the drone. I think it highly likely it has numerous resources for gathering energy from its environment.'

'Ridiculous idea,' said the man. 'And quite likely you'll damage the relict!'

'I don't think so,' Rune replied. 'It's undamaged, as far as we can see, from having been swamped in lava.'

'And what precisely do you expect that to do?' asked the woman snootily.

'I expect we'll perhaps see some activation of some of its parts,' Rune replied. 'We can then continue from there. We will learn something at least instead of simply recording what is easily evident.'

'And what is easily evident?' she asked.

'That it is a rugged war drone made in the shape of a scorpion and all but impenetrable to the technology we have available.'

'In your expert opinion,' the man derided.

'And,' said the woman, 'supposing this does manage to activate something, it could be very dangerous.'

Rune focused on her. 'Are you saying that a Polity relict could be dangerous to us?'

She suddenly looked scared and shot a glance at Eller. The man looked too – both of them unsure of their ground now. Eller had watched all this with an amused expression and now bowed his head in thought. Without looking up he said, 'We will do this.' He looked up. 'Presumably we have a suitable way of controlling the current?'

'I don't know that we have anything like that,' said the man. 'And, Hand Eller, we should be proceeding with extreme caution at this point.'

'So you *do* feel this Polity relict might be dangerous to us?'

The man swallowed dryly. 'Of course not. It is certainly God's plan for us to find such things and to have found this.'

'If I may interrupt,' said Rune. He pointed to a large metal box on wheels over by one wall with cables strewn all around it. 'That looks to me like an arc welder – perfectly suitable as a controller.'

Eller looked too, then gave Rune some consideration before turning back to the other two. 'We will take it from here. I suggest you head back to the College and do some more research. Perhaps, if I allow you to return, you'll have some useful suggestions?'

'Sir! The Bishop instructed us –'

'The Bishop put me in charge,' Eller interrupted. 'Until he says otherwise I say what happens here. I suggest you leave now before I have you removed.'

They really did not want to go, moving off to have a whispered conversation over by the personnel door beside the main entrance doors. Rune had no doubt that they would be going directly to the Bishop and quite possibly he would intervene, though possibly not since the Hand had the man's confidence. It didn't matter. Any intervention would come too late now. Certain events would have occurred, or they simply were not going too.

'The cables for the welder are long enough,' said Rune, as the two departed. 'It must have been used for fixing any of the stationary machines in here.'

'Cold forges,' Eller replied. 'Now in another factory underground – used for making shell casings.'

'Very well.' Rune headed over. Upon reaching the welder he spotted the heavy plug lying on the floor with its cable coiled underneath it. He picked the thing up and towed its cable over to the buss bar nearest the drone, pushed it in and secured it with one twist. Eller had followed him and together they returned to the welder and pushed it over to the drone, dragging its power cable with it.

'Everyone away from the drone,' Eller called. 'It's about to be live.'

Never a truer word spoken, thought Rune.

The clamp for holding thick arc rods opened wide enough to close firmly on the drone's sting. The other clamp for the item being welded he pulled round to the front of the thing and closed about the tip of one claw. He then returned to the welder. On the upper face was a rotary rheostat switch, four position switch and one large power switch. In a concession to Eller's concerns he clicked to the lowest of the four settings and wound the rheostat down to zero before turning the thing on. The box jerked as it hummed into life. He wound the rheostat up to its top setting then back down before clicking the four-position switch up to its next setting. As he wound the rheostat up again some sparks dropped from the clamp on the claw. That, he knew, would damage the clamp and not the drone's armour, but he turned the welder off to go and check anyway, shifting the clamp to a more secure position. Up through each power setting nothing much happened until he reached the top one. As he wound the rheostat up on that the drone shuddered and shifted.

'My God,' said Eller, but with excitement in his voice. They walked over to see what had moved. The scales on the jacks had dropped to zero for the thing now supported its own weight. Checking the claws he found a piece of card and slid it underneath, showing that they too had risen from their jacks. He turned to head back to the welder.

'Look!' Eller exclaimed, drawing his attention back.

The tail began to rise, slowly coming up off the floor towing the attached power cable with it, then with a flash and shower of sparks the clamp came off, and with a crash the drone slumped. The dials on the sides of the jacks shot up again, and one of them released a squirt of oil from a faulty hydraulic connector.

'Damn,' said Rune. 'I'll have to wire those in place.'

'But we have results,' said Eller.

'We certainly do, but I suspect it will be a long while before we get any more than this. It will have to sit on charge.'

'What makes you suspect that?'

Rune waved a hand at the drone. 'It's very heavy and I can only assume that its power supply must be immense, perhaps something we haven't seen before.'

'Very well.' Eller turned away from him to the workers standing around watching. 'Who's in charge here?' he asked.

After a moment a man walked over. 'You are, sir,' he said.

Eller smiled. 'And below me were our two friends I sent away. Who is next down in the chain?'

'That would be me,' said the man.

'What's your name?'

'Gaston.'

'Very well, Gaston.' He pointed to Rune. 'While I am gone you are to take instructions from this man. You do whatever he tells you.'

'You're going?' Rune asked.

Eller grimaced, and waved Gaston away. When the man was out of earshot he said, 'I need to report to the Bishop as I've no doubt Glade and Reynolt have gone to him. He needs to know that we're getting somewhere here without them. I wasn't too pleased about the idea of

College researchers in charge here – too concerned about religious matters, rather than military ones.'

'Curious to hear that from the Bishop's Hand,' Rune noted.

'I am a curious fellow,' Eller replied. 'Get back to work on this and do what you can. I am hoping you'll have more for me when I return tomorrow.'

'I hope so too,' Rune replied.

As the day drew to its close Rune found himself in charge of a lot of workers and little idea what to do with them. He told Gaston this and the man sent many of them away. The remainder Rune got to work on making two good solid clamps for electrical contact with the drone's sting and one claw. Others he had working in close with small chisels, taking out the stone hardened in various holes all about its exterior, like the barrels of the obvious weapon attached to one claw. By the time the clamps had been fashioned and tried out, one of the workers had cleared out two square holes just behind its head on top. He refrained from pointing out that plugs could be made to push into these and inject power more directly, because obviously that would show he knew far too much.

'Okay!' he called once the clamps, with cables attached, had been positioned and tightened. 'Stand clear!'

The remaining five workers hurriedly moved away, and he switched on the welder and quickly wound it up to full power. The drone shrugged and raised its weight again, and this time when the tail rose it did not shed its clamp. With Gaston at his side and the others trailing, he walked round it making a visual inspection. This time the eyes were a deep dark red, as if they had filled with blood. Pieces of stone still in some of its orifices now fell out. The air around it felt prickly, telic.

'I think we should call it a day now,' Rune said. He had noticed one or two of those remaining looking at a clock over on the wall beside the main doors. 'We'll leave it charging like this overnight and see what the morning brings.' They all stood watching him. 'You can go home now,' he added.

Back in his apartment, Rune first prepared and ate a light meal. The changes continuing inside his body needed their fuel just as the drone needed power. He also emptied out his pockets of items he had picked up in the warehouse: the swarf of a wide variety of metals, plastics and carbon, a mixed bag of metal salts and other chemicals he had found while apparently making an inventory and deciding what might be needed for work on the drone. These he now wrapped in bread and swallowed, because the changes in his body were not what they would describe here as wholly organic. His digestive system, being about the first to upgrade, handled these without problem, while his nanosuite and much changed body quickly began distributing them where required.

He went to lie on the bed and, not needing sleep, next focused his vision inwards. The mechanisms of this aspect of his full being were coming along nicely, and soon communication with his full self would re-establish after three years. It amused him to think of the reaction of Eller and the like should he allow them to take a look inside him with one of their primitive X-ray machines.

As the changes continued his temperature rose but, adapted for this, he did not need to reduce it. Sweating would not have worked in that respect anyway, since he was now wondering about getting off the bed and stripping off his clothes before they scorched. But all the while, as the changes continued, he kept his external appearance as locked down as he could. Four hours later he realised he needed more materials for the changes inside him, so stood and headed back to the warehouse, taking a loaf of bread with him.

A stair led down from his apartment directly to a door into the warehouse. On the level just below his apartment a window had been inset and, through that, he saw guards patrolling outside. As he entered the warehouse he wondered if they would be there too, but could see none, and he could see clearly, too, without needing to put on the lights. He began walking around, senses now tuning up so he could recognise the things he needed should he see them. He scraped up copper, magnesium, iron and aluminium swarf, made selections from the chemical store, noting a need for potassium and calcium salts. Steam rose from his clothing and tremors in his muscles seemed to hint they might explode. He walked back to the door leading up to his apartment and beside it shed his clothing, stacking it neatly on a crate. It didn't matter if someone came in now, anyway, since he had grown enough chromatophores and other technology in his skin to render himself invisible.

He returned to searching out the things he needed, at one point opening a crate and taking out an artillery shell, using the tools here to open it and ingesting the contents. The prime chemical he needed from it was phosphorous, which he mixed carefully with machine oil before drinking down. Internally his density had now increased to five times that of a standard human being and yes he did feel ready to explode, but still he had to maintain the facsimile of something approaching the humanity of this world for a little while longer. Finally deciding he had taken himself as far as he could for now, he decided it was time to go back to his bed and turn himself off for a few hours. But first he went over and stood before the drone.

Now, his senses enhanced by a range of spectral scanners growing throughout his body, he could see a little more of the war drone. To many of his new senses it was still utterly black because that armour blocked most EMR, but, gaining some data from neutrinos zipping through his immediate environment from the far sun, he could see what looked like a warm blush inside as it sucked up and stored power in laminar capacitor batteries, steadily accumulating enough to kick start its scattered network of fusion nodes. As he watched, power flashed out from that blush, highlighting a network like veins. Its eyes glimmered and if shifted, and then it spoke.

'You are,' it said, in a language only found on this world in the oldest writings and spoken only occasionally by a few academics in the Divinity College. It then slumped. It simply did not have sufficient power yet. But Rune felt this brief activation to be a good sign, because forming words likely meant its mind was still intact. He turned away and headed back to his apartment.

In the morning the Bishop arrived with numerous soldiers, a retinue of ecclesiasts, the two from the Divinity College and with Eller at his side. They arrived just after the workers, which was good, because Rune had no idea how to keep them employed. He stayed back with those workers, noting their nervousness, since it was never a good idea to be around the higher ups. At some point he supposed Eller would summon him over; for now he just watched.

They milled around the drone, seemingly reluctant to get too close, then one brave soul abruptly stepped forwards and rested a hand on it. Eller shouted a warning, then seemed embarrassed when nothing happened. Had the drone just been a normal lump of metal sitting there, on the slightly damp floor, that individual would have now been stuck in place frying nicely. But the thing processed the power input efficiently. No one was likely to get an electric shock unless they touched one of the clamps. Rune considered walking over and making that warning, but Eller got there before him, urging caution, and the people backed off. Rune, of course, could hear every word spoken. He could even hear the beat of their hearts and the rush of blood through their veins.

'Rune!' Eller finally called.

He walked over and, as he should, went straight to the Bishop and down on one knee before him to receive a bored touch to the forehead. The Bishop's eyes widened, boredom dispelled, and he retracted his hand and stood back. Rune stood up meekly, his head bowed, but he noticed some of those who had gathered closer now backed off too – sensing, as did the Bishop, at levels below the conventional that what stood before them was not quite human, at least in their terms.

'So it was your idea to attach the power cables?' said the Bishop, shrugging himself and trying to regain dignity. Of course he sensed something, but the likes of such men were masters at making mental adjustments to put others below them.

'I did indeed, your reverence,' Rune replied, his gaze straying to the drone, and other senses abruptly going to high alert. Changes were taking place in it and power distributing. New systems within the thing were coming online.

'What do you hope to discover by doing this?' the Bishop asked.

'I hoped to reveal active systems within the drone and thereby learn more about it than would be garnered by merely measuring it.'

The Bishop frowned. 'According to my –' he began, but then his words just trailed off as it seemed the air around them thickened and began fizzing with energy. Rune detected a rise in radiations one of their new detectors would have registered, were they not large immobile machines sitting in the divinity college. Collating scan data he observed, in a multi-spectrum view, singular glares igniting at various points in the drone's body. Almost at once the radiation spill began to fade, as the fusion nodes settled to a steady efficient burn. Then, in eerie silence but for the crunch of its feet against the floor, the drone rose higher and walked forwards.

Yelling and chaos immediately ensued as some just ran, others backed off, and guards grabbed the Bishop to pull him to safety. The drone kicked one of the jacks in passing, sending this item, weighing at least two tons, crashing across the floor. It turned, flipping its tail and snapping the cable there, the thing sizzling and sparking across the floor, just as Eller reached the welder and turned it off. The drone flipped its tail again and the clamp there came off in a flat trajectory smashing a hole through one wall. It turned, scuttling round, feet gouging holes in the concrete. Facing the retreating people with Rune ahead of them, it pointed one claw – the one with what Rune knew to be a Gatling cannon fixed down the side. It held that claw there for a moment, but then reached across and stripped the power clamp off its other claw.

'We will talk,' it said in that language ancient here.

Rune dipped his head in acknowledgement.

Everything now seemed to tighten, as if the world were taking a breath. The drone rose from the floor and Rune felt the wash of its grav engines, then it shot up towards the roof and smashed through, and in the oily yellow glare of dirty-burning thrusters, disappeared from sight. Rune just stood there smiling as chunks of roofing material fell all about him.

'Arrest that man!' the Bishop shrieked.

A rifle butt smacked against his head and he shifted it in consonance with that, as if the blow had actually moved his head, and staggered as if the blow had affected him. In that moment he decided not to ape unconsciousness because the moment they tried to pick him up they would know something was very wrong. Further blows ensued and he staggered some more, yelped and protested, then finally they cuffed his hands behind his back, and shoved him into motion.

Outside the warehouse the Bishop and others were climbing into big luxurious cars. The guards dragged him over to a van, threw him down on the floor, and sat on the seats along the sides. He listened to them talking about the drone in awed tones, then one of them poked him with a rifle barrel.

'So what happened there?' the man asked.

Rune coughed and wheezed like someone injured, then replied, 'I have no idea.'

'I'll bet you'll be having all sorts of ideas later,' said another. This inevitably was a source of amusement for which Rune needed no explanations.

After a short drive the guards quickly dragged him out on a road beside bubble grass lawns with buildings rearing all around. Some were old and Gothic in appearance, while others were new boringly blocky structures. He noted the gun installation at the centre of one of the lawns, gun turrets up on the roofs. Some spectators stood nearby clad in long leather coats and thin-brimmed black hats. If recognition of his surroundings had not been enough, their presence would have been. He needed neither since he now had utterly perfect knowledge of his location. They had brought him to the Divinity College.

They took him into one of the older buildings, along corridors with polished stone floors and through thick old doors of apple wood, down steep stairs into gloom, soon dispelled by big fizzing electric lights. In this cellar stood a row of cages along one wall, with doors in the wall opposite. Here in the College they corrected and reinforced religious thought, but also interrogated enemy prisoners. They tried to throw him into a cage and much puzzlement ensued when he didn't stumble and fall satisfactorily. Afterwards he allowed them to beat him to the floor with rifle butts and give him a kicking for good measure. Then they departed.

Rune sat up and crossed his legs as the lights went out. He searched the darkness around him, seeing with perfect clarity. In the cage at the far end lay a dead woman – he had heard her breathing turn ragged when the lights came on, then stutter to a halt while the guards were kicking him. In infrared he could see her body cooling. He knew his position perfectly on a map of Foreton, this continent and this world in his mind. With his enhanced senses he could probe beyond this cellar, seeing the people above, in the lecture halls and class rooms or strolling in cool sunshine. He could build a schematic of the College's electrics, water and gas supply and see the line of workers carrying shells up to the roof. But this was not enough, for beyond a certain point his vision faded as the data became more difficult to collate. And he wanted to know where someone was. He turned his vision inward. Now had come the time to push to connect to the whole of himself.

Growing tougher and tougher his body now etched in and grew circuitry on the surface of his bones, while laminating new meta-materials inside them. His blood, packed with nanites running in a lubricant, no longer resembled blood at all. It was moving much more slowly now and no longer shifting about oxygen, which his body required less and less. Dense and fibrous muscles were switching over to electrical activation, while organs had begun serving new purposes or were being completely displaced. Half of his liver and three quarters of his lungs were gone and in their place laminar power storage and other devices steadily grew, along with the expansion in complexity and utility of his gut. He wryly observed those places where fusion nodes had begun to grow, and how much of what he could see here resembled what the war drone already had. Quantum storage crystals were blooming throughout and tough nanoptics and superconducting nanofibres were connecting the whole. Once that network completed, his organic brain would become surplus to requirements. But right now, what he really wanted was firm connection to and activation of the U-space transceiver in his chest.

He concentrated resources around it, drove the growth of superconductor to connect there and to a portion of the laminar storage that had become useable. Annoyingly the processes were using up his resources and he needed to eat more of a variety of materials, but of course none were available here. Instead he scavenged elsewhere in his body – reversing some processes to get what he required where he required it. As the optics connected to quantum storage his capacity for data processing – for thought – shifted to them and increased, so he began breaking down the fats and proteins of his brain for their energy and materials. Finally the superconductors supplied power, while the optics already in place could feed data to his now distributed mind, and he activated the transceiver.

Connection.

That majority of himself sitting in U-space adjacent to this world both absorbed him and returned to him. If he so wished, he had the option to simply dissolve into it and abandon this body. But that was not his purpose here. He fined the connection down and limited it to the demands his self here on the planet required, and that was the sensors of his whole self: omniscient vision.

He could now look upon the whole world, and in as much detail as he required. He studied the Islands, noting some islands turned over to be airstrips entirely, the dwellings on land and spreading into the sea, the ships that were floating towns, the factory and processing vessels. He focused on the missile barges, assault craft and warships and allowed a brief smile. Options would be available to the one making the decision, but he suspected he knew what its choice would be. At the mainland he studied the villages, towns and cities, the airfields there, though not so many as the Islands, and the industrial complexes supplying defensive guns but whose greatest output went to the sea forts lying all along the coasts facing the islands. Little had changed. The war ground on, depleting both populations and their resources, while they continued pulling more resources out of the ground here and out of the sea over there. And people grew up and joined in with the killing. But war also drove innovation and as Rune had already surmised that innovation would result in it ending in utter disaster for all.

He now looked elsewhere for particular energies not produced by this civilization. At first he could detect nothing and suspected that the drone, as was often the nature of such machines, had grown paranoid and hidden itself too well. But then a brief intense flash of radiation deep in a sea trench reflected off a surface, whereas elsewhere it just passed through. He focused his instruments there, bringing scanning heads out of U-space in that location and gathering data.

The drone was doing precisely what he had been doing back in the warehouse when it first spoke to him. It was gathering up resources. In its case this wasn't to initiate new growth, but to replace materials and energy that had been depleted and pack it into the dense technology of its body. The flash had brought down an undersea cliff, exposing deposits of pitchblende. This puzzled him for just a second, in his earth-borne mind, but his whole mind supplied the answer. It did not need uranium to supply its power since it ran on fusion. However, the dense radioactive metal served as a good precursor for making the hyper-dense beads of its material ammunition. It had also, Rune noted, been grazing on metallic nodule deposits on the bottom there. These no doubt supplied the correct particulate for its particle weapon. He considered contacting it right then, but felt such a conversation would be too distant, too inhuman. He had after all come here as much for the interaction as to do some good. He would wait until it came to him. He withdrew scanning heads into U-space, leaving just one in place to warn him should the drone's activity change in any major way.

Time passed.

Outside, the sun rose on a new day but there was no sign of it down in the cellar for any without the senses Rune possessed. Two guards came, stopped to peer in at him, then went down to the cage at the end to drag out the body and carry it away. The corpse would go into the town composter without ceremony – all part of the cycle here. A little later the lights came on again and he could hear someone struggling, blows being delivered. A new prisoner really did not want to end up down here and should have begun his fight a lot earlier than this. The guards dragged the man down the stairs. A last effort from him had one of the guards crashing down the stairs and hitting his head, sprawling on the floor unconscious. The remainder beat their prisoner into unconsciousness too and dragged him the rest of the way down, then along to the cage right next to Rune's. They threw him inside and then kicked him while he lay on the floor, but being unconscious he wasn't so entertaining, so they left.

Rune listened to the man's breathing and the beat of his heart. Looked through his body at its functions and saw that though the man had received a beating no bones had been broken. Inspecting his skull, he saw no bleeds beyond those from a light concussion. He turned his attention elsewhere, watched the world, watched the drone, considered and then dismissed old options. Finally the man regained consciousness. He moved against the floor, swore, vomited and then finally heaved into a sitting position.

'I'm sorry you ended up here,' said Rune.

'Who is that?'

'It's Rune, Eller – the relict digger.'

They came in the late afternoon: four guards with batons and the interrogator with his clipboard and sheets of paper no doubt detailing the questions he must ask. They opened Rune's cell first.

'Get up,' said the interrogator. 'If you resist it will be bad for you.'

At this Eller laughed bitterly and the interrogator frowned at him.

Rune stood and walked out of the cell, whereupon the guards grabbed him and struggled to drag him across to the door in the opposite wall. Again they were puzzled about their difficulty in moving him until he moved with them, allowing them to get him to the chair bolted to the floor. They took off his cuffs and then sat him down in it, pulling across leather straps to secure him there. Ahead of the chair stood a desk and the interrogator took out a cloth to prissily wipe the chair behind that before sitting down. Rune studied the implements on the walls – obviously there to scare the life out of a prisoner and no doubt to be used when required. He hoped they did not use them because the moment they did they would know he was no longer... normal. That would mean the necessity to act, when he had wanted to keep a low profile. But then, in retrospect, he realised it did not matter either way.

'You are Rune the relict digger, a graduate of the Divinity College,' said the interrogator.

'I am indeed,' Rune replied.

'Then perhaps you can explain to me how it is that though your name appears in the records, no one remembers you? Perhaps you can also explain how in your submission papers to the College, you have recommendation papers from people who have no knowledge of you?'

Rune shrugged. 'I don't understand the problems with the paperwork. I do understand that because of my appearance I was avoided here and that is why people do not remember me.'

The interrogator stared at him then inclined his head slightly. A guard stepped forwards and brought his baton down hard on Rune's leg. He yelled, just for form's sake, and twisted up his expression in pain.

'How long have you been working for the Groogers?'

This was interesting. Obviously they had decided he was a spy. He chose to run with this and see where it went.

'I don't work for them,' he protested.

He kept the protests up through the beatings that would have shattered bones in the arms and legs of a normal man, then finally conceded that he had been recruited by the Groogers at the age of eighteen. Next, gasping in pain every time a guard probed his apparently broken bones with a baton, he spent the next hour whining out his story of recruitment, secret organisations in the mountains, spying in Foreton and reporting the positions of factories via a radio concealed in his house in Meeps. He then moved on to the instructions he had received concerning the drone – how he needed to infiltrate here and ensure they fed it power. He wove a tale then of the Groogers finding a drone some years before and how by connecting it up to a power source the Groogers had activated it, whereupon it had sunk a research barge. He took his cues from the interrogator – measuring his heart rate, micro changes of expression, shifts in neurochemicals, pupil dilation – but it could not last.

'How long has Hand Eller been working for the Groogers?' the man asked.

'I didn't know he was.'

The interrogator raised a finger. 'Bring in Eller. I think it will be instructive for him to watch this.'

Eller fought as they dragged him in and hooked his cuff chain through an iron wall staple back and to the left of the interrogator. He hung there looking at Rune, terrified and in pain from the beatings, but also angry.

'Now,' said the interrogator. 'You will immediately and succinctly answer each question I ask. For every wrong answer you provide, Efton here,' he gestured to the guard who had supposedly broken Rune's legs and arms, 'will cut off one of your fingers.' The guard grinned at Rune as he took down a set of bolt croppers from the wall display. 'When we run out of fingers, he will cut off your toes, then your penis, your balls, your nose and ears.'

Rune just stared back at the man. Obviously this interrogator and the four guards in this room had done this kind of thing before, perhaps many times. He felt no sympathy for them. In fact, in that part of his being some of his kind would see as primitive, he quite relished the prospect of what must now ensue.

'Now, I will ask again: How long has Hand Eller been working for the Groogers?'

'Oh, just a couple of years,' Rune replied.

The interrogator showed a flash of annoyance at that. 'Who recruited him?'

'I did.'

'You're lying!'

'What lie would you prefer me to tell?'

The interrogator nodded. Efton stepped forwards, pulled up Rune's left forefinger and got the jaws of the bolt cropper around it. He looked straight into Rune's face then proceeded to close the croppers. His expression of cruel satisfaction changed to puzzlement as the handles simply would not close together – the sharp jaws denting Rune's skin down to the bone and stopping. He opened them again and pulled them away, tried them in the air and they closed easily.

'What are you doing Efton?' asked the interrogator.

'They jammed – seem okay now.'

He tried again to cut off Rune's finger and again the croppers just would not go through. Rune sighed.

'Oh well,' he said. 'Play time is over.'

Rune snapped the straps securing his left arm, slid his finger out of the cropper, raised it and stabbed it straight into Efton's eye, deep inside and hooked it to hold him there. He snapped the straps holding his right arm as he pulled Efton's head down to the left chair arm, then delivered a punch that crushed his skull and bent the metal underneath. The man dropped away bonelessly as Rune stood, snapping further straps as he kicked clear of the chair. A baton flew at his head. He caught it, snatched it from the assailant's grip, snapped it in half and drove one half into the man's mouth so hard that splintered wood stabbed from the base of his skull in a spray of blood. The second half he swung back, leaving it imbedded in another guard's chest. The last guard now came in swinging his baton. Rune took that blow on the head, grabbed the front of the man's uniform and threw him at the wall, where he hit hard enough to leave a corona of blood before peeling away and dropping to the floor. This took just a matter of seconds, and the interrogator was still in his chair, gaping in shock.

Rune walked over and leaned on the desk, hands on the edge. He then just pushed the desk to the wall. The interrogator tried to stand and got high enough to trap his hips between the wall and the desk. His pelvis crunched and he screamed, but Rune supposed that wasn't an unusual sound down here. He kept pushing, bones splintering, the gap growing narrower and narrower, flesh parting and blood, urine and shit spurting out. The desk was just an inch from the wall when it broke, the upper surface bowing up and shattering. Rune stood back as the man collapsed, almost separated from his legs. He tried to crawl and Rune stamped on his head. He was no torturer. He then returned to the guard gasping and bubbling with half a baton stuck in his chest, and backhanded him, shattering his skull and relieving him of his misery.

'Well that's messy,' he said, looking at the blood up the walls, on the floor, spattered on the ceiling and all over him. He felt a twinge of annoyance. He really should have killed them all bloodlessly. Now as he got out of here his state would draw notice.

'What... the fuck are you?' said Eller from where he hung from the staple.

Rune stepped over to him and Eller flinched away. He reached up and snapped the chain between cuffs. Eller dropped to his knees staring up at him and Rune stepped back. The man was waiting to die, but when he realised that wasn't going to happen, his mind kicked into gear. Rising unsteadily to his feet he walked over to one of the corpses, searched pockets and came up with a key to take off the cuffs.

'What now?' Eller asked.

Rune reviewed exterior events in his mind. The drone had risen from the ocean trench but was still under the sea. He doubted it was collecting materials there, just ruminating and probably sulking. He then surveyed inland. Back from Foreton rose hills and then some of the highest mountains on the continent. It seemed an appropriate place.

'I'm going to the mountains,' he explained. 'You may do what you will, though I suggest that you do not stay here.'

Eller looked around at the corpses. 'I'm coming with you.'

'Why?' Rune studied him.

'Because I want explanations. Because you know too much and you just did things no normal man could do.' He grimaced. 'And because I now have nowhere else to go.'

'Okay.' Rune nodded. 'Let's go.'

'Wait,' said Eller, then went over to the corpse of the interrogator, searched through his pockets and came up with a heavy cylindrical key. 'Now we can go.'

Rune walked over to pull open the door and lead the way out of the cellar to the stairs. They climbed in electric light then stepped out into corridors now lit by gas lamps. Locating himself, Rune turned to head for the most direct route out of the College and towards the mountains. Eller caught his arm.

'This way.'

Rune nodded. Of course – the key Eller had taken. As they moved through the corridors a group of divinity students came towards them, accompanied by their lecturer. As the two approached they moved quickly to the side to let them past, goggling at them all the while. Perhaps seeing people coming up bloody from that cellar wasn't usual, but not so unusual as to cause alarm. Rune felt a sneer twist his lips. He did not like this place and all it represented, and considered acting on that. But then he shook himself and dismissed the idea. He had aimed to be just the catalyst here. The ensuing reaction he had no intention of controlling.

Soon they exited the main door out into the central area of the college. The troop truck parked over on the far side had presumably brought the four guards below. Directly opposite the door, under a gas street light, sat a large well-polished sedan. Leaning against it was the driver, drinking from a lidded cup, sandwiches open on the bonnet next to him.

'We're taking the car,' said Eller, walking up to the man.

'Where's Amb –' the driver began, then the breath went out of him as Eller chopped him across the throat, then thumped him hard in the torso, before shoving him stumbling to fall on the bubble grass.

They climbed into the car and Eller started it – a big engine grumbling into life – and took off in a spray of gravel. He turned on the lights as they headed out through the College gates, where he negotiated streets obviously familiar to him. Checking his internal map Rune saw that the man seemed to know where he was going so desisted from giving directions. They finally reached a clear road heading out of Foreton; moths and bats flitted through the headlamp beams, and Eller relaxed back from the wheel, for until then he had been hunched over it.

'Now tell me how you managed to do what you did back there,' the man said.

Rune considered ignoring him, or maybe weaving a fabrication as he had with the interrogator, but he saw no reason why he should. Why not tell the truth? Few would believe Eller if he survived what was to come and told his story, and even if some did, that didn't really matter. He pondered on where to start and, since they would be driving for a few hours, decided to start with a historical error here.

'The Polity did not fall, you know – not in the sense you people think of it.'

'What?' Eller shot a look at him that seemed like panic.

'There was a war against monsters. They were called prador and, being vicious, xenophobic, amoral crustaceans the size of this car, "monsters" is a suitable description for them. The war lasted many decades during which worlds were destroyed and stars detonated. Billions on both sides died, and then, because of usurpation in the prador kingdom, an uneasy truce ensued.'

'How do you know this?'

'I've picked up a few things over the last few thousand years,' Rune replied.

'I don't believe you.'

Rune shrugged and continued, 'But like I said, after that war there was no immediate fall. Integration and radical changes fractured the Polity society, along with a vast diaspora.'

'I don't understand.'

'There are so many things you don't know, for example, humans did not really rule the Polity but artificial intelligences did.'

Eller looked around at him again. 'Artificial intelligences?'

'Machines that could think, and could think a lot better than humans. From their rise, way back during the Quiet War in the Solar System, they could have easily abandoned humanity and gone their own way, or they could have exterminated it. They hung around instead always trying to push humanity to catch up with them – rather like the young trying to teach ageing relatives modern things.'

'And did they catch up?' Eller looked at him pointedly. Rune enjoyed the man's perspicacity, nodded and smiled.

'It started with the mental enhancements – machine additions to the human mind to improve communication and function – but these were mental prosthetics, if you like, to begin with. It was difficult to combine human mind and AI as they were then. The first was organic and slow while the second was crystalline and fast. An early human tried it once and did some brilliant things in the brief time it took his mind to burn out while connected to AI. But things changed as hard material technology blended with organic technology. For many years there were the haimans who were a buffered combination of human and AI, and you had people loading to crystal and AIs loading to organic minds. New substrates arose on which intelligence could be written. Change was a gradual thing. And after some thousands of years no one could distinguish between AIs and humans.'

'You became gods…' said Eller.

Rune looked at the man – that perspicacity now surprising him. Rune had expected lengthy diversions and explanations. Or perhaps

Eller simply did not grasp it or believe it, and thought Rune a lunatic to be calmed.

'As you would see it, yes,' he said. 'Control over their existence and great swathes of material technology fell into the grasp of individuals. This was essentially your "fall" because individuals being so able there was little need for the organisation called society, little need for its infrastructure, for the means of maintaining populations, for factories, piped water or power. Also a diaspora had commenced. Individuals being so immensely powerful, and little needing the company of each other, drifted away like seeds on a breeze. Those that needed company often retreated into virtual worlds written into the cores of neutron stars. Trillions of humans just evaporated from the Polity.'

'Humans?'

'As such. It has always been accepted that the AIs were post-humans. The individuals that came next, whether arising from AI or human, could be described as post-post humans, but humans nevertheless.'

'And you claim to be one of these creatures?'

'I went away for a long time – there was, after all, a galaxy to explore and, at some point when I was ready, other galaxies. But my explorations have brought me full circle to the ancient ruins of the Polity, and here I find primitive human populations arising from the landings of ancient colony ships, engendered by birthing machines on some worlds, woken from underground storage on others, or growing from just a few who did not choose to be what I am. Here on this world your population arises from a crash-landed colony ship whose machinery took a millennium to self-repair before waking your ancestors.'

Eller's hands were tight on the wheel as he turned off the main road onto narrower more winding roads up into the mountains.

Rune added, 'That colony ship is remembered in your sacred texts as the ark ship, of course.' Eller grunted, as if Rune had just punched him in the stomach. Rune continued, 'Your ancestors were a religious group and, as with many such, infighting soon started. They wrecked the technology they had brought and dropped back into semi-primitivism out of which you people are beginning to rise.'

'What are you doing here? Why the drone?'

'Take a right here.' Rune pointed.

'There's nothing up there,' said Eller. 'Just the Flat Top.'

'I know.'

Eller turned and drove up a track that soon lost its metalling and became a gravel one. They were silent for a while, then he asked again, 'Why are you here?'

'Your war has stagnated,' Rune replied. 'Your sea forts prevent invasion by the Groogers, their sea power prevents you invading them. Neither of you have weapons powerful enough to do more than just tear at each other. It would be nice to think you would just tire of it and that the war would die a natural death. But it engenders hate with every generation and just continues.'

'It would never end?' Eller asked quietly.

'That's not the problem. You and the Groogers now have technology within your reach that could end it. The problem is that the scenario I predict will result in billions dying and your whole society dropping into a primitivism worse than that of your ancestors after their particular fall.'

The track took them up and up for miles, finally opening out on to the flat top of a mountain that looked like it had been sheared off with a blade. In fact it had been sheared off even while the colony ship, sunk out in shallow seas by the Islands, had still been slowly repairing itself. This world had been a battle ground during the prador-human war and this was why so many artefacts could be found here. The mountain top had been sheared off by a particle beam capable of cutting through the crusts of worlds.

Eller stopped the car and they climbed out. No lights up here, but the star-sprinkled sky gleamed bright, and green light from the moon turned their surroundings into black blocky shadows and shades of emerald. They walked over to where a waist-high wall had been built across the top of the drop down the side of the mountain. From here they could see the plains below, the lights of hundreds of villages, of Foreton and other towns, and factory complexes extending into misty distance. The lights of the sea forts were bright red, perhaps that colour being a warning or a threat. They stretched from out of sight on his left and studded the coast to his right for a hundred miles, ending where other mountains stepped down into the sea. Cheever was a fortress as such. The Groogers could evade the sea forts and land elsewhere on the continent, but to get to the heart of military production would require passing through mountains all around. They could not bring armour for that purpose, and fortifications in the mountains would make mincemeat of any land army.

'Some say that if we were to concentrate on air power, the war would be winnable,' Eller commented.

'Grooger air power is growing at near the same rate as yours,' Rune replied. 'Already you are building your attack planes to bring down their gunships and they are doing the same with yours. Both sides would also get round to deploying ballistic missiles that could reach each other, but the war would continue.'

'So what is this technology that could end the war?' Eller asked.

Rune glanced at him, feeling brief disappointment. Was he trying to learn the 'secret' that could win the war for his side? He studied the man for longer on other levels, analysed his reactions and tracked the signalling in his brain. Out of the whole of his observations he reached a single conclusion. Eller, after being sent to be tortured, felt betrayed by his own side. He considered himself an outsider now and had no loyalties beyond his personal ones.

'On your side it would be atomic weapons.'

'I have heard theories about these,' said Eller. 'That mass can be turned into vast amounts of energy.'

'Quite – you would be able to build bombs to depopulate islands in a single blast.'

'And the Groogers?'

'Biological weapons. Plagues they could sow from their gunships that would have your people coughing out their lungs and depopulate most of the continent.'

'And you will not allow either of these.'

The drone had risen from the sea now and begun looking around. He had no doubt it was absorbing and translating radio transmissions, in fact it had probably learned all the languages here within just half an hour of leaving the warehouse. He now sensed its scanning, which was on the same level as his own. It reached out to the islands and in towards the continent. It would be analysing the cultures here, assessing their technological capabilities. Because of its nature it would first be looking at the weaponry and of course it would know they were at war and who was doing what to whom. But it would be seeing and understanding a lot more than that. Rune did not in the slightest underestimate its intelligence, understanding and wisdom. The thing was, after all, older even than him and throughout its long existence had upgraded itself as desired. It had even fought in that long ago war against the prador, which he had only learned about as a child in school via the growing implants in his brain.

'It is not a case of either or,' he told Eller distractedly. 'You and the Groogers will develop these weapons at around the same time. Or, the more likely scenario, you will use nuclear weapons against the Groogers and that will compel them to use biological weapons they will have developed but will otherwise be too frightened to deploy.'

The drone began cruising in towards Foreton now. Their primitive radar installations would not detect it unless it allowed them to, in which case the sirens and searchlights would come on and the guns begin firing, all to no effect. As it passed over the sea forts, Rune realised it had made itself invisible to them. It came to a halt over the city, no doubt directly above the warehouse in which it had woken. There he sensed its scanning becoming more intense. It then began shifting inwards towards the centre – to the Divinity College.

'And that will result in most of us dying?' Eller asked.

Rune turned to him. The drone was low down. He had no doubt the bodies in the cellar had been discovered now. He also had no doubt the drone had scanned that cellar and was listening in on various conversations, perhaps thousands of conversations.

'Do you know about mutation?'

'Yes, I understand the theories,' Eller replied.

'You are widely read, then.'

Eller nodded agreement.

Rune continued, 'Radiation increases mutation rates. The plagues the Groogers would sow, which would be bad enough by themselves, would mutate. This would result in more than three quarters of the population of this world dying. Social and technological collapse would be another consequence. It would probably take you five hundred years to get back to the level you are at now.'

The drone began moving out of the city. Rune wondered what it was tracking now: the micro impressions of tire treads in the roads, fragments of conversation concerning sightings of their car, or perhaps it had begun following the military vehicles heading out of the city along the road they had taken. As it came above those vehicles he felt the wash of terahertz scan and the flash of a vortex laser passing over their car, and then Eller and himself. The drone accelerated with a flash of bright thrusters – now no longer burning dirty at all.

'What was that?' said Eller.

'A friend is coming,' Rune replied, reaching out and resting a hand on his shoulder. 'Let's give him room to land.'

Eller went with him as they moved back to stand beside a monument that had been erected here in the far past. The thing looked vaguely like a Celtic cross and was one of the early symbols of the Cheever religion. Eller rested a hand against it and stared wide eyed at the sky. The drone came faster and faster, then slowed over the mountain with a wash of grav. It descended, utterly black in this light, and only visible to Eller when it reached twenty feet above the ground.

'God in Heaven,' said Eller.

'No, not really, Rune replied.

The drone came down gently for something weighing many tons. But when its feet touched and it turned off grav, it sagged briefly, feet splintering stone as it scuttled round to face them. After a moment its eyes glimmered red, then other things began to happen. Blue light emitted from patches all over its surface, lighting up the area. Light gleamed from within joints. Its surface swam with waves of colour, finally settling on a grey and brown camouflage pattern. It then just stood there watching them.

'What does it want?' Eller asked.

'At this point I have no idea,' Rune replied, which was part of the excitement of it all really. At his words the drone shifted, it then spoke.

'Human,' it said in the old tongue.

'Use their language,' Rune replied. 'It's rude to do otherwise.'

The drone made a sound suspiciously like a snort. It then rose up a little and directed the claw with the Gatling cannon on it towards Rune.

'Show yourself to me, Polity man,' it said.

Rune glanced over at Eller for a moment, then turned his attention inward, assessing his condition. All his internals were compacted and hyper dense now, which in turn hindered full function. His external appearance remained stable with very little showing through. He realised that the drone could not see him completely and, though it had said 'Polity man' wanted to be utterly sure.

Rune relaxed his chameleonware and the self-imposed strictures on his physical form. Concertinaed and collapsed growth expanded, bones opened out along shear planes, organics spread and bulked, densely compressed oxygen and hydrogen combining into water for that purpose but also providing energy for other changes. Systems unpacked themselves and spread, fusion nodes expanded and then fired up, flooding his body with energy. He felt the baggy overall grow tight on him and within just a few seconds he stood a head and shoulders taller than Eller. He tore off the sleeves so his arms would not be constricted, felt buttons ping away down the front of the overalls and their legs split as he kicked off slippers now too small for his feet. Looking at his arms he saw the flesh translucent and grey but with optics gleaming from within, bionic threads shifting, bones as dark shadows with silvery tech etched into their surfaces. He looked down at Eller as the man backed off, utterly bewildered and terrified, crouching down by the monument as if it might offer protection.

Meanwhile Rune's links to the whole of himself, threaded through underspace about this world, strengthened. Via this he also connected to those parts of himself he had left monitoring other worlds, swimming through nebulae, etched into dark planetoids and tumbling around bright suns. And the whole of himself focused in on the body here.

'Seen enough?' he asked.

The drone grunted dismissively. Then turned away and walked over to the edge of the Flat Top and peered down at the primitive civilization spread out below. Rune shrugged, smiled and gestured to Eller to stand up. The man did so, then followed him as he walked out to stand beside the drone.

'What's your name?' Rune asked.

'I think you know,' the drone replied. 'Just as I know you.'

'You recognise me?' Rune asked.

'You were a Polity brat creating war virtualities who interviewed me. Later you were a man who travelled with me, while you decided on virtual existence or real. I see you made the correct decision.'

'Good times,' Rune said, nodding. 'And you're Amistad, perhaps one of the oldest drones still in existence.'

'I wouldn't go that far.' Amistad reached forwards and gently tipped over a rock. It tumbled down out of sight. 'Plenty of the old guard still about.'

'How did you end up underneath that lava flow?' He gestured to Eller. 'Here they would think it happened during the Fall, the war, but we both know better.'

'Ah the war – the good old days, Rune,' said Amistad. 'When dangers still threatened and an old war drone could find useful employment. But after most of your lot all but sublimed things ceased to be so interesting. I came here when the humans here were stumbling out of their cold coffins in their old colony ship. They had a hell of a time getting their stuff out and onto a nearby island. I hung around to watch.' Amistad gestured off in the distance. 'The volcano erupted and lava flowed down towards me. Didn't bother to get out of the way – there seemed no point.'

'I would have thought such an intelligent entity as yourself would have been able to find something to occupy his time.'

Amistad shrugged. 'We are creatures of action and physicality.' He tapped his claw against the ground for a moment, then continued, 'Why did you dig me up?'

'I felt it was time for you to engage with the physical world again.'

'And take actions,' said Amistad.

'You've seen how things are here?'

'I have. Why don't you correct those things?'

'Free will – stuff like that.'

'The intricate thinking of AI and now Polity humans,' said the drone. 'Why push a stone off a wall...' Amistad did just that again. '... when you can play snooker with asteroids half a light year away, finally altering the course of a small one so it will enter atmosphere few hundred years later and do the job for you.'

'You exaggerate.'

'Do I really?'

'Tell me what you see here.' Rune gestured towards the plain below and out towards the islands.

'Exactly what you see: warfare, biotech and fissile weapons, perfect storm putting them back into the Stone Age.' The drone then pointed a claw behind. 'I also see lots of heavily armed soldiers driving up the track to here.'

Rune nodded contemplatively. 'Then I'll stop the word games. I want you to end this war in such a way that unifies the peoples here.'

Amistad dipped, perhaps in acquiescence, perhaps just acknowledging the confirmation of what he had expected. The drone then turned round to face back across the stony ground. 'And what about those soldiers?'

Rune focused his attention – all of his attention – down the track from where Eller had parked the sedan. Eller could not see them because trees and part of the mountain were in the way, but Rune, via his whole self, could see two trucks and another sedan. Twenty soldiers in the trucks and in the sedan the Bishop and some of his retinue. He considered letting them get up here and allowing the drone to deal with them then, but it would be pointless grandstanding.

'Don't kill them,' he replied. 'Just stop them.'

With a smacking sound a streak of light issued from Amistad – the tail fire of a small missile. It took a looping course outwards and then down. In the track ahead of the vehicles it shot straight into the cliff made when the track was carved out. The detonation seemed to shine through the rock, highlighting its cracks in bright light. The cliff bulged out and then collapsed dropping tons of stone across the track.

'And now, about this war...' said Rune.

'Okay,' Amistad replied. 'I will stop this war. I'll endeavour to keep the casualty count down and I'll unify them, since invasion and subjugation are a form of unification.'

The drone abruptly rose in a wash of grav, and then fifty feet in the sky fired up his thrusters and shot away towards the coast. Rune looked into Eller's stunned expression and gestured to him. They walked over to the edge again to look out.

'It's going to fight for us?' he asked.

Rune shook his head. 'It is going to do precisely what I asked it to do, and there is a relatively simple way to do that, which I suspect it will take.'

'End the war,' Eller said, then looked at Rune shrewdly. 'If that drone had been somewhere on the islands you would have been talking to one of them right now. The fact that you are here with me now is just because its location was here in Cheever.'

'Exactly.'

'What happened back there?' Eller gestured to where Amistad had fired the missile.

'Your Bishop and some soldiers – Amistad collapsed the cliff beside the track to stop them.'

'It killed them?'

'No.'

'So we are trapped here and they will come.'

'I think they will shortly have other more urgent concerns.'

The first blasts lit up the factories around Foreton, then further explosions lit up the harbour. Rune observed an armaments barge exploding, then further ignitions as it tossed its contents all around. But this was just the warm up – Amistad was just testing how to blow up munitions using the least amount of energy, since the drone did not have an endless supply. A moment later a blue line cut the air out to sea, then a massive explosion cut a hole in the side of one of the island sea forts. He analysed scan data. The drone had used a particle beam to burn through into a munitions store there. The next sea fort, one of those built up on steel legs, exploded leaving only its legs standing. Another blew out its sides and its legs twisted toppling it into the sea. Next came a pause. He wondered if the drone was allowing the bad news to travel and then checked radio transmissions. The personnel of all the sea forts were now receiving correctly coded orders to abandon their positions. The drone would give them the time for that.

'It's destroying our defences!' Eller objected.

'It is indeed.' Rune glanced back. The soldiers were clambering over the rubble down there, while the Bishop's car was turning round to take him back to Foreton. He reached over and grabbed the back of Eller's uniform, hauled him up and slung him over one shoulder. He then jumped the wall, hit the steep slope and bounded down it, initiating grav and slinging out force fields to control their descent. With Eller yelling all the way they finally reached a copse on the side of the mountain, just beside where the track wound down, where Rune deposited him.

'Amistad will destroy all your sea forts,' he told the man. 'Wait here.'

Rune walked out into the middle of the track as the sedan came down into sight. It braked hard, skidding on the gravel, then doubtless in response to an order from the Bishop, accelerated again. He ran to meet it, shouldering into the front of the thing, feet cutting grooves in the track as he brought the vehicle to a halt with the engine stalling.

Guards piled out and one opened up on him with a machinegun. The bullets dented his skin to simply fall out smoking as he moved in, back handed the man to deposit him on his back on the track. Two others never even got to fire their weapons as he stepped up to them and slammed their heads together. He then reached in and took hold of the cowering Bishop and threw him out on the grass at the side of the road.

'Why?' Eller asked. He had not stayed in the copse.

'For you.' Rune gestured at the car.

Eller nodded as he moved forwards, stooped and pulled a sidearm from the holster of one of the guards.

'For me?' Rune enquired, eying the weapon.

Eller turned and fired once, the shot hitting the Bishop in the centre of his face and blowing his brains out the back of his head. He then turned back, pointing the gun at Rune.

'You told me the drone will destroy the sea forts.'

'It will, all of them, and then it will work inland steadily destroying your weapons factories and stores. Just a few hours after the forts are gone the Groogers will know about it. I expect it will take them three days to launch their invasion. They'll want to prepare, but they won't want to leave it too long and give you time to set up new defences.'

'And the war will be over.'

'It will be hard here for a very long time.'

Eller nodded, tossed the pistol away and stepped over to the car. 'I think, once I've collected my family, I'll take your house in Meeps,' he said. He shrugged. 'The Groogers have their relict diggers as do we.'

'I wondered if you might,' Rune replied.

'You didn't wonder at all, did you, really?'

'No, not really.' Rune dipped his head in acknowledgement, turned and walked back up the track. He would disarm the soldiers and send them on their way and up there he would await Amistad's return. Then perhaps they might ameliorate things here, maybe ease the transition of power, help the Groogers establish their rule, help the Cheevers accede to it and drive eventual integration.

Or perhaps not.

Okay, I have a confession to make. It's not like I wrote every one of these stories during lockdown. My get-out is that it is during this time I decided to publish them in a collection. Some while back I wrote "Snow in the Desert" – a Polity story that owed much of its conception to spaghetti westerns. "Snow" was going to be turned into a short CGI film by Tim Miller for a project called Heavy Metal. That fell through but Miller has since moved on to doing something similar called Love, Death and Robots on Netflix. Since "Snow" had been so well received (apparently Tom Cruise said it would make a good film by itself) and since I thought it a good idea to write some more stuff with L,D&R in mind, I wrote this sfnal riff on High Plains Drifter. Nothing to lose by doing it since surely I could aim to get it published somewhere. "Monitor Logan" was first published in World War Four edited by Sam M. Phillips and Adam Bennett in 2019. This is not that version but an extended one in three parts.

MONITOR LOGAN

<u>Part 1</u>

The crawler– a car-sized vehicle running on caterpillar treads out on arms – hammered down the track from the mountains, kicking up dust and skidding on the corners. Monitor Enders L Trepanan watched it for a moment longer then stepped over to his jeep and, grabbing the roll bar, swung inside to drop in the seat. He started it, the engine whirring softly, then took off across the jigsaw-cracked mudstone of the Flat, the jeep's treads kicking up flakes of rock and dust. Meanwhile, the crawler had reached the Flat and was accelerating. He shortly swung in parallel to it and eyed the figure behind the bubble screen of its cockpit. The man looked over and Enders gestured for him to stop. He didn't.

Enders accelerated, pulling ahead of the crawler, and with his right hand on the joystick drew his rail-beader from his left holster. The weapon, attached by a cable to a power supply on his belt, was all smooth white metal with polished chrome inlay. He held this up for a moment for the driver to see, then fired into the ground ahead of the crawler. The weapon crackled and mudstone erupted in a line before the vehicle but it swerved and still did not stop. He fired again, closer, spraying the front screen with broken stone. The crawler swerved again, hit a pothole then skidded and jounced sideways. Its turbine started to wind down and the driver lowered his head to the control console. It settled in a cloud of dust.

Enders circled round to bring his jeep in close and parked. Holstering his beader, he climbed out, but now took a laser carbine from the inside pocket of one door before walking over. As he drew closer, the man inside looked across at him. Enders rested his carbine across his shoulder and beckoned. After a pause, the man stood up and headed back into the body of the vehicle. A door popped open in the side and he stepped out. Enders studied him.

He was tall and thin and clad in overalls, his skin grey, tendrils depending either side of his mouth, shifting slightly. The man's face had no nose and his hands were three-fingered. He held these out to the side to show no weapons, and stepped forwards.

'Big hurry,' Enders commented.

The stone man gazed at him steadily with amber eyes, then said, 'You are Monitor Trepanan. You have no power here. Earth jurisdiction is to be rescinded.'

Enders acknowledged that with a shrug, and replied, 'Earth jurisdiction of the Flats and Godrun does not end until the day after tomorrow. I'm the Monitor here until then. Why are you running, stone man?'

'I run because that is all we can do now.' He gestured back towards the crawler. 'The arthrodapt is back –Trader John is back with his janglers. Now there is no law here they are doing what they always did before.'

'Trader John,' Enders said tightly.

'Yes. He has opened his mine again, like before. And the other owners are following his lead.'

Enders stared at him for a long moment then stepped past him to peer inside the crawler. A woman and a child of the stone people sat inside. They did not look round at him. Their heads were dipped and their wrists and ankles tied. He stepped inside and studied them, the stone man followed behind him.

'Who are they?' he asked.

'My wife and child – I took them from a mine.'

Enders turned and held out his carbine. 'Hold this.'

The stone man took the gun reluctantly, held it as if it might bite him, then hurriedly put it down beside the door. Enders tipped the woman's head back and studied her face. She looked utterly blank while a triangular device attached to her temple blinked a green light.

'Induction thrall,' he stated bitterly.

This accounted for the bonds. The mind-control device enslaved someone to another's will. Even though these were the man's wife and child, if he hadn't tied them it would have returned them to whoever controlled them.

'The janglers are taking my people again,' said the stone man.

Enders nodded then opened the utility pack on his belt to take out a small remote control with inset screen. He tipped back the child's head and studied the thrall there, then held the device over it and triggered it. Code ran on the screen, while a green light began flashing on the device to match the blinking of the one on the thrall. Both lights turned amber, then after a moment red before going out. He reached down, clicked a button on the face of the thrall and detached it, putting it in his pocket. It left a sore triangle of skin with puncture marks evenly scattered across it. The child became conscious again, looking round in bewilderment. He did the same with the woman and she gasped the moment the lights changed, then gazed up at him, tears welling in her eyes.

'But there are others,' said the stone man, drawing a knife from his belt to cut their bonds, 'and you can do nothing. It will be as it was before: my people enslaved in their mines and Trader John in control out here.'

Enders handed over the device to the stone man. 'Maybe you will find this useful,' he said.

'You will not use it again,' stated the stone man.

Enders picked up his carbine and stepped to the door. 'I'm sorry,' he managed, and stepped down to tramp angrily back across the mudstone to his jeep.

Enders drove up a metalled road from the flat, the town of Godrun coming into sight around one curve. Here cylindrical foamstone houses clustered on either side of the river valley with narrow streets running between. A series of bridges crossed the river while here and there raised car parks were dotted with crawlers. At the top end of the town warehouses and factories served the various mines scattered throughout the mountains.

The road took him in past a few houses then to a bridge over the river. Many more people were about than usual – men and women in mine worker overalls, weather gear and envirosuits – and he noticed how they paused to watch him as he drove past. The news had spread that Earth jurisdiction here was ending and that he, the single enforcer of Earth law, would soon be out of a job. He grimaced in annoyance as he finally drew his vehicle to a halt outside the station house.

Little different from others in Godrun, the foamstone building stood like a grain silo punctuated with windows, with a front portico to one side of a ramp leading up from the underground garage. However, the front door was armoured and as he stepped up onto the portico a disc-shaped security drone dropped on its power cables from the rain roof and swivelled to inspect him.

'Any problems?' he asked.

Red lights flickered around the drone's rim then it replied, 'More people coming past to take a look here. Who knows what they expect to see?'

'Nothing will happen today,' said Enders. He shrugged. 'Tomorrow all bets are off.'

'I can still defend this property even then,' the drone stated.

'Of course, but try not to kill anyone.'

'It will be their choice.'

Enders nodded then said, 'Open.'

The armoured door clonked and then swung open ahead of him.

Not yet dressed, Enders sipped from a cup of coffee as he gazed out the window across the town. Shots rang out and he transferred his gaze down to the street where revellers were leaving a saloon and firing their weapons into the air. He glared at these and after a moment turned to put his cup down on a side table.

'We should get out of here now,' said his wife, Emily, from where she sat on the bed pulling on her leggings. 'They're already celebrating.'

Enders glanced at her. 'I'm not finished until sunrise tomorrow morning.' He headed across the room and jerked open his wardrobe, harder than intended.

'Really?' She stood, watching him carefully. 'Even now Earth jurisdiction is limited in the city to the Embassy. You know Trader John has city officials in his pocket. How else did he get out of prison so early? And here? The town council and Mayor Gavon are all mine owners and have always been in his pocket. You have no backup anymore, Enders.'

'I know,' he conceded.

'You should have shot him in the head,' she stated flatly as she continued dressing.

'He's an arthrodapt and tougher than I realised.' He shrugged, taking out a shirt. 'He should have died, but money talks here. Even with the murder charges he still managed to buy off-world medical care.'

She shook her head. 'The guy is a creep, and a dangerous one. He thinks he can buy *anything* he wants.'

'He couldn't buy you.' Enders observed, pulling on the shirt.

'Yeah,' she said.

'I shut him down before and I'll shut him down again.'

She looked up. 'Why? We're done here.'

'Because it is my duty to enforce the law until sunrise tomorrow morning,' he said flatly.

She grimaced. 'Always the soldier.'

Enders turned back to the wardrobe, pushed aside the shirts to reveal a uniform jacket. He ran his finger along the service ribbon on the breast. 'The war was simpler,' he said, closing the wardrobe then concentrating on buttoning up his shirt.

'Of course it was,' she replied. 'The evil alien prador against you and your soldiers.Black and white.'

Enders smiled wryly at his reflection in the mirrored wardrobe door. 'When things got really nasty we brought in the heavy mob – the war drones. Shame that's not an option here.'

'You knew it would be complicated – political – when you took this job.' Emily gestured to the window. 'Here you're a lawman, not a soldier, and here you're dealing with humans, not evil aliens.'

'Are the prador evil anymore since the truce?' he asked tightly, turning. 'Apparently we must negotiate with them and appease them.'

He walked over to a nearby table, took up his gun belt and strapped it on. While Emily watched, frowning, he drew the rail-beader from one holster. He checked its display then holstered it again before drawing the other weapon from its holster – a long-barrelled pulse gun. He gazed at it, expression blank.

'Anyway,' he said, 'tomorrow morning I will no longer be a lawman. I will no longer be Monitor E L Trepanan of the shitty little mining town of Godrun.' He turned to Emily. 'I shut down Trader John and his janglers. I brought order here. And now, because the prador don't want Earth forces on a world this close to their border...' He shrugged.

'They can't seem to distinguish between monitors like you and soldiers like you were.' Emily shook her head. 'Perhaps the distinction is a fine one.'

'I think there's more involved,' said Enders, ignoring the jibe. 'I would bet Trader John has been feeding them bullshit – he has the contacts.'

'But there's nothing you can do about it now.'

After a long pause he replied, 'I cannot allow it all to be for nothing, Emily.'

She looked up at him, gentler now. 'Where are you going?'

'Out to the Flat again.'

'Please don't,' she said.

'I have to,' he replied, holstering the pulse gun and turning for the door.

Emily leapt from the bed and moved in front of him, wrapped her arms around him and kissed him hard.

'Then go careful,' she said as they separated.

He nodded, disentangled himself from her and strode out the door.

The river wound across through the mudstone of the flat towards the city, which glinted with lights in the early evening, a fairy citadel transplanted to this backwoods world. Enders drove over a bridge across it then along a metalled road beside it, tracing its course until he saw his destination.

The ovoid house stood on double-jointed legs, rather like some huge animal dipping its feet into the water in preparation for crossing, for it overhung the river. The motorised home was capable of walking on those legs to another location. However, judging by its surroundings, it had established itself here some time ago. A jetty protruded below with boats moored against it. Surrounding mudstone had been dug up and gardens planted – adapted palm trees scattered here and there amidst the shrubbery, the whole enclosed by a high security fence. A short drive ran up to the double gate in the fence, with a parking area to one side.

As he turned into the drive, Enders gazed across at a raised area back from the jetty. People were gathered there and soft music waxing and waning with the breeze. It seemed Trader John was eating alfresco today with guests.

Enders brought his jeep up to the mesh gate, noted the palm reader on a post to one side, then took his carbine from the door pocket. He fired, blowing away the hinges in sprays of white-hot metal, tossed the carbine down and drove at the gate. Clinging only by a few tags of metal it collapsed before him and he motored straight off the short drive and into the gardens, heading for the raised area. Slewing to a halt beside a palm tree, he climbed out, took out his pulse gun and altered its power setting, then took up his laser carbine and, resting it across his shoulder, began striding towards the steps leading up.

'Hey you!' someone shouted.

He glanced over as two heavies stepped out of the bushes. Without hesitation, he fired twice. Pulses of ionised aluminium dust hit them both in their chests, electrical discharges leap-frogging down their bodies to earth in the ground. They stood shuddering for a moment then just dropped, thudding into the succulent groundcover. He strode on, ignoring them. Another thug appeared at the head of the steps and he just shot him. Bullets zinged into the shrubbery nearby and two smacked into his chest sending him staggering – shock-absorbing fibres flowering from his flack-jacket. He brought his carbine down and fired it one-handed, earth erupting and shrubs catching fire. Two leapt for cover but he nailed a third with a stun shot from his pulse gun. Finally, he reached the top, stepping over the one he had stunned earlier.

Guests stood in shock about a table laden with food, still clutching forgotten drinks. Some other heavies ran up into the area but seemed unsure of how to act now he was in sight of these others. Two others appeared, these clad in combat armour, visored helmets concealing their faces and heavy carbines clutched across their stomachs. Enders eyed them and knew that stun rounds would not bring them down.

Then one big individual amidst the guests raised a hand and they all halted. This man turned. He looked like he wore armour under his loose white shirt and slacks, but that was the carapace of the arthrodapt. His bald head sported saurian ridges running front to back, while mandibles folded out to reveal his human mouth.

'What do you want, Trepanan?' he asked.

'Justice and peace everywhere,' Enders replied, still striding forwards, 'but right now you are under arrest.' He came up before Trader John and pointed his carbine at the man's chest.

'This is interesting,' said John. 'How do you think this is going to work?'

'I'll take you into the city and present charges, as usual,' said Enders.

'And then what happens?' John looked at a fancy watch on his wrist. 'In ten hours there will be no Earth law here.'

'Hold out your hands.'

Trader John glanced around at the people here, then towards the various heavies around the top of the mound. He smiled, rattled his mandibles. Focusing on the two armoured guards, he called out, 'Do nothing – just stand as you are.'

Enders noted weapons being lowered, hands drawing away from holstered guns.

'Very sensible,' he said.

'Of course,' said Trader John, and held out his hands.

Enders watched him for a long moment, then stepped forwards taking a snake tie from his belt. He slapped it around the man's wrists then caught hold of his biceps and began marching him towards the jetty.

'I suppose you hoped I would resist,' said John.

'It crossed my mind,' Enders replied.

'I understand your need to do your duty,' said John. 'You were a soldier after all, but you understand that this is a futile demonstration.'

'We'll see about that.'

They clumped along the jetty to the boats. Enders paused beside one. 'Get in.' He unwound the rope from a bollard and tossed it in. 'You take the wheel,' he added, as he climbed in after John.

They motored out into the river, John steering the boat with his tied hands. Soon the jetty, with people gathered on it, disappeared behind a curve of the river.

'How is that lovely wife of yours?' John asked.

'She's fine – looking forward to a break from Godrun and the Flats, to be honest.'

'I think I'll take her when I go back to Godrun,' said John. 'After I've killed you, of course. There's little enough entertainment to be had in that place.'

'Over there,' said Enders, pointing to the edge of the river where a small channel cut into the mudstone.

'Really? I thought you were taking me to the city?'

Enders did not reply – jaw locked.

'You're not thinking of doing something illegal are you, monitor?'

'Take the fucking boat in,' Enders spat.

John shrugged, apparently unconcerned, and guided the boat into the channel, finally bringing it to a halt where it ended.

'Out,' said Enders.

Trader John climbed out of the boat. Enders followed, struggling a little to get from the boat to the rocky edge while holding his carbine. A hand reached down to assist him, free from its snake tie. Trader John smiled then heaved him up over the edge. Enders landed hard on his back and looked up in time to see John holding the carbine. He snatched for his pulse gun and fired, hitting the man on the shoulder. John staggered back, discharges all down his body, but instead of collapsing, he raised the carbine and fired. The shot hit Enders' arm, flaying away smoking flesh. He grabbed with his other hand for his beader, but John moved in, stepping on his wrist, then slamming the butt of the carbine into his head.

Monitor Enders woke with a groan and immediately struggled against his bonds. Trader John stepped over and hauled him up onto his knees facing the river. He walked round and squatted down in front of him, holding the pulse gun by the barrel.

'You set it to stun for my guards. That doesn't work on me.' He tossed the gun aside, then pulled open his shirt to reveal three scars on his chest carapace, which he peered at, then prodded with a finger. 'Not like last time.' He looked up. 'Have you any idea what they had to do to keep me alive in that hospital?'

Enders eyed the scars. 'She was right. I should have shot you in the head.'

'Your wife,' said John. 'Her attitude will change.'

Enders glared at him and said nothing.

John waited for some further response then reached out and picked up the carbine, continuing, 'So what was your plan? Was I to have an accident on the way to the city?' He waited again, then said, 'Not very policeman-like of you. Thinking you were a soldier again?'

Enders just turned to one side and ignored him.

John held up the carbine. 'I like these. All the different focus settings can be so useful. Narrow beam for distance shots, and then there's this.' He altered settings on the side of the weapon, then unscrewed a short end section to the barrel. Pointing the carbine at a nearby shrub he triggered it. The entire shrub glared red and then burst into flame.

'Do you think that lovely wife of yours… Emily… do you think she would look good wearing an induction thrall?'

'Fuck you,' said Enders, swinging back.

'No no no. Fuck her. When I'm doing that I'll fondly remember this moment.' He turned the carbine and pointed it at Ender's stomach. 'I would like to take some time with you, but I'm a busy man. You know, stone people to collect and put to work, mines to run, money to be made. You understand?'

'I understand that you're –'

John triggered the carbine and the disperse beam hit the monitor's stomach. Enders started screaming, his clothing and his flesh smoking as John played the beam up and down. He burst into flame, oily black smoke boiling from his body. The screaming turned to a rough sawing sound as John burned away his throat, but left his face intact. Then that stopped as with a wet crackling sound he bowed forward and down over the fire. John shut off the beam and watched as Enders continued to bow, still burning, his forehead jarring against the stone.

'And in the real world this is what happens to heroes,' said Trader John.

With a sigh, he stood and put the carbine aside. He then stepped over to the still burning body and with one hand easily picked it up with the cord binding wrists to ankles. He carried the body over to the river's edge like a suitcase, swung it back and forth a couple of times and tossed it into the water. After watching it floating and bobbing as the current took it, he gazed in the direction the river flowed, towards the city.

'Give them my regards back there, Monitor E L Trepanan.'

He headed back to the boat, whistling tunelessly.

The village consisted of dome houses fashioned of foamstone sprayed over a wooden skeleton, doors and windows cut afterward – the doors made of composite and the windows out of multi-glaze chainglass. Gazing through his monocular at this, Kraven noted the power cables running from an oblate fusion reactor, the pump station for groundwater and a satellite dish for full media connection. Here and there, some modern crawlers and Flat scooters were parked. All this was irrelevant of course. They may have taken advantage of some modern technology but the stone people were still primitive and sub-human.

Some residents were visible loading supplies into one of the crawlers – probably for an expedition on the Flat, hunting for the same star gems for which the mines in the mountains had been sunk. Some others were tending food crops in gardens cut out of the mudstone. They had no animals here, since any form of killing was anathema to them. This made the job for Kraven and his associates so much easier.

'All quiet?' asked Deela, standing beside him.

He glanced at the woman. She looked hot in the tight envirosuit she wore but he knew better than to hit on her. Other janglers had made that mistake.

'Seems so,' he replied.

She lowered the mike on her headset. 'Status report,' she demanded then tilted her head to listen. After a moment, she turned back to him. 'Dreyfus and Holse are in position. Let's do this.' She strode back towards the crawler and he followed.

The crawler sat with its main body down on the ground and chameleonware paint turning it the same colour as the surrounding mudstone. He stepped inside after her to where Frax and another jangler waited. Frax was playing with his power whip while the other checked over their stun guns.

'Frax,' said Kraven, heading for the cockpit, 'stunners only. We want them all and we want them undamaged.'

'They might get a bit antsy,' said Frax hopefully.

'They're stone people,' interjected Deela from the cockpit. 'They don't know how to be antsy. But I can personally guarantee that if we lose any, Trader John will not be happy.'

'But if we knock them out we have to carry them,' Frax protested meekly.

He preferred to round them up and herd them into the transport and use stunners on them once they were inside. But stone people, though non-violent, could be stubborn. This would always result in Frax having to use his power whip, often with the consequence of missing eyes and other damage that cut down on the working life of the catch.

'Stunners only,' Kraven insisted, glancing to Deela.

Frax sighed, put his power whip to one side and picked up a stunner. The short weapon resembled a shotgun and was the weapon of choice for janglers everywhere. It fired a blast of narcotic beads that punched through the skin and rendered the victim instantly unconscious. There might be a few deaths if they hit someone old, or sick, or maybe the odd child, but that kind of loss Trader John expected.

Kraven dropped into the driver's seat and hit start, Deela now in the seat beside him. The crawler body rose up off the ground on hydraulics and he shoved the joystick forward, taking them towards the village. Even as they approached, he saw other janglers moving in on foot. One of them had entered the garden area – probably the Marsman, Dreyfus – and he could see the stone people there dropping, unstrung puppets. By the time he entered the village, two other Janglers were putting down those around the crawler – that would be Holse and his party of janglers. Kraven brought his own crawler to a halt, then stood and followed Deela back. He took up a stunner, then followed her outside, Frax and the other jangler close behind.

Things were beginning to stir up – stone people coming out of their houses. A woman stepped out of a doorway nearby, a stunner thumped and she staggered back with her hands up to her face and keeled over.

'Body shots, Frax!' Deela warned.

Frax ignored her as he kicked open the door and entered the house, his stunner thumping repeatedly once he got inside.

'That guy is going to have a bad end,' Deela stated. She didn't have a stunner, just stood with her hands on her hips and watched the surrounding activity. She then turned to Kraven. 'What are you waiting for?'

Janglers were kicking open doors all along the row of houses. Kraven moved off to do his part and, as he reached his chosen door, a child stepped out. He hit the kid with his gun butt and stepped over him – the children could be useful at the sorting troughs, but they tended not to last very long, so Trader John had given instructions to leave them behind this time. The supply of induction thralls was limited at present.

Inside the house, he saw a man and woman sitting at the table and another young heavily built man standing in an open kitchen area, holding a knife. He shot that one first, the blast throwing chopped vegetables and a couple of saucepans to the floor. The man at the table began to stand when the second shot took him in the chest and flung him back against the wall. The woman was quite attractive so he waited until she stood before shooting her in the legs. He didn't want to spoil her face – he had a private deal with a bar owner in Godrun for one of his catch.

Once sure there was no sign of further movement from them he walked over, put his weapon on the table and took a packet from his belt pouch. Opening this he took out three induction thralls and pressed one against the woman's temple. It crunched as its bone anchors went in, the red light coming on. After a moment, that changed to amber as it scanned her skull for the correct neural networks in her brain. When it changed to green this indicated it had found them. He did the same with the man who had been at the table then walked over to the kitchen area.

'Shit,' he said.

The young man here lay face down in a pool of blood. Kraven stepped up to him and turned him over. The fool had fallen on his knife and was now coughing blood. Damn, he was big and fit and would have been perfect for the mines. Grimacing, Kraven drew his pulse gun. Stone people were sub-human, but Kraven wasn't without feelings. Best to put this one out of his misery. He shot the man once through the forehead, burning a smoking hole through and blowing steaming brains out the back.

A moment later, as he stepped out of the house and scanned around, Kraven saw that the big transport crawler had arrived. Holse came up beside him pulling a grav-sled loaded with three bodies.

'Good catch,' he said. 'Thrall count is twenty-four units.'

'Twenty-three,' said Kraven. He gestured back to the house he had just left. 'One in there I'm selling in Godrun. The rest go to the mines.'

Holse glanced over at Deela. 'You cleared it with that bitch?'

'She's taking her cut.'

Emily gazed out at the sunrise over Godrun, the cylinder houses casting blocks of shadow on the ground as the sun cracked through a slab of cloud over the mountains. Her arms tightly folded across her chest she closed her eyes as if in pain then opened them and shook herself. With determination, she turned away and headed over to the console against the wall in the sitting room, sat down and made a call. After a short delay, a face appeared on the screen before her.

'Emily Trepanan,' said the uniformed woman before her. 'This comlink was reserved for your husband until this morning.'

'I know, but I have to speak to someone,' said Emily.

The woman looked bored, her attention drifting to something over to one side, probably another screen.

'About what?'

'Enders headed out to the Flat yesterday,' said Emily, trying to keep calm. 'I tried to contact him yesterday evening but got no reply. I've been trying to get a call through to you all night and there was no response…'

'The change in jurisdiction has caused some problems…'

'Still, Enders is one of your officers. It is your responsibility to respond to this.'

The woman swung her attention back to Emily. 'As of just half an hour ago Enders L Trepanan is no longer our responsibility. The monitor division has been disbanded. Do you wish me to file a missing persons report?'

'You can find him,' said Emily tightly. 'He has a locator beacon implant!'

'That is no longer the responsibility of city police, and with the changeover we no longer have the time or resources to mount a search.'

'This is crazy! You just have to ping his beacon!'

'Do you wish me to file a missing persons report?' the woman asked again, robotically.

'Yes, I want you to file a report! You have to find him!'

'The matter will be attended do. Is there anything further?'

'Look, if you don't have the manpower just give me his location!' Emily wiped away angry tears.

'That information is restricted to police personnel only, and certainly not available to those who do not have full citizenship,' said the woman, smiling nastily. 'Now, I have other matters to attend to. Further calls from your console will be blocked.' The image winked out.

Emily gaped at the screen for a long moment, then put in another call. The response was immediate: a chromed face appeared on the screen.

'Earth Embassy AI.'

'This is Emily Trepanan. My husband went out yesterday and I've not been able to contact him since yesterday evening. The city police will not help me, even though they can locate him with his beacon.'

After a pause, a young shaven-headed man replaced the chromed face, 'Hi, Emily. Do you know what Enders was doing? It was his last day...'

'Janssen!' Emily talked quickly. 'He headed out to the Flat, that's all I know for sure. But the janglers are taking stone people again and he definitely was not happy about Trader John's release... Why are the city police being so... pig-headed?'

Janssen looked to one side. 'I'm running a trace on his beacon now.' He operated controls out of sight. 'A lot of the city police and bureaucrats here are in Trader John's pocket. The imposition of the monitor division from Earth pissed them off, beside the fact that the monitors were not citizens of this world. They are being deliberately... obstructive.' He paused for a second. 'There. I have it. Enders is about five miles outside the city on the River Spill. I'm sending coordinates to you now. Load them to your personal unit. I'll pull together some men and meet you there.'

A map displaced his image, with a winking dot on the snaking course of the river. Emily stood, taking her unit out of her pocket. She pointed it at the screen and the same map appeared on its screen. She pocketed it again as Janssen reappeared.

'Thank you, Janssen.'

'We owe this to you both at least, though Embassy interference in local matters is now illegal. I can scrape this past during the present chaos… I suggest you just bring along the belongings you most value and can carry. We'll take you both straight to the Embassy.'

Emily frowned. 'Are things so bad?'

'When I said "obstructive" I was being a little disingenuous,' said Janssen. 'There are people looking for pay-back and it's getting dangerous out there. You may not be able to return to Godrun.'

'Okay, I understand.'

'Get moving, Emily, and go careful.'

The screen blinked out.

Dressed in a jumpsuit, a pack slung over one shoulder and a gun holstered at her hip, Emily moved fast down the stairs of the monitor station. She went through the door at the bottom into a garage with a roller door at one end and headed over to the scooter parked there. Opening one pannier, she dropped her pack inside, closed it and mounted. She started the thing, its turbine winding up to speed and the control console between the handlebars lighting up. Sorting through the options on the touch-screen, she chose one and hit it. A motor started ahead of her and the roller door began to rise.

Sunlight flooded in and she blinked against the glare. A ground car partially blocked the exit, two men sitting on the bonnet. They leisurely pushed themselves away from the car and began walking forwards. Emily made her calculations. Returning inside the defences of the station would only buy her a little time, and nobody would come to rescue her. She wound back the throttle, shot forwards drawing her pulse gun and fired at the ground in front of them – multiple shots splintering up hot smoking stone. One of the men dived to the side, while the other yelled and went down clutching at his shin.

She swerved for the narrow gap beside the ground car, shots from the uninjured man slamming into the scooter's caterpillar treads. She smashed into the gap, ripping off the panniers and scraping a deep dent down the side of the car, the vehicle jerking sideways. Then the scooter began jamming. She revved up the turbine, caterpillar treads spinning and tearing up the road, sparks showering out, then with a thump that tore off the back bumper of the car she shot through. The scooter weaved as she fought for control, the street now in sight. But the scooter shed a tread, the handlebars twisted right round and it went over, flinging her to the road.

Emily shoulder rolled but still landed hard. She lay there dazed for a moment, then struggled to get up. The shadow of a man fell across her and she looked up with fearful recognition.

'Good try,' said Trader John, pointing her husband's pulse gun at her. She grabbed for her own weapon and had it halfway out of its holster when the stun round hit her in the chest. Wreathed in electrical discharges her world went black.

Seated inside the spider, Trader John gazed around at the mine workings. Dust hazed the area from the conveyor shifting rubble from the sorting troughs to a spill pile. A group of stone people – mostly men – was trooping towards the mine entrance shouldering power chisels, heavy power packs on their backs. Others – mostly women – were at the sorting troughs. His mandibles open he smiled at all this busy industry.

'Let's go take a look down there,' he said to his companion. 'What do you think my dear?'

He glanced aside. Emily Trepanan still wore her jumpsuit, but the medic had cut part of it away to apply dressings to her injured shoulder and arm, while tags held together the cut on one side of her forehead. On the other side of her skull, over her temple, clung an induction thrall, its light winking green. Her mouth was open, her expression blank.

'I think it is a good idea, John,' she said without inflection.

John took hold of the joystick and pulled it up. The spider rose up on its legs and then began making its delicate way down the slope when he pushed the joystick forwards. Reaching the narrow valley leading to the mine entrance, stepping over strewn power cables snaking across the ground from the reactor, finally brought them to an area to one side of the sorting troughs.

'Here,' said John.

He lowered the spider and opened the door, stepping out. Emily opened the door on her side and walked round, moving to stand just a pace behind on his right. He gestured to her and she followed as he went over to the nearest trough. The women here were picking up chunks of mudstone and running them under the terahertz scanner. Most of these then went onto the spill conveyor, but occasionally they would toss a chunk onto a smaller conveyor running to another sorting-trough. John walked over and watched the work here, Emily close behind.

Some women were moving chunks of stone to an auto press to break them, while others were using vibro-chisels to dig out the contents of smaller chunks – the whole purpose of this mine. He watched as one woman broke open a large chunk of mudstone, ran the pieces under another scanner, discarded most of them then handed over one piece to another woman with a vibro-chisel. Stone falling away in dust and flakes, she revealed a small misty blue ball and finally freed it. She carefully placed this in a box filled with other orbs whose colours ranged across the spectrum.

'The women are useful for this work,' John said. 'But it's not for you.' He turned and studied her. 'Some new clothing, I think, and a prettier thrall for that fine skull of yours.'

'Thank you, John,' she said.

'Only the best for you,' he said. 'I don't think your husband appreciated you as much as he should have. You know they found his body washed up near the city docks and took it to the Earth Embassy?'

'You told me,' she said. 'It is unfortunate.'

'He was a soldier before he became monitor here,' said John. 'He died heroically.'

'Yes, I am sure he died heroically, John,' she said.

Trader John frowned. 'Aren't you sad about that?'

'Yes, I am sad about that, John.'

John studied her for a while then walked over to the box to pick up and inspect a pink orb the size of an eyeball.

'Star ruby,' he said. 'What do you think?'

'Never look much until they are polished,' said Emily, but she wasn't looking at the gem, just at his face.

'They are wealth,' said John, 'and wealth translates into power.'

'Yes, they are wealth, John.'

With a flash of irritation, he tossed the gem back in the box, eyed the stone people working here, then turned away and headed back towards the spider, Emily walking obediently behind.

Enders Trepanan's face was just about recognisable – eyes closed as if in sleep, head tilted forwards. He had been gutted with fire – a burned-out husk – his corpse now sitting at the focus of massed medical technology. A skein of tubes and wires ran from his skull into the surrounding hardware, another skein plugged in under his jaw. His burned body had been pulled wider open for the admissions of numerous probes, pipes and clamps.

All around robot arms terminating in intricate hardware twitched and shifted in anxious anticipation. Tanks held variously coloured fluids. One tank held something that looked like a human spine sculpted in metal and wound with cords of washed-of-colour muscle. Another tank held a similarly constructed human arm. Janssen surveyed all of this through the clean room window then switched his attention to the technician seated at her complex console with its displays for the indicators of human life.

Everything was flat-lined.

'You don't get much deader than this,' she said.

'I disagree, Lily,' said Janssen. 'True death is when there's nothing left.'

She conceded that with a shrug.

'You can begin,' he said.

Lily nodded once and began working her consoles. Screens flickered and changed, loading bars expanded. After a moment, she sat back and crossed her arms.

'Automatic now,' she said, 'unless it finds something that needs my attention.'

Numerous robots arms folded in to Trepanan's corpse and began cutting, pulling and levering. These arms began conveying away burned flesh and organs, chunks of charred bone like the detritus from some grotesque barbecue. If was fast, AI fast, and soon the body was a completely empty cavity. Another arm brought in a bar trailing skeins of wires and pressed it down on the exposed spine. This issued thousands of connector-like insect legs that folded in and pushed between the vertebrae.

'When can I go in?' asked Janssen.

'Any time now,' Lily replied. 'There's no need for an aseptic environment in there, nor will there be.'

Janssen moved over to a door beside the window, palmed the reader on the wall beside it and stepped in as it opened. He walked up to the surgical table, robotic arms shifting out of his path and folding away.

'Enders Trepanan,' he said.

'One moment,' said Lily via the intercom. 'Okay. Now.'

'Enders Trepanan,' Janssen said again.

The corpse opened its eyes, the head tilted further with the pipes feeding in underneath it shifting as they took pressure. Trepanan saw his body and groaned, bloody fluid flying from his mouth. This then cut off, air hissing from his mouth, and his eyes rolled up into his head.

'Just some adjustments,' said Lily. 'Oh yes – didn't shut off the afferent nerves. You can try again now.'

'Enders?'

Trepanan's eyes came back down again and he focused on Janssen.

'What?' he asked.

'You're dead,' Janssen explained. 'However, your services are still required.'

Enders just moved his mouth wetly, fluid running from one side.

Janssen walked closer and sat on the edge of the table, arms folded. 'Now, tell me about Trader John...'

Part 2

Logan gazed through his monocular out across the flats. A crawler, just running on solar and moving slowly across the mudstone, had stone people walking along on either side, probing for potential wash holes, which showed on the surface only as dimples or smaller punctures in the rock. They were looking for star gems – sapphires, rubies, diamonds and other precious jewels.

They were a family unit, a trailer behind the crawler containing their equipment and their self-inflating tents for this expedition. But it wasn't them Logan had been tracking. He swung his monocular to the side. The janglers had halted, four dismounting from Flat scooters and more stepping out of their crawler. Of course, all of them were heavily armed. Perhaps they had stopped for a beer or two before getting down to business. Logan lowered his monocular and walked back to his scooter. He unbuttoned his long coat, folded it and put it in one of the panniers. Now he could easily reach the pulse gun on his right hip and the rail-beader on his left, its power cable plugged into its battery on his belt. He mounted his scooter, made sure his laser carbine was free in its holster beside the pure water fuel tank, and started the vehicle.

Caterpillar treads biting into the rock, he shot out across the Flat, kicking up a cloud of dust behind him. A short while later the stone people saw him coming, but they did not react much. They thought they were perfectly safe.

As he drew closer, he spied the patriarch of this family. He was easy to spot: a tall thin man with long lip tendrils and grey skin. Old and tough, but gentle. Logan slowed and pulled up nearby. Climbed off his scooter and walked over.

'What are you?' asked the man.

'I'm Logan – I am the new monitor,' he replied.

The old man shook his head. 'Earth lawman?'

'Yes, and you've got janglers ranging further from Godrun. There's a hunting party of them here now and they've been watching you.'

The old man tilted his head and gazed at Logan suspiciously. 'Janglers here... So what good is an Earth lawman to us?'

'Earth law again applies in the city and out here, and in Godrun,' Logan stated.

'For how long?' the old man looked bitter. 'Can we return to our homes in the mountains?'

'It's different now,' said Logan tightly. 'The prador have agreed to Earth law applying here so long as there is no big military presence. That agreement has been locked in for a century.'

'Tell that to Monitor Trepanan.' The old man eyed Logan carefully. 'Or what you can find of him after Trader John fried him with a laser.'

'It will be different now,' Logan insisted.

'We will see...'

Logan cooled. 'Whatever way it goes, you should stay off the Flat for a while.'

The old man dipped his head in grudging acquiescence. 'And you?'

'I'm going to talk to those janglers.'

The man turned and whistled, waved his three-fingered hand above his head and his people started heading back towards to crawler.

'Luck,' he said.

Logan smiled without humour. 'It's not me that needs it.'

The janglers were packing up their temporary camp. They seemed in no hurry, knowing their vehicle could catch up with their prey quickly. They'd set up a table and yes, there were bottles of beer on it, a cooler on the ground beside it. Three sat in deck chairs by this table, others sat on the mudstone checking over stun guns.

Logan drove in slowly, aware of hands on or reaching for weapons. He halted, climbed off his scooter and pulled off his goggles, pausing for a moment in introspection. Then he sauntered over, assessing them. A thickset guy, with Marsman tattoos on his face, sat at the nearest the table, while the woman sitting nearby clad in a modern envirosuit he knew had been born on Earth. Others were local humans and one a stone man hybrid who had cropped his tendrils and had some cosmetic work to build him a nose.

'Do you know why you are called janglers?' he called as he approached the table. He came to a halt, hands on his hips.

'Because of ancient slaving techniques,' replied the woman.

He studied her. Deela was tough and pretty with an envirosuit that clung to her curves. She was the boss here, but he'd known that for a long time, just as he knew her name.

'Quite.' He nodded. 'The chains you use to manacle your victims… they jangle.'

'We don't use chains,' she replied.

'No, nor will you use inducers or slave collars today, or ever again.'

Deela stood up from her deckchair. Meanwhile the Marsman drew a pulse gun from his hip and put it on the table before him. Logan tracked all this, just as he was aware of the two moving round behind him.

'Says who?' she asked.

'Says Polity monitor Logan.' He paused and looked around at them. 'That would be me.'

The Marsman cleared his throat. 'Last lawman didn't do so well. And Earth has no jurisdiction here.'

Logan smiled. 'You haven't been keeping up on events. That changed precisely one hour ago. This world is now under the jurisdiction of Earth. It was just a case of a little negotiation with the prador. They don't really care what happens here – they just don't want a big military presence this close to their border.'

'So Earth sent one monitor,' said the woman, grinning at this madness.

'Seems so,' said Logan.

'Dreyfus,' Deela said the Marsman, 'shut this idiot up.'

'Predictable,' said Logan.

Dreyfus snatched for his pulse gun.

Logan tipped his left holster forwards so the weapon pointed behind him, and pushed it back. It hummed and spat, shooting out of the bottom of the holster as he turned, drawing his pulse gun with his right hand. He heard the fleshy impacts and oomphs of surprise from behind as he fired his pulse gun three times. Dreyfus flew back, following the back of his head to the mudstone. The hybrid in the other deckchair similarly followed part of his head to the ground. Logan dropped and rolled, automatic fire cutting above him. He shot under the table taking out the Deela's kneecap, shot twice and brought down another jangler. Then he came up with a weapon in each hand. Short bursts from the bead gun had two twirling in atomised blood. Another ran for his scooter. Logan was about to open fire again when three shots hit him in the chest. He staggered back, but fired once with his pulse gun, blowing away Deela's elbow. She shrieked, dropping her weapon. He walked round. One man was crawling along the ground leaving a slime trail of blood. He shot him through the back of the head, then glanced over at Deela. 'Don't go away now.'

'Body armour,' she spat.

Logan probed the bullet holes through his shirt. There was no blood.

Returning to his scooter, he drew his laser carbine and calmly checked it over. After a moment, he flicked up the sight, shouldered it, and aimed at the now distant escaping jangler on his scooter. He shot twice, the carbine crackling, impacts to the right of the scooter. He adjusted and shot again. A short burst. The scooter and its rider tumbled, shedding debris in a cloud of dust. He put the carbine away and returned to Deela.

'Now, time for us to chat.'

'Fuck you,' she replied, obviously in a lot of pain.

'Medicate yourself,' he said.

She stared at him for a long moment then reached to take an ampule from her belt pouch. She stabbed it into her biceps and after a moment sighed with relief.

'Again. We chat.'

'Why should I? You'll kill me anyway.'

Logan shrugged. 'You're a jangler. You know the routine. Do you want me to torture you and pump you full of serum?'

'Just let me live.'

'Okay, why not.' He waved a dismissive hand, apparently not bothered. 'You answer my questions and I let you live. Now, where exactly is Trader John?'

'He's out at Riverside – at his house.'

'But I guess if his operation starts falling apart he'll be back soon enough?'

'You guess right.'

'How many stone people enslaved in the jewel mines now?'

Deela shrugged, then wished she hadn't. ''bout a thousand.'

'Where is Emily Trepanan?'

'What?'

'Emily Trepanan – the wife of the previous monitor. You know. The monitor who shot John in the chest but didn't finish the job. The one he laser-burned and threw in the river.'

'What?'

'Where is Emily Trepanan?'

'How the fuck should I know?'

'Okay.' Logan stood.

'You said you wouldn't kill me.'

'Quite.' He drew his bead gun and fired short burst into the jangler's remaining scooters, one of which caught fire. He fired a longer burst into the crawler and shuddering and spraying debris it seemed to deflate on its treads. He must have hit a battery because power also arced to the ground.

'You might survive.' He shrugged. 'People have survived much worse.'

He headed back to his scooter.

Logan gazed at Godrun and frowned. Only one way to do this, and that was to just go on in and take the long vacant position of monitor – the lone lawman, the sheriff of this town.

He started up his scooter and continued along the road, entering Godrun, studying the people on the pavements. Many janglers were evident, also town residents and workers from the top end. He slowed by a party of stone people trudging along in a line. They were clad in heavy but ragged work clothes and all wore induction thrall devices attached to their temples. Their handler strode ahead of them – a big ugly brute with a cattle goad he really did not need. That, Logan decided, would be stopping very soon, but he needed to prepare.

Finally, he arrived at a single cylindrical building with wide chainglass windows and bullet holes in the walls. As he drew up, it surprised him to see the front door still intact, but then it was armoured. He dismounted, took a rucksack out of one pannier and walked up to the door. Looking up he saw the security drone dangling from its power cable, one of its lasers hanging out and bullet holes through its crablike body. However, it activated as he drew close. Red eyes ignited on its rim, it swivelled as best it could to face him.

'Good morning,' it grated.

'Good morning, drone,' he replied. 'Polity monitor Logan reporting for duty. I've come to fill E. L. Trepanan's shoes.'

After a long pause, the drone said, 'Yeah… right.'

'Has this station been breached?'

'Nah, some janglers used me as target practice but otherwise weren't interested.'

'Very well… open.'

Locks disengaged all around the door and it swung inwards. Logan entered a reception area: seats all around, a chainglass window and an office lying beyond. Though only one monitor had ever attended, the station could take more staff. He headed to the door at the back, placed his hand against a palm reader and it opened for him. He climbed the stairs, entered a large apartment and dumped his rucksack on the sofa. Walking over to the window while stripping off his shirt and gazed out. Already gawkers had appeared. The news of an arrival here would travel fast.

His shirt off revealed his naked chest. He inspected circular scars on his skin then folded his forefinger in to touch one of four skin controls on the palm of his hand. The bullet marks just faded away. Next entering the bedroom, he opened a wardrobe and studied the clothes inside. He took out a uniform in blue and white and inspected it for a moment, then shook his head and put it back. He found a T-shirt and put it on. Another wardrobe revealed woman's clothing.

'Like you never left, Emily Trepanan,' he said, closed the wardrobe and turned away. Over at a wall he gazed at a picture. Here stood Monitor E L Trepanan in military uniform, Emily at his side with her arm linked through his.

He reached out and touched the picture, then closed his eyes for a second. His face rippled and his cheekbones and jawline shifted, his nose sagged a little and his eyes changed colour. But for his dusty blond hair he now looked exactly like Trepanan. He smiled.

'Hello Enders,' he said.

After a moment, the smile faded. He took his fingers from the picture and turned away, his features shifting again and returning to their earlier setting. Seating himself at a console, he turned it on. A film screen rose out of the top and flicked on to show the monitor logo. He passed his hand across in front of it and it flicked to the image of a chrome face.

'Logan,' it said.

'You,' he said.

'Evidently,' it replied

'I expected Janssen, not the Embassy AI – is your oversight necessary?'

'The situation is complicated here,' said the artificial intelligence. 'Earth law needs to be established, but we cannot be too heavy handed, since that might aggravate the prador.'

'Very well.Monitor Logan reporting in.'

'Yes, your arrival has been noted,' replied the AI. 'The woman you left alive called for help and other janglers picked her up. Now, Trader John is aware that his profit margins might be threatened, and has put a price on your head.'

'Then all is as it should be.'

'Do you require back-up now?'

'No more than I asked for. You're sending me a deputy?'

'Yes, I am sending you someone who was in the service – from the heavy infantry.'

'That's interesting. Who?'

'He's an armoured antipersonnel unit.'

Logan said nothing for a moment, then, 'I asked for something a little less… effective.'

'You asked for a deputy.'

'You also said you did not want to get heavy-handed and annoy the prador.'

'There are innocent people to be protected.'

Logan raised an eyebrow. 'In Godrun?'

'I am aware of your opinion of this town and its people,' said the AI. 'When I say innocent people, I am talking about the stone people.'

'Very well,' said Logan. 'But this drone must stay covert. I need time. I need Trader John to come out here…'

'I know what you need. But I must make my own cold calculations.'

'Very well. Speak to you later.' Logan cut the connection.

The offices of the town council stood out from the foamstone houses all around. The ugly block with wide marble steps leading up to a colonnaded entry looked out of another century. Wearing the monitor uniform, Logan strode up to the panelled double door, noting a security drone depending inside the colonnade. He tried the door but found it firmly closed, so he stepped to a com panel beside it and hit the buzzer. The screen came on to show a mousy blonde-haired woman.

'How can I help you?' she asked.

'Polity monitor Logan,' he replied. 'I am here to serve notice of jurisdiction. Net notice has already been served so you are aware of this.'

'I'm sorry, but the Council is in session with the Mayor – they cannot be interrupted.'

'Under net notice you will be aware that I have right of entry into all public properties. I suggest you open the door.'

A flash of anger crossed her features. 'You have no rights here!'

'On the contrary –'

'You cannot come in.'

The screen blinked off and above him the security drone whirred, its eyes igniting. Logan sighed, then in one smooth motion drew his pulse gun and fired, blowing the drone into pieces. He walked over to the doors again, stepped back and shot out the locks, then stepped rapidly forward driving his boot against them. They crashed open and he marched into the lobby. Two security guards ran out of a back room as he switched down a setting on his weapon.

'Those doors...' said one of them, while the other reached for the gun at his belt.

Two shots and they froze issuing electrical discharges, then dropped bonelessly. Logan walked up to the reception window. The woman sat inside, gaping at him.

'Where is this meeting?'

'You can't –'

'I can,' he cut in. 'Now are you going to tell me or must we be uncivilised about this?'

'The Polity can't just make demands like this –'

He dialled his pulse gun up again and shot a hole through the window, just to the right of her face. She sat there frozen for a long moment, then decided defiance sat above her pay grade. She pointed to a door on the other side of the lobby. Logan walked over, tried the handle and found it locked, kicked it open and stepped in.

Five councillors sat at a glass-topped table, the Mayor at the head – a bulky shaven-headed man packed into expensive businesswear and chuffing on a cigar. The councillors – three women and two men – were of a similar kind. A bottle stood on the table and they were all drinking.

'This is a private meeting!' said one of the women.

Logan walked over to stand beside the dark haired, thin and sour-faced female. He picked up the bottle and studied it.

'Earth monitors don't take much notice of privacy or individual rights,' said Mayor Gavon, putting down his cigar and leaning back in his chair. He was sweating, nervous. 'Trepanan was just as arrogant.'

'This is Earth import bourbon,' said Logan. 'Expensive tastes here.'

He took the bottle and one glass, walked to the other end of the table, sat and poured a generous measure. 'I guess the mining operations here are making a lot of money. Maybe more money than Trader John knows about.' He smiled humourlessly.

They watched him in silence as he sipped then put down the glass. It seemed they had no comment on that.

'Well,' he began. 'You are all aware that Godrun and the Flats are now under Earth jurisdiction again, but I thought a courtesy call was in order – just to make things clear.'

'Courtesy,' spat one of the men.

'Yes,' said Logan, 'courtesy. I have the power to enforce the law without political oversight. I did not have to come here. I do not have to deliver warnings.'

'Seems Earth law is what your kind chooses it to be,' said sour-face.

'You might not like it, but it is a fact of your lives now.' He drank some more of the bourbon – it was very good. 'But I am prepared to be lenient when it comes to minor infractions – we are after all in a period of transition. What concerns me at present, are the major ones.'

'Like what?' asked Gavon.

Logan focused on the man. 'Like the law against enslaving sentients. What was it you said about individual rights?' Gavon had no reply and Logan continued, 'Also, like the laws against extortion, murder, rape and torture. The major ones.'

A sharp-looking man in an expensive grey environment suit spoke up. 'You're talking about the stone people.' He sat back and turned his bourbon glass on the table top, inspecting its contents.

'In part,' Logan replied. 'How they have been treated is not unique.'

'They're animals,' said sour-face.

'They're adapted humans who arrived here before you in the first diaspora from Earth. As such, under Earth law, they have more rights on this world than you.'

'You'll destroy the mining business here,' said another woman.

Logan gave a tight smile, studying his own glass. 'There are machines that can do their job better. All it will take is some reinvestment of your profits.' He looked up. 'You will free the stone people working in your mines. Though you are already breaking the law under the net notice, I will give you until this time tomorrow to get it done, then I act.'

'That's not enough time!' one complained. 'We need to get new infrastructure organised. That'll shut down the mines!'

The one in the environment suit stood up. 'My stone people left this morning,' he said to Logan. 'I trust that I will have no problems?'

Logan spread his hands. 'You know the laws. Don't break them.'

'Fuck you, Pallen, you've got machines,' said the whiner.

Pallen glanced round at her. 'Because I knew this was coming.'

'You never were one of us,' said sour-face.

'I know,' Pallen replied. 'I don't possess that special degree of stupidity to think Trader John could keep Earth from taking over here, and nor did I think the percentage he demands is enough to keep him off our backs.' He paused and surveyed the table. 'And do you really think he hasn't noticed that you've been skimming the profits? That he's not been getting the percentage he demanded...? Later.' He headed for the door and out.

'Sensible man,' said Logan, also standing. 'You have one day.' He too headed for the door. There was no reply from the table.

'Pallen,' Logan called.

The man turned halfway across the lobby and waited.

'They will turn on anyone who breaks ranks,' Logan said.

'They were already turning on me,' he replied. 'I took the slaves they used up, gave them medical care then paid them a wage until they were ready to leave.'

'I know,' said Logan. 'Watch your back.'

'Watch *your* back,' Pallen replied. 'Trader John has a bounty on your head and every jangler here will want to take a shot. You know what happened to E. L. Trepanan?'

'I know.'

'I just hope Earth is prepared to move in here with more than just one man. This is all about to get very ugly...'

'You think?' said Logan

Pallen eyed him for a long moment, then nodded towards the council room. 'They don't know who to be the most scared of, you or Trader John. He'll come, you know... and he'll come hard. He almost certainly knows what they've been doing.'

Logan shrugged. 'There's always a heavy price when you make a deal with the devil.'

'Quite,' said Pallen, and headed away.

Trader John studied the sweaty face of Mayor Gavon staring at him from the screen. He then glanced to the curved windows of his home, across the river and out across the Flat towards the mountains.

'He's delivered notice of jurisdiction,' said Grade.

'Yes,' said John, 'of course he has. We knew this was going to happen, but thus far there is only him there, and thus far the political situation has to be tested.'

'You said you could keep Earth out of here,' said Gavon.

John swung his attention back to the screen. 'Are you complaining? My agents fed the information to the prador that led to Earth being shunted out before and I got rid of Trepanan.'

'But a monitor is back, and it's looking a lot like Earth law is here to stay.'

'We will see,' said John tightly.

'So what do we do?'

'Some of my men will test this Monitor Logan,' said John. 'I have information about him that leads me to think they will be unsuccessful. I then have other options to bring into play.'

'What can we do here?'

'Nothing, for the present. Just sit tight.' John waved a hand over the screen and it blinked out. He stared at it for a long moment then reached out and tapped it. The screen blinked on again but this time just showed a revolving sphere. 'House, detach services and move to pre-set location.'

'As you instruct,' replied a robotic voice.

The house rumbled and began to move, the view through the windows shifting. John tapped the screen again and the sphere disappeared. A touch brought up a list of names and he touched one of these.

'Chinnery Grade,' he said.

After a short pause a face appeared. Below white spikey hair, half of it was conventional human while the other half was metal.

'You've decided?' asked Grade.

'Yes, I've decided,' John replied. 'Meet me out on the Flat as detailed.'

Grade nodded once and his image blinked out.

'Why are we moving?' a female voice enquired.

John looked over his shoulder. 'Business,' he said, 'just business.'

Trader John's house rose higher on its hinged legs. It then raised one of them, terminating in a big flat foot, and took a cautious step into the river. More sure now of its footing, it took another step, then another. Soon it was wading across the river, then stepping up out the other side and heading out across the Flat.

The drone dropped out of the darkness like a nightmare scorpion fly, writ large in nano-chrome armour etched with black superconductor. Its legs were thick and shiny and terminated in four-finger hands. Its wings were spread effector plates running from grav-engines in its back. Laser ports dotted its body, a missile launcher jutted from the thorax below its head. It hung above the building for a moment protruding two Gatling cannons, and revolved to inspect the town. Next, it folded the cannons away to come down with a heavy clattering thump on the roof of the monitor station.

'Hello, monitor... Logan,' it said.

'Hello, drone. What do I call you?'

'Call me Sting. It's what they called me in my old unit, for reasons that should be quite obvious.' The drone wiggled its scorpion sting.

'More detail than I require,' said Logan flatly.

'Just making conversation,' said Sting. 'You have work for me?'

'Yes, I do. I gave them until tomorrow afternoon to free the stone people. I want you to ensure that they do.'

'Oh good...'

Logan shook his head. 'What I mean by that is that you'll use your induction warfare systems to knock out every thrall device and explosive collar throughout the mountains.'

'Oh... and if they start killing stone people?'

Logan grimaced. 'Yes, that is a possibility, but you can intervene subtly. You must not reveal yourself. If Trader John realises something like you is here he might not come. And I want him to come.'

'That could be... difficult.'

'I have every confidence in you.'

'The stone people even now are under Earth protection,' Sting observed.

'Yes, I understand. I'm just asking you to at least try.'

'I will try not to reveal myself,' said the drone, 'but if the janglers start killing they start dying.'

Logan nodded. 'Then I would prefer them to die quietly.'

'That can be arranged...' said the drone. 'So what are you going to do now?'

'Make my presence fully known and stir the pot a little.'

'Don't get yourself killed.'

'What, again? I'll try to avoid it.'

The drone snorted in amusement then launched from the rooftop and disappeared into the night.

The saloon was ersatz eighteenth century USA. Logan pushed through the swing doors to the sound of a piano, only he noted that the player was an android that had lost most of its syntheskin. He walked up to the bar.

'Bourbon,' he said.

The bartender was one of the stone people – a woman in a simple dress with black hair bound tightly back, tendrils cropped and skin pale blue. An induction thrall clung to her temple like a flattened metal tic, a green loading light glinting across a small rectangular screen in its surface. She served his drink and he paid with an octagonal coin. She was about to move off.

'One moment.'

She paused, obedient but wary.

Logan gazed at her steadily, held out his hand and pressed his midfinger down on one of the touch controls on is palm. The woman's thrall beeped, the lights turning to orange then red and going out. Her mouth dropped open in shock and she reached up to touch the thing.

'Don't do anything now,' he said, speaking low. 'At the end of the evening you can take it off and just leave. Stay safe.'

She nodded, tears filling her eyes, then moved off to serve another customer, her movements unsteady. Logan turned, bourbon in hand, and surveyed the saloon.

There were janglers here and others. Whores ran their trade from soundproofed booths along one wall. At gaming tables, holograms or small robots fought gladiatorial battles. One man hung in gimbals in a VR suit, perhaps, by his movements, fighting another battle. One group was lounging around a hooka, the air around them striated with rainbow smoke. Logan sipped his drink, noting that the four who had followed him from the station had spread out about the room and were now making their way towards him from different directions. He smiled coldly and turned back to the bar – watching the room in the mirror behind it. Now a fifth entered. Logan recognised the big ugly man as the stone people handler he had seen earlier in the day – the one who felt the need for a cattle prod, which presently hung at his waist.

'Hey, monitor,' said Ugly.

Logan turned and eyed the man.

'I hear you're a coward and wear body armour.'

'Where did you hear that?'

'Seems some of my friends ran into you out on the Flat.'

'Oh, how unfortunate.'

The man just glared at him.

'But you asked about body armour.' Logan pulled down the neck of his T-shirt to expose bare chest. 'Only when I'm working.'

'Bit stupid to come in here without it.'

Logan shrugged. 'My working day is over. This is a saloon, and I'm a customer.' He stepped a little way out from the bar.

Breaking glass...

One came at him from the left wielding the bottle he'd broken on the edge of the bar, jabbing it towards Logan's face. Logan caught his wrist in his left hand, pulled and grabbed his shirt, spinning him into the one coming in from the right. Ugly came straight in, cattle prod crackling. Logan advanced, chopped it sideways, taking a jolt to his arm, but delivered a heel-of-the-hand blow to the man's nose, shattering it. He fell back. Another, from behind, smashed a length of iron pipe against his back, sending him staggering. He came in for another blow but Logan turned and delivered and uppercut to his ribcage, lifting him from the floor and bowing him over. One hard chop to the back of his neck dropped him. Cattle prod came again, this time Logan grabbed it and turned it into his guts, crackling and hissing. The man screamed, until Logan head butted him, twice, kneed him in the guts then as he bowed over slammed his head hard into the bar. Logan turned. Three men now surrounded him and had decided to upgrade. Logan eyed their selection of weapons. Two had knives. The third had his hand on the pistol at his hip.

'I will meet violence with equal violence, until I really start to get annoyed,' he said.

The two with the knives came at him. He knocked one stab aside and caught the wrist of the other, pulled and shoved driving the knife from one into the guts of another. The gunman drew and fired, but

Logan ducked and turned one of the knifemen in front of him, who took the shots in the back. He threw him towards the gunman and rose, a knife he had taken held in one hand. The gunman now tried to take careful aim, and a moment later was gagging on blood, the knife imbedded in his throat. He took a step, and then dropped.

The music had stopped now and all in the saloon were watching. Four were down unmoving, a knifeman was sitting on the floor holding his bleeding guts. Logan stepped over to the bar and picked up a bar towel, wiped blood from his neck and from his hand. He then threw the bar towel to the bleeding man.

'Here, put pressure on with that,' he said. 'You might survive – people have survived worse.'

He finished his bourbon

In his cab, Kraven peered at his screen. 'What you saying, Caber?The whole system?'

'Yeah, it shut down.'

'The stone people?'

'Just dropped their tools and started fading into the mountains.'

'Why didn't you stop them?'

'I ain't paid enough to start shooting the fuckers – not with an Earth monitor in town.'

'That worries you?'

'It should worry us all.'

'You make me want to puke, Caber.' Kraven switched off the screen, grimaced at it then looked up to survey his surroundings.

One party of stone people trudged out of the mine shouldering power drills running from heavy packs. They walked out beside a conveyor loaded with broken rocks. Other stone people awaited assignment, while among them fellow janglers were on patrol. He grunted satisfaction – all was as it should be – and returned to work. Guiding the moveable section of conveyor, remote controlling it from the cab of his spider, Kraven filled up another sorting-trough. He then keyed another control. Stone people, mostly women, who had been waiting to one side, jerked as if prodded, some of them reaching up to the thralls on their temples, then headed over to the trough and began sorting.

Kraven now set his spider in motion, and it walked delicately down the slope amidst the exterior mine workings. He then turned it to head over to the punishment frame where two stone people were hanging. Parking it on the ground, he climbed out, and sauntered over to Holse and Frax.

'Hey Frax!'They high-fived. 'So what's this?' He indicated the two on the frame with a nod.

'Thralls packed up and they tried to run.' Frax shrugged, snapping his power whip back and forth.

'John says don't waste them,' Kraven warned.

'They're about done anyway – maybe three or four days left in them.'

'Really?' said Kraven. He eyed the two. They were nothing but skin and bone, and were covered with whip marks. He shrugged. 'Might all be over soon anyway.Earth jurisdiction now. Four mines have released their workers.'

'Yeah, Pallen's mines.Fucking coward.'

'There's that but I just heard, over on Tulse Mountain, Caber's system went down and his workers just left.'

'He let them leave – Caber's a chicken.'

'It's a little concerning – the Earth monitor…' Kraven drew a pistol from his holster and toyed with it.

'One monitor in Godrun. What can he do? I bet Caber shut his system down himself because he's shitting himself.'

Kraven nodded agreement. 'Anyway, we should at least keep things neat and tidy here.' He nodded to the two on the frame. 'Get rid of these two.'

Frax turned and looked at them. 'Yeah, I guess.'

With casual indifference, Kraven raised his weapon and shot the stone man on the right through the head. The man jerked and kicked for a little while, despite most of his skull being missing.

'Damn but they take time to die,' he said.

'They're tough, adapted – that's why they make useful workers.' Frax grinned. 'Gut shoot the next one, an' let's see how long it takes.'

A low humming then penetrated the air, followed by a thump as of someone beating a giant carpet. Something passed through the mine workings raising a cloud of dust.

'The fuck?' said Holse.

They scanned around. The stone people were looking about in confusion. Then those carrying power drills just dropped them and began shrugging off their packs. Kraven looked over to the sorting troughs. The stone people there had stopped working and seemed confused. He watched a woman step away shaking her head. She then reached up and took hold of her thrall. She pulled it off her head, discarded it, and began walking away.

Kraven holstered his pistol and began backing away, scared. With a hissing sound Frax's power whip activated.

'What the hell!'

Frax barely seemed able to hold onto the thing, it was thrashing about like a trapped snake, then it abruptly snapped back, wrapping itself around his neck, and began strangling him. He went down on his knees, gagging.

'Sir?'

Spinning round to face one stone man, Holse drew his weapon and aimed it. A crackling ensued and he found himself gaping at his severed wrist, his hand, still clutching the weapon, on the ground. The stone man backed away, hands held out to his sides to show he was unarmed. Shooting then, from across the workings. One of the janglers had opened up with a carbine. Hissing cracks filled the air. The man's carbine crumped and shed fire and he fell back screaming, his hands and forearms burned down to the bone. Other weapons were just detonating. Kraven saw a jangler beating one stone man abruptly beheaded by something invisible. The conveyor went over. Equipment exploded and fires bloomed all across the workings. Stone people were discarding their thralls and running.

Kraven ran for his spider and climbed inside, setting it into motion. It dodged across the mine workings then hit the slope, climbing fast.

'Come on. Come on!'

He reached the top of the slope then headed across the ridge and down the other side. Another slope took him up to a peak where he turned the spider so he could look back at the mine workings. Yes, all was chaos, but he had no idea what was causing it. He turned the spider, ran it further, scrabbling along above a cliff. Something rose up the cliff and turned to face him. His spider just stopped, its controls becoming inert. The thing out there looked like a giant steel hoverfly with a scorpion tail.

The drone folded down two Gatling cannons and opened fire, disintegrating the cab of the spider, and Kraven along with it. A moment later just legs and a few broken hydraulic motors stood on the cliff top.

Sting turned away, muttering to himself. 'Every confidence in you...' He paused, hanging in the air. 'But I did try,' he added.

He accelerated away.

Part 3

Logan sat up on the low wall rimming the monitor station roof and gazed out across the town. A couple of fires were burning out there and, as he watched, something exploded. He grimaced, held out his right hand and pressed his little finger down against one of the touch controls.

'Is that you?' he asked the night.

A green light flickered on in the darkness. Whining, it scribed a circle and out of this, translucent, appeared the nightmare head of the war drone Sting.

'It's me,' it said.

'What's happening?'

'I shut down the thrall units and explosive collars of all the stone people in Godrun,' the drone explained. 'There were some objections to them leaving.'

'But no objections now?'

'No objectors,' the drone replied.

Logan tilted his head in acknowledgement.

'You are aware,' said the drone, 'that events draw to their close?'

'Tell me...'

'Trader John moved his house last night – he's down on the Flats.'

'I see.' Logan paused for a moment. 'You will take no actions yet, I assume.'

'You were given control. I await your orders.'

'Limited control of you,' said Logan.

'I will not act until you have located her,' said the drone. 'But your time for that *is* limited.'

'Thank you, Sting.'

The image before him winked out.

The mercenary, Chinnery Grade, was a short individual with white spiky hair, but whether he could be called a man was debateable. Not only was half his face metal, so were his hands. He wore an armoured combat suit and his helmet, with its HUD visor, sat on the table before him. He hadn't brought his weapons in with him, but Trader John was aware that this 'man' was more than capable of killing without them. However, on the table beside the helmet rested a squat esoteric looking gun with a ring-shaped magazine.

'You understand the situation?' asked John.

'I understand the situation,' Grade replied. 'You want full control of Godrun. You want its head cut off, that monitor out of the way and the mine owners there dead. What I don't understand is why – they ran their mines and paid you a nice percentage.'

'They are no longer satisfactory – they allowed just one man to disrupt my operation.' John grimaced and clattered his mandibles. 'They also neglected to mention to me how well their mine workings have been doing lately. That was a fatal omission.'

'Why do you care?' asked Grade. 'This is one of your smaller operations…'

'Profit is always an issue,' John replied, scratching below part of his carapace armour. 'Reputation is a bigger issue still.'

Grade shrugged. He looked doubtful. 'I still don't know where you are going with this, but I'll do your job.' Grade's attention strayed to the two standing behind John's chair. Here were two big men clad in heavy combat armour, their faces concealed by opaque visors, heavy complicated looking carbines clutched at port arms across their chests. 'Nor do I understand why you hired mercenaries, when you have your own people.'

'It is not necessary for you to understand.'

'Quite – it is only necessary that I be paid.'

'You have been paid well, and your second payment will come on completion.'

Grade tilted his head in acknowledgement.

'Good,' John smiled. 'Then get to it.'

Grade stood, taking up his helmet. He then reached down, picked up the weapon and inspected it closely.

'And Grade…'

Grade looked up. 'Yes?'

'I don't mind what you use against Godrun and the people there when you take control, but you go careful against the monitor. Be sure you understand.' John pointed with one claw. 'That weapon is key.'

'Understood.' Grade rested the weapon across his shoulder. 'It's quite clear what he is.'

Grade departed.

Trader John sat idly in his chair for a while longer, his yellow eyes narrowed. A moment later, a woman walked in. Emily Trepanan was as beautiful now as when he first saw her. She wore a simple toga and had loose long brown hair. The thrall unit on her temple was a decorous silver thing that looked more like a piece of jewellery.

'And I don't understand what you're doing,' she said, her expression void.

'No?' he smiled, exposing sharp teeth. 'It's simple really – Grade goes in full force. He captures the monitor and takes control of Godrun and the mines. I test how far Earth will go in enforcing its laws. If it responds in force and the prador are okay with that, then the whole operation can be written off.'

'A costly exercise,' she said, still blank.

'True, but the prador might not be all right with a strong response from Earth here, in which case Earth might lose jurisdiction, and I have full control here. Alternatively, if there is no response, the result is the same.'

'Grade and his men... if the Earth forces go in?'

'Expendable, of course.'

John picked up a remote control and operated it. Blinds hinged open all along one wall to expose the Flat, lying beyond his relocated house. Out there Grade and his mercenaries were preparing to leave in four armoured raptors – things that looked like attack helicopters but lacking in rotors. One of them took off while they watched.

'But I don't understand why it is important to capture the monitor alive,' said the woman. 'Nor do I understand why we had to come out here.' Her words were leaden – no feeling in them.

Trader John eyed her coldly, fingering the mass of scar tissue on his chest carapace. 'There are many things you don't understand, my dear Emily. Suffice to say that this Monitor Logan is not quite as he appears and that I have... business with him.'

'So you wanted a private meeting,' said Logan, gazing across the wide real-wood desk at the Mayor. The man was nervous and sweating again, and Logan studied him carefully.

'Yes, a private meeting,' said Gavon. He reached over to his humidor and took out a cigar, began tapping it against his desk. 'Trader John arrived here last night – his house is out on the Flats.'

'That's interesting, but gets me no closer to understanding what you want.'

'We want an accommodation.'

'You speak for the whole council?'

'All but Pallen.'

'Then why aren't they here?'

'They're in the building, but I thought it would be better if I spoke to you first.'

'Then speak.'

'Trader John is here, while only you are here in Godrun…'

'Yes…' Logan sat back, knowing what this was about.

'If Earth is establishing jurisdiction here, then why only you? Yes, you've used some Polity device to knock out the thralls, but surely there should be more monitors… soldiers… mechanisms…'

'Oh I see now,' said Logan. 'You're scared of Trader John.'

'When he gets what he wants he is perfectly reasonable. When not…' Gavon spread his hands. 'The situation has to be one way or the other. Either Earth in full control or him. Any other way is chaos.'

'And of course John wants his full cut of your profits, and not the rather reduced amount you have been sending him…'

Gavon lit his cigar and puffed on it in agitation. 'Yes, John can be… excessive.'

Logan leaned forwards. 'Let me tell you how it's going to run. John's people will come here seeking to, just as you put it, push the situation one way or the other. He'll come after me but he'll come in strong. He'll want to be sure regarding whether Earth has full jurisdiction or not. He'll push for a reaction and people here are going to die. The first to die will be those who haven't been paying him what he feels he is owed.'

'You're the Earth monitor – you're supposed to protect us.'

'I protect the innocent.' Logan stood. 'From where I am standing there is not one person in this town who has not been part of the enslavement of the stone people, and who has not been culpable in many other crimes, including murder.'

'That's bullshit,' said Gavon. 'Others work here who have nothing to do with the mining.'

'Everyone is here for the money the mining generates, and all have neglected to notice the crimes being committed around them.' Logan shrugged.

'That's it? That's your final word?'

'That's it,' said Logan, turning away. He paused at the door and glanced back. Gavon was already pulling a small com unit towards him. Logan smiled again and headed away.

The lobby was clear of people, even the woman behind the glass, still punctured with a bullet hole, was gone. He exited through the colonnade, out onto the street, turned and began heading back towards the station. Then a shot rang out, and the impact flung him sprawling face down on the stone walkway. He rolled onto his back, then rolled again to drop from the kerb between the treads of a parked crawler. Smoke was rising from his back – a big, burned hole there. He dragged himself past a tread and peeked down the street. About twenty janglers were coming up the road. The one in the middle, a tall thin man in a long duster, was cradling a flack-shell carbine with a telescopic sight.

'You got him?' asked a man at this one's side.

'He ain't getting up,' said the tall man. 'I just blew his spine out.'

Logan rolled out, came up into a crouch and levelled his rail beader. A short burst flipped over five men in clouds of atomised blood. He fired again dropping two more, but then return fire threw him back, bullet after bullet slamming into his body. He lay there, perfectly still for a moment, then abruptly sat up. He held up his beader again and triggered it, but nothing happened. He peered down at the severed power cable.

'What the fuck are you?' called the tall man.

He and the remaining janglers were now crouching or had taken cover behind crawlers. Logan surveyed the numerous weapons pointed at him.

'I'm your worst nightmare. I'm a monitor who just won't die, guys.' He began to stand, but then heard a roaring from behind.

He looked round to see an armoured raptor sliding down the street. Its guns roared tearing up men and crawlers in a running explosion of blood and debris. The tall man just disintegrated. The firing stopped and the raptor came on past Logan and opposite the council building, the effect of its grav engines flicking up dust and scraps of clothing. It turned, facing the offices, and fired two missiles. These gutted the building, but the raptor just sat there in the back-blast unaffected. Logan stood, watched it for a moment, then holstered his beader.

'Welcome to Godrun, Trader John,' he said.

As the raptor swung towards him, he turned and ran.

At the controls of his raptor, Grade watched the monitor running along the street. He opened up with the Gatlings, tearing up everything behind the man but not actually hitting him.

'Trader John said not to kill him,' said, Shafer, the mercenary beside him.

'We might kill him,' said Grade, 'but it would have to be a very lucky shot.'

Shafer looked over, curious.

Grade reached down beside his seat and picked up the weapon Trader John had given him: a short wide-barrelled thing with a ring-shaped magazine. He pulled one of the glassy shells out of that magazine and held it up for Shafer's inspection. Its nose was a ring of short barbed spikes, while electronics packed its translucent body.

'Disruptor bullet,' said Shafer. 'So he really is…'

'Yes, he is,' said Grade. 'And tactically that's how we regard him.' He now spoke into his headset. 'Keep him running. We want him out in the open when we take him – drive him towards the square.'

'Ah fuck,' a voice replied. 'He just ducked into –'

'I see it,' said Grade. 'Take that building apart. Start with the top floor and work your way down.'

'Civilians?' someone enquired.

'Not our concern, and if they are this monitor's concern, he won't use their houses for cover again.'

Another raptor fired a missile that blew the top off one of the foamstone houses. Just as Grade instructed it worked its way down. By the time there was little left of the house, people spilled out the back and ran. Grade's HUD picked out the monitor running close to the row of houses. He strafed behind the running figure, then swore as Logan turned and kicked down a door entering yet another building.

'Seems he doesn't care much for the civilians,' Shafer observed.

'Okay,' said Grade, calling up a town map in his visor. 'We run him up Sapphire Street. Incendiaries in every building along there. Keep him running.' He paused. 'I'm loading tactical data constantly so watch your HUDs.'

Two raptors flew along Sapphire Street shooting missiles out of side cannons into each building as they passed. Behind, the buildings gouted fire from their windows and some of them came down. At the end of the street, one of the raptors turned and hovered. The other shot up and over and began to demolish the house the monitor had dived into for cover.

Grade, now high up, gazed down at another explosion in the town and marked another tick on the map displayed in his HUD.

'That was the monitor station,' said Shafer.

'Yeah,' Grade agreed, 'but for the monitor himself this place is headless now.'

'Bit harsh, don't you think, Trader John?' Grade looked at him and he continued, 'The council building, the homes of every semi-independent mine owner plus business premises?'

Grade shrugged. 'He wanted us to be harsh. Seems you don't take more than your fair share of his profits.'

'You sure it's just that?' asked Shafer.

'Not for me to be sure or otherwise so long as he makes that final payment.'

'I guess...' said Shafer.

The monitor staggered out of the ruins of the latest building the raptors brought down. He looked to the far end of the street where one of them hovered, then turned and ran in the opposite direction. It began shooting up the street behind him. He kept going, past buildings burning inside like furnaces.

'Okay, he's heading for the square now,' said Grade. 'All units close in and ring-fence him. I've updated you all on tactical so you know what to do.'

Logan ran on down the street, paused by a scattering of burned human bodies, gazed at them blankly then ran on when the raptor coming behind opened fire again. He stumbled out into the Square – lawns here patterned about a central monument. Glancing aside he saw running refugees, and looking around he saw pillars of smoke rising from Godrun.

'You deal with the Devil and the price can be high,' he muttered.

He turned to head to the right but another raptor appeared and turf erupted in front of him. He glanced to the left and saw yet another of the things rising up over the buildings, and he moved on. Soon he leapt a small garden, rounded a pond and headed towards the monument. Here stood a statue of a big wide-shouldered and heavily adapted man – a man who looked like one of his parents might have been a praying mantis. On the pedestal the name read: Trader John. He stopped beside it, resting a hand on the cold stone, and eyed the raptor down on the lawns ahead – battle-armoured mercenaries piling out and spreading into a line. To his left and to his right the other raptors were also landing and spewing mercenaries. The same behind.

Logan drew his pulsegun, took aim at those approaching behind and began firing. Return fire slammed him back against the monument. He staggered forward again, shots slammed him back again, his weapon trashed and issuing discharges. He discarded it and just stayed where he was. A moment later Grade was standing before him.

'So John employed mercenaries to do his dirty work,' he said.

Grade shrugged. 'He has the funds.'

'And you have done my work too.'

Grade tilted his head, curious.

Logan gestured to the devastated town all around. 'This place does not deserve to exist. You've done a good job here.'

'Apparently so, then,' said Grade.

'It's a shame you won't live to collect your fee.'

'Really?'

Logan thrust himself up, horribly fast. Grade triggered the weapon he held and stepped smoothly aside. Logan staggered past and turned, a glowing cylinder embedded in his chest. It pulsed, issuing waves of white fire that spread over his body like the burning edges of fuse paper. He stood shuddering, power discharging from his legs into the ground. Then the cylinder went out and Logan just froze, smoke rising from him. Then he went over, crashing to the ground like a falling tree.

Holding the weapon Grade had returned to him, Trader John watched the raptor depart. He then turned and trudged up the ramp, which his house had lowered on the Flat, and inside, his two guards close behind. Walking through the plush corridors of his home, he came to a door and rapped on it. Emily exited and walked meekly a pace behind the guards as he moved on.

'Come see our Earth monitor,' he said.

They entered his main living area. John walked over, dropped into his steel chair and put the weapon down on a surface beside it. Emily paused to look at a sheeted figure lying on the floor, before taking her place on one of the sofas in the lounge pit, folding her legs underneath her.

'Stand up, monitor Logan,' said John.

The figure on the floor moved, then stood, the sheet falling away. The two guards lowered their weapons from port arms and pointed them at him.

'But he's not human,' Emily said, her words devoid of emotion.

'Doesn't look it, does he?'

Heavy manacles bound Logan's wrists and his clothing hung in rags. His upper torso lay bare and his trousers were in tatters. This exposed his loss of skin and flesh. It was gone from his right arm from wrist upwards, from his shoulder and across his chest. Gunfire had stripped one leg too, and a portion of his scalp was missing. This exposed his ceramal bones, corded white electro-muscle and various interior mechanisms.

'Is he an android?' Emily asked.

'No,' said John. 'He is in fact partially human – a cyborg.' He pointed. 'Do you see, on his skull?'

Emily studied the monitor more closely. 'Induction thrall.'

'That would not work if he was an android,' John explained. 'It does work because there is a human brain inside that metal skull.' After a pause John continued, 'Logan, look up.'

Logan shuddered, jerked his head from side to side, then up. He gazed at Trader John blankly, then transferred his attention to the woman, his mouth moving silently.

'Emily,' he finally managed.

She turned to John. 'He knows me?'

'Perhaps you'll understand better if he wears his real face.' Trader John allowed himself an ugly smile. 'Logan, return your face to its base setting.'

Logan's face changed and for the first time Emily showed real emotion. Her mouth opened in shock.

'Emily Trepanan,' said Trader John. 'Meet what is left of your husband, Enders Logan Trepanan.'

John now stood up and walked over to Logan, grabbed hold of his face in one clawed hand and turned it, staring at him closely.

'I dealt with you once and now I'll deal with you again,' he said. 'But what satisfaction do I get from that? You can die, but you can only feel pain if you choose to do so.'

'I can feel satisfaction,' said Logan. 'Your operation here is over, and you will not be leaving.'

John stared at him and clattered his mandibles. He stepped back, fingering the mass of scar tissue on his chest. He looked round. 'Emily, come here.'

Obedient to his will, Emily stood and walked over. As she did so, John operated a control at his wrist, bringing over a hoist in the ceiling and lowering a wire with a hook. Placing this through a hole in Logan's manacles he hoisted him up into the air. He then stepped to Emily and put his arm around her.

'I think I will fuck your wife now,' he said. 'Afterwards I might kill her in front of you.' He shrugged. 'Who knows? She's not so interesting any more – too long under the thrall and they lose their... novelty.'

Logan just hung there, watching them go. Once they were out of sight he looked up to his hands, reached down with one finger and pressed one of the touch pads on his palm. Green light flickered on his face and he gave a tight smile.

'She's here in his house,' he said. 'You can take the gloves off now.'

Sting sat atop a boulder on a mountaintop looking down at Godrun. He focused on particular areas, putting frames over whatever interested him and magnifying the image. First, he studied the town square. Here the mercenaries had erected a scaffold and were leading some people towards it at gunpoint. He focused on faces and identified them. 'Jangler Edmondson: murder, enslavement, torture – guilty. Mine-owner Jefferson: murder, enslavement, torture, theft, perjury – guilty.'

109

Not finding one innocent amongst them, he watched as the mercenaries strung them up, then swung his attention elsewhere.

Putting a frame over a raptor, he analysed it: miniguns, seeker missiles, particle cannon, anti-munitions lasers, EMP disruptors, ceramal impact armour, super-conducting impact foam… He snorted dismissively and turned his attention to another raptor, then concentrated on the individual who had stepped out of it.

Chinnery Grade: multiple murder, insurrection, terrorism, torture…Guilty. Sentence: death. Sting rattled his feet against the stone impatiently, extruded his Gatling cannons then retracted them, sighed and then tilted back.

'Patience, drone,' he muttered to himself. 'Tactical considerations first.'

He now observed mercenaries driving a crowd of people towards the outskirts, occasionally shooting in the air. Crosshairs appeared over every mercenary, then winked out. Sting spread his effector wings and rose from the boulder, revolving slowly in mid-air, picking out the other two raptors. Frames and crosshairs multiplied around them, then again went out. Words appeared in his vision: Assessment Complete.

'Gloves off,' he muttered.

He tilted and roared down towards Godrun.

Logan hung from the wire utterly still, then raised his head and looked around. Trader John was coming back. The big arthrodapt returned to the room – his ever-present guards following him – and stood gazing out at the Flats, elbow supported by one hand and claw against his cheek.

'I've been thinking,' he said. 'About revenge…'

He lowered his hand and operated his wrist control, lowering Logan to the floor. Another stab with one claw opened the manacles. Without looking back, he began heading towards the exit. 'You will follow me.'

Logan turned and trudged slowly after him, but the guards came up swiftly behind him and took hold of each of his arms. They walked him behind John through the rich corridors of the house, then down a ramp and outside. Here stood Emily. She rubbed at her arms and her expression was puzzled as she searched her mind for memories. She turned.

'I'm cold out here, John,' was all she said.

Trader John smiled nastily. 'Don't worry, that won't be for long.' He swung round towards Logan. 'You know, when you shot me, I came the closest to death I have ever been.'

Logan watched him steadily and said, 'Death is not easy to define. There was not much left of me when they pulled me out of the river.'

'Yes… quite.'

'You were alive when they took you to the city hospital,' said Logan. 'It was some time before I was found…'

John waved a dismissive claw. 'Fuck that,' he spat. 'You nearly killed me and I made you pay, now you, and Earth, are screwing my operation here and you have to pay again… but apparently I cannot hurt you.' He gave a cruel smile. 'However, under the thrall you must obey my every word.' He waved another hand and the two guards released Logan.

'Is that the only way you can command people, by controlling their minds?' asked Logan.

Trader John retained his smile as he drew a knife from his belt. He tossed it down on the ground before Logan.

'Mind control has its satisfactions,' he said. 'Now pick up that knife and gut your wife.'

Sting spat two missiles, one after the other, and tracked them down. The first struck the top of the building, demolishing it. The raptor parked there, rose up on the blast, then engaged its effectors and turned, issuing missiles of its own. The second missile struck it in the belly and blew a glowing hole. The raptor slammed back into the building opposite smashing a hole in the wall, then peeled out and crashed to the street.

'I bet that hurt,' commented the drone.

Cruising on, the drone fired lasers from its body ports blowing up the missiles the raptor had fired, turning them into hot explosive streaks across the sky. He then fired three more missiles, which hurtled out towards the other raptors already launching into the air. Two exploded before reaching their targets – taken out by anti-munitions – the third blew the tail off a raptor and it fell, spinning.

'I'll attend to you later,' said Sting.

More missiles came hurtling back and Sting dropped behind a building at the last moment. These struck the face, blowing a glowing hole. One of the raptors came in towards this, then rose up to go over the building. Sting came out through the hole, tilted upright and opened up with Gatling cannons into its underside. It shuddered under multiple impacts shedding debris, then abruptly tilted and shot to one side. The drone extruded another weapon and hit it with the royal blue of a particle beam, tracking it. The thing glowed and smoked, pinned by the beam, which finally punched through. The raptor hit the street burning and bounced along it, coming to rest on the steps of the demolished council building.

Amazingly, two people rolled out of the thing, flaming. They came upright with extinguishing gas from their body armour putting out the flames. Sting hit them with one Gatling cannon – two short bursts and they disappeared.

Shots from below…

The drone took fire, bullets ricocheting off his carapace, then tilted, observing mercenaries further along the street. Targeting frames bloomed over them, with identification tags, and his lasers stabbed out, turning human beings into hot explosions of blood and flesh. Briefly, as they disappeared, the words 'Sentence Executed' appeared over each.

Then a missile struck him, flinging him back. He hit the top of a building, bounced and fell down into the street beyond hitting the road on his back.

'Fuck,' he said, flipped over onto his feet and shook himself.

The tailless raptor now rose into sight, firing with everything it had into the road. Sting shot in hard reverse, turned and fired three missiles down a side street, then went in hard reverse down the street opposite. He rose up and the tailless raptor rose up before him. They hit each other hard with Gatling cannons, but then the three missiles shot up out of a street behind the raptor, looped over and hit it all at once. It blew to pieces.

'Okay, just one more,' said the drone, now revolving in the air.

Further shots hit him, and bounced off. Almost negligently, he targeted mercenaries and took them out. Cruising across the town, he put frames over those herding citizens along, narrowed the focus of his lasers and killed them with head shots. He cruised in over the square and dealt with the mercenaries there likewise.

'Come on – don't be shy.'

The fourth raptor came at him from underneath, firing all its weapons. He spun nose down, fired with all his own and accelerated towards it. The raptor shed debris, but nothing seemed to affect the drone as he took slugs and lasered missiles before they hit him. He and the raptor crashed head-on then fell into the street and bounced apart.

Again, on his back with his legs in the air, Sting said, 'What a rush!' And flipped upright. Turning now to face the wrecked raptor, he waited. Eventually a door banged open and a man stepped out. His armour was smoking and broken in places, glowing in others. He had lost his helmet and the human part of his face was bloody.

'Chinnery Grade,' said Sting. 'Always the best for last.'

Grade spread his hands. The drone surged forwards, sting looping over and jabbing. It impaled Grade and lifted him, shrieking and smoking orange vapour, then flipped him away. He thumped to the ground, inert, vapour rising from him still, his skin blackened.

'Sentence executed,' the drone added.

Logan stood still for a long moment, fighting the thrall. He then squatted and took up the knife.

'I cannot, yet, disobey your instruction,' he said. 'But the thing about such a degree of control is that you must be precise in your instructions and, more importantly, tell your slaves what they cannot do.'

Logan held out his hand and pressed a finger against one of the touch controls on his palm. The tracking green light on his thrall turned to amber, then to red, and then went out. Emily gasped and went down on her knees, and reached up with a shaking hand to her thrall. Its lights were also out.

Logan allowed himself a nasty smile then turned and drove the knife straight in through the armour of one guard, lifting the man off his feet. He turned him and threw him at the other guard, sending them both crashing to the ground. The second guard then tried to rise and bring his weapon to bear but Logan kicked him savagely in the head, knocking away his helmet. The man looked up at him, stunned. Logan punched him twice, hard, caving in his face, then snatched up his weapon. He turned then to face John.

Trader John was just standing with his arms folded. Logan watched him in puzzlement, then glanced across at his wife. He held out a hand. 'Emily...come here.'

She looked up at him, her expression unreadable, then reached up and detached the thrall from her head. She then swung her attention to John as she climbed to her feet. After a moment she turned away and fled waveringly towards the ramp.

'Emily!'

She ignored him and entered the house, moving out of sight.

'Like I said,' said John. 'They lose something under the thrall.'

Logan swung back towards him, really angry now. 'Fuck you!' he spat and then opened up with the weapon. Explosive shells hit Trader John, wreathing him in fire and blew him back across the Flat. Finally, he spun round and went down, still smoking and burning. Logan stared at him and then dropped the weapon. He stared at the mobile house, all his dreams about rescuing his wife now dust. Then he took a breath and followed her inside.

'Emily?' he called, gently, nervously.

He came towards the main room.

Explosive shells hit him in the back throwing him into the room. He crashed down and a big hand reached down, hauled him up and slammed him hard into the wall. And Trader John was there delivering punishing blow after blow.

'How?' asked John, 'Did you think I was repaired?'

The earlier shots had burned and blown away most of Trader John's arthrodapt exterior. Exposed now was his metal body, its electro-muscle and internal devices. He threw Logan hard against the wall again, then pounded him into it. Stepping back, he slapped a hand against his own chest and said, 'And this, believe me, is the best that money can buy!'

Logan flung himself forwards to fight back, but John hammered into him again. Logan was outmatched. As he rained blow up blow on Logan, Trader John continued:

'Yes... you are... right,' he said, punctuating his words with further blows. 'It is stupid... to rely... on thrall technology.' He paused to stab a finger at Logan. 'But it is equally as stupid to think yourself invulnerable.'

'Quite right,' said a voice behind.

There came a thump and a flash. John turned with bright fire traversing his body like the smouldering edge of fuse paper, a glowing cylinder pulsing in his back. He tried to reach it, but then finally froze and crashed to the floor. Emily walked up to stand over him, holding the weapon with its ring-shaped magazine.

They sat on the Flat some distance from the house, in twilight.

'You are my wife, and I owed you this,' said Logan. 'But I will understand if you want nothing more from me.' He gestured at the exposed workings of his cyborg body. 'Do you?'

She gazed at him expressionlessly. 'You can feel if you want to and, when you are repaired, you can be human in every way. You are still you inside.'

'But what about –' He broke off as a shadow fell across them then, with a deep thrumming sound the drone Sting settled on the Flat.

'So you saved her,' said the drone.

Logan nodded, not smiling.

'And what about Trader John?'

'He's inside his house.'

'Dead?'

'Still alive, since he's mostly machine like me.'

'That's not so bad,' said the drone, 'but sentence must still be executed.' He rose into the air and turned, then spat a whole series of missiles straight at the house. They shot in through the ramp door. 'Get your heads down.'

The missiles exploded inside the house, first blowing out all windows and gutting it with an inferno, then tearing its apart. Smoking debris bounced across the flat. One big leg spiralled up in the air and came down with a crash. Then after a while, all was calm in the orange glow of the burning wreckage.

'You didn't answer my question,' said Logan.

Emily reached out and rested a hand against his face. 'You are still you inside,' she said. 'I don't know what I am, inside, any more. And I don't yet know what I want.' She smiled tiredly. 'That's the best answer I can give.'

I had a nightmare once of standing on a bridge and seeing what I thought were trout in a stream, until they raised their tubular thread-cutting mouths out of the water. There was a deep green jungle above a white sand beach too, out of which improbably long blue hands reached out to grab someone. And then a bowl of stone on a mountainside in which lay three people who had been skinned and were still alive. This turned into a short story called Spatterjay, and when I wanted to write the next thing after Gridlinked I turned to it, and another story called Snairls, and out of these the book The Skinner was born. Many of my readers love the planet Spatterjay with its hostile life forms, and its immortal, indestructible Old Captains and so do I, so how could I not write a story set there?

BAD BOY

Sand grated against the side of my sore face and my hands were burning. My legs hurt badly and I really did not want to look at them because bones might be sticking out, though of course they would not have penetrated my monofilament suit. But still, as the terror steadily receded, I celebrated the victory of surviving the swim to shore, which was practically unheard of in the seas of Spatterjay. Usually such a swim would be akin to one through a mincing machine.

I rolled onto my back to gaze up at blue-grey clouds against a purple-blue sky, reached down to a thigh pocket, unclipped it and pulled out a medpack. This provided me with a container of analgesic wet-wipes also laden with sprine. First my hands, wiped thoroughly all over and into the cuffs of the suit, then my face, scalp and neck, also wiping down into the collar. Relief from the burning sensation quickly ensued. The usual ocean predators had fled this area from something larger and nastier, and so the water had been free of leeches with their plug-cutting mouths and the snappy claws and other sharp limbs of glisters and prill. But it still swarmed with the microbes of Spatterjay, and the burn was them eating my skin. The analgesic killed the pain, while the sprine killed the microbes as it did all the virus-infected life of this world.

I finally tossed the wipe away and eased up into a sitting position to gaze down at my legs, and yes, broken bones were jutting against the fabric of the suit. Looking out to sea I eyed the distant floating bubble-metal wreckage of the grav platform. It had supposedly been a safe method of travel, but we'd got too close to the sea. The huge stony tentacle had speared up from the surface and slammed down on the thing, catapulting me into the water. I scanned down the beach hoping my driver had survived, but no one was in sight. I then looked up at the wall of jungle, or dingle as they called it here, interspersed with peartrunk trees, and knew that crawling up there would offer no more safety than here – less in fact since the place would be swarming with leeches. And I tried to avoid thinking about just how long I might manage to stay alive alone in this place.

'The bugger was not happy,' said a voice behind me.

Happy and relieved, I eased round to find the source. Captain Smurk stood where the waves lapped against the sand. His canvas clothing hung ragged on his huge frame.

He added, 'Deliberately and –' He coughed and spat something into the sea, finishing with, '– visibly bad.'

He was referring to 'Bad Boy', but what he *implied* by that statement I had no idea.It wasn't unusual for Old Captains to make obscure statements. He had lost one of his hobnail boots and his hat – the bald dome of his head now revealed with its circular blue leech scars. I blinked, trying to figure out what else was wrong about this image, then saw it when the captain turned towards me. The man's right arm was missing, torn off, ligaments and shattered bone protruding through broken virus-toughened and bloodless flesh. A large chunk was missing from his torso below his ribcage and with his remaining hand he held his guts in, while the front of his right thigh had been ripped right down to the bone. But even now exposed flesh was shifting, oozing across that thigh bone, closing up where his arm had been torn away and incidentally expelling the mangled head of his humerus from his shoulder. After a moment he took his hand away from his guts, a cloudy skin having drawn across to hold them in place.

This meant: my situation had not improved with Smurk's arrival. The cold fear I had felt swimming in from the grav platform wreckage nudged my spine.

'It's not usual,' I replied, struggling to keep my voice steady. 'We knew that when we came out here.' I enforced calm, trying to tell myself that Smurk obviously had it under control for now. But I needed to get mobile quickly, so opened the medpack again, took out a small diagnosticer shaped like a pre-Quiet War computer mouse and pressed the rubbery thing against my neck. The device sucked into place as I leaned forwards and carefully, with hands only shaking a little, undid the stick seams attaching my trousers legs to my boots. Blood poured out, but the pain started dying as the diagnosticer keyed into my internal nanosuite and made adjustments, numbing the nerves from halfway up my thighs down to my feet.

'It grabbed you?' I asked, unable to stop my voice rising to a high note at the end.

The Captain grunted dismissively and tramped round to stand in view. As the man's injuries rapidly healed Smurk was also growing thinner, bluer, and didn't look quite so calm and centred as he had been before. Even though I knew about this change, actually seeing it happening kept the fear nicely topped up. This was dangerous. As a xeno-biologist I had studied this transformation and could not deny the reality. Hoopers like the captain had been rendered practically indestructible by the viral threads weaving their bodies together as tough as towing cable. However, the action of the virus was not necessarily good for its host.

In a mutualistic arrangement with the leeches of this world, it kept its hosts alive as a reusable food resource for the leeches, who in turn disseminated it to other prey. This arrangement had resulted in just about everything here being infected by the virus. Besides making its hosts improbably tough it also retained an eclectic selection of their genomes. With this it made changes to enable a very badly injured host, like the captain, to survive. They developed a serious hunger. Infected humans so damaged also lost grip on what little sanity they possessed. The long list of life forms on this world that might see me as dinner had now grown by one: Captain Smurk.

'Got a tentacle on me and took me down,' said the captain. 'Started on me till it recognised the taste.' He waved his remaining hand at the nub of flesh protruding from his shoulder. 'Didn't do anything to you,' he added, with just a hint of accusation.

Recognised the taste? I felt no inclination to question him on that because his voice had begun to slur and he couldn't keep his eyes still. His tongue had changed and, in one immediate and somewhat redundant change the virus made to injured humans, Smurk had begun growing a leech mouth at the end of it.

I *really* did need to get mobile. The pain relief now made it easier to roll up my trousers to expose the compound fractures of fibula and tibia of both legs. The injuries required more than the diagnosticer and nanosuite could provide.Reluctantly reaching up to the chrome comma of the augmentation behind my right ear, I pressed a fingertip against it, turning it on. I had closed the thing down so as to get more of a feel for this place before conducting my chore here. But survival had now become the primary objective.

The net opened up – a thousand worlds within a world, all the information of the Polity a thought away, communication with anyone, anywhere, available with just a blink and a word but, most importantly, much more finesse of control over the diagnosticer and my nanosuite. With what seemed a third eye I gazed upon the multi-layered menu and with a hand of invisible fingers made a selection. The diagnostic feed came up to my inner vision, showing a three dimensional image of my body with injuries highlighted. Only seeing that did I feel an area in my chest the suite had numbed, where my ribs had been broken. I searched for solutions to the broken legs. My nanosuite could rapidly knit carbon fibres to stick bones together but it could not position them. I looked up at the captain.

'It didn't grab me because the impact threw me some distance away,' I said. 'If I'd been a hooper I could probably have clung on and would have gone down with the platform like you.' I paused for a second and felt a bit selfish adding, 'And my equipment.' Right then I wasn't thinking of the scanner, analysers or field nanoscope, but the Spartech assault rifle in one of the cases.

'So you say,' said Smurk, now looking just a little bit crazy.

'I need some help here,' I finally said, scared of what that help might lead to.

Smurk's eyes rolled, his head nodding and jerking, but then he seemed to get a grip and peered down at my legs.

'You need 'em pulled and straightened,' he said.

'Should take the nanosuite a few –' I began, but Smurk stepped forwards, squatting down to press his knee into my right thigh, then got hold of my foot to pull and twist. The muted pain still made me gasp, eyes watering. After a moment I managed to focus on that internal vision, observing splintered bone retracting into my legs. I quickly input an order to have the nanosuite hold off from automatically threading together the breaks, and studied the image.

'Twist my foot to the left, slowly,' I instructed, calm as possible, aware that at any moment he might decide to rip my leg off.

The captain made a strange gobbling sound but complied. Fragmented bone in the tibia closed up, but then opened out a bit as the fibula break lined up.

'There,' I said, knowing that would have to be enough and initiated nanosuite repairs in that leg. A loading ring appeared, counting round. 'Hold it there…'

The captain snorted agreement, a strand of saliva shooting from his mouth.

The ring completed its circuit. I waited a moment more before saying, 'Okay, the other leg now.'

When the captain released that leg to move over to the other the internal three D image showed the bones of the first flex a little but stay in place. The leg would not bear my weight yet, but the repairs continued. I checked the stats as Smurk pulled on my other leg, and saw muscles with their artificial additions quickly knitting together too.

'Twist to the left,' I instructed, watching the image of the second leg. 'Hold it there.'

The nanosuite continued to work its wonders and the second ring wound round to completion, but before then Smurk released his hold and quickly staggered away. The break collapsed a little but then firmed. Another readout showed an alert then nanosuite adjustment via the diagnosticer as it seized control of my leg muscles and set them stretching to straighten the break. I eyed the captain, who was stooped over with his chest heaving, took out another wet wipe and cleaned my legs exposing bright red scar tissue and one slowly closing split. In some respects, with the nanosuite, I possessed the same ability to heal as Smurk, though without the drawbacks. Groping in the sand around me, my hand came down on a large rock. Then the stupidity of that impacted and I choked down a giggle. Smurk was an Old Captain – that meant even shots from a Spartech assault rifle would only make him tetchy.

'Howzz longzz?' Smurk managed, then turned towards me. The man's tongue oozed from between bright blue lips, a hollow opening in the end like a lamprey mouth. His pupils were pinpoints. And a knotted baby fist protruded from his damaged shoulder.

'Half an hour and I'll be mobile, but slow,' I replied, my mouth dry, and back suddenly feeling chilled.

'Howzz long till you runzz?'

I swallowed that dryness. 'Maybe an hour.'

The captain pointed up along the beach. 'I goezz there.' He then pointed the other way. 'You runzz.' He staggered off, fighting his biology. With a surge of adrenalin I pushed myself to my feet despite the alerts from the diagnosticer. I would probably cause myself some damage doing this, but not half as much as would a hungry Old Captain.

With their propensity for understatement the hoopers called it the 'Bad Boy'. Spatterjay's seas swarmed with hostile life inclined to eating just about anything that moved or a least taking a tasty chunk out of the same. That life ranged from microbes that could strip away a swimmer's skin if the leeches did not get there first, through vicious arthropods like glisters and prill, to the giant fish-like heirodonts and ocean-going leeches the size of blue whales. But above all these in terms of size, sheer destructive power and voraciousness, was *whelkus titanicus*. Some of these giant molluscs had been confirmed by Polity underwater drones to be incredibly ancient – probably even the first creatures infected when the virus took hold on Spatterjay over five million years ago. Some of them were so packed with the virus their squid-like bodies were as hard as stone and as durable as steel. Fortunately their feeding grounds lay in the ocean depths and they rarely ventured above the surface. When any of them did. the consequences were inevitably disastrous, but they never stayed long – usually returning to their abyssal home in a few days. Until Bad Boy.

The giant whelk first came ashore on a c-shaped atoll hoopers used as a harbour far from the larger islands of the world. Bad Boy was immense, fully a hundred feet to the top of its shell and with tentacles a hundred and fifty feet long. Fortunately it came up on the outside of the atoll to begin its depredations. It ate everything, macerating down trees as well as land-going heirodonts and leeches. Knowing the danger, the hoopers took to their ships fast, but still it reached the harbour before all could depart and smashed three ships. I could only assume that no one had died because of the sheer ruggedness of hoopers. Other crews rescued those in the sea as the whelk seemingly lost interest and went back ashore. One survivor of this event was Captain Smurk – beats me why he volunteered to take me out to the giant whelk that had destroyed his ship.

By the time Bad Boy returned to the sea a second time it had all but denuded the atoll of life. The thing had even scooped soil rich in organics into its maw. Satellite imagery showed the ocean turning black shortly after it submerged and a sampling drone rendered the useful information that the thing had just taken an immense shit under the sea.

The whelk went on to denude two more atolls and seemed, by a circuitous route, to be heading in towards the larger inhabited islands. The Polity warden, the AI set to watch over Spatterjay but with contractually limited ability to interfere in events on the surface, offered assistance. A conclave of Old Captains, now linked by Polity comware, refused this help. The sails, being the indigenes of the world and thus having a larger vote in the Conclave, agreed. That was until it next appeared on the stony shores below the Big Flint – a monolith of stone protruding from the ocean on the top of which the organic sails – large batlike creatures that served, under contract, as sails on hooper ships – had made their home long before humans arrived on their world. The satellite railgun strike that all then agreed on knocked the whelk from its hold halfway up the Big Flint, whereupon it crawled back into the ocean.

Yes, something needed to be done.

I managed to get up to a slow trot as, with the sounds as of giant earth-movers digging the foundations for some mega high rise, the peak began rising up on the far side of the island,. I gazed at this, then turned to look back down the beach. Thus far Smurk had managed not to turn around and come after me.

'Gather data, they said,' I muttered. 'Be careful, they said.'

On my aug menu a comlink icon began flashing. The source was the AI Warden, or at least one of its subminds, so I opened it.

'You seem to be experiencing some difficulties,' the Warden observed.

'Uhuh. Difficulties...Bad Boy just smashed our grav platform depositing all my equipment on the bottom. Smurk and I got ashore, but my nanosuite is dealing with compound fractures in both my legs, meanwhile Captain Smurk is falling out of the giggle tree. And there's that.' I pointed to peak rising on the other side of the island – the top of Bad Boy's shell. 'But of course I'm telling you nothing you don't know.'

The Warden, now apparently distributed throughout the system of satellites in orbit, had an omniscient view of the world below with cams that could distinguish the grains of sand on this beach, and a mind capable of counting them.

'You were lucky,' the Warden opined.

'What?'

'At your behest the captain took you too low to get a look at Bad Boy. It destroyed your platform in passing on its way round the island to come in from the other side. If it had come ashore where you are now, we would not be talking.'

'You have an interesting idea about lucky,' I grumped. Now talking to the Warden I felt safer, even though that was illusory. The AI's ability to intercede on the surface remained as limited as before. By the time it got permission to act it would probably have watched in minute detail how one of the creatures here dismembered me.

'Also your assessment is incorrect,' said the Warden. 'Your equipment is not on the bottom of the ocean but inside the giant whelk. But it's not all bad news either. Captain Smurk just caught a fleeing land heirodont and is eating that.'

'Shiny,' I replied. 'Any chance of a satellite strike any time soon?'

'Firstly, I do not have permission and doubt it will be forthcoming; secondly, no other action I take from up here will drive the whelk back into the ocean; and thirdly, killing the creature is contraindicated.'

'Contraindicated?'

'We have discussed the matter and are not so blasé about terminating a life form that may be millions of years old and may well be a Class Four or upwards intelligence. The Conclave is also reluctant to permit this until the results of your study are in.'

'That's just a little bit unlikely now, don't you think?'

'I repeat: your equipment is inside the giant whelk.'

I halted abruptly. 'Oh.'

'Quite.'

I contemplated the equipment he had brought: I had the tools for analysing that whelk shit and any organic detritus it might shed, but my main aim had been to stick a hardened multi-scanner in its path to get that scanner precisely where it was now: inside the whelk. I wasn't thinking straight else I would have got that the moment the Warden said my equipment had been eaten. Perhaps the possibility of me being eaten at any moment was interfering with my rationality.

'My relay console is inside too,' I said. 'I'll need something to boost signal strength and an aug upload for translation.'

'Thankfully the Conclave has given me permission to intercede in this small matter,' the Warden replied. 'SM17 will be arriving at your location shortly.' And that was the end of it, because the AI cut the link.

Walking again, I contemplated questions unasked. Being a xeno-biologist in a Polity swarming with AIs could be a thankless and annoying task. Any studies I might want to make had usually already been conducted by remote drones then assessed, collated and extrapolated from by AIs. This was why I had jumped at the offer to come here and make a study of the giant life form currently grinding its way across this small island towards me. However, this begged the question of why? Why had the Warden not pushed for permission to send one of its drones down to stick a multi-scanner on or inside Bad Boy? By now they could have all the information needed to figure out why the giant whelk was behaving so... badly. The only conclusion I could come to was delaying tactics. For some reason the Warden, and thus the AIs of the Polity up to and including Earth Central, wanted the whelk's depredations to continue for a while longer. And that usually meant politics, though I had yet to parse what was actually going on.

My legs now much improved, I trotted for a short distance along the strand,scanning my surroundings and ~~thinking of~~considering what to do next. Just ahead, and a little way into the jungle, a jagged rocky mount reached for the sky with a small patch of vegetation on top of it. All being well, I accelerated, moving up closer to the dingle where the sand lay hard packed. But just as I settled into a steady pace a land heirodont broke through the vegetation ahead and I skidded to a halt, adrenalin surging and nerves jangling.

The thing looked like a lizard made in the shape of a rhinoceros, but only vaguely so. It walked on four legs terminating in huge flat pads. Its head horns repeated in rows along its neck, and it had no tail. Mandible limbs lay folded under its three-cornered mouth. I noted the pock marks of healed leech scars all over its hide and, recognising a herbivore, felt calmer. This creature's feeding usually resulted in leeches dropping from the trees to feed on it. It was the ultimate expression of what the virus did, for it kept the creature alive as that reusable food source.

Lumbering out onto the sand it cast me a mournful glance with compound eyes before coming to a halt at the water's edge. There it huffed for a while before turning and heading off staying close to the sea. Maybe it would escape the devastation here if it could keep from the reach of the whelk's tentacles. But it was also a warning for me because other creatures would be on the move this way as they sought to escape.

Breaking into a run again I came opposite that jagged stone peak and then eyed the dingle. Mats of vines hung from trees and other large plants, draped over cycads and lay in thick tangles on the ground. Blue reed sprouted amidst this interspersed with nodular growths like yellow puff balls. I searched along the edge until finding a stick of tough fibrous wood, was about to pick it up then remembered to do something I had not had time to do when the whelk attacked the grav raft. I removed gloves from their pouches at my wrists and slid them on, closing stick seams about the wrists, and unrolled a hood from my collar and tightened it over my head. From the front of the collar I could pull up a transparent visor with air holes down the sides, but didn't bother with that. Taking up the stick I carefully began to forge a path through the growth, also prodding at suspect areas in case something was lurking there.

Within just a few hundred yards I began to see them. Leeches the size of a finger clung to the trunks or spread leaves of some plants, while one the size of an arm crawled onto my boot and I kicked it away. Beyond the first line of dingle the vegetation began to thin out but the going became more precarious with a layer of oily bubble grass over the ground. I paused, spotting movement over to one side. Like a flock of sheep, a number of large whelks, each shell standing a couple of feet tall, were making their way towards the sea. Frog whelks? No –

they would have been moving as their name implied. The whole flock halted and stalked eyes oozed up to observe me. Vibration through the ground signified these were hammer whelks – creatures that used their armoured feet to bash in the shells of their prey. A blow from one of these could kill a man, but after a moment they moved on, more interested in surviving than feeding.

Reaching the foot of the mount I began to climb. Something whickered at me from a crevice and I skirted round that. When higher I watched a creature like an onion the size of a man's head, with spider legs, climb out and head towards the ground. Higher still I peered down at what looked like the backs of a herd of water buffalo heading towards the sea, until I reassessed and saw these were huge leeches. Thankfully I was not in their path, because almost certainly they would have attacked with plug-cutting mouths the size of buckets. The climb became steeper and soon I had to use my hands. I had begun working my way up an almost vertical face when the visitor arrived.

'So what are you doing now?' a voice asked out of the air.

A metallic-blue seahorse watched with red eyes as it floated in the air just a short distance away. From nose to tail the thing was three feet long. It tilted its head to inspect me, flicked its tail and drifted a bit higher, blinked.

'Climbing to get a better view,' I replied. 'You're SM17 I take it?'

'I certainly am,' the drone agreed.

The Warden of this world had a particular kink. When it fashioned subminds of itself it loaded them to drone bodies aping the life of the seas of Earth and other worlds. It also tended to give them a loose leash and did not often reload them into its own mind. Many of them, over the years, had become distinct entities and applied for and gained independence… of a sort.

'Are you armed?' I asked.

'Minimally so,' the drone replied. 'It's much easier to just get out of the way.'

I grimaced and continued climbing.

'You have something for me?' I asked.

In response a new icon appeared in my aug menu.

'Tell me about this while I climb,' I instructed.

'It's an aug upgrade that also links into discrete processing within me. You'll be able to use me in place of much of the equipment you lost, and you'll be able to assess the data from your hardened scanner.'

'Signal boosting?'

'Yes, that too – through me.'

'Okay, I'll look at it when I get higher.' But now I found a ledge below the peak and crawled onto that to gaze across the island. 'Um, maybe no higher,' I added.

The ledge gave a clear view of the further shore and of Bad Boy. The giant spiral shell had a rocky coralline appearance and certainly looked like a large version of a terran whelk's shell. Below this its head section protruded, showing two huge red distance eyes towards the centre with smaller auxiliary eyes either side. From the bulge of this head its skirt had spread across the ground for fifty feet all around and with its tentacles starring out from this. It kind of annoyed me that these things had been named whelks since, despite the shell, they more resembled cephalopods from the family Nautilidae. But the first humans to come to this world, being pirates and their prisoners, probably hadn't been that bothered about correct taxonomy. Anyway, that wasn't so easy when it came to alien life.

Sweeping up jungle and tearing down trees as it steadily trundled inland, the whelk fed masses of vegetation under its skirt to the awaiting maw. While I watched a heirodont, like the one earlier, broke from cover and ran. The giant whelk lashed out a tentacle to bring it down, coil around it and pull it in. Bad Boy had cut a swathe four hundred feet wide leaving rocky ground and black soil behind. This time it did not seem to be eating the topsoil so perhaps it wasn't quite so hungry? I watched for a while, tracking the thing. It was moving marginally to my right so the way to avoid it and come in on its trail, was to continue along the beach in the direction I had been heading. I nodded to myself, then eased down to sit on the ledge with my back to the rock.

'Okay,' I said. 'Let's see what we can learn.'

The seahorse drone SM17 settled on the ledge over to one side, impossibly balanced on its tail. I opened the new icon.

First the feed from my aug simply blanked and it was as if my third eye had been blinded. An archaic icon appeared: an egg timer. I sighed, half watching it while most of my concentration was on the island. I wondered where Smurk had got to and if the man had enough sanity to keep clear of the giant whelk. Only then did I realise my own danger. Walking along the beach would take me from the creature's path, but right now it still headed nominally towards me. It had taken me an hour or more to climb up here and would take as long if not longer to get back to the ground.

'Fuck,' I said, scrambling to the edge and heaving myself over to climb down.

'What are you doing now?' asked SM17.

'What does it look like? I'm getting back to that beach as fast as I can.'

'Oh I see.' The drone floated out from the ledge to watch me. 'I had assumed you were being tardy because you knew about the other option.'

'Eh? Other option?'

The drone floated closer, well within reach. 'Grab my tail.'

I stared at it for a long moment. The thing wasn't big and grabbing its tail seemed rather like clutching at the string of a party balloon to slow my descent. However, gravmotors could be powerful and the drone must be packed with hardware to dense tech levels, and probably had microtoks or fusion nodes as power sources. I reached out and grabbed the tail with one hand – rough ridges giving me a good grip and then the tail winding around my hand. I then reached out and grabbed hold above that with the other hand. No give in the drone as it took some of my weight and none when I finally pushed my feet from the cliff. SM17 began to descend.

'I won't take you right round the island,' it said. 'This is draining my laminar storage and I'll need to charge it up again from fusion.'

'Understood.' The drone carried me out from the cliff and down. I looked over towards the whelk again and noted something seen only in rare instances in the recording from the other islands the whelk had attacked. Here and there, huge coiled heaps stood steaming in the afternoon chill. Of course, even a creature this size needed to shit, especially when digesting the organic mass of an entire island.

The drone passed over the band of jungle and began to descend, then abruptly altered course because leeches scattered that area of beach like basking seals. It finally came down towards clear sand, unwrapping its tail from my hand and then the tail turning slick and dropping me just a foot to the ground, which was enough to elicit a warning from my diagnosticer. I started walking, away from those leeches and towards the back trail of the giant whelk, incidentally removing the diagnosticer and shoving it in a pocket.

'Scan data coming in now,' said the drone.

the egg timer still hung in place, but with the upper glass bulb nearly empty. It then blinked away and a whole series of menus appeared. All were familiar, the same as those on the screen of my relay console. I went straight to a three dimensional image scattered with data links: the lower body of the whelk – its head, skirt, tentacles and underlying maw. Above this the image steadily expanded in transparent blocks filling with the creature's internal structure. A glowing dot just to the back of the maw marked the scanner itself.

'The scanner is low down,' I noted. 'I would have thought by now it would be in the main intestinal tract higher up.'

Floating long beside me SM17 said, 'It seems its digestive processes are moving a lot faster than normal – hence the faeces scattered behind it.' It added, 'Anus and mouth are close together.'

'I have an old scan for comparison in my relay console,' I replied. 'I'm presuming you have access to something similar?'

'I do – presently downloading it from the Warden.'

I nodded then concentrated on the image about the scanner. A great deal of macerated vegetation and other objects surrounded it, and I recognised other items in there. I mentally focused in, highlighting them, and saw two of the plasmel cases containing my equipment, then a couple of regular chunks that looked like parts of the grav platform. Pulling back again, showed the overall image had expanded to include the bulk of the whelk's body in its shell and much of that shell too, but loading had slowed down now.

'And that's it,' said SM17.

At that moment the glowing spot of the scanner and much that surrounded it dropped down as the whelk heaved up off the ground. As it then moved off this new mound of faeces, the scan image managed to build a few more blocks then froze. I had lost ultrasound and sonar and was now only getting EMR bands to which the virus hardened flesh and stony shell were resistant. The whelk shifted on.

'Shut it down for now,' I said.

Rounding a small peninsular revealed where the whelk had come ashore. I broke into a run again on the hard ground at the head of the beach. Here I leapt a long leech with a body as thick as my waist and it snapped at me like a striking cobra, but missed. I spotted a cluster of those onion creatures down by the waterline and then a herd of land heirodonts on a rocky islet just out from the nose of the peninsular. Soon I ran past where the dingle had been torn down, having to jump deep furrows in the beach, and then reached the point where no dingle stood at all.

The ground here looked like it had been turned over by robot ploughs and broken up by disking machines. In the distance the whelk was heading away but, turning in to walk its path, I saw that it had by no means completely denuded this place of life. Its tentacles could reach out and snatch creatures that came close, but they did not have infinite reach. Over to my left a squat leech massing like a hippopotamus oozed along, and ahead a different kind of land heirodont the size of a dog wandered round a great steaming pile of the whelk's shit, saw me and ran off. I paused, looking around, then moved on again when a leech crawled out of the ground by my feet and began thumping its mouthparts against my leg.

'I need to get to my equipment,' I said, but was again thinking more about the Spartech assault rifle rather than the other tools of my trade.

SM17 drifted along beside me, effortlessly. I felt a flash of annoyance with the thing spectating while I tramped through the mud.

'Over to your right,' the drone replied.

I pulled up menus and used one function to get a ping from the hardened scanner as confirmation, then used a mapping program from the conventional aug software to initiate an icon. Now, every time I looked towards the scanner's location, a representation of the device appeared above the ground with an arrow below it pointing downwards. Trudging on, I soon saw the pile of faeces the arrow was pointing at.

'It seems strange to me that this hasn't all been sorted out already,' I said. 'Obviously the Conclave did not object to the Warden sending you, so why would it have objected to you or some of your fellows scanning and analysing Bad Boy?'

'They would not have objected,' said SM17. 'In fact they themselves made just that request. The Warden told them that a human expert would solve the puzzle a lot more quickly.'

'The AI said a human would be better?' I asked disbelievingly, coming to a halt and turning to face the drone.

SM17 swung round to me. Its head shifted and eyes that had previously been on the sides of its head moved round to the front to give it binocular vision.

'So what the hell is going on then?' I asked.

'I think you know the answer to that already.'

I stared at the drone, not having expected such a direct answer. and now realised that SM17 must be one of those drones that had obtained independent existence from the Warden.

'Politics,' I said.

The drone dipped in agreement. 'The Warden is withholding assistance and pushing for political gains, such as an agreement for it to send its drones down at any time, or be able to deploy orbital weapons without consultation in emergencies, but mostly small detail, like bringing the laws here more in line with those of the Polity.'

'Small detail,' I repeated.

'Horse trading,' said SM17. It swung round to face towards the distant whelk. 'The pressure increases the closer this creature gets to the inhabited islands.'

'That's dirty.'

'You thought Polity AIs were clean?'

'I guess not.' I turned and started walking again.

As we drew closer to their target faeces pile we passed others along the way. Despite the danger all around I now began to think more like a xeno-biologist. Stopping by one pile, I used a stick hauled out of the mud to probe it, levering out pieces of vegetation and wood, a chunk of fatty flesh and a length of bone with stringy flesh still attached that I identified as heirodont. I even found a couple of live leeches in the mass.

'This is not right,' I said. 'It's eating hugely but not properly digesting its food.'

'Perhaps because it's the wrong kind of food?' SM17 suggested.

I tossed the stick aside. 'No – they are omnivores in the ocean deeps and the vegetation and animal life of the islands is not that different. It seems likely they also have a sprine bile duct like the big ocean leeches and pelagic heirodonts. Those leeches should have been dead.'

'So all this devastation because it has an upset stomach?'

I grunted dismissively and moved on. Further remaining life became evident. Another land heirodont the size of a domestic cat, sporting six limbs and a trumpet mouth, heaved itself from a shit pile and moved off. Seeing green items pushing through the soil I walked over and saw new sprouts. An earlier passing thought about surviving heirodonts starving, I now dismissed. Not that they would die anyway – the virus would not allow that. Finally I reached the requisite pile of faeces and dismissed the icon.

'Give me a local scan,' I instructed the drone.

The scanner initiated briefly and loaded a three dimensional image for inspection. I could see myself standing by the pile – all my organs visible if I cared to concentrate on that image. SM17 hung in view too, but inspecting its internals was not so easy – so densely packed were they. Assessing relative positions I began digging at the pile with another stick. The first case was about five feet in, with a large globular object, three-feet across, in the way. If I could get to that and heave it out, I would quickly reach the case.

In this pile the whelk's digestion had worked a bit more efficiently. Chunks of wood and vegetation were bleached white amidst brown excrement. Collapsing the side of the pile, revealed the surface of that globular object. The pale rubbery skin of it yielded only slightly under the digging stick for it seemed as taut as a drum. Some sort of egg perhaps, or a scooped up life form of a kind I did not recognise? I dug round it and, getting a grip, heaved it out a little way, but it was too heavy and rolled back. I dug around one side to clear an area to stand in so as to get better purchase and tried again. This time the object came free and rolled out, bounced and then settled in the mud. But it also shifted. I pulled up the scan data again. Something was knotted up inside the thing and, seeing no openings or methods of locomotion I decided the thing must be an egg. I would inspect it later. Right now I wanted that case. Digging again revealed the edge of the case – its plasmel pitted by stomach acid but the handle conveniently facing towards me.

'Bugger fuck!' exclaimed SM17.

I turned in time to see the egg deflating as a creature shot out of it like a jellyfish sting. A long neck the width of my own, with fins flapping down its length, terminated in a blunt eyeless head, which opened a mouth full of square sharp teeth. The mouth clamped on SM17 and the neck whipped, sending the drone end over end through the air to stab in the ground ten feet away. The rest of the creature pulled clear of its egg – body folding out like a huge flatworm with fins rippling down its sides. I tugged frantically at the case, pulling it partially clear, then had to dive aside as the neck hooped and that mouth stabbed down at me. It thumped into the ground beside my leg, then came up with a lump of wood jammed in its teeth. On hands and knees I crawled clear, but the thing came after me fast, hooping up ready for another strike.

'Deckz squirtzz,' said a voice, as another figure loomed into view.

The creature stabbed down again but a big hand snapped out to catch its neck, stopping it dead, fingers digging in. The creature turned its head to snap at its attacker, but Captain Smurk pulled his head back, then abruptly forwards, his forehead slamming hard into its teeth and breaking them. It hung there for a second, dazed, and he did not give it time to recover. He turned, sweeping his arm in an arc, heaving the creature up off the ground and then slamming it down again. Next, releasing the neck, he delivered a hard kick to its body. The creature landed twenty feet away and with a great thwump simply exploded, spreading its internal organs and slimy yellow juices in every direction.

'Captain Smurk,' said I, climbing to my feet. I looked over at the creature's remains, then peered down at the remains of its egg. The thing had been huge. It had expanded from the moment it left its egg, so what was that all about?

'Squirtzzz,' said the captain.

I studied him. Took in the baby arm sticking from his shoulder, the blue of his skin and the way he was twitching, then quickly headed back to pull my case clear. I tried to undo the latches just as fast as I could, but they had been corroded by stomach acid and wouldn't budge.

'Need...helpzzz?' said the captain, suddenly close and looming over me. The man's eyes would not keep still and didn't go well with his crazy grin. Then his tongue protruded from the side of his mouth, opening out like a trumpet at the end to reveal rows of lamprey teeth. He stooped closer and I scuttled back, but the captain just reached down, snapped off both latches as if dead-heading flowers, then stepped clear. I moved in and flung the case open. The Spartech assault rifle sat in shaped padding in the top since I had expected that if needed it I'd want quick access to it. The thing was only a foot and a half long and quite light. A turn of its energy canister powered it up. I shoved a magazine in one side and another in the other, and stood up feeling just a little bit safer.

'Be needin thatzz,' the captain observed. He waved a hand at our surroundings. SM17 heaved from the ground and zoomed up high, while below pale shapes slid across the ground, long necks waving and teeth snapping. Hundreds of what Smurk had named 'deck squirts' were all around us.

'Deck squirts you said?' I moved out from the pile, but also away from the captain.

'They haul them up from the deeps occasionally,' said SM17 settling back down to hover beside me. 'The pressure differential makes them blow up like balloons if they're left long enough. Hoopers will usually equalise the pressure with whatever sharp implements they have to hand.'

'Hence "squirts",' I said shakily.

'Behind you,' SM17 warned.

One of the creatures came scuttling on its body fins round the shit pile. I fired once without making an ammo selection and an explosive slug hit the ground beside the thing blowing open a smoking crater. I had all but missed but some chunk of debris must have penetrated the creature's hide. A jet of slime shot out of the hole cutting a urine-yellow arc through the air. With its head waving from side to side the thing rapidly deflated, skin sinking back against lumpy internals and what looked like a proto-skeleton, neck growing thin and finally slumping, head nosing into the ground.

'Come you buggerzz!' Smurk strode away to where the creatures seemed most concentrated. He backhanded one that tried to bite him and the force of the blow flipped it over, its neck thrashing and the ruins of its head acting like a sprinkler for that same slime. He moved onto another, stamped on its body, the thing exploding under his foot and sending its neck and head tumbling through the air.

Other squirts where heading toward me so it seemed about time to improve the accuracy of my shots. Auging into the weapon, I brought up cross hairs to my vision. Since the things were vulnerable to just about any penetration of their hides I selected soft bead ammo, targeted the nearest creature and fired at its body. The semi-liquid metal bead spread out as it travelled, and blew a hole the width of a hand in the squirt. It exploded, flinging proto-bones and organs in every direction. I lowered the gun, now no longer vulnerable and suddenly ashamed to be killing the creatures.

'They'll die anyway, you know,' said SM17. 'The few samples we've seen indicate a very low viral infection level and inability to withstand the pressure differential from the depths.'

'Give me what data you have on them,' I said.

'Not very much, unfortunately.'

I responded to the comlink request and got a surprisingly brief file. Almost without thinking, I fired at another creature drawing too close, then wiped jellied lumps of slime off the front of my suit.

'Hoopers only catch them rarely,' SM17 explained. 'By the time one of us got to examine the remains of just one of them there wasn't very much left. The crew concerned threw it back in the sea and most of it was eaten.'

'One of those occasions when you had permission to come down here?' I suggested.

'Of course,' said the drone, but I knew it was a lie. Though the drones weren't supposed to come down to the surface without permission, they had their methods of concealment. I rather doubted the Warden allowed local politics to get in the way of data gathering down here.

Smurk was steadily wiping out the population of creatures in the surrounding area, his chore becoming progressively easier as they were getting slower, while some spontaneously burst open and spread their insides. I studied those creatures nearby and focused on the first one he had shot at. Having relieved its internal pressure through just one hole it seemed the most intact. I would start there. But not yet. I looked towards Smurk. The man seemed to be losing interest now the squirts weren't putting up a fight and had started wandering back.

I called up that shit pile scan image while grabbing a collapsible trenching tool from the first case. Digging into the pile I quickly unearthed the second case, thoroughly aware of Smurk standing nearby watching me. Breaking off the latches with the shovel, I opened it, sorted through sample bottles to find one with a pale red fluid in it. As Smurk loomed at my shoulder, I held the bottle out.

'Diluted three hundred to one,' I said. 'It was for me if I got infected by the Spatterjay virus. Though infection has its advantages, Polity technology can give me those.'

Smurk peered at the bottle. 'Sprinezz,' he said.

When the predators of this world got large enough they tended to swallow their prey whole. This caused problems because virus infected prey did not die in the gut and could cause damage. Evolution had provided sprine for large ocean-going leeches, heirodonts and, it was speculated, the giant whelks. Issuing from the bile duct it killed the virus in their prey thus enabling digestion. Hoopers, like Smurk, hunted large leeches and rendered sprine from their bile ducts. It was much prized by them as practical immortality had its drawbacks too, and sprine enabled them to die. However, for a hooper in the captain's condition, diluted sprine retarded viral growth. It could bring Smurk back towards the nominally human and prevent him from turning into something nastier.

The captain took the sample bottle in his only hand, stared at it in irritation because he could not undo it, then shoved the whole thing in his mouth and crunched down. I expected him to spit out the tough plastic but he just kept crunching and swallowed. He then grunted and jerked, his massive hand closing into a rock crushing fist.

'And these,' I said hurriedly, handing over a pack of protein bars.

Smurk shuddered, forced his fist open, took the pack and walked away.

I glanced to the horizon where the sun was guttering out, turned to the case again to find water and food for myself. Weariness pummelled me after I'd eaten three protein and vitamin bars. Luckily the case contained my spare heat sheet for the night.

It had been an interesting night. I'd rolled myself in a spare heat sheet but the activity nearby kept pulling me out of slumber. Smurk's yell woke me first, alerting me to a late hatching of squirts. I took the floater lamp out of one case – a device of bubble metal almost as light as air – turned it on and tossed it into the air. Using its micro-propellers it settled three feet above my head and maintained position, while I sat with the Spartech across my lap. None of the creatures got close – they were much slower now and leaking body fluids even as they hatched. Later still a squealing woke me, whereupon I saw the captain dismembering a small heirodont and eating it raw – he had already eaten all the protein bars. The man kept grabbing hold of his tongue to push morsels past it. In the early morning I woke to movement in my heat sheet and had to throw out a leech that had come to spoon me. Sunrise revealed the dismembered and still weakly moving remains of two big leeches the captain had caught in the night. The captain himself sat on a rock nearby. He did look a bit less blue now.

Time to get to work, I decided.

Now, with all the equipment retrieved, I chopped a small sample from the squirt and inserted it into a compact genomic analyser the size of a coffee mug. Linking to the device I tracked its start-up routine, then watched it steadily building a map of the creature's genome. All the data I would need should come from this, but I would only get some basic information now since detail would require heavy processing. As I peered down at the deflated deck squirt I didn't want to wait for that, however, so grabbed up a hand scanner and ran it from the thing's head all the way down its length. I had retrieved the hardened scanner, its case battered and etched by stomach acid and the thing still functional, but it was a bit too high powered for this chore. I mentally explored the image of the initial scan and, running the scanner back up and down, viewed further detail being filled in. After a moment I took up a vibro-knife and split the creature from the base of its neck to its back end. On the basis of the scan I made two more side cuts and folded over a large flap of skin, split open an inner layer and studied the organs there revealed.

'And the purpose of this?' enquired SM17.

'Occam's razor,' I replied. 'The whelk is behaving in an unusual manner. It is eating hugely and not properly digesting its food. It has, as you said, an upset stomach. Meanwhile its excrement is loaded with these things.'

'Two plus two equals five,' said the captain from where he sat on a rock nearby, staring into the distance.

Smurk had lost that tongue buzz to his words, but I still did not trust his sanity. I dipped to the remains and cut out an organ vaguely resembling a bright green human heart.

'Joseph,' said SM17, but I ignored the drone to run the hand scanner over the organ, and accruing more detail dropped that into the overall image.

'I think maybe it's time,' said 17.

I shook my head in annoyance at this interruption and ran comparisons between this creature and data on other creatures of this world, steadily building up a picture. I linked to the growing genome data and enlarged that picture.

'Equals five!' Smurk shouted, leaping to his feet.

I came back to myself, abruptly aware that the ground was vibrating. The captain pointed – unnecessarily because Bad Boy loomed large and was coming fast across the denuded ground towards us. SM17 shot from the top of the shit pile to hover above me.

'Grab what you think you'll need – not too much since we'll have to move fast,' said the drone.

I just stood there holding the organ, then dropped it. So deep had I gone that I'd all but forgotten the danger here. And why the hell was the whelk coming towards us now? It was crossing ground it had already fed from and there was plenty of other vegetation and animal life all over the island.

'Move!' 17 prompted.

Out of one of the cases I took a backpack, quickly slinging inside a number of items. With the pack full, and heavy, I looked down at all that remained in the cases. Took an expensive remote laser spectrometer out of the pack and, after a moment, replaced it with a short reach atomic shear, since self-defence seemed more important now. I shrugged the pack on, then turned to follow Smurk, SM17 floating at my shoulder. We began tramping back to the shore.

'Do you have anything yet?' asked SM17.

I kept up with Smurk's fast walk and, glancing back over my shoulder, saw the whelk's tentacles groping across the ground towards us. It was moving faster than us, but we should be able to get ahead of it on the hard ground at the top of the beach. I looked into those dark eyes sure I read malevolence there, but that was probably just imagination. Looking away, I dipped my head and returned to analysis. Data was falling into a place in my programs – building a loose hypothesis.

'Complex biology as it always is with parasites,' I finally said as I laboured and stumbled through the mud.

'Parasites?' said Smurk, looking over his shoulder.

'The things you call squirts are mobile oocysts and in the deep ocean feed and grow multiplying sporozoites inside themselves.' I grimaced. 'I'm using words that only loosely apply. Their purpose at this stage is to be eaten – probably by ocean-going carnivorous heirodonts.'

We reached the top of the beach where Smurk turned left. Ahead leeches lay on the sand beached-seal style again. The captain widened his stride on the harder ground as did I, now regretting some of the items in my pack but not the weapon, even though it now felt heavier.

'Inside the host's gut the sporozoites encyst,' I said. 'We know that ocean heirodont's are one of the whelk's favoured prey.'

'And inside the whelk the things you incorrectly label sporozoites hatch out and produce more eggs?' suggested SM17.

I looked back towards the giant whelk. Was it my imagination that it had changed course to line up with us?

I shook his head. 'I'm not sure. I would need AI analysis of the genomic data. Inside both the heirodont and the whelk things are complicated.' I peered up at SM17. 'Here is the genomic data.' I sent a link.

SM17 blinked, opened the link and the parasite's genomic data flooded across. I wondered if I was doing the right thing. Did the drone have the mental capacity to analyse the data or would it send it to the Warden, who, apparently wanted to delay things as long as possible?

'I'll need that other whelk scan you downloaded to make comparisons,' I added.

A link arrived in my mind and I opened it to begin running comparisons with the scan of Bad Boy.

'Something here doesn't quite make sense,' I said. 'Parasites had a difficult time of it with the rise of the virus. Their purpose at each stage of their life cycle is to produce huge amounts of offspring to offset predation and the likelihood of not reaching their preferred host, but the virus kills off competing parasites. I submit that in the heirodont they do not venture out of the intestines but encyst on the wall of the throat – anywhere else and sprine or the virus will kill them.'

'And in the whelk?' SM17 asked.

I held up a hand and closed my eyes for a second, trying to get it all straight. 'It's complicated. You said the parasites are weakly infected by the virus…'

The scan data was rendering results. Bad Boy's insides were scarred, with lines of damaged tissue leading away from its gut, tightly wrapped with viral fibres. But most of these terminated somewhere in its flesh. I decided these must be the paths of the parasite stages that had come out of a consumed heirodont. And it occurred to me then that I might be seeing scar tissue millions of years old.

'Looks like it kills most of the next parasite stage,' I said.

'Which doesn't explain the quantity of eggs this whelk has been excreting,' said SM17.

'Do you have anything for me yet…or does the Warden.'

'I am doing this myself. I don't think the Warden would be helpful.'

I nodded an acknowledgement as an image came through the link. I saw a larger version of the squirt, with longer jaws, bigger fins and sensory spicules down its back. This was the creature the heirodonts would eat extrapolated from the genomic data.

'As expected,' I said.

'We're getting to an explanation of the parasite,' said SM17. 'But that is not our most immediate problem.'

I glanced back seeing a massive tentacle slam down on the beach. Bad Boy loomed huge now, closer than I had expected. It turned, its stony skirt rippling across the sand and observed us. Then it came in pursuit.

'Maybe time to run,' I suggested.

'It won't stop,' said Smurk.

'Why the hell is it after us?' I complained.

The captain looked back at me. 'It knows,' he said.

The comment seemed to drop into my mind like a lead weight into mud. I didn't know what to do with it for a moment but, still in analytical mode, started to put things together.

'The squirts die up here,' I said. 'It came up here so they would die.'

'Why would it do that?' asked SM17.

I fell into confusion for a moment, then said, 'It's maybe a Class Four intelligence or upwards the Warden told me. That might mean some altruistic motive. If it dumps its squirts up here they will not reinfect it or infect it or its fellow's prey…' But that did seem a stretch.

Another image arrived in my mind. This was of a sharp headed worm with fins turned to blades down its sides. I mapped this across to the image of the whelk and saw that in size and form it matched those scar tissue tracks. However, the virus killed these so where were the eggs coming from?

Smurk broke into an easy trot and I copied him. This was crazy. We would end up running round and round the island to keep from the whelk's clutches until I finally collapsed from exhaustion. Could SM17 carry me as far as another island? I guessed this was something I would be finding out unless…unless Bad Boy decided to return to the sea… I now set about building a small program to run over the whelk image, tracking every one of those scars, but even at that moment another image arrived in my mind. This one was large: coils of wormish body, a variety of tubes protruding, closer images of boring mouths, a long hard tubular spike labelled as an ovipositor.

'That's the final egg-laying stage?' I asked, to be sure.

'It is,' SM17 replied.

My program now showed its results. One scar tissue path arrowed up through the whelk's body without a terminus, and exited through the muscular mantle in its upper shell. Because the image had not completed before the whelk shit out the scanner I had only seen a portion of the structure up there, but had no idea what it was. Now I knew. I overlaid the final form of the parasite on this and got a match. The egg-laying portion of the parasite lived in the creature's upper shell. I shivered, remembering my earlier speculation about millions of years. Had the thing got there before the whelk was fully infected? Had it been there so long?

'I think I know what's happening with it,' I said, incidentally sending the matched images to SM17. 'And I don't see this ending anytime soon.'

'Why no time soon?' asked Smurk, looking back at me. He now appeared about as sane as he had when he brought me out here.

'There's a large egg-laying parasite lodged in its upper shell,' I explained. 'The whelk is eating fast and excreting fast to rid itself of the eggs that thing is laying in its guts.'

'Killing the squirts,' the captain opined.

Yes, it seemed the captain's mind was working better now.

'Exactly: it's killing the squirts,' I replied. 'Unfortunately, extrapolation from the genomic data tells me this is a vicious circle. The parasite feeds on the whelk's chyme supply around its intestine to make more eggs it then injects with its ovipositor. This process, perhaps in some past age before the Spatterjay virus, would have resulted in the whelk eventually dying. It won't die. I don't see this process ending.'

'Bad Boy does,' the captain replied.

Before I could pick the bones out of that comment, a tentacle with an end like a spatula slapped down hard on the beach behind, throwing sand and debris over us. Just like a squid, the whelk had two of these longer tentacles, yet it had misjudged its reach? I thought about how easily it had snatched up those animals that had come close to it, and I thought about its complex eyes and evident spacial awareness. Now when I looked at those eyes I did not see menace, but intelligence.

'Time to run,' said Smurk.

We did that thing, putting a good distance between us and the whelk before slowing to a walk, but I hardly noticed my surroundings as all sorts of facts competed for my attention. The whelk had attacked an atoll where hooper ships had been anchored and destroyed three of them, but it had killed none of the crews from those ships, instead heading ashore again. It had attacked other atolls. I'd seen recordings of hurried evacuations of inhabitants, seeming near misses and narrow escapes, yet still the whelk had killed no one. It had here knocked our platform from the air and destroyed it, grabbing Smurk in the process. Yes it had taken his arm, but then, oddly for a thing with such an appetite, released him.

'How intelligent is Class Four?' I wondered out loud.

'About that of an uplifted dog,' SM17 replied. 'Though assessments are difficult when it comes to alien life forms.'

I thought about that. An uplifted dog could use language and understand somewhat of its world, but would have seemed quite thick to even a pre-Quiet War human of half a millennium ago.

'But Class Four is also the minimum classification for the giant whelks,' SM17 added. 'More of a guess really.'

I turned to the captain. 'Why did you volunteer to bring me out here?'

'To witness the ending – one of us has to do it.'

The captain hadn't spoken much on our way out to this island and had seemed to show little interest in what I might discover. I thought about what it meant to be an Old Captain. He was centuries old, probably very wise and had 'managed to live into the calm', as they say on this world; that is, had managed to achieve great age without taking a sprine overdose and killing himself. Had he seen all of this before, or otherwise known about it? I thought he had. I thought about some of his odd comments and data began combining into a complete whole in my mind.

'It knows what's happening to it, doesn't it?' The captain merely shrugged. I turned my attention to SM17 as if I might be able to read some expression on its face. 'The Warden knows too, and the Conclave. That whelk is deliberately threatening the human population here because it knows that by doing so that population will eventually respond. It's committing suicide.'

'The other one did a lot of damage,' said Smurk. 'But we had off-world trade by then and bought a nuke.'

After this confirmation I stared at him. There had been another whelk like this they had killed with a nuclear weapon. Did the Warden know this?

'And now, because of what we have learned here, that might not be necessary in this case,' said SM17 before I could fully absorb the implications. The drone bobbed in the air as if excited. 'And now you understand, beyond the politics, both the Warden's and the Conclave's reluctance to act.'

That ticked the last box for me.

'It's not killing anyone.'

'Yup,' said Smurk. 'The other one didn't, but it also didn't know we could end it. This one knows different.'

I looked back at the whelk again, still trundling along the shore towards us, but now stopping occasionally. I looked closer. Yes, each time it stopped it tilted back to peer up at the sky. The whelk knew that threatening the humans here could result in its death, and it knew precisely where that death would come from. I turned back to SM17.

'Are you capable of lifting the both of us?' I asked.

We again ran to put some distance between us and Bad Boy, then halted. I emptied out my pack and inspected the contents. Thankfully

I'd made my choices based on survival. I took out some items to reduce the weight but left in the short range atomic sheer and a floater lamp, which I would certainly need. I handed a vibro-blade over to the captain, who took it with his new small hand. He grimaced, fumbling the grip, then took it in his other hand to insert it into his belt. He then eyed SM17 in a way I could only describe as acquisitive. I didn't know what that was all about until later. I then pulled out the strap for the Spartech and hung the weapon over my neck and shoulder, secure at my side.

'Aim for the top,' I said. 'That's where it will be thinnest.'

I moved closer to the captain and looked across at SM17. The drone was vibrating and I noted a red gleam showing through between the ribs of its shell. The thing had powered up to maximum for this task. It floated in above us and I could feel the strong backwash of grav from its engine as it hooked its tail above us. Smurk reached up and closed a hand around it, solid as a spaceship docking clamp. He would not fall. I reached up and grabbed, the tip of the tail closing over one of my hands and roughening for grip. With his other yet adult hand, Smurk reached out and grabbed the front of my suit, pulling me close. With a deep thrumming sound, SM17 rose into the air. As my feet came off the ground I did not feel so sure about my grip so wrapped my legs around the captain. Close to, I saw his tongue peek out and it still hadn't closed up. I swallowed dryly.

We sailed up into the sky and then along the beach. One of those spatula tentacles reached up towards us then halted twenty feet below, the end snapping open and closed. We passed over this then down towards the giant shell. The spiral of this thing was ridged and caked with coralline growths and blooms of limp blue seaweed. I hoped that stuff wasn't slippery as we rapidly descended. SM17 brought us in to the top part of the spiral curving and sloping down at fifty degrees.

'Let go of me,' said Smurk, as he released his grip on my suit. I unwrapped my legs and he simply released his hold, dropping to the sloping surface. He hit then began to slip on the weed, but then just slammed his fist down into the surface, sending porcelain chunks tumbling, and got a grip. SM17 got me in closer, in over an area free of weed, and loosened its grasp on my hand. I landed, my boots gripping, then fell forwards to sprawl against the surface scrabbling to find a grip. The peak of the shell lay twenty feet above. The fear that had initially tightened my guts began to fade and I realised this was no worse than my earlier climb, in fact easier and with a lot more handholds.

'A little higher,' I told Smurk. 'The older the shell the thinner it should be.'

We worked our way up with SM17 hovering just out from us and finally reached an area I deemed appropriate.

'Here.' Even as I said that the shell's steady shift under us changed. The whelk shrugged, nearly dislodging me, dropped and jerked up again. When this movement ceased the whelk was no longer traversing the shore.

I took out the atomic shear and turned it on – the thing extruding its emitter, starting to vibrate and then the shear field shimmering into existence about the emitter. Next, peering down towards the ground, I saw tentacles rippling against the sand. It wouldn't take the whelk long to realise something was going on up here and we weren't out of its reach.

'You watch,' said Smurk, holding out his hand.

I passed the shear over and readied the Spartech, crosshairs in my vision, laser and explosive slugs selected. One-handed, Smurk drove the shear into the shell below us, dust exploding out all around the thing, clouding out and down, settling white and nacreous nearby. Down below the tentacles stopped moving for a moment, then started again, like someone rattling their fingers against a table top in impatience.

Smurk had cut a circle when the two spatula tentacles curled up off the ground and back to grope around the shell lower down. Of course the whelk could not see us, and surely had no idea where we were or what we were doing. It searched around as Smurk swore, realising the shear had not cut through to the inside. He began slicing out chunks so he could cut deeper, them bouncing down the side of the shell to the ground. As pieces of these hit below, the two tentacles abruptly began to track higher.

'Perhaps I can distract it,' said SM17, abruptly dropping.

The drone hurtled down towards the two tentacles and came to an abrupt halt opposite them, backwash from its grav engine tearing out a cloud of weed fragments. The drone hung there for a moment and I saw flashes of red, only revealed as a laser by the steam they raised from one of the tentacles. The drone was armed, I thought with annoyance, then reconsidered. This was probably only a spectroscopic laser ramped up to maximum output. I hoped SM17 would retain enough power in storage to get us back to the ground.

'There,' said the captain in satisfaction.

He'd broken through, pieces of shell falling into a dark cavity, and began to cut around the circle again. Below, still flashing that laser, SM17 dropped into the whelk's line of sight. The thing began to thrash at it with its other tentacles while the two that had been coming up towards us just paused in place.

'Damn and bugger,' said the captain. Looking over I saw that where he had broken through had been a thin spot merely a foot and a half thick.

Smurk started carving out further chunks sending them tumbling down after the others. This set those two tentacles in motion again, but only tentatively. I continued watching SM17's antics until one tentacle whipped in from the side unexpectedly and hit the drone. I watched it, trailing smoke, tumble end over end to splash into the sea.

'That's not so good,' I said, but felt the urge to giggle, as if, though uninfected by the virus, the madness of this place was getting to me. Behind me Smurk swore again as the whine of the shear dropped to a low grumbling. I looked round as he held the device up, showing me its small diagnostic screen. The battery was flat. He discarded the thing then began bashing the cut circle with the flat of his hand. I was about to assist – using my weapon's laser – but now those two tentacles were coming up towards us. I fired explosive shells that hit one of the spatulas, but the blasts just raised fibrous splinters like bullets hitting a tree. Laser shots next set one of the spatulas smoking as the two tentacles zeroed in on me, as if they had some form of vision. A hollow crash resounded behind. A big hand closed on my shoulder and dragged me back. As I fell into darkness I had one last glimpse of the tentacles – they had stopped, poised just out from the shell. I only remembered then that they could have come straight for us right at the beginning because they did have sight – they were covered with an equivalent to retinal cells.

A brief slide over slick shell took us down into darkness until we hit a ridge in the floor. I looked up at the opening now twenty feet away and maybe ten feet up. I shed my pack then hooked the Spartech strap over my head so as not to lose it. Delving inside, I took out the floater lamp and initiated it. The light flared off beautiful nacre all around us.

Setting the lamp to float just a yard behind us, it cast our shadows down into the depths.

'Down we go,' I said.

Smurk now held the vibro knife and looked decidedly piratical. We clambered over the ridge and slid down further to another one, the space we occupied growing steadily wider and the slope not so steep. After the third ridge we could no longer slide and so crouched our way down until we could stand upright. Though the tunnel grew wider the ridges grew bigger all around the inside of the tunnel. We crawled through the hole at the centre of one only to find the next one along closed across completely.

'Protect your eyes,' I said, closing up my visor. Smurk dipped his head as I opened fire. Explosive slugs shattered the nacre wall, but it took a lot of them, as did the next, and the next after that.

'Air is not good,' said Smurk.

Yes, it was getting difficult to breath and I damned myself for not wearing a full environment suit here with its own air supply. We kept on around another curve, the spiral tunnel now twenty feet across, and then we saw the back end of the whelk.

A great fleshy tail ran along one wall, steadily growing thicker as we progressed until it filled half the tunnel. Thereafter it developed splits and webs of flesh running like bird bones across the tunnel. This looked like damage to me. We were close. Then, ahead, we saw a thick wormish body, its hue dark brown in the surrounding pale flesh. So what now? I hadn't really thought much beyond this point. We needed to kill this thing. Before I could do anything, Smurk pushed past and through gaps in the fleshy web to drive his vibro knife into that body. He sliced across, opening up a big split in thick fibrous skin to expose shifting guts, yellow ichor like that from a squirt bubbling and jetting out. The whole worm thing writhed, hoops of it shifting through our surroundings. It was a chore – we needed to get on with it.

I started firing at the exposed coils using up the last of my explosive slugs. They blasted fist-sized holes in the thing as Smurk kept on carving, but no sooner had I thought to be making some headway than the coils shifted to expose new undamaged ones. Then, abruptly, the whelk shuddered, its movement throwing me back against some fleshy mass, feet slipping in pools of yellow slime. I crawled to a point between two of the flesh growths and braced myself as the shaking continued, switched over to the laser and began burning the coils. Hot smoke boiled and I soon stopped that, wheezing and panting and my vision blurring. Soft beads next, but they just opened shallow hand-sized craters that did not seem to penetrate the outer tegument. All I had left was a few hundred hard beads that punched deep inside and I began using them, but the coils were disappearing around us and I saw a spiked saurian tail whip from sight. All at once there were no more targets left.

Smurk stood panting, soaked from head to foot in yellow slime. He appeared crazy again as he looked round at me, but joyfully so.

'Reckon we've pissed it off enough?' he asked.

A deep hissing chattering sound replied from where the thing had disappeared, then something began pushing into view through the fleshy webs. The wide head was blunt at first – smoothed down for pushing through flesh. It paused, questing here and there before zeroing in on us. It seemed blind but now somehow sensed us – I did not have the time to check the data on this thing. A momentary stillness ensued, because even the whelk had stopped moving.

'Well,' said Smurk.

In the still smoky air a red laser cut through from behind us, hit the head and tracked round leaving a smoking burn. I glanced back to see SM17 there, floating in a hole through those webs. The shot seemed ridiculous. The head was fully five feet across and the laser shot seemed like squirting a water pistol at an elephant. It shook itself, and then it opened like a flower bud into four jaws and emitted a stinking chattering shriek. I'd thought that leech mouth at the end of Smurk's tongue bad enough and the actual mouths of leeches too, but this seemed an order of magnitude worse. Back-facing teeth lined the thing, jointed hooks opened out from the jagged lips, deep in its hellish throat what looked like workings of some ancient clock, rendered in bone and red flesh, turned against each other.

It surged forwards and I opened fire, switching the Spartech to automatic. Beads slammed into the thing, shattering teeth and cutting away hooks. Knowing the captain's craziness I expected him to then attack, but instead he turned round, pushed through to come opposite me.

'We get out,' he said.

We backed through the damaged body of the whelk and I kept firing, SM17's occasional stabs of laser lost in the chaos. The head advanced and retreated as we stumbled clear of the whelk's living body into more open tunnel. Hard beads ran out and I switched to soft. Then something surged through underneath the head. I felt Smurk grab the back of my suit and he jerked me aside with bone-crunching force. A long black tube a foot wide, on the end of worm body, passed where I had been crouching and slammed into the tunnel wall, tearing up nacre. I'd forgotten about the ovipositor. With this is laid its eggs inside the whelk's guts – away from the sprine in its stomach – they doubtless went through it elongated and soft then expanded to their normal size in those guts. I fired at that body, but then the Spartech ran out. Laser now, I thought, but Smurk pulled me aside again.

'Time to run,' he said.

We turned and headed upslope, SM17 shooting along ahead of us. I glanced back, only vaguely seeing the parasite past the glare of the floater light. The thing was coming after us – of course it was, this was Spatterjay.

'We will need to rethink this,' said SM17.

'We won't…get up…that last slope,' I managed to wheeze out.

'We will,' Smurk replied easily.

It seemed a lot further up than it did down with that monster chattering and shrieking behind us. We went through the walls I had earlier shot down, up and up, and then, beyond another ridge, I slipped over on my face. I felt a hand close on the back of my suit and then I was sliding along the floor, different light beginning to impinge on my surroundings. I managed to look up to see Smurk sliding along ahead of me. I really hoped his new hand had a good grip on me because it was with his old hand he clutched SM17's tail. I looked back, seeing the parasite was having problems with the slippery shell surface, but was managing to progress through sheer squirming rage. Then all at once I was in the air, then out into daylight.

Smurk discarded me on the outer shell. I slipped on weed until slamming up against something, raised my weapon set to laser and aimed at the hole, but then scrabbled at my visor to get it open and gasp at fresh air. I realised Bad Boy was on the move, trundling along the beach again. Smurk crouched near the edge of the hole, still holding SM17's tail.

'If you must,' I heard the drone say, and saw it seem to contract a little and tighten up.

The monstrous head surged out of the hole a moment later. I opened fire on it, burning it where I could but to seemingly little effect.

'Now y'bugger!' Smurk bellowed, and hit the thing with SM17. The crashing blow split one of its jaws and it retreated a little as if stunned, that chattering shriek stilling. Smurk hit it again, then again, but now it recovered and pushed towards him. He retreated up the outer spiral, still hitting it, but slipping on weed and struggling not to fall. Its thick body oozed out after its head and I fired on that, still burning it, but hardly penetrating. It seemed we simply could not kill the creature and in a depressing moment I realised that though the primary of this creature did not have much of the virus in it, this thing was probably loaded. We probably could not kill it. Smurk would eventually fall and, quite probably, it would turn on me. I would fall too, since I had more chance of surviving that than this thing. Then I saw movement to one side and glanced over.

One of Bad Boy spatula tentacles rose up like a cobra, hooped over and in. In one swift movement it wound around the body of the parasite behind the head like a tightening hawser. It then pulled. The head snapped away from Smurk, out and down. I saw him slip and fall, hurtling towards the sea, but halfway down SM17 shrugged and, jetting smoke and sparks, applied grav. Obviously not functioning correctly it did still manage to slow their descent, swing them in from the sea they had been heading for and both crashing down on the beach. Smurk could survive that. I turned my attention back to the parasite.

Bad Boy kept on pulling, drawing out the parasite's body like guts being pulled from a torso. Frilled slabs of muscle came out of the hole and stumpy limb-like protuberances. A bulbous section came out to with another wormish body branching from that, terminating in that ovipositor. This whipped out and stabbed into the spatula tentacle, actually penetrating the tough flesh. But the parasite was now in reach of shorter tentacles that coiled up around it, pulled the egg-laying tube out and snapped it. Finally the tail of the thing I had seen earlier came out too and the giant whelk had in its grasp a parasite that had probably occupied its shell for millennia – a parasite that had driven it to the brink of suicide.

The whelk raised the thing up then brought it down hard, and now seeing our location I saw its target: that rocky promontory, now devoid of land heirodonts. It took maybe half an hour of repeated blows against the rocks, worrying and tearing, before the parasite lay in shreds over the rock and in the sea. In that time I saw Smurk stand up and go over for a closer look, but SM17 just sat down there jabbed into the sand. Finally it was over and Bad Boy could not find anything large enough to shred further. But Smurk and the drone were down there and I was up here. I turned to look for a way down, not much liking the idea of having to get past the whelk's tentacles if I managed to get down there without falling. I then saw what had stopped me falling when Smurk released me: Bad Boy's other spatula tentacle.

I stared at the thing, wondering what the hell to do now. Before I could decide, the thing folded in around me and hoisted me from the shell. It then lowered me down to the ground and deposited me beside SM17.

Another night passed and Bad Boy kept trundling around the island eating and shitting, but I soon saw it was inspecting its own excrement. The thing certainly seemed intelligent for I felt sure it was waiting until it passed the last of the squirt eggs before it returned to the sea. Peering out from the beach I watched two ships approaching, but the grav rafts arrived first.

'So we did actually help to kill something that was very old?' I enquired.

SM17 sat with its tail jabbed in the sand. Every now and again the drone leaked a little smoke, but it continued self-repairs and would soon have its grav engines back online.

'That scar tissue was ancient,' it replied. 'It seems likely the giant whelk acquired its parasite when young and the thing grew with it and very slowly – only recently attaining sufficient mass to lay so many eggs.'

'Unless the egg laying is cyclic in nature and shuts down after a period.'

'The data indicate otherwise,' SM17 said dismissively. 'The captain comes.'

I looked back in towards the island to see Smurk strolling towards us. Carrying a large chunk of wood he'd decided to track the whelk, and had spent most of yesterday and the night killing squirts. I didn't quite understand why, since the things would die anyway. I noted that now his new arm was about the same length as the old.

'Still, we did help kill something that was quite ancient.'

'And unintelligent,' said the drone.

'Oh, so it's not some snobbery about the lives of parasites having less value?'

'You are bored and looking for an argument.'

I grimaced. I guess I was.

A large raft settled on the beach, guided down by a hooper woman in ratty blue overalls. Most of the space aboard was taken up by a large tank running a pipe to a thing like a gun mounted on one rail. Further around the rail another gun-like object had been attached and could be classified as such. Exactly to my specifications, I thought, as I stood up.

'Soon be heading away from here,' said Smurk strolling up. He pointed to the two ships then added, 'But I want to see this done.'

'Killed all the squirts?' I enquired.

'No more coming out,' he replied. 'Bad Boy's just stopped over there.'

I gestured to SM17. 'The drone tells me reinfection is unlikely due to the age of the whelk and its concentration of viral fibres.'

'But it's still more likely while that hole stays open,' said Smurk.

'Quite.'

He reached down and picked up SM17 and tucked the drone under his arm where it vibrated for a moment making a sound like a bee in a can. We walked over to the raft.

'All you need,' said the hooper woman. She leapt from the raft and headed towards where another settled to the beach. Talkative sort. I climbed aboard and the captain came after, held the drone down by the rail where with a buzz and a clang it stuck itself, head peering over the top rail. Smurk took hold of the pedestal-mounted joystick and pulled the platform into the air.

We were soon passing over the devastated island, but it had not been completely denuded, for dingle still stood to the left and the right – Bad Boy had just taken out a strip across the centre. Ahead, the giant whelk had reached the far shore. As we drew closer I could see its tentacles splashing in the sea and again wondered just how intelligent the thing might be. Was it waiting? It then slowly turned, grinding up the beach and tilted to look up at us. A moment later those two spatula tentacles rose up and I just knew that through them it was inspecting us too.

'Take us down in front of them,' I said.

Smurk looked at me with a raised eyebrow, but complied. The tentacles stretched towards us as he took us closer and brought the raft to a halt. I let them inspect us for a while then walked over to the gun device, tilted it to point to part of the beach free of tentacles and just beyond Bad Boy's skirt, and triggered the thing.

The jet that shot out was pure white, like milk. Where it hit the beach it formed a pool then began bubbling and expanding, turning yellow as it did so. Within just a minute it had expanded into a large globe and solidified. Bad Boy reached out and probed it with one tentacle, set it rolling, then snared it and bashed it with another tentacle. It didn't break and when the whelk bashed it again even harder the thing escaped it grasp and bounced out into the sea. It looked ridiculously like the giant whelk was playing with a ball. In the sea it started to sink, because this ceramic-base crash foam expanded with a hexafluoride gas almost the same density as water.

'Okay, I guess that's the best we can do. Take us in,' I said.

Smurk complied, bringing us over the area of shell where we had entered, close to the hole he had cut. The whelk's two spatula tentacles followed us in, watching intently. Peering down into that darkness, I thought about how close I had come to dying, then pointed the crash foam gun at it and triggered. A white line disappeared into dark. I kept firing it for a few minutes, glancing at the gauge on the tank, then stopped and waited, timing it. When it all should have expanded and hardened I fired again, because now that tunnel inside must be blocked and further foam would come up to the hole. When the tank read three-quarters empty I saw the foam bubbling and expanding inside and shut off the jet. After minute or two it began expanding out of the hole forming a great globule that eventually hardened.

'Closer now,' I said, moving over to the other gun – in fact an industrial laser.

Smurk positioned the platform just right over to one side of the globe. I fired up the laser, the beam punching into the globe then revealed as bright green by vapour. I began cutting, slicing through the thing close to the shell, hexafluoride gas running like water down the shell. The thing took a lot of energy to cut through such being the resistance of this foam, but eventually I got through and the globe slid away, tumbled down shell, bounced off the whelk's skirt and rolled out onto the beach. Behind it left a clean glossy face – the laser having melted the ceramic into something like glass there. Smurk backed us up.

'So that's it,' he said.

With a clunk, SM17 detached from the rail and rose up – grav obviously back online. 'I will stay with this creature,' it said. 'I have permission to remain and study it while the Warden has permission to intercede immediately should another of its kind come to the surface like this.'

'So we're all happy,' I said, looking out at those two tentacles. And then, just to dismiss any uncertainties about its intelligence, Bad Boy applauded us, slapping the spatula ends of those tentacles before turning and heading back into the sea, SM17 floating along behind.

Smurk departed the platform on the beach to watch a rowing boat coming in from one of the now moored ships.

'What next for you?' he asked.

I shrugged. 'I'll find something.'

He clapped me on the shoulder and wandered off. I flew back to what could be called civilization on Spatterjay, my shoulder aching.

Far future Polity again where digging things up might be helpful and might not. You could say this is an sfnal take on Robinson Crusoe. I never thought that while writing it – only in retrospect. In The Bosch I depicted a far future biotech world and here we get a look at another one. What to say about it? As with them all I just started writing and used what my subconscious delivered. In this case it delivered some on the delights of getting older, the destructive squabbles of humanity and how perspective changes ultimate goals.

PLENTY

A whickering sound cut the night, followed by a long drawn-out hiss. Ben rolled onto his back but could not summon the energy to get up. What could he do, anyhow? If the Stalker attacked the house again and managed to break inside, he had his carbine within reach and, if that didn't work out, he simply was not well enough to fight in any other way. He stretched out his hand to the weapon, but then realised how light the room was. It wasn't night time and the sounds he had heard had been yet another nightmare. He sighed and, like so many times before, drifted back into haunted sleep.

His house stood on the edge of the plain with low hills rolling behind towards the haze-green mountains whose name had been long forgotten. The location was good since potable water rose in a spring nearby, the stream from that running down into the plain and disappearing, while easy sources of food lay all around him. Sack bats hanging in the turtle tree copses in the hills provided a ready source of meat while edible mushrooms grew in the carapace shade of the trees. Wide varieties of greens and roots could be found all around, the occasional gnapper snake and of course his main source of protein: the mantids. On the plain grew other edible plants and fungi and, most importantly, that's where he found podules always filled with a cornucopia of delights. Even without his almanac and Snooper, food was no problem here. But it seemed likely other problems would curtail his survival.

Ben woke again but this time to the sound of distant mantids scraping together their serrated forelimbs. He lay in his cot summoning up the courage to move, then slowly tipped himself out of bed, his back and his joints aching and creaking, his stomach roiling and nausea hitting him. Sitting upright with his feet down on woven rugs on the stone floor, he congratulated himself on having got to this position without his back popping and the agony that had made getting himself moving after sleep an hours' long task. He looked to the end of his bed for his clothes, but then realised he was wearing his battered envirosuit – he often went to bed wearing it now because of the problems he faced putting the thing back on when he woke. He stood, pain stabbing his back, and walked past the low divider into his kitchen area. Opening his fridge – one of the many items salvaged over the years from the crashed shuttle – he took out a bowl of mantid meat and a couple of large pea pods containing peas that tasted of orange. As he sat at his table eating these, and washing them down with cold coffee, he knew he needed to head out collecting again. The fridge was all but empty, and in another twenty hours the three hundred hour night would arrive, and he didn't want to be outside then, not with the mantids out hunting, and definitely not with the Stalker.

'Snooper, activate,' he said.

Over the other side of the room Snooper unfolded from its alcove. The quadruped robot was battered and worn now after twenty years of perambulating around this area with him. Fortunately its capacitor battery had only lost a quarter of its functionality and the solar panels he had taken from the shuttle served to charge it up in just a couple of days. Briefly, it looked like an eager headless dog as it came upright and moved towards him, but with a body like a section of a wide cylinder – the legs attached to its circumference – the illusion disappeared when it squatted in waiting position.

Heaving out of his chair, Ben wandered around inside his shack collecting the things he needed. His laser carbine still worked as intended and still charged up from the solar panels on the roof, though of late it had developed a strange colour change. The beam, which used to shine red if it hit any vapour or smoke to reveal it, was now shading to purple. A weapon being a necessity outside the shack, and this change to his carbine, was why over the last night on this old biotech world of Afthonia, he had made a crossbow, which he also took up. This weapon did not shoot standard bolts but chevrons of metal he had cut from the shuttle's hull and spent a long time sharpening with corundum gritstone out of a podule. It was perfect for chopping through the neck of a mantid, should his shooting be accurate enough with his failing eyesight and the tremor his hands had developed. How it would do against the Stalker he had no idea. He had never, in all the long years he had been here, seen the thing clearly.

He collected up his backpack too, strapped on his belt with its carry sacks, then went to the door, opening it carefully and checking outside down the sight of the carbine, then moving out as quickly as he could to turn and take a look at the roof. Nothing nasty had moved into the location, so he returned to the door to close and bolt it. He paused, catching his breath, and looked around. The Stalker confined itself to the night and its visits were infrequent. Perhaps he should consider himself lucky that a thing that size – he knew it was bigger than a man – did not come out in the day. Or perhaps he should consider that unlucky, because in daylight he would have had a better chance at killing the thing.

He went round the shack closing the shutters and finally arrived at his lean-to. A dirt turtle that had taken up residence at the back stuck out its head to peer at him for a moment, then swiftly retracted it. He left it alone since though the meat of the creature tasted sour, its proximity might provide emergency rations. Within a few years of being stranded on Afthonia his need for food had grown enormously. He did not know why but speculated that maybe the food here was not as nutritious as it seemed.

In the lean-to sat his barrow loaded with tools. He uncovered it and, putting his carbine and crossbow in with the tools, trundled it out. Only when he had walked a few hundred yards did it register with him that he had taken the route out onto the plain. It wasn't the best choice for victuals with night approaching, but stubbornness kept him going.

He followed the path he had tramped down over his years of journeys out onto the plain, Snooper walking silently behind him. Near his shack, bubble grass, herbs and other low-growing plants cloaked the ground. He often collected many of these for flavourings but little grew here of any nutritional value because he had denuded the area in the early years. He had walked a couple of miles before seeing anything different and potentially edible but, even so, the plants were sparsely scattered and their growth did not look healthy – growths from pieces of root he had left in the ground, or small bulbs to fiddly to peel – and certainly there were none of the familiar sprouts of podules so close to his shack.

The walking helped ease away his internal aches and pains but aggravated the sores and other lesions on his skin. Even so, as he warmed up, he began to feel positively buoyant for the first time in a while. He decided to put a good distance between himself and his shack today, but then hesitated when he saw the thick sprout jutting from the ground. There would be a podule below, but the green and black chequered leaf had yet to unfold and there were no old stalks on the ground around it, so the thing was newly grown and had yet to pack itself with…whatever it happened to contain.

'No,' he said, then looked around as if he had expected someone to overhear. He kept going, through an area where more sprouts protruded and where some had opened out leaves that harvested sunlight to power their chemistry but also sunlight to turn into electricity to run some of the other processes inside. Further on he passed low mounds free of vegetation and kept a more wary eye on his surroundings. Next passing another such area, he saw three big mantids rise up to watch him like nightmare meerkats. But they stayed precisely where they were. He grunted dismissively. In his first years here the mantids had always attacked on sight, but now they had learned that this particular moving protein source burned off their heads and took them home for lunch. Or rather, surviving mantids had learned that's what he did with their less fortunate fellows.

Finally he reached and area where the path hardly showed through the vegetation and branched off in many directions. He hadn't come out so far in many days – those 'days' consisting of three hundred hours of darkness and the same of daylight, but with seasonal variations of eighty hours. Around him he recognised the foliage of edible roots, of podules, and berry bushes, but here he only stopped to examine a ring of grey-topped mushrooms similar to edible ones he had picked before.

'Over here,' he said, taking a laser pointer off his belt, triggering it and selecting one of the mushrooms.

Snooper scuttled up beside him then stalked forwards like a cat getting ready to pounce on a mouse, but instead stepped daintily over the mushroom he had selected and squatted. After a moment the screen on the robot's top turned on and began running an analysis that was mostly opaque to him. He knew he was missing out on a great deal because of this, for Snooper was detailing useful chemicals and perhaps pharmaceuticals, but as a shuttle engineer the language was as much gobbledegook as the code he understood would be to a bio-technician. After a short while the readout came to an end and awaited instructions. He input what he had managed to learn via the touchpad and received a terse summation. The mushrooms would not poison him but their nutritional value was low. He moved on, again considering another attempt to hook up the almanac to Snooper. In previous years it had not been an urgent consideration. His body had been tough standard human and ran a basic nanosuite which meant that without suite adjustments or visits to a doctor AI he could live, barring accident and exotic maladies, for over a hundred and seventy years. He had lived for a hundred and twenty years. In the last twenty he had suffered accidents and poisonings that should have been no problem for the suite. However, it seemed he had also somehow returned to some ancient age whereby sicknesses afflicted him with irritating then worrying regularity. And now it appeared he was suffering the maladies of age – that accumulation of damage – early, and some pharmaceuticals might come in useful.

After a while he turned from the half-seen path, passed some mantid mounds and moved into an area he might have visited before but, by the quality of the growth here, not for some time. He dug up black parsnips and blue potatoes that Snooper told him were non-toxic and nutritious, found a large puffball the same and packed a bag with spinach-like greens. He then focused his attention on one of the podule sprouts, its leaves well spread and crinkling at the edges. Old growth of previous sprouts dry and brown on the ground around this indicated a podule that had been growing for five or six 'days'. He took his shovel and pick from the barrow and began digging. Within a few minutes he revealed the upper tough rind of the thing which, by its curve, indicated an oblate podule maybe two feet across, and he thanked the gods of biotechnology. Carefully digging around it he cut through soft wet roots then finally cleared enough soil to get his shovel underneath it. As he levered the thing out of the ground he knew he would pay for this later and the next time he climbed out of bed it would be to an hour or so of suffering.

With the podule up on the surface, large and heavy as a sack of potatoes, he called Snooper over and had the robot do its thing. Immediately a light flashed up in the corner of the screen, which then ran a long list of the thing's contents. The green light indicated all the contents fit for human consumption, so he heaved it whole into the barrow, then peered towards the pink bloated sun sitting above the horizon. Sixteen or seventeen hours of daylight remained. Call it fourteen hours, since he wanted to be home before the lengthy twilight brought out the innocular flies. However, he had plenty of time to dig up another podule.

Fifty or so feet away another mature sprout poked from the ground. As he headed over, the barrow wheel bounced over something and he spotted a shiny object sunk in the earth. Pulling the barrow back he used his pick to lever up a short pipe of bright metal. After inspecting it for a while he put it in the barrow beside the podule. It might come in useful, though he acknowledged that similar finds of old tech had risen into a heap behind his shack of which he had only used one or two pieces. Next setting to work around the sprout, he revealed a podule smaller than the previous one but, by the dark honeycomb pattern on its skin. knew it might contain items more useful than food. He felt a brief surge of excitement as he chopped through the roots around it and in his eagerness it took him a moment or two to realise he wasn't managing to cut through one of the roots, though he did break through a thin tough membrane. Peering at the thing in puzzlement, he took in its odd shape, then puzzlement turned to shock as he recognised the membrane as badly degraded plas-wrap about a human hand.

Ben just stared for a long moment – his reasoning no longer as fast as it had once been. This could not be a corpse buried here because the ground had obviously lain undisturbed for a long time. Any human corpse would have decayed to bones by now. Quickly coming to a decision, he further dug around the podule, levered it out and put it in the barrow beside the other one. He then began digging back from the hand, revealing more plas-wrap about an arm. He took out a chainglass knife and tried it on the wrap, and it split open as it should not have, so it had to be very old. After closely inspecting the skin on the arm he made a small cut to reveal inner layers, confirming what he had first thought. He had found part of or the whole of a Golem android. He kept digging, wincing at the prospect of how he would feel later, but unable to stop. He revealed a shoulder then a head, all tightly wrapped. Finally he had the thing revealed in total, face-down to the ground. He split the wrapping and pulled it away to reveal the body of a Golem clad in a monofilament overall. Silvery hair dropped away in tufts from the head when he touched it. He now saw at the lower back where the monofilament and artificial skin and flesh had been burned away right down to composite bones inlaid with meta-circuitry. More artificial flesh had been burned from the lower legs and, when he managed to heave the heavy thing over, he saw that *she* had also lost half her face covering and that the burn he had seen on her back had resulted from a shot at belly level from the front. It looked like she had been hit with a laser carbine.

The sensible thing to do now would be to leave her here on the ground and get back to his shack. He could return after the long night to collect her, for she would receive no more damage than she now had. Another sensible thought, immediately dismissed, was that he was wasting his time here. A burnt up Golem that had not managed to repair itself wasn't much use to him. Quite probably the crystal mind in her chest had been fractured, the power supply had become depleted or wiped out, her micro circuitry corroded by exposure through damaged syntheskin to the environment. But the stubbornness that led him out here and to which he also attributed his survival on Afthonia, persisted.

He pulled his barrow as close as he could and set about heaving her onto it. She was heavier than a human of the same size and he struggled for some time, at one point tipping the barrow over and spilling out the podules. Immediately on top of this he felt a sick flush through his body and broke into a hot sweat. His chest hurt and then the pain spread to his neck and left arm. He knew exactly what that meant but ignored it, for what could he do? Instead he went and sat on a nearby tuft of stringy grass and thought about how he should deal with the Golem.

During the long rest to let the pain ease, he had time to ponder, and next went over to kneel on her with his knees on her hips, grabbed her shoulders and pulled. Some little movement indicated he was on the right track and he kept at it, her hip joints slowly bending as if set in hardening glue. Finally he got her into a position sitting upright with her legs out in front of her, and she showed no sign of collapsing back down. He emptied the barrow of podules and tools, ran it up behind her and tipped it, bringing the front down against her buttocks, reached over and grabbed her under the armpits and pulled her back into the barrow. As her weight entered the thing it tipped back towards him and down on its back two wheels. She rested inside firmly, backside down in the bottom of the barrow, legs sticking out the front, one arm out to the side and the other sticking straight upright.

Ben again rested, then wandered about until finding some cranberries, ate them and then wished he had brought water. Returning to the barrow he loaded the podules on top of her and jammed in the tools and weapons where he could. Next, conceding to his urge for neatness, he went to work on her arms, pushing against intransigent joint motors to bend them until her hands rested down on the podules. He then worked on bending her knees so her legs did not stick up so ridiculously, and later, looking at her sitting there, wondered if what he had done had been more about making her look more dignified than about neatness.

He began the journey back to the shack, tired and thirsty but still warm enough from the work not to ache yet. A glance at the horizon showed him the sun just touching it and he knew he would not get back before the innocular flies were out. The barrow was heavy and lifting it up on the forward wheel made it unstable, so he turned it round and towed it down on all three wheels, wondering if it would stand up to the punishment, since he had made it from a luggage loading trolley from the shuttle, which he had been pushing around for a lot longer than its intended life. He took frequent rests, aching now because of his unnatural position reaching back to grasp the handles. At one point he stopped and tried fashioning a towing strap out of his belt. This worked for a little while until the barrow tipped over, dragging him to the ground and twisting his back – it clicking ominously as he struggled to his feet. Again he loaded her and the podules and tools. Again he set out.

As the hours passed he began to feel quite unwell, and knew that if he was back in his house to set the almanac screen to mirror he would see a complexion that looked almost grey. When the light turned to pink Champagne close to twilight, he considered dumping her out and just heading home with his other finds. The first innocular fly landing on his neck and digging in made him yell in frustration. He slapped and crushed the thing, pulled it from his neck and inspected it. It looked

164

like a big mosquito with a tiger-striped body and, recognising the type that caused pain, he knew the exposed skin of his arms and head would be covered with itchy bumps from the ones that did not cause pain and were hardly visible. He hated the things and found the effects of their bites disturbing. Sometimes he would break out in horrible rashes or end up suffering some nameless malady. Other times he slept like the dead afterwards and woke with one or other of his maladies in remission. And yet other times he felt variously drugged – sometimes as if with amphetamines other times as if with an opiate. But as he continued on, he soon saw that the innocular flies were the least of his problems.

With the light fading and shadows stretching out towards infinity, he glimpsed movement to his right and left. Mantids did venture from their burrows during the day to hunt, but they much preferred the night. He counted perhaps two of them over to his right and one to his left that had edged close enough for him to see its almond shaped body, thorny limbs and, above gyrating mandibles, two bulbous compound eyes studying him. He put the barrow down, reached for the crossbow and then hesitated. He had used this weapon only once before and it had proved very effective. But it had then taken him a couple of hours to find the sharpened missile. It took a great deal of work to make each of them and he did not want to lose them. In this light he was sure to.

Instead he selected the carbine, turned it on and noticed that the charge bar was not at maximum as it should have been. The sight of that made him nervous, but obviously the sight of the carbine made the nearest mantid nervous too, for it quickly scuttled away out of sight. As ever he wondered at their intelligence. They were obviously capable of learning but, seriously, how much knowledge could a brain the size of a shelled walnut retain? Looking over at the other two he saw that they had frozen in place. Should he fire a shot to scare them off? He didn't like the idea – now thinking his carbine had a limited number of shots remaining. He hung the weapon from his shoulder by its strap, hoisted up the barrow and trudged on. He then had to stop to bat away an innocular fly that had landed on his nose. A mantid, lying flat to the ground beside the path, chose that moment to attack.

The thing was on him before he could even get to his carbine. It reared up and brought its serrated forelimbs down on his shoulders and only his instinctive grab for it, closing his hand around its 'neck' prevented the mandibles from tearing into his face. Awkwardly, with his left hand, he reached across and grabbed the carbine, aware that the other mantids were closing in. He thrust the weapon forwards and just as awkwardly got a finger to the firing button. A flash of red and purple partially blinded him and the creature jerked away, leaving one of its limbs still gripping his right shoulder. It thrashed on the path before him and he kicked it as hard in the head as he could, flipping it over onto the side of the path. Bringing the weapon stock up against his shoulder he fired again at half seen movement to his right, and saw the mantid there retreat in flames with a whickering clattering sound. Turning left he saw another rising and this time managed a head shot, the head exploding in burning fragments and the thing dropped away. Taking a breath, he peeled the limb off his shoulder and discarded it. A switch seemed to click down then and looking to the horizon he saw the last of the sun wink out. Darkness would descend very quickly now. He turned to Snooper.

'Go home,' he instructed the robot, and it quickly scuttled ahead of him along the path. Hopefully it would distract any mantids ahead until, by some manner he had yet to divine, they realised it wasn't edible. He then grabbed up the barrow and, charged with adrenaline, towed it just as fast as he could after the robot.

Finally his house came into sight, while around him he could hear the stalking mantids and other sounds indicating other unsavoury night denizens. It surprised him to get right up to the building without being attacked. There he unbolted the door to let Snooper inside, turned the barrow round and readied himself to push it in, but as something landed on him from above, he realised that he had not checked the roof. He swung at the thing with both fists, the impact on carapace sending him staggering because this one was bigger and heavier than those he had seen earlier. A smell like perfume impinged and the sound of clattering mandibles. He swung the carbine round and fired, hitting the side of the mantid's thick almond-shaped body. Its feet clattering on the wooden porch; it shifted sideways, mandibles dripping, and of course more terrifying now the light had faded.

The thing skittered back and raised its long saw-tooth forelimbs. Smoke boiled from the wound in its side, but not enough. He fired again, burning into its thorax, but the shot did not have the effect he expected and merely seared the surface. The creature backed off again, however, so he turned and pushed the barrow over the threshold into his shack. Inside the door he turned and fired again as the mantid lunged at him. His shot seared it again and it veered away, thrashing its body against the ground, its stunted wings lifting. He fired once more and in the smoke the laser spread like a torch beam, merely lighting the creature up in all its grisly magnificence. Ben quickly grabbed the door and slammed it just as the creature hit it from the other side. Shouldering against the wood as it jerked against him and threatened to throw him across the room, he managed to slide one bolt across. On the next blow this half tore out its fixings, but he managed to slide another across, then another, then finally drop the first of two locking bars into their loops, then the other.

The mantid thumped against the door twice more, then he heard it moving around the house clattering its mandibles. He breathed out a sigh of relief but then, abruptly the clattering transitioned into a stuttering squeal, terminated with a crunch, then further crunching and the sound of fluid trickling to the ground. A short while later, almost expected, he heard a familiar whickering out in the darkness, then a measured heavy tread coming up to his door, the floor shifting as its weight rested on the porch. It pushed against the door for a moment, the wood creaking, then the Stalker hit it hard raising splinters and dust from the inside and nearly lifting one of the locking bars out. He should go back and put his weight against it, hold that bar down, but found he could not move. The thing out there took a long sniff at the door, then hissed. He heard it moving away but did not trust that for a moment. He just stood there until he found himself shivering, then pushing himself into motion again.

He stared at his carbine, its power now down to zero. Had the thing known, somehow? The last time it had been around here had been another occasion when he came back late and the innocular flies were out. He'd glimpsed the thing out in the darkness and simply fired at it without any other consideration. It had made a horrible grunting and he's seen fire before it disappeared from sight. Later it had attacked the house trying to tear through a wall, before going away again. The next day he found long splinters torn from the logs but nothing that needed repair. Or, he wondered, was it always out and about around here in the darkness? He turned and looked at the contents of his wheelbarrow, and wondered if his find had been worth this new insight. His sleep might not be so good now. Nevertheless, he staggered over to his bed and crashed down on it, and was asleep before even considering a more comfortable position.

Ben woke in darkness and panic. Had he properly locked the door? And had he closed the window shutters before he went out? He just didn't know because these being tasks he had done so many times he did them automatically. He tried to move but his body felt sore from head to foot and his limbs fizzed with a sick heat. He lay their trying to get into motion but instead fell asleep again.

The second time he woke was to the sound of something squealing out in the darkness, and adrenaline got his legs off the bed and his feet on the floor before he realised how much pain he was in. Yet, oddly, because it was not the specific pain in his back nailing him in place, but in every joint *and* his back, it seemed somehow more bearable. In pitch black he reached over to the head of the bed, found the light switch and clicked it on. The single panel in the ceiling glowed to life flooding the shack with sun-bright light. He had only felt it necessary to use one panel at a time of the five he had recovered from the shuttle. He was now down to three. The things did not fade or change colour like the beam of his carbine had, but just blinked off after maybe ten years of use, and nothing he did could get them working again.

Thinking on that he turned his attention to the carbine lying on the floor, and with slow care stooped to pick it up. A brief inspection showed him the battery so depleted it could not even fire up the display on the side. Perhaps that had been the problem? Perhaps if he could replace the battery the beam would return to its usual colour and coherence? His gaze wandered to the load in the barrow. Perhaps that smaller podule would provide? He shook his head and listened. Was the Stalker still out there? Would it try to get in? Was it even the same creature as he had first seen?

It had been fifteen solstan years ago, after he had built the house. The prior years had well taught him that you did not go out at night and during his first year in the house he made a thicker and more secure door and window shutters. The windows themselves had no glass, but retrieving metal from the shuttle he did give them bars. He had been out digging up podules as usual but was late returning. He had been relatively fit then and confident and so stayed out later – mainly to lure in some mantids to complement his food supply. Then the visor of his envirosuit had not been so hazy and he felt that adequate protection against the innocular flies. At first when he saw it, he thought rescue had arrived, for a big human stood on the plain gazing towards him. He raised a hand, suddenly joyful, but the man stooped forwards and, down on all fours, came charging towards him like a silverback gorilla, grunting and whickering. This was no man. He opened fire on the thing, hitting one shoulder, the flash lighting up carapace and gleaming metallic eyes. The creature swerved and disappeared behind a clump of podule foliage. Not so confident any more he pushed his barrow back to the house and closed the door. The next day he found mantid remains scattered all about the area and had to hunt further afield for them until their population grew again, sure in the knowledge now that they weren't the apex predator here.

Perhaps that was it? Perhaps this creature was a roving hunter and had only returned here because the mantid population was once again high. And of course he had no idea if the one he had just heard was the same one he had first seen, or that other sightings were of the same creature. He didn't really know which case was the more frightening. Damn it. He just had to continue. The thing had failed to get to him and he would take more care about getting back to the house before nightfall for he had never seen it out and about in daylight.

Anyway, now he had work to do.

Putting aside the carbine he grimly heaved himself to his feet, went to the barrow, took out the larger podule and, struggling with its weight, brought it over to his kitchen table. He took an ever reliable and sharp chainglass knife from a rack and careful not to cut too deep sliced through the tough rind from the top, the cuts dividing the thing into four quarters. He then used a blunt metal knife to work under that rind, peeling it away from white pith, exposing translucent 'seeds' much like those of a pomegranate but each the size of his fist. With the rind folded down to the table he stripped away much of the pith and discarded it in his waste bin, for he had not yet found any use for it. He then used the knife to open gaps between the top seeds, shoved his hands inside and peeled the thing open.

Some of the seeds were completely opaque, others translucent with objects visible inside. Snooper had already green-lighted the podule so he knew everything here was edible. He recognised some of the seeds: the pale green ones contained a paste like avocado with a hint of orange, the dark brown ones were like raw beef, objects inside some of them were spherical nuts with familiar tastes, and all the variations on yellow were like cheese. Those he did not recognise would be a taste adventure, though he would try them with more caution than he had used when trying a red paste that turned out to be chilli. He freed them all from their pith, wiped them with a damp cloth and piled them in ancient plastic boxes in the fridge. Then he cleaned down the table and went to get the other podule.

This one opened up just like the first, contained seeds similar to the other but darker and often with a hint of metal. Once he had them all cleaned and laid out on the table he inspected each carefully, putting aside those whose contents he knew. Snooper's green light here had really been no help, since it only indicated that the podule had produced what it was supposed to produce. Edibility wasn't the question. All those seeds he could not identify he put over on a counter for later investigation. He did not hold out hope of finding much, but occasionally they contained items or substances he could recognise and use. Many other items that had utterly baffled him he had stored in one of his large collection of cupboards, while pastes and liquids he had found he had put in a growing number of containers he collected from bottle bamboo growing near the mountains. All these were a source of activity for him during the long nights – taking them out and trying to figure what they were.

With those that remained he began with three metallic grey seeds, stabbing in the chainglass knife till hitting something hard then cutting round it. He opened each, spilling out small stacks of grey rectangles which, when he separated, revealed their metallic plug-in connections. He now had more capacitor batteries to plug into those he used to store power from the panels. He eyed the carbine, wondering if he should make the attempt at changing its power supply. The thing was security sealed and would be a bastard to get inside, and he was pretty sure that with the density of its power supply he would need a carry pack of these capacitor batteries to power it, supposing that it was its power supply that had gone wrong. Later, he decided.

Another seed, translucent with something jet black inside, revealed another stack that immediately fell into separate pieces. These had post plugs and sockets along the edges and mated together there. He put them in a cupboard with the rest. When he had enough he would climb up on the roof and plug them into the growing solar panel up there – a useful addition since the ones from the shuttle were steadily losing efficiency. Other seeds revealed connectors, transformers and other plug-and-play electronics. He found one containing small light squares that fitted into his rechargeable torch. Still more rendered varieties of ceramic items he could use for fixing this and that, but had little idea of their original purpose. Some looked like plumbing fittings, while others looked like components that might fit in Snooper. The remainder he put aside unopened since they contained liquids and pastes he knew.

Finally, with all the seeds opened and their contents cleaned, he tried to stand up to put them away, but his legs felt numb and his back registered pain right up to the base of his skull. He looked over at the Golem android still lying in the barrow and knew that though he wanted to set to work on it, he couldn't right then. Swearing and wincing he pushed against the pain and paralysis, managed at last to heave up from the chair and stagger over to the bed to lie down. Sleep finally arrived after a long uncomfortable time, and it felt like dying.

The pain had diminished when he woke up again, and he did so damning himself for not turning off the light, though also recognised that it had felt reassuring to have it on. He eased up into a sitting position on the bed and gazed again at the Golem android, but deferred setting to work on it. Instead he commenced the lengthy procedure of removing his envirosuit and underclothes. Thankfully he had no catheters to pull out since he had cut them from the suit long ago, along with related recycling equipment. As soon as he undid the suit and began pulling it off, his own stink made him wince. Then he got angry and despite the aches and pains quickly shed the thing. Before putting it to one side he inspected it. The various patches he had made from seat material from the shuttle were still in place, stuck with excellent podules glue, as were the boot soles, made of slices of turtle-tree leaves. He turned the suit inside out ready for cleaning and put it aside.

His underclothes – absorbent white trunks that extended down to his knees and a long-sleeved tight fitting top – were stained with the exudations from the lesions on his body. Removing them was painful, and one wound on his hip started bleeding when he peeled the material away. He dumped them in a heap beside the suit.

Next stepping into his shower, he allowed a little water over his body before turning it off again. He did have a solar water heater on the roof, but it wouldn't be working now and the only warm water he had left would be a few gallons in a small insulated tank. With his body wet he washed himself with a sponge and liquid soap – both taken from a podule some 'days' before. He cleaned his nails until no sign of dirt showed, used scissors he had made from hull metal to crop his hair and beard as close to his skin as possible, brushed his teeth and then finally rinsed himself down.

When he stepped out he felt better – that being a relative thing. He dressed the lesions using leaves he had collected stuck in place with more podules glue. It probably wasn't best to help them heal, but it did prevent the stains in his clothing. He then dressed in jeans and ever-white shirt turned a shade of yellow from his store of clothing. He had no idea who the shirt belonged to. Probably it had been Mickonsel's – the last to die.

He pulled on slippers he had woven from plant fibre – stuck together with some podule glue too – then turned his attention to the inside of his body. Using some of his battery power, he heated water for the rare treat of coffee – again from a podule – but decided not to cook anything since he might need the power when he set to work on the android. Instead he ate a selection of nutritious pastes, nuts and some bright yellow cheese that tasted lemony. Now he was ready.

Ben moved a chair into the middle of the main room, tipped the android out of the wheelbarrow then lifted her into the chair. It seemed much easier to move her this time, probably because he felt a lot better. He put a strap around the chair seat and over the legs to hold her in place. Next pulling over his tool box from the shuttle and boxes of other tools he had made or taken from podules, he paused to give her a long inspection.

The plasmel wrapping she had been in had decayed and he knew that stuff did not decay over any stretch of time he had known. She must have been in the ground a long time. However, that wrapping had obviously protected her because her syntheskin and flesh showed no signs of breakdown. He set to work removing first the remains of overalls then charred sytheflesh and skin, cutting back with a chainglass knife to where it wasn't burned or otherwise cooked. His back soon beginning to ache he pulled over another chair and sat as he worked, and soon had the burned half of the face cleaned down to the composite skull, revealing white teeth and an eyeball with a blue iris. It was a start. As a shuttle technician he knew the best way to approach work like this was to clean all the crap out first so he could see what he was doing.

Setting to work on the lower torso, he found little that had not been cooked, so ended up stripping away all the syntheflesh and skin from below ersatz breasts to the composite hip bones and pubis. Pulling this away revealed a packed mass with burned optics, fused and melted electronic and mechanical components, and others he had no idea about. He inspected some fibrous white strands wondering if they were part of her system. No. He began pulling them out – long thread roots probably from podules. Certainly she had a venous system and quite probably nano-factories for making nanites to send out into that to reach throughout the body, but they weren't it. He started to realise that some of the stuff wasn't actually melted but had been made that shape – spread over and connecting other components like growths of metallic fungus. Perhaps he was wasting his time, but then, he had time to waste. He decided he would first just stick with what he knew – the gross electrics and optics – and see where that got him before fiddling with anything else.

Next, even though he did not relish the prospect of getting down on the floor, he did the same for the burned lower legs. Finally he had her sitting clean with all the damage exposed – a sad combination of human facsimile and the truth of exposed and broken machine. Now he knew the real work would begin.

He took a break, lying down on his bed and drifting into a doze, woken again by something dying noisily out in the night, heart thumping and breath short. He sat up bleary and unenthusiastic, knowing it would take him an hour or so to be properly functional again. Then stabbing pains in his chest further woke him and spread a hot tingling sweat down his body from the crown of his head. He sat there wondering if this was it, if his recent efforts had finally pushed something to breaking point, for he had no doubt that his heart no longer beat as it should. He then stood, because that's what you did: you kept going until you no longer could. The pain faded as he picked up his chair and took it over to where the almanac sat on charge, and noted in passing that this time there had been no pain in his left arm so it probably hadn't been due to his heart – more likely muscle strain from heaving about the android.

The almanac looked like a slab of black glass a foot square, but it had massive data storage and sub-AI processing. He sat down with it propped up on a wooden stand he had made for it, with its shielded s-con charging cable still plugged into one of the wall sockets of the house power supply. A touch turned it on, centre screen bringing up the last thing he had been looking at – which plants of Afthonia might provide heart medicines, as it happened – with sub-menus on the subject to either side. After swiping that away he brought up the main menu, and input a search on Golem androids. He hoped for at least a few pointers from the general database, though this device mostly contained stuff about Afthonia. But his luck was in because it contained a whole chapter on Golem, and even schematics. He settled himself to read and absorb as much as he could, but after just an hour or so, with what he had learned, he became enthusiastic about getting back to work.

Turning the almanac off again, he returned his chair to its original position, then went into his kitchen area and hauled out the table to put it beside the android. The noise he made must have alerted something because he heard a whoosh of breath as if from a large animal. He paused, listening, then eyed the carbine again. Perhaps his choice of night-time activity should be fixing that? He pondered that for a second then dismissed it. The android interested him and he was damned if he wanted to keep being scared. Anyway, during the daytime his other weapons were sufficient – his crossbow and machete – he only needed the carbine when things got hectic as darkness fell, and he had no intention of being out in the dark ever again.

He knew his reasoning was faulty, but dismissed it as he went to fetch his tool boxes.

On the table he laid out a wide selection of tools, but left one space. Next he retrieved the almanac, unplugged its charging lead and brought it on its stand to sit on the table. Inspecting the burned interior of the Golem he could see some things he could do now. So much of a Golem's system was about emulation, and so much of that could be removed to give him access to the really important stuff. She did not, for example, need the digestive system there, nor the nodular bioreactors that acted as a backup to extract energy from anything she ate – all that stuff was badly burned anyway. He selected tools and set to work.

Over the next few hours he removed a coil of ribbed tube with something dry inside it that might have been her last meal, along with skeins of tubes connecting to bioreactor nodules. He removed a cylinder that produced a form of bile, along with other items that fed into that – a distributed liver, kidneys and facsimiles of other organs that served the purposes of digestion and excretion. All the while he took extreme care not to break any of the optics or s-con wires and, each time he did break one turned frangible by fire, he connected it back up with string, or tape, or blobs of glue. This was not to maintain any function, but just so he knew what connected to what. He also took care with that metallic fungi and other stuff he did not recognise, trying his best not to displace it, and angry with himself every time some section of it came away.

By the time he had finished removing everything surplus to requirements the Golem looked partially gutted. Of what he recognised remaining inside were optics and wires, nodular junction boxes, shunts, transformers, temporary distributed power storage and small processing units. Some optics and wires connected to the spine and ran down into the pelvis and legs. Where they spread from other items in the torso they each had a yellow ring around them. Checking the almanac he identified these as leading to joint motors. Others marked in red ran into syntheflesh and skin and many had pulled out of what he had removed, either connected to small nodes or broken. They were for a sense of touch, emulation of muscle movement and all other changes visible to others, and they were not necessary to him. Most important were two things: an ovoid power-supply about two hands across attached to the inside of the spine and from which most of the s-con wires ran, and which also ran a thicker wire down to a socket above one hip bone, and an object only partially visible in the lower part of the chest.

Numerous black boxes were gathered around this upper object making millions of connections to its surface. As far as he could see nothing there had burned, but he needed a closer look. Fetching his torch, he leaned in close and turned it on, trying to get a glimpse of what lay inside. Light reflected from crystal and he could detect no cracks or discoloration. This was her mind: a crystal gridded through with nanowires and laminated with sapphire, hugely complex meta-materials intersecting. He wanted to inspect it more closely, but dared not. He just had to hope it was still functional and still contained the person this had been if he managed to power it up again.

Now he returned his attention to all that wiring and the other items in her torso. Something about it had been nagging at him for a while and now he saw what. The junction nodes looked familiar. He went over to the cupboard where he had stored podule finds and took out a large bottle-bamboo pot to peer inside. The thing was full of nodes he could use to replace the damaged ones inside her. From the same cupboard he took out skeins of optics that looked about the right length and had the requisite plugs at each end. A further search rewarded him with a reel of s-con – a little thicker than the stuff inside her, but maybe suitable. Everything labelled as s-con wasn't actually a superconductor but had levels of conductivity near to that.

Upon his return he stared into the interior again. He was tired and aching but at least wanted to make a start. He worried about pulling things apart and then not remembering where they went, then he had an idea that should have occurred to him right at the start. He turned to the almanac, flicked back to main menu and chose a function he had once used then grown tired of, and took a couple of pictures.

Now he was ready. He chose one damaged junction node and traced the wires and optic from it. With infinite care he unplugged those he could and then taped them in position. For those burned connections he had to cut he took more photographs and even resorted to the finger sketching function of the almanac. It took him a long time before he was satisfied he knew the location of everything and finally removed the node. A sort through his pot gave him one that looked exactly the same. Old and new both had bar codes and the almanac could read them, but the damaged one's code was half burned away. He reinserted those wires and optics that didn't look like they were about to break, then traced one fried optic snaking between components right up to the Golem's mind, measured a replacement against it, then pulled out the old and put in the new. He sat back, feeling at last he was getting somewhere, but now the somewhere he wanted to be was snoozing on his bed.

The long night continued and what at first had seemed an almost impossible task became a mundane chore. Ben replaced most of the damaged superconductor, all the junction nodes and most of the optics – as for the last he decided he would take a trip to the remains of the shuttle and see if he could find some there, in the daylight. As he worked he noticed other 'black box' devices that he had in his collection. He replaced just one of these sitting on the power supply – some kind of controller – all the rest he could see were undamaged. Just four of the distributed capacitor batteries were damaged. He replaced these with those he had been saving for house storage, using connector plugs found in his collection. He had no idea if they would be right, but this was the best he could do. Finally he reached a point where he had burned and broken optics and wires extending from junction nodes, or other devices, or the Golem mind, but no idea, should he replace them, where they might plug in. He did replace them, then taped all the loose ends together in bunches and tied them off to one side.

He got down on the floor and set to work on the legs, replacing all he could there, tied off some loose wires, and abruptly realised he had gone as far as he could with this task. It was now time to look at that power supply. He turned on his torch again and inspected the thing. It was blackened on one side but at a point where no wires plugged in. He could unplug everything and take it out? The prospect of getting to the thing and doing such intricate work appalled him and, rather than make a decision then, he decided it was time to see to his own needs.

He heaved up from the floor, gripping the edge of the table, but a dizzy spell washed over him and his legs, like rubber, sent him staggering. He grabbed for the chair to support him but knocked it over, and, arms flailing, fell heavily on his side.

'Fuck fuck and fuck!' He pushed himself up with his hands to hear a thumping tread approaching the house. The Stalker crashed into the wall beside one shutter, then whickered and hissed.

'And fuck you too!' he shouted.

The shutters began rattling and then it hit them hard enough to have dust and splinters dropping away. With the surge of adrenalin he managed to get up on one knee and peered across the room at his machete, propped against one wall, then got shakily to his feet. The adrenalin began to fade as quickly as it had come and he felt weak. The sensation was familiar. He had long ago grown tired of the fear and it seemed to arise only briefly now – he just did not have the energy for it. The shutters stopped shaking, but he knew the thing was still out there. Going over to pick up the machete, he took it with him into his kitchen area, and put it down on the counter while he fetched himself something to eat and drink. The whooshing breath ensued, sounding almost disappointed, and he heard the creature move away. He finished eating and subsequently felt numb and weary, and simply went for another sleep. Even as he got into bed he acknowledged he had not brought the machete, and could not be bothered to fetch it.

After waking Ben felt a bit more energised. As he returned to the Golem he soon realised he had been too tired before to note that access to the supply would be easier through her back. Fighting her joint motors he hinged her forwards until her head was resting on the table. From the back he photographed the supply and, as he did do, he spotted that three distribution plugs had been pulled out. This made him realise he need not detach individual wires but could take off the distribution plugs they entered. But why were those three plugs out? He shook his head. The shot must have somehow done it – pointless to wonder now.

Using a screwdriver he tried levering out one of those still in place. It came out with a crack and he thought he had broken it until inspecting the bayonet that entered the supply. A quadrate pattern of connectors covered its surface and they were dulled by corrosion. More work, but also some indication of how long this Golem had been in the ground. The connectors looked like copper but he knew them to be a corrosion-proof meta-material version of it. During his work on shuttles he had never seen the stuff less than gleaming. In fact most metals where treated this way and this made him look inside the Golem again at all the dull metal. She'd been in the ground a long time, a very long time.

Detaching each plug in turn, he cleaned them with a fine grinding paste and solvent, knowing he would somehow have to do the same for the sockets in the supply later. Once all were removed he turned his attention to the thing itself, and found that laughably primitive nuts and bolts fixed it to a bracket. He undid these and soon had the thing out, but cleaning those sockets turned into an hours' long chore during which he wished one of the podules had provided him with a magnifying glass. Finally he reached the point of being worried to do any more in case be broke something.

Time to test it.

A wire with a standard charging plug on the end from his house supply went into the socket that had previously been positioned above her hip. Here he really did know what he was doing because such supplies, though larger versions, were often used in shuttles. He turned on the power and, finding the requisite socket on its surface, plugged in a testing tablet he had often used to check his domestic needs. He got nothing to start with, then the screen blinked on and displayed a series of loading bars only one of which showed a sliver of energy. Flicking over to numeric he saw it charging, scratched his head, then switched over to the specifications of the supply. He nodded to himself. Even if he could not get the Golem running this power supply alone was a hell of a find. He quickly pulled out the charging lead – it had been sucking on his house supply, would have emptied it in an hour and only moved up one of those bars to halfway. Of course, Golem burned a lot of energy and he suspected this thing was highly advanced laminar storage...

He paused to inspect the surface of the thing again. There were some holes there and now he recollected removing a mass of melted composite from nearby. Pure water supply he had taken to be part of digestive emulation, in fact was part of that because the water would have been filtered from the gut. The damned thing had a fusion node inside! He abruptly went back to the Golem and inspected the interior, but could see no sign of other nodes. Perhaps they had been torn out, perhaps there were others in other parts of the body he had not looked at, maybe the skull? He shook his head. The disheartening reality was that all the components packed in there probably concealed further nodes, but also concealed further damage he had not repaired.

Ben again wondered if he was simply wasting his time. Really he should be searching through the almanac looking for medicines to keep him going or trying to figure out some way to re-programme his nanosuite, or perhaps send more messages from the shuttle radio in the hope that some passing ship might hear him. There were so many things he should do to increase his chances of rescue... so many things he had done here for decades... He fought it, but could feel the depression trying to settle on him. It arrived every time when he spent so long stuck in his house throughout the night. He pushed back to work, because he wasn't tired yet. He fixed the power supply back into place and began reconnecting the distributor plugs, satisfied with the way they went in after he had cleaned them. Then the Golem android moved.

He jumped out of his chair and stepped back, a moment later thinking he must have imagined it. But no, the head was up when before the forehead had been down on the table and, even as he watched, the shoulders twisted, as if she was trying to get a crick out of her back. Then it stopped, and ever so slowly the head dropped back down to the table again.

'Yes!' Ben punched the air, then wished he hadn't when that sent stabbing pains through his lower back. He stood there anxious to do something more, before realising he had come to a temporary impasse. He needed to get more optics from the downed shuttle and he needed to charge up that power supply. Both of these required daylight.

He walked over and checked the calendar and clock on the almanac and saw twenty hours yet remained until sunrise. Next, he cleaned the table and floor of debris from his work, cleaned and put away his tools, then spent some time sorting through his previously unknown podule finds to see if anything there was recognisable from the Golem, and to refresh them in his mind. Finally he went to bed, and to sleep.

Over the next two waking periods Ben spent much time reading and trying to memorise all the Golem stuff in the almanac. This resulted in him sitting for too long, so he took breaks to set about various domestic chores. He cleaned the inside of his envirosuit, cleaned himself again and his clothing then, between reading sessions, set about cleaning the interior of his house. The cleaning created a lot of noise and at one point, when he dropped something on the floor, he paused to listen for activity outside. Nothing, no movement. He recollected that this had always happened when the Stalker was about: it left many hours before sunrise. He supposed it must have a hide or a cave distant from his house.

Later he returned to tinkering with the Golem – replacing another damaged component he had recognised in his collection, and managing to put back one of those fungus-like pieces he had managed to knock free while working – when the almanac chimed, telling him he had an hour before sunrise.

He finished what he was doing and set about preparing for another venture outside, first collecting the tools he would need and putting them in his backpack. Checking on the laser carbine he saw that despite it being on charge throughout the night, it had retained nothing. He grimaced, fetched his crossbow, and then the machete he had made from shuttle hull metal. After donning his envirosuit, he turned off the light and waited. In a short while he could see light through the gaps in the shutters. Walking over to listen he could still hear the buzzing of innocular flies so just went and laid down on his bed. A seeming fraction of a second later he opened his eyes to bright light beaming in through those gaps.

Ben hurriedly gathered up his pack and weapons and headed for the door. Something niggled at him and he came to a halt, wondering what it was he hadn't done, and recalled previous fears about forgetting to close the shutters. Then he looked round at the Golem. Of course. The solar panels up on the roof would be charging up his power supply even now. Putting his stuff down he went to find a power lead, plugged it into the house supply and then into the Golem. After that he paused to consider the risk of fire, then dismissed it. There really wasn't much inside the android that could burn – her previous damage only possible because inflicted with a high-intensity laser – while the lead and the house power supply were s-con and simply would not heat up. He turned for the door.

Stepping out into a new morning was always an adventure. He got out quickly, machete ready as he turned to look up at the roof. No mantids in sight. He checked around the house and found the broken open and scoured out shell of the dirt turtle and guessed that had been the Stalker's midnight feast because no mantid could break a shell like that. He then found carapace remains of a large mantid and guessed it to be the one that had been on the roof, and that it too had fallen foul of his other night-time visitor. Inspecting the outside of the house he saw that though there were claw marks on the walls, they weren't deep enough to require repairs. As he took the wheelbarrow out, heading towards the mountains, he saw carapace, still wet with ichor and shreds of flesh scattered here and there, the bloody spine of a gnapper snake, its skull lying on a clump of grass nearby, the scattered rib bones of some sort of graser and a short distance further on the ears of a hare. All these confirmed what he had learned long ago: you don't go outside in the darkness. Readox had been his first lesson in that respect.

The track wound around between hills, the path well-worn from his previous journeys. After a little while the slopes got steeper and the hills taller. He passed a copse of turtle trees – wide ropey trunks supporting thick leaves the size and shape of turtle carapaces – from the branches of which sack bats burbled at him. And then, after a few hours, the crash site came into view.

The shuttle had been of a simple design – just a slab of a thing with a rounded nose ahead of the cockpit screen, a compartment behind for passengers and/or cargo, turret steering thrusters jutting from its body, two fusion nacelles protruding from the sides at the back and a grav engine within the body. Now the main body of the thing lay half dug into the ground sans nacelles and steering turrets. It had carved a trench as it crashed and left those and numerous other chunks of itself in a line of debris. Most of those he had been able to carry were piled behind the vehicle now, while the trench had overgrown with brambles and was now the home of a colony of rabbits. He could still see one of the nacelles he had been unable to move, a hundred yards back from the main body, jutting up a chunk of the hull it had torn away. Bright green vines cloaked it now.

As he drew closer he saw that the antenna he had fashioned for the radio lay tilted over and something had shit all over the solar panel he had left in place to power it. Closer still and he saw the screen he and Mickonsel had fashioned out of branches tied together with shuttle optics and wiring was still in place. He still had no idea where the chainglass cockpit screen had gone. It had popped out at some point during the crash and would have been unlikely to have broken, but though they had searched they had not found it. He walked up beside the vehicle, dumped the wheelbarrow and, picking up crossbow and machete, walked around the other side. The grave markers were still standing, though tangled in green vines too. He considered clearing them but knew they would be back by the next time he came here, and doing so would do no good for the occupants below. He squatted, looking at Redox's marker.

The crash had been hard. The catadapt woman Grace, the pilot, was dead. She had not put on her safety harness and her impact with the front console had told him she was dead before he later checked her pulse. Just he and Mickonsel had been relatively uninjured because they were the two who had put on their safety harnesses. Readox was a mess: broken arm, mashed face, and when they got him outside he noted that he could not feel his legs. It was late afternoon of a long day when they crashed and, while Mickonsel kept trying to call the *Falcon*, Ben went off and collected wood from a nearby copse. He made a little camp, brought out food and heat sheets bags for them to sleep in. They had only just begun the survey and hadn't seen anything that might be a problem so why not sleep under the stars while they waited for rescue? This was after all an old biotech world fashioned for human habitation, so it seemed unlikely that those who built the ecology had included nasty predators.

'I'm getting a ping,' Mickensel had said, 'but they're just not responding.'

Twilight brought the innocular flies as he and Mickonsel sat around the fire while Readox lay in a drug-soaked haze. They closed up their envirosuits and discussed what might have happened, and assumed some fault aboard the *Falcon* itself. But surely, once they solved their problem, they would be in contact? Surely, once the shuttle had not reported in they would move the ship over the locator beacon and see what had happened?

Then the mantids came.

It all happened so fast Ben felt he must have fallen asleep and straight into some virtuality nightmare. The things swarmed over their camp and they simply had no time to do anything other than fight a retreat using lumps of wood as clubs to the shuttle, and to the sound of Readox screaming. Once inside with the door closed they had the things coming through the front screen. Only the distraction of Grace's corpse gave Mickonsel time to get the carbine out of the weapons locker. He shot those in the shuttle and coming in through the front screen, then climbed out that way, Ben behind wielding the long drill bit of a ground auger. By the time remaining mantids retreated the area was littered with their smoking almond-shaped bodies, like leaves. Of Readox very little remained, and by the time that long night ended, nothing but a skull, which made the second grave when daylight returned.

They rigged up a tarpaulin to cover where the screen had gone missing, but always one had to be on guard while the other slept. They simply ate, drank and slept, and periodically tried the radio. They used the shuttle toilet till it malfunctioned and started pushing their waste back at them, then resorted to a large sample cylinder. When day finally arrived they were stinking, tired and frightened to go out. But in the end they did, first to bury Grace who had begun to stink more than them, then Readox's skull.

'We need to block that screen,' Mickonsel had said – their first implicit admission that help might not come.

They used a shearfield cutter to slice wood from the copse to block off the screen. Ben really missed that cutter – it had been a very useful tool. They sorted their food and agreed to ration it, checked through their supplies to see what was useful. And days and nights passed. Ben took Snooper out to check local plant life and found their first podule, Snooper also passed mantid meat as fit for human consumption and Mickonsel relished hunting the things down. But water began to run out. They began searching the locale, found a stagnant pond whose water they boiled, but it began to dry up. Ranging further and further from the shuttle they found the spring, from which they began hauling water, but it was a long and tiring trek every time. They discussed relocating there and Ben surveyed the area. He marked ground far enough away from the spring not to be too soft and wet. They cut wood and hauled stone in the days, argued about design, discussed construction techniques and always wondered what had happened with the ship above. When at the shuttle they kept trying the radio regularly. Nights were long and both frightening and boring.

Only in retrospect did Ben realise Mickonsel stopped talking at about the same time they ceased to be able to ping the *Falcon*. That was four solstan months after the crash. Probably he did not notice because he wasn't talking either, as depression sank over him. He remembered the day, two months later, quite distinctly. He had gone out with his barrow and Snooper and found a large podule and a great load of blue potatoes. Perhaps they could plant some of them? He would have to discuss it with Mickonsel. Ben now found his own dark mood had passed. First he smelled burned meat as he climbed inside the shuttle, then he saw Mickonsel sitting in Grace's seat. Even from the back he could see what the man had done, because from there he could see the charred hole in his skull. Ben walked up and studied him. Mickonsel had stuck the carbine under his chin and pulled the trigger. Ben was angry with him, shouted at him, even slapped him across the head. He then searched for a note, in the almanac, in one of their various recording devices, even written by hand, but found nothing. But really, what was there to say?

Ben dug the third grave, then went back to simply living. He built his house, saddened by defeats and collapses, celebrating successes. It took him over three years Earth time because he did not hurry and paid attention to every detail. Podule harvests made it easier to complete the power supply and the water supply, as did some of the other biotech plants here like bottle and tube bamboo. Finally the house was built and the water system ready to start when he removed the pump from the shuttle toilet and installed it there. Doing so would be a final step and, on realising that, he also understood he had been procrastinating. He spent the next two long days hauling things he would need from the shuttle, including the clothing and belongings the others had brought along. When it finally came time for him to sleep in the bed he had made in the house, he understood that by leaving the radio at the shuttle he was maintaining one connection with hope. And then, as once spoken of in ancient literature, he began the long habit of living.

Ben stood up from the grave, frowned down at it for a moment, then transferred his gaze to the sky. Still, after all these years, he had no idea what had happened up there. He had his theories. They had used probes to collect samples from the planet so perhaps something had escaped. Perhaps the *Falcon* had swarmed with mantids or some disease he had thankfully not encountered had spread. The ship had been old and in need of constant maintenance, so maybe some drastic failure had killed them all. Ben had actually written out a list of the possibilities, and there were many in an old spaceship. Perhaps the ship had been attacked by another. There were still hostile aliens out there, and pirates, though encounters with either were rare. But in the end one thing had him dismissing all of these, but also wondering if he was venturing into conspiracy theory.

The crew had been a mixed bag of soldiers of fortune and experts in many disciplines, but self-discipline wasn't one of them. They argued with Captain Constance and her subordinates and there had been talk of seizing control by some. He, and the other three that had been aboard the shuttle, had been vocal supporters of Constance and of the status quo. Readox had been quite harsh with those arguing for change. Grace had been one of the crew and ever at Constance's side. Mickonsel had been harsher than Readox and even beaten unconscious someone who had been campaigning for a change of leadership. While Ben had spoken out against those who wanted to put their leadership to a vote. Perhaps a mutiny had occurred up there. Perhaps it had been planned long before and when the four of them went out in the shuttle it had been sabotaged because, though the vehicle had been old, it had been meticulously maintained. He knew because he had done the maintaining.

Ben snorted, turned and headed back to the shuttle. It struck him as highly likely he would never know the truth. Pulling open the door he checked the radio and saw that it was still working, but the power low. The signal would also be rubbish, so he collected a lump of cloth, went outside again and climbed up to first clean the panel and then erect the aerial again. A return inside showed it up to power already, so he tried sending a call for help – words he and Mickonsel had repeated time and time again. The words sounded strange to him and his throat hurt just speaking them a few times, so unaccustomed to speaking had he become. Next he checked the beacon function of the radio and saw that it was still on – still broadcasting this location. Enough. He got his tools and set to work inside the shuttle stripping out optics and, as ever, found other items that might come in useful. By the time he had finished he'd filled the wheelbarrow – this happened whenever he came here.

During the trek back he saw two mantids watching him from their mound. Perhaps it was the memories of what had happened at the shuttle all those years ago that compelled him to dump the wheelbarrow and go hunting. He loaded the crossbow, hung the machete from a belt loop and walked towards them. At first they showed no reaction other than to watch him. Then they started to get agitated, shifting about and raising their forelimbs towards him in their 'you wanna fight?' pose. He raised the crossbow and fired, the projectile making a whirring sound as it shot through the air. It took the head off the mantid on the right but, as was usual, the creature kept moving about and waving its limbs for a while before keeling over. He kept an eye on the course of the projectile beyond it, seeing it thump into some low-growing glossy-leaved plant. The other mantid turned and inspected its fellow as Ben dropped his crossbow and broke into a stumbling run. It finally looked up in time to take the machete through its neck. He walked round it as, headless, it lunged at where he had been standing. Keeping his eye on that glossy plant he walked over, used the machete to chop through it and finally found the projectile.

By the time he returned to the mantids their bodies had both caught up with the news that they had no heads, and they were still. Grabbing their back legs he dragged them to the barrow, picking up the crossbow on the way. Some of the flesh would be a nice addition to his next meal and, since he had a whole day ahead of him, he decided he would dry the rest into biltong. It tasted good – a bit like prawns.

Finally getting back to his house he felt oddly reluctant to go inside to expected disappointment. He unloaded his barrow and returned it to its lean-to, dropped the mantids outside the front door, then walked round opening all the exterior shutters. Then he took the optics, his tools and a few other possibly useful items inside. She still sat as before with her head down on the table. He scanned over her carefully, hoping for some sign that she had moved, but could see nothing. As he leaned closer to inspect her back he detected a faint humming and could feel warmth against his face. He touched items there and found that the metallic fungi had warmed up. Next he heaved her back into a sitting position. He could now replace the remainder of the damaged optics but the prospect of such work, after spending the night in here doing the same, did not fill him with enthusiasm and, anyway, he had his chores to do.

First he dealt with the mantids while sitting on a chair outside, cutting off carapace and separating out the body meat and tasty organs to dump in a bowl which he took inside to his fridge. Next he brought his barrow back around and loaded up the debris, carted them from the house and tipped them in the hole he threw all his waste in. Tank work ensued. He had removed two tanks from the shuttle – one for fuel and one for potable water – and over two days dragged them here to install them, long ago, when such a task had not seemed impossible. One was up in the roof of the house and he would get to that later, the other was as low down as he could manage without burying it and then being unable to drain it. He got a bucket below the tap he had made and opened that. His sewage ran into the bucket and, since it had been some time since he'd emptied the tank, he took ten bucket-loads over to dump on the mantid remains, shovelling over some earth to kill the stink.

He next walked off to the right of his house then down, taking two fresh buckets – the product of squat growing bottle-bamboo – to the spring. Here he followed the course of meticulously joined tube-bamboo. Many years ago he had used another pump from the shuttle, connected to a solar panel over by the spring, and had piped the water to his house through this. When the pump gave up he resorted to this measure because he had no replacement. He still had the pump and had taken it apart, but had never got round to searching for replacements for its components. Perhaps that was a task he should now get onto, since hauling buckets had become a painful chore rather than invigorating exercise.

The plants around him grew taller and greener, then rocks displaced them and revealed a cleft at their centre. The spring bubbled out here scaling moss, growing in its flow, with deposited calcium. Below, a short waterfall fell onto a flat slab that hadn't been there originally – he'd put it there to make filling the buckets easier. Beyond this it turned into a stream, which wound between rocks and turf to disappear into the plain. He filled the buckets and trudged back with them, went round to the back of his house and climbed a stair he had made ten years ago when he decided he no longer liked climbing the ladder. This took him up to the shallow slope of the roof, tiled with turtle tree leaves which turned hard and glossy when they dried, and which might have been designed for the purpose, and these mostly covered with solar panels from the shuttle and the one he was building from podule finds. He climbed up steps in the roof between panels to the peak, put the buckets down on a platform nearby, then reached down and twisted off the stopper for the filler hole into his main water tank. It took forty buckets to fill the thing, with a long rest every ten buckets, and the return of pain throughout his body, now accompanied by strange sweats, nausea and black dot floaters in his eyes.

Back inside the house he checked on the Golem and saw no change, then went to his bed and slept, subsequently finding he had been out of it for six hours. He ate and drank, dozed some more after that, then went outside again.

In his garden he managed to grow blue potatoes and black parsnips and many other crops besides, but here they produced a meagre crop often infested by white threadlike worms. He supposed that when the ecology had been engineered here the crops had burgeoned without any need for pest control, but this was an old biotech world, long abandoned, and the life had run out of control with natural evolutionary pressures but mostly some plasticity to the modified genomes of what grew here. How else to account for the mantids and the night Stalker? They could not have evolved in the thousand or so years since Afthonia was occupied. Then again, maybe someone had done something here – some form of bio-terrorism. He had as much chance of finding out about that as he had of finding out what had happened in the *Falcon*, if it was still above.

He weeded and dug up blue potatoes, throwing away half of them because they had the black spots on them that told of insides eaten out by thread worms. He brought his haul to the house in two buckets, opened the door then held it open with his boot as he entered. The Golem looked up.

'Hello,' she said.

Ben dropped the buckets spilling potatoes across the floor and stared in shock. She was still sitting in her seat with the power cable plugged in. As the shock began to pass he took in the scene. He had left the optics on the floor at her feet and now she had some of them strewn across her thighs. His tool box was on the table beside her and, now he looked properly, most of the table was strewn with components. She appeared more gutted now than she had after he had pulled out what he had. Even as he watched she reached down and grabbed something, a fizzing click sounded and she removed a lump of that metallic fungus – a long piece like the hardened spill of molten metal from a crucible. She put it down on the table.

'Hope not mind,' she said, waving a hand towards the box of tools.

He tried to choke out something, but his voice felt rustier now than it had when he used the radio back at the shuttle. Also those were words he had used many times before, so rehearsed and easier to find. Right now he couldn't think what to say to her.

'You repairs made,' she said, 'Thank. Continue them.'

Finally his vocal apparatus jerked into motion.

'Good,' he managed, then groping round for more. 'I did what I could. Was out of my depth.'

'Did enough.' She smiled, but that only looked frightening with half her face gone. 'Shot put safety mode. Something else happen.' She looked around the cabin and he recognised the emulation. 'Internal clock. Long time.'

Obviously she had something wrong with her voice synthesiser or, more worryingly, the mind that drove it.

'How long?' he asked.

'Twelve year,' she replied.

He stared at her, puzzled until he realised she was talking about Afthonia's years and not solstan. He didn't need to spend time figuring that out because one of Afthonia's years was close to a century solstan.

'Long time,' he agreed, stooping down to pick up the potatoes.

They both worked in silence for a while. He retrieved all the potatoes and took them over to tip into one of his storage boxes. Again he was struggling to think of something to say. She spoke instead.

'What situation yours?' she asked.

He walked over, grabbed the other chair and moved it round to sit astride it in front of her. 'I have been marooned here for about twenty years, solstan. I'm a descendent of humans who decided to stay human as the Polity was breaking up. I and others came here in a ship on an expedition to survey Afthonia and catalogue its resources.' He swallowed dryly. That was the most words he had said in an age and it really did bother his throat. He abruptly got up, went and got himself a glass of water and returned.

She had taken more pieces out of her torso and as he watched she plugged in optics at such speed he could not quite see how she was doing it. She was cutting the things to length too but how she was dealing with the plug and socket he had no idea. The only explanation that fitted was that she would deploy nano-technology later.

'I have more components here you might find useful,' he said.

She glanced over to the barrow, shook her head, then pointed to his cupboard full of podule finds.

'I take what need?' she asked.

'Yes, help yourself.'

She dipped her head in acknowledgement but her hands did not slow or hesitate.

'How marooned?' she asked.

He told the story, interspersed with sips of water. She dipped her head on occasion to confirm she was listening. About the time he told her of the death of Mickonsel her hands abruptly grew still. She looked over to the cupboard, shifted her feet then slowly stood. He pulled his chair back, abruptly concerned, but she just reached down for the power lead, flicked it over the table and walked over to the cupboard and squatted before it.

'You know my name,' he said. 'What's yours?'

'Anna,' she replied.

'So what happened to you, Anna?'

She opened the cupboard and began taking things out.

'It is history now,' she replied, her diction abruptly improving. 'They had a civil war here using biotech weapons and hard tech. I was on one side. One of those on the other shot me and thereafter I have no memory.' She looked round at him. 'The shot should not have been enough. I should have woken.'

Some facts clicked into place in his mind. 'Whoever shot you disconnected your power supply.' He paused for a second then added, 'Someone also wrapped you up in plasmel and maybe you were buried, so that protected you some.'

'Maybe someone buried me when they found me shot,' she said, grimacing. 'There was a plague at that time – altered brain structures… I don't think anyone is left?'

He shook his head. 'No humans here.' Standing, he walked over as she opened containers and removed a selection of items. There were odd-shaped nodules, small cylinders that looked to be made of brass. While he watched she began inserting these inside her torso and he could hear the sound of them plugging into something.

'What are those?'

'For my nanotech – unprogrammed nanites, microfactories, specialised meta-materials.'

He shrugged. It was no wonder he had never been able to divine what they were.

Once finished with these she put various containers back, but retained a series of fist-sized eggs of various pale colours and some thin chrome-like rods, and cradling them, stood up again.

'And those?'

'They contain synthemuscle and skin substrate.'

'Oh right.'

Returning to her seat she began plugging in the items on the table, rapidly, her torso filling out again. This done she took up a pale green egg, took up one of the rods and pushed it into the end. How it went in he had no idea because he had closely inspected those eggs looking for some way to open them. Raising the egg and rod to her face she began moving across it depositing green fibrous material. It was precise – like a printer bot running – and while he watched the shapes of muscles appeared. He could think of nothing to say, just continued watching in fascination as she cloaked the bare metal-composite of her skull with muscle. It was changing colour too, darkening and turning red like bloody meat.

'So you have no way off Afthonia?' she said, and this time she did it without her mouth moving at all.

'The shuttle is a wreck,' he replied. 'I know I could repair the thrusters and maybe I could get one fusion drive working, and that's a big maybe. Grav engine is screwed too and of course I stand no chance of repairing that.'

'And now any of this is too difficult for you,' she said.

She finished with her skull and set to work on her torso. The absolute precision of it fascinated him. He had seen Golem before, but with their emulation they always moved like humans, not like the machines they actually were.

'Yes, it's difficult. Things seem to have become a struggle lately.'

'That's because you are dying,' she told him.

When he woke again, the conversation rushed back at him. It was surprising he managed to sleep after hearing that, yet he had been so very tired. He lay there running through it all again. Just as she had looked into his cupboards with senses way beyond human she had looked in him and found his problems. That his heart was failing hadn't been a huge surprise, but confirmation of the fact was unpleasant. The other news was even more unpleasant. Apparently his nanosuite must have been under a huge load while he was here fighting off the dregs of biological warfare of over a thousand years ago. It had also had to deal with strange compounds that were a result of that war too. She told him that the innocular flies had been a way of addressing biological weapons. When he told her of their effect on him she posited that in the intervening time the substances they produced had probably changed. To some extent they had responded to the changes in the wartime viruses and bacteria in the environment, but there would also be a lot of mutation. This accounted for them sometimes improving his condition and sometimes not. They were best avoided, however, since they did inject programming changes to nanosuites and that was dangerous territory to get into.

The upshot of all this was that his nanosuite had, within a few years of him being here, reached the stage where it ideally needed to be reprogrammed and upgraded. It was no longer repairing his body as it should and in some cases was attacking it like an auto-immune disease. So his heart was failing, but he also had tumours in his lungs that had metastised and now spread to his liver and bowel. His brain was clogging up with misfolded proteins and his arteries were hardening with the same crosslinking that spread throughout his body. It was hard to judge now what *would have* killed him first but she submitted that it would likely be his heart. It was, as she put it bluntly, ready to go pop.

Would have...

He told her he would sleep on it. It had all come as too much of a shock and just... too much. Now, as aching and nauseous again he swung his legs off the bed, he was ready, but as his vision cleared as much as it was wont to, he saw she was no longer in the house.

He slowly eased himself to his feet and walked over to the table. A number of items where there from his collection: things like brass marbles, some more of those chrome rods, an odd item like a knuckle duster and a stack of objects like coins made out of bone. She had also brought over the almanac, his circuit tester and, as far as he could see, had assembled a number of optical and s-con leads. He stared at all this, daring to hope and terrified of that. But of course it made sense. If the podules produced the kind of nanotechnology and components her body required, then why not stuff the human body needed as well? The population here, if any of the history he knew from way back in Polity times was right, would have consisted of a great deal more humans than Golem.

He headed for the door and opened it. Stepping out, he looked around for her, but she was nowhere in sight. Walking a circuit of his house he saw his barrow and tools were gone. Returning inside he saw his crossbow and machete were still where he had left them. He doubted she would have any problem with mantids or any other creatures she might encounter in the wilds. But why had she gone?

Next he eyed the sun, now halfway to zenith. So much had happened he had neglected to go for his usual morning food collection. All he had left was blue potatoes and too much mantid meat. It would have to be enough for now since its importance had dropped to irrelevance. He considered topping up the water tank and emptying the sewer tank. Neither of those jobs were really required, but they would keep him busy. But then he shelved the idea, remembering her comment about his heart going pop. Silly to kill himself when suddenly it seemed he had a chance of life. He made coffee from his dwindling supply and sat outside watching the plain for some sign of her, though he had no idea if that was where she had gone. Finally, with a bank of cloud rising on the horizon and wisps of it crossing the face of the sun, as he sipped his third cup of coffee, he saw her coming back.

Anna was pushing a wheelbarrow improbably loaded with podules. At one point she turned to look at something and he saw she had his pack on, stuffed full, while bulging carry bags hung round her waist. She drew closer and closer and he noted that she had taken some of his supply of clothing: Grace's envirosuit he had used for spares for his own until they ran out. As she drew closer still he saw that her face was now completely intact. He knew she hadn't enough of the skin substrate to do her whole body and understood why she had concentrated on her face. Golem were usually cautious of scaring the humans – that was what their emulation was all about. She did have enough of the muscle substrate so likely had covered her body with that. She probably did not look that great naked.

Finally she brought the wheelbarrow up to the house and put it down. He saw that two of the podules were the food variety while the other three where those filled with tech.

'You've been busy,' he commented.

She nodded, picking up two podules with ease, going in through the door and putting them in the house. When she returned she had also dumped the pack and carry bags.

'I went to have a look at the shuttle,' she said.

He stabbed a thumb over his shoulder. 'The shuttle is that way.'

'I went there first.'

He nodded, accepting that. He had to remember the reality of Golem and of emulation. She had probably run inhumanly fast to the shuttle first – probably there and back in less than an hour. The time she spent there to learn what she wanted to know had almost certainly been minimal with her ability to scan.

'So what do you think of what you found?'

'There are possibilities,' she replied, fetched the last of the podules and took them in the house. He stood up and followed her inside and she continued, 'It may be possible to repair the grav engine.'

He considered that. Such a task was utterly beyond him but then he wasn't a Golem. If it were possible then everything else followed. He could repair steering thrusters, one fusion drive nacelle and maybe the other with her help. But then what? The shuttle would only be capable of getting to orbit…

'I wonder if the *Falcon* is still up there?' he said.

'That is something we must investigate, just as repairing the shuttle is something to investigate further. But all of this is irrelevant to you if you are dead.' She stood by the table for a moment, then walked over and picked up one of the sacks. Out of this she took some dark roots he had once dug up and then been told by Snooper were inedible, and other plants he again recognised but had never utilised in any way. Taking these over to the kitchen area she cleaned them.

'What are these?' he asked.

'Medicine,' she replied. 'It will help you until we can make more radical changes. Do you have a large container for liquid?'

He went to the cupboard and searched out a smaller version of his bottle-bamboo buckets. By the time he brought it over she had pulled over the table and found one of his larger knives. Dumping the vegetation and roots on the table she began dicing, but so fast the knife was a blur and it sounded like an engine running. As she worked she discarded some items. Some were precisely the same as others she chopped almost to paste and he could not think why, but then realised she was measuring the quantities. The paste went into the bucket, which she then filled to halfway with water, and stirred with a knife.

'Let it stand for one hour, stir it again, then fill the cup you were using to the brim. Drink it all and then drink the same every eight hours.'

'What will it do?'

'It will ameliorate the pain and thin your blood. It also has anti-viral and anti-bacterial properties for the microbes of Afthonia. It will reduce the bacterial infections and help with the lesions. It will also improve your intestinal biome.'

'Right.'

She put the knife to one side then crossed from the kitchen area to plug the charging lead back into her body.

'I need to recharge and continue with self-repair now. I will be temporarily shut down.' She sat down in the chair by the table.

'Shut down?' he enquired.

She acknowledged that with a nod. 'My focus will be inward and most of my processing taken up with nanotech programming and repairs.'

'Okay.'

Her head dipped and she became completely still.

Ben stared at her as if expecting something further, then turned away to be about some chores. He first checked the time and set the almanac to sound a bell in one hour, then dismantled the food podules and filled his fridge. He had just finished that when the almanac rang its bell. Fetching his cup he filled it, then remembering her instructions, tipped it back and stirred the contents of the container. It looked like one of the vegetable soups he had made when boiled so often it had turned to slurry. Filling the cup again he braced himself then gulped down the whole cup before the expected awful taste hit him. It was bitter and dried his mouth out once it was down. His stomach seemed to just hang like a lead weight for a moment, as if in shock, and then it started grumbling and bubbling.

He gritted his teeth, thinking he might throw up, but then pushed himself into motion again. Opening the remaining bags and the back pack, he cleaned the stuff she had picked or dug up and filled the fridge to bursting. Some he recognised as food and some he did not. It occurred to him then that being a resident Golem on Afthonia she probably had the equivalent of the almanac in her crystal mind, and much else besides. Glancing at Snooper, he wondered if he would ever need the robot again.

Next he opened up the non-edible podules, began sorting and cleaning items to put them away. The first time he went over to the cupboards to squat down and put things inside, he noticed just how easy he found it – how little his knees and back hurt. Many items, liquids and pastes he left out – not sure if he should open up the 'seeds' containing substances he knew for maybe she had some use for them that required them to be sterile.

He started to feel good, really good, and began cleaning and tidying his house. Before he knew it everything was back where it should be and he had swept the floor. Outside he further weeded his garden and considered, then dismissed the idea of planting some more potatoes. When he stood up, dizziness assailed him and a wave of sick weariness overcame him. Fool. He returned inside, prepared and ate some mantis meat and raw vegetables. This multiplied the weariness and he hardly remembered getting to his bed.

'I have initiated fusion,' she said.

He stared up at her, utterly baffled, his eyes open but nothing going on behind them. He blinked, then remembered he had supposed she must have a fusion node in her capacitor battery. A *good job* thought arrived a moment later when he realised how dark it had become and how this would affect his solar panels. Panic arrived on top of that and he pushed himself up to swing his legs round to sit on the edge of the bed. He could hear a steady rumbling and hissing sound and could only think of hordes of mantids as dizziness and nausea arose driving a brief dry heave that set his eyes watering.

'The shutters,' he managed. 'The door…'

'I have closed them.'

He sat there baffled again until realising he had thought it night time – hence his panic.

'The rain, you know,' he said, not wanting to admit his confusion.

The monsoon came every day. Obviously she had closed the shutters to prevent water getting into the house. He sometimes did that, sometimes not. The torrent always came straight down and never really splashed through the windows and door. Often he took a chair and sat in the doorway to watch it – especially when the thunder and lightning commenced.

As his vision cleared to its usual crappy condition, he saw she held his cup. The thought of drinking what it obviously contained did not please him, but he took it anyway and gulped, only managing half a cup at first, then the second half while his body broke out into a hot sweat.

'We must begin now,' she said. 'Remove your clothing and come and sit at the table.'

'You should at least buy me lunch first.' He surprised himself by managing to find that much humour.

'I don't suppose you feel very hungry.'

'No, not really.'

As he pulled off his clothes he just felt tired and ill, but when he came to his underclothes he felt suddenly bashful. She was a Golem android but now, with the skin back in place on her face, she had the appearance of an attractive woman. It then occurred to him that despite the nausea and the weariness, perhaps some things in his body had changed, because his mind had ceased to wander into that territory more years ago than he could remember. He left on his pants and, painfully aware of his gaunt stringy frame, pale loose skin and leaf-covered lesions, walked over and plumped down in the chair.

Now he saw that the table looked paler than it had been. She must have scrubbed it down with something. Laid out on its surface were numerous items: the contents of podules, a selection of his tools – also cleaned until they gleamed – containers of various fluids and pastes.

'Looks like some ancient surgeon's table,' he observed.

'There will be no gross surgery, if that is what concerns you.'

He felt slightly reassured, but that went away when she picked up an object she had obviously fashioned. It was a bloody great big syringe with a needle as long as his hand. He tried not to think about why the needle had to be so long, instead wondering how she had made it. Probably she had paid a visit to the shuttle again and found some micro-fluidic pipe from one of its cooling systems.

'First I need to ascertain what has happened to your nanosuite and, since it shows regional changes throughout your body, I must sample from those regions.'

'Oh, okay.'

She put the syringe down on the edge of the table, took up a jar of some sticky green paste and began to gob lumps of it on various parts of his body. By the time she had put on the third lot the area underneath and around the first began to grow numb, so he didn't need to ask what she was doing. Knowing something of human anatomy it looked like she was aiming for lymph nodes, but then she strayed and he began to get the nasty idea that his liver, kidneys and other internal organs were targets. By the time she had finished he looked spattered from head to foot with the stuff. Next she began taking the paste off in precisely he order in which she had put it on. Just for a second it concerned him that she might forget where she had put some, or might have missed a place, then silently swore at himself for being a fool. An oily substance followed, rubbed into the skin of those areas, astringent smelling and probably some kind of disinfectant, though whether from a podule or from the plants she had gathered, he did not know. She retrieved the syringe.

The sampling injections didn't hurt, but they were not exactly pleasant. She worked her way round his body, each time injecting the sample she had taken into one of those brass marbles, then sluicing the syringe through with that oily substance. He didn't know how she got the needle into those marbles, just as with the eggs he had inspected them closely trying to find a way to open them or at least to ascertain their purpose. By the time she had finished she had twenty or so of them lined up on the table, and he was beginning to feel sore and aching from head to foot, he had also begun to shiver as the temperature dropped. Outside thunder rumbled, but he did not feel inclined to go look at the light show. He sat there just feeling awful, until the light came on making him jump in shock – he hadn't realised how dark it had become.

'You can put clothes back on now,' she told him, walking back from the light switch.

He eased himself out of the chair, staggered over to his bed, picked up his clothing and dumped it to one side when he decided to use the shower. Much freshened after that, he frowned at the lesions. They already looked better and he decided to leave them uncovered, dressed in old clothes and returned.

She sat at the table with the almanac and his testing tablet linked together with optics she had made. These also linked to that thing like a knuckleduster in the supposed finger holes of which sat some of those marbles. Scientific text ran on the almanac screen while code ran on the tester. He tracked the larger combined optic and s-con skein off the table and into a hole in her forearm. While he watched, she removed some of the marbles from the duster, put them to one side and inserted more. He went and made himself a coffee, thankful there had been more in one of the podules she had brought. He felt he shouldn't interrupt her, then realised he was anthropomorphising again – she could more than handle whatever she was doing and conduct a conversation.

'So what are you finding?'

'I am finding that your nanosuite is at war with itself and your immune system. I had hoped for some easy fixes, but it looks like I will have to take it down to base,' she said, adding, 'You will not feel good.'

She went through all the marbles – much quicker now and probably just confirming what she already knew. Once finished, she selected three other objects like large chrome almond seeds and plugged them into ceramic rings. He had done that once, but never figured out the purpose of doing so. With a ring about it, one of these objects fitted perfectly into one hole of the knuckle duster. The almanac screen blanked for a moment and began running incredibly complicated schematics at great speed. Only after watching them for a while did he recognise molecular schematics – nano-machines. He turned to her to ask her about these, but she was utterly still and her eyes had faded to a weird metallic grey. Now he knew, but was not sure why, he would receive no answers.

Now also seemed like a good opportunity to deal with something annoying him since his confusion when he woke up. He found his waterproof jacket, opened the door and went outside, walked round the house opening all the shutters, then returned inside. Checking the time he saw he was an hour past time for his medication so scooped some more out of the small bucket and drank it. Next he made another coffee, brought his chair to the door and watched the storm.

The monsoon continued to hammer the ground. Thunder rumbled constantly and lightning webbed the sky. He always found this enjoyable. Some atmospheric effect gave lightning streaks in primary colours – a bright red being the rarest. These storms had concerned him in the early years and he had put up a lightning conductor on the house, but in twenty years he had never seen it strike ground. It stayed up high and entertained him.

'First it needs to go back to base,' she said behind him.

His cup was empty and on the ground and he guessed he had been sitting for some hours. He lost track of time here and often was glad to do so. He looked round at her and saw eyes still dark and somehow menacing. She held the syringe.

'Where?' he asked.

'Your torso is best.'

In her other hand she held that pot of paste. He eyed it for a second then eased to standing, stiff, but not so much as usual. He pulled up his shirt. 'Just do it.'

The injection was fast and painful. As she retracted the syringe their surroundings lit up actinic bright and the crash of the lightning strike was a deafening bang. In that light her eyes returned to normal. He looked around seeing a fire burning on the plain, smoking and steaming as the rain rapidly put it out. He laughed, looked up at the sky.

'Who the fuck ordered the omens?' he wondered.

The monsoon passed and, as she had warned him, he began to feel a lot sicker than he had before. His nanosuite had begun to turn off. The nanites she had injected were finding the micro-factories scattered throughout his body, shutting them down and erasing their programming. They would no longer produce the nanites of his suite – that combination of what had once been considered 'hard tech' and biotech. Meanwhile, those machines still loose in his body would be breaking down as they reached a set point obsolescence. It would take, she told him, twenty hours.

After six hours the storm ended, abruptly – cloud breaking up like broken pottery. He walked outside to do some jobs, but started to feel so awful he felt in danger of collapsing. Returning inside he observed her for a while, her eyes metallic again as, plugged into the external computing, she worked on his new nanosuite program. He watched the code running on his tester and the rapidly changing molecular schematics on the almanac screen, drank another cup of medicine, then went to his bed.

He lay there with his body fizzing, a deep ache in his skull like a sore, and aches of a different kind throughout his body. He felt abruptly thirsty, but also busting to empty his bladder. Struggling to get upright again he nearly pissed himself and only just reached the toilet in time. His urine, he noted, had turned green. In his kitchen area he drank cup after cup of water and returned to the bed feeling bloated, expecting to lie there just a few minutes before needing the toilet again. However, he sank into a world of weird dream where he conducted conversations and did things that frustratingly made no sense, then slid from that into a frightening blackness.

Wakefulness came with a full bladder, not a surprise, but he felt completely paralysed. Finally toilet training beat his leaden body into motion and he staggered to the toilet, his body feeling like it had been burned from head to foot. His urine had gone from translucent green to cloudy green. When done, he staggered back, noticing fractured capillaries on his arms and strange rashes on the backs of his hands. When he touched his face it felt lumpy with spots. His teeth ached and there seemed rather more crap floating about in his vision than usual. He lay down, desperately hoping to sleep. It came for him like a mugger. On his second waking he saw Anna standing over him. Her expression showed nothing until he looked at her, then it showed compassion. All emulation.

'How are you feeling?' she asked.

'I thought Golem had superior minds,' he muttered.

'I was just trying to pay the usual courtesies,' she replied, her face returning to beautiful indifference. 'Microbial activity in your body has increased and your immune system, surprisingly, has managed to respond to the burden. In the long run it would do no good and you'd be dead within forty hours. You precisely feel that reality.'

He reached up to her. 'Help me up.'

She gripped his arm and pulled him up, but his legs felt like jelly and collapsed. In an instant she had his arm across her shoulders and her arm about his waist, easily supporting him. With his feet hardly touching the ground she walked him to the toilet – up the two steps onto the platform it sat on. Doubtless her omniscient gaze had seen his inflated bladder. He undid his trousers one handed, but couldn't piss with her supporting him. Previously urination had not been a problem while she was in the house and he had managed the other business when she was not. He tried to relax, tried to remember she was a machine, visualised her in pieces and with half a face. Eventually something worked. His urine was green still and it hurt to pee. Finally done, she took him back to the bed and sat him down on the edge of it. He remembered the early history of Golem had been precisely this: as carers of the old and infirm.

'I'm watching you internally,' she confirmed for him. 'If your heart fails I am ready.'

He glanced across at the table. Items were there, clean and gleaming, including most of his knives it seemed. He really didn't want to think about that. His arm hurt where it had been across her shoulders. He noted large blisters on the backs of his hands and when he rolled up his sleeve he saw that they had burst on his arm to leak bloody plasma. Turning he flopped down on his back, then wished he hadn't when his head ached like he'd hit it with a hammer.

'How much longer?' he asked.

'Another six hours, to be safe.'

'So time for more medicine…'

She brought him that and supported him like an invalid while he drank it, then did the same with the copious amounts of water he needed afterwards. Lying back again, slower this time, he just sweated, with some twist to his perception and odd open-ended thought trains running through his mind like in the earlier dreams. Feverish and dislocated, sleep evaded him. He was aware of her moving about in the house, then not there for a while. He felt a hand against his back lifting him again and she fed him soup. It tasted like chicken soup, though he had no recollection of anything tasting like that in all his time here. At first he gagged on it, but got it down, which ignited hunger and he kept drinking it until she brought no more. The world faded with the effort of digestion. Went out.

'I've injected the reprogramming nanites,' she told him.

He lay there unable to figure out if the words had woken him or if he had woken just before them. He now felt dried out, his skin tight – a dry atomy sprawled on the bed.

'How long ago?' he rasped.

'Four hours.'

He needed to go to the toilet again but doubted he had the energy. However, the humiliating thought of her helping him there brought him up into a sitting position and he swung his legs off the bed. The blisters on his hands, he saw, had deflated, leaving wrinkled skin.

Carefully standing up he expected dizziness, but his motions were hers: dry and exact as a machine. He used the toilet than headed to the kitchen where she was busily at work. Watching her, he drank cup after cup of water. She had cooked and otherwise prepared food and placed it in a turtle tree leaf. On the leaf sat a pile of steaming mantid meat, boiled vegetables, assorted greens, sliced cheese, and now she was making coffee. Even though he ate more on Afthonia than before, this seemed too much for him. Had she reinstalled her digestive emulation?

'Sit and eat,' she instructed.

He peered at her, visualising her in a frilly apron, but the image did not really fit. Only retrospectively did he note the turtle tree leaf was on the table, which she had cleared of the tools she might have needed to save his life and moved back into the kitchen area. A brief flash of joy arose at what this meant – he was now getting better – then it dissipated into puzzlement. Sitting, he picked up a carved spoon and set to work. The nausea he felt transformed on the first mouthful to ravenous hunger. He ate fast, too fast at one point because he bit his tongue. Fear of terrible indigestion – something he had suffered many times – arose and dissipated too. It just did not seem relevant at all.

In a very short time he had cleared the leaf. She put down more hunks of cheese, nuts, bowls of paste and a cup of coffee. He ate the cheese like eating an apple, scooped up the paste, crunched the nuts and washed it all down with the coffee. Finally his stomach seemed to be full. Gulping the last of the coffee he stood as intense weariness bludgeoned him and without a word he went back to bed.

Darkness had arrived by the next time he ate, and then went straight back to bed. And going through this routine two more times he wondered if she had already planned for this when she fetched the food podules. More mantid meat appeared on these occasions, but only when she provided gnapper snake and sackbat did he realise she must have been hunting while he slept.

'Be careful out there,' he told her when he saw her heading to the door for one of her outings. 'Take a weapon.'

She looked askance at him. She was Golem of course, unhumanly strong and fast, but strong enough and fast enough? The Stalker was big and had been fast, and she was an old Golem and perhaps more... brittle. His own decision to avoid even the twilight before dark was predicated on that and the fact his carbine was kaput. He wouldn't like to face that creature even with the weapon, let alone a machete.

'The mantids and other creatures are no problem,' she reassured him.

As a Golem, she was also observant and had perfect recall.

'You've seen the claw marks on the outside of the house?'

She paused for a moment, blinked and then nodded.

'There's something else out there.'

'Describe it to me.'

'I haven't really managed to get a close look at it. When I first saw it I thought it a man, but it was up on its hind legs. It came down on all fours and charged at me like a… like a big gorilla. I winged it with one shot but that did not put it off. It's been lurking around here for over a decade – feeds on the mantids.'

'You have no further detail?'

'Looked like it had carapace, but breathes… and sniffs like a mammal. That's all I can tell you.'

She stood there looking thoughtful, then wandered over and picked up the machete. On the one hand he was glad she had armed herself, but on the other, it concerned him that on his brief description she had taken his advice. Perhaps she had done so to reassure him. It hadn't really worked.

The skin peeled from his hands and arms in sheets, the stuff underneath newer and fresher looking than it had been for a long time. One of his teeth fell out – one that had been bothering him on and off for years. Probing his mouth he could feel the budding new tooth in the gap. He remembered that old style humans had not had this facility – their teeth only replacing once. For him this had not occurred since he had been on Afthonia, so he took it as a sign of his body again beginning to work as it should. A glance at the almanac screen, set to mirror, showed him a face he recognised from twenty years previously, while the sparse white hair on his skull sat like clouds over black stubble growing underneath.

'You've saved my life,' he told her.

'Yes,' she agreed with a nod, as he returned to cutting the bamboo he had stored in the house. Anna was meanwhile weaving, at highly improbable speed, the vines she had collected out in the darkness. He'd heard shrieks and clatterings out there, but she returned only with the vines, and some ichor spattered on her envirosuit.

'I need to find some way to repay you for that.'

He began joining the bamboo, delighted by the way his hands were working, the lack of that gritty feel to his finger joints and the stiffness, delighted by the lack of pain in his back, delighted by his strength and endurance.

'Nonsense,' she said. 'I have repaid you. If you hadn't found me and dug me up, how likely was it that I would have been found?'

He nodded agreement as he took the assembled screen over to the toilet and used wire to bind it to the side of the toilet platform. It was make-work really – something to keep them occupied throughout the night. His suggestion that they go to the shuttle in darkness had been met with a brief consideration then a negative. Yes, she could kill anything out there that chose to attack them just like him swatting away innocular flies, but it would all be too inconvenient. She added that the innocular flies themselves were still a danger too – they still might inject reprogramming nanites that could cause problems with his present suite.

He fixed up the first woven sheet, securing it with vine ties she had left protruding for just that purpose. It of course fitted exactly. He made the other screen and the door, and by the time he had those fitted she had made the rest of the woven sheets and returned to other jobs. She had already made preparations for their morning journey, assembling numerous connector leads, altering some of his tools and then disassembling his tester along with personal computer hardware from his dead friends, then reassembling these into new computer items. Now she took apart his carbine and, by the time he had fitted the woven sheets, had reassembled it and put it on charge, and next set to work on his old water pump. He eyed the weapon and, despite feeling so good, felt a shiver of cold.

'Did you see anything out there?' he asked.

She looked up. 'I saw tracks. It appears, as you said, the creature can travel on four legs or two.' He hadn't said that – he'd just said he'd seen it standing upright like a man. She continued, 'I followed the tracks and found where it had dug up a mantid nest. It had killed and eaten four of them.'

He nodded. 'I searched through the almanac but I could find no animal like it. They had no large predators here.' He shrugged. 'The mantids were there but smaller. Do you know different?'

'No, they did not have large predators. Tell me again of your encounters with this creature.'

He described his snap shot at the thing, his other glimpses of it when tardy about getting back to the house at night, the way it lurked out there and had tried to get in.

'I think you have been very lucky,' she said.

'For a debateable meaning of "lucky". But I'd like you to explain that.'

She grimaced and he wondered about the difference between emulation and real expression of a feeling. 'I don't know yet but, seeing how it uprooted that mantid nest, it strikes me that if you had not hit it with the carbine that first time it would have been in here.' She gestured around the interior.

'But you have no idea what it might be?'

'I have no idea,' she replied.

He watched her blank expression, and wondered if his own paranoia was giving him the idea that she knew something she wasn't telling him. He let it slide because whatever the Stalker was, he now had an ally should it pay another visit... and he had his carbine back.

After a pause which paranoia told him was due to her wanting the subject dropped, or might have been his own reaction, conversation started up again – him at last remembering how to conduct this social interaction and her complementing him. The war here had been a ridiculous disagreement between purists on how things should be run. One side said that 'pure' biotech only could be used and gross mechanical technologies were anathema. The other side disagreed, feeling that though they should use biotech their goal should be the permanence of hard tech. She had fallen into the second camp, mainly because the first had decided that all Golem should be shut down and dismantled. She told of old friends and enemies, of battles with microbes and tank-grown monsters and of the final plague released by the other side and to which they had mistakenly thought themselves immune. They called that the 'dumb plague' because it thoroughly altered the brain and skull structure of those infected, and reduced them to the level of animals.

'I don't know what happened to the others,' she said at one point.

'The other Golem,' he surmised.

'Yes. They would have survived the plague and there were hundreds of thousands of them. I would have expected at least some to have remained here.'

'My understanding of history is not the best. As the Polity broke up a lot of Golem went the way of other AIs – loading to virtual collective substrates in neutron stars, heading off into the universe, combining with human minds.' He shrugged. 'There are a lot of Golem amidst remaining human populations now. Maybe those that didn't upgrade and up sticks need to be around humans.'

She stared at him with a raised eyebrow, then her face broke into a grin that he felt to be truly genuine.

'It seems you are well enough to take the piss out of me now,' she commented.

'Only a little,' he admitted.

They continued in this vein and, not wanting to spoil it, he did not pursue something that had been niggling at him since she said it. She had mentioned *tank grown monsters*. He felt, at some point, he must return to that subject and discuss it with her, sure now that there was something she wasn't telling him.

Morning arrived after he cropped the white hair from his head, scrubbed down his body to be rid of improbably quantities of dead skin, and slept again. The dawn was like any of the hundreds he had already seen but now filled with exciting possibility, and just a hint of... something else.

'We will need to make two trips, minimum,' she said.

He nodded while stuffing his face with food and washing it down with plenty of water. He then put aside his plate, unfinished. His appetite had increased but it seemed he became satiated sooner. He returned the food to the fridge.

'Two trips?'

'We can get a lot of the work done on the first trip,' she said, 'but if we are successful and can repair the grav engine, it will of course need power.'

He pondered that for a moment, then said, 'The house battery. While we work out there it'll charge up here and we can take it out next time.'

'Precisely.'

He collected his back pack and filled it with some of the tools they had selected. He also filled a water container and hung it from his belt, as an afterthought filling a belt bag with some food. Anna went outside, a little early he thought, to open the shutters, and came back with the wheelbarrow. They loaded the rest of the tools in that, while Ben kept a careful watch for innocular flies. Finally, with the sun breaking over the horizon, they set out.

As usual in the morning the remains of creatures that had met their end in the night scattered the landscape. He wondered just how many of them Anna had sped to their end – scavengers then hollowing out the remains – and how many were the result of that other visitor. There did seem rather more of them than usual around the house. As they walked she moved ahead of him along the track and he found himself staring at her arse. Her human emulation being near perfect, he found a response stirring in a body that had long been numb to such. Shaking his head and telling himself not to be stupid, he tried to summon up visions of what lay underneath that clothing: skinless pseudo muscle. It didn't seem to help. He then considered raising the subject of *tank grown monsters*, but sunshine and his reborn health made him reluctant. It seemed a subject to be left back in the night with the shadows.

Finally they reached the shuttle. She looked over her shoulder as they stepped inside. 'I'll get to work on the grav engine now. If I need any help with that I'll call you.'

'I'll collect up some of the stuff outside and bring it there.' He pointed to the rear of the shuttle's crew compartment. 'Then set to work on that steering thruster.'

'Not too much stuff in here, mind,' she said. 'I'll need to take up most of the floor.'

'Okay.'

'And there's something else we could really do with.'

'That being?'

'The front screen.'

He grimaced, remembering his constant searching of the area, nodded and headed out. Even as he reached the door she had stooped down and begun undoing with her fingers numerous plunge bolts he would have needed a special tool for.

Outside, he peered at the pile of debris he had collected, then abruptly changed his mind about the order of business. Instead, he went over and shifted things aside to expose three steering-thruster turrets and cleared a space around them. He first inspected them closely looking for damage, then heaved them over to inspect the undersides. Most of the damage was where they had been torn away. Checking each closely, he selected the most intact one, then fetched tools and began disassembling broken components. Hoses supplying the chemical propellant had been snapped – power leads and control optics too – hydraulic rams fractured, the cog wheel that engaged in one of the cog rings still hopefully in the shuttle had been shattered, but one of the other turrets had an intact one. Once he had removed all the broken components he then began taking apart the other two turrets and replacing the broken with the unbroken. He even found some hoses not snapped, but which had pulled out their connectors. He knew as he connected them up to the turret his work had only just begun, because he would find equal damage in the shuttle itself.

So involved had he become in this work that only when he got up to go into the shuttle in search of a tool Anna must have been using did he realise hours had passed. She had stacked all the seats outside, having unbolted them from the floor. Inside, the floor plates were all up and leaning against inner hull, and she was down in the space below. The grav engine sat in the middle – a great lump of a thing webbed with cooling tubes, nested in optics and power supply and with numerous subsidiary mechanisms attached. It was heavily braced to stop it tearing free and attached by brackets and heavy wave guides to two effector bars running along either side parallel to the hull. She was sitting on one of these, optic cable running from her arm into the tangle of technology before her, other devices plugged in here and there. On one floor plate, laid out flat just along from her, she had heaped optics and burned devices. He took in the chaos, her metallic eyes, found the tool he needed, picked it up and departed.

Outside again, Ben had his lunch then returned to work on the thruster turret. Finally reaching a point where he had done all he could, he climbed up onto the top of the shuttle to find the socket they had chosen for the thruster. Up on top would give them the most use out of it along with the grav engine, since underneath the shuttle wasn't an option. The damage was bad, but with a rediscovered enthusiasm for his old job he began removing it. The cog ring was shattered, but he found a complete one in a side socket. He replaced everything else he could and finally sat back to contemplate his work. He had done all he was able to for now; the rest would need the turret in place – a task he could not perform alone. It was time now to check the fuel supply.

The thrusters were a simple design powered by hydrogen and oxygen. The system had a lot of safety cut offs to prevent leakage in case of damage. He had considered taking out the water cells that used minimal power and layered meta-materials to crack water into oxygen and hydrogen, to use in his house, but they were heavy and once emptied he would have needed to purify water to recharge them. He also had no real need of that power source either, what with the shuttle panels and the increasing amount of the same he had been accruing from podules. Checking, he found the fuels cells to be half full, while there was still pure water in the feed tank. He smiled at that as he climbed down from the shuttle, acknowledging that taking the cells from a system he could repair would have been one further sign that he was stuck here.

Nothing more to do now. He went in to check on Anna.

The grav engine looked even more in pieces now and he frowned at the mess. She had opened the thing up and he could see packed coils and plates and the shimmer of pseudo-matter. This was the kind of work where he simply stopped. As a shuttle tech you left a grav engine to the shipyard where computer and sometimes AIs, if any of the few remaining were available, got to work – those AIs of course including Golem like her.

'How's it going?' he asked.

'Slowly,' she replied. 'The damaged exterior components are no problem.' She waved a hand at those he had seen earlier removed. 'But internal field tech went out of balance and shut down.' She paused for a moment, then shrugged before getting back to work. 'It does, as you surmised, look like sabotage.'

'Virus in the control software?'

'Seems likely.'

He grunted at that. 'I'm about done with the thruster turret and will need you to help me get it into place. I'll go take another look for that screen.'

'Yes, you do that.' She looked up again. 'Check those copses again. The screen would not have popped while you were in flight but when you hit, so I doubt it went far.'

He nodded and headed out, collected up the carbine then studied his surroundings. He had walked the path of the crash site many times, in the first months checking the ground for disturbances on the theory that if he could not see the screen above ground perhaps it had penetrated below the surface. He'd dug into some disturbed areas and come up with nothing at all. Steadily widening the search, he'd checked the area on either side of the crash scar for a couple of miles in either direction. The thought of starting again depressed him. He shrugged and swore. He wouldn't check all of where he had looked before but beyond it because maybe the screen had been flung for miles, though he would, as Anna suggested, check the two copses of turtle-leaf trees again because there were plenty of places something could be lost in them.

He set out, walking at first, then annoyed with how long this would take, breaking into a jog. The joy of his functional body dismissed depression. With rabbits scattering in the low vegetation ahead he shortly reached the first copse. Walking round to one side of it he chose the trunk of one tree as his starter mark and walked through trying to keep to as straight a course as possible. Familiarity returned as he recognised a big old stump covered in bracket fungus and as hardened leaves shattered under his boots. Out the other side he moved twenty paces to his left and walked back in. All the while he looked for some glassy glint, some hint of the screen, but saw nothing.

How many hours he spent there he had no idea. The sun seemed to have hardly moved in the sky and he carried no com unit to show him the time. He did begin to feel tired and thirsty by the time the copse had become a map imprinted on his mind, so stopped to eat the last of his food and drink some more water. In the next copse he searched similarly, and felt the same disappointment he had felt many times before. The screen wasn't here – as he had hypothesised it had been flung a long distance. He must now search beyond where he had searched before and the thought of that began to depress him again.

Returning to the other copse he felt weariness in his bones. His nanosuite might now be working to repair the years of damage, but he still needed the old cures of food and sleep. Thinking on that, he felt hungry again and eyed the fungus. The brackets had been white when he first came here but were now an odd veined yellow. He knew they were edible because he'd checked them with Snooper, but were they still edible now? Reaching out to snap a piece off he saw his hand turn yellow too, and realised the coloration of the fungus had more to do with the quality of the light than its age. He held his hand in that light, studied its changes and the shadow underneath.

Realisation came in a wave of gratitude and extreme annoyance at his own stupidity. All his searching here and in the other copse had been at ground level – a ridiculous mistake to make for someone who had spent large parts of his life in zero gee – flatlander thinking. He leaned in close to the fungus and looked back towards the sun and there, caught in the top of a tree, was the chainglass screen from the shuttle. His annoyance dissipated as he considered how Anna had suggested here was the best place to search, and he wondered if she had found the screen already, but wanted him to have this little victory. It was the kind of thing Golem did.

'I am absolutely wiped out,' he said. 'I need food and sleep.'

'And obviously I am not.'

They stood outside the shuttle, both looking towards the screen he had dragged all the way from the copse. He turned to look at the shuttle. She had put the turret back into its socket on top but had left connecting the thing up to him.

'I'll go back to the house.' He felt reluctant to go and leave her working, but he had to accept that she ran on fusion and capacitor batteries and had no need of sleep.

'Take the wheelbarrow with you and, when you return, bring your house power supply.'

'You'll have the grav motor ready by then?'

'I don't know,' she replied, which he felt was an odd thing for a Golem to say. Usually they could have everything calculated out to the second.

'Anything else you'll need?' he asked.

She looked at him with an amused smile. 'Just go.' Turning away she headed back inside the shuttle.

He collected the wheelbarrow but didn't bother with any tools – unplugging the house supply he could do easily without them. Getting it into the wheelbarrow would be a bit of a chore, however because the thing was so heavy. He would have to separate the stack and carry it in pieces. Already thinking on that work he was soon out of sight of the shuttle.

When he finally reached the house he dumped the barrow outside and immediately went in to see to his needs. He ate a large amount, but still not as much as he had been used to eating before, drank a lot of water then made himself coffee. Sitting outside, he watched the interminable day and relaxed. Once he had finished his drink it was time to hit his bed. He undressed this time, because he could, because it was easy now, slid under the old heat sheets and fibrous blanket, and remembered no more.

After waking he cooked some mantid meat and vegetables, and made more coffee, mainly because he was feeling anxious about detaching the power supply. Finally ready, he went and opened the back cupboard and gazed in at the stack of capacitor batteries. The first three quarters of the stack consisted of single slabs a foot across and they were the ones he had taken from the shuttle. The remaining quarter consisted of plugged-together units taken from podules. Should he take that remaining quarter? He thought so because, not being resupplied by its own system, the shuttle would likely need a lot of power. These capacitor batteries also acted as convertor cells for the peroxide that had been stored in the tank that now contained his sewerage.

Reluctantly, he turned off the switch to his house power and pulled the two leads. Out to the barrow and back; in five trips he had the whole stack loaded. He looked around. Nothing else to do really, so shutting the door he set out.

When he arrived at the shuttle, Anna was up on the roof doing something with the steering thruster. As he drew closer she turned and jumped down, already knowing beforehand he was approaching. The drop was ten feet but she landed and straightened as if jumping down from a fraction of that height.

'I didn't know whether to come to you or wait.' She eyed the battery stack. 'We need to connect that up and run a brief test, then I'll probably need to make some adjustments.'

Inside the shuttle the grav motor was sealed up again, all its components back in place and all the wiring and optics as neat as if fresh out of a shipyard. They carried in the battery stack, opened a panel in the floor of the cockpit and installed it, including the podules cells. With the extra content the panel would not close, so Ben put it to one side. He then stooped, his hand hovering over the power switch.

'It's just occurred to me how many shorts there'll be in here,' he said.

She shook her head. 'I've isolated it to power the grav motor only. Later we'll have to check things out when we run power to the thruster turret.'

He clicked the switch over.

The shuttle lurched briefly, and he could feel the backwash of the grav engine.

'Okay.' She reached past him and shut off the power. 'I'll run some tests, secure everything and ensure the controls are working. You need to get that turret installed.'

He nodded, grinning, and set to work, first moving a floor plate into position where he needed it, then finding something to stand on. He took down ceiling panels for access to the underside of the turret, first secured the turret and engaging the cog wheel. Next he connected up the hydraulics. By now Anna was back down in the floor space finishing up some work there. Optics and power supply next, then finally the flexible fuel hose. It all went easily, surprisingly so. He had expected to have to find some leads or hoses elsewhere in the shuttle but got them all from the other turrets and their sockets. Finally he stepped down, his back and arms aching, but it was a muscular ache and satisfying.

He watched Anna; having finished below she was now putting the floor plates back. He assisted, briefly, to put two in place and bolt them down at the back, then went outside. Here he began transporting inside all those pieces he had collected over the years. By the time he started to run out of room on the two plates, Anna had finished securing the rest. She joined him outside, stepping over to stoop and pick up one of the thruster turrets as easily as if it was made of foamed plastic. He took chairs back inside for they had parts that might be useful – struggling with each yet them weighing a third that of the turrets. She then picked up the one fusion nacelle he had been able to drag here. He watched her carry it, her boots sinking into the ground. He had just about been able to lift one end of the thing.

'We're getting there,' he said, eying the diminished pile as she returned.

'We certainly are. Let's hope we don't have to take it all out again… here at least.' She grimaced then wandered off, heading back along the old trench the shuttle had carved.

He continued loading the rest, glancing at her occasionally. He saw her bowed over the ripped off fusion engine and its attached chunk of hull, then the thing heading back towards the shuttle, with only her lower legs protruding below it. He swore as he absorbed this salutary reminder of what she was, as if seeing her carrying the other nacelle had not been enough. With its strut and attached lump of hull, that thing had to weigh close to a ton.

As they worked he eyed the bank of cloud now rising over the horizon. Anna had picked up the screen and taken it to the front of the shuttle. A moment later he saw the wooden screen he and Mickonsel had made arc through the air and thump into the vegetation. Returning, she said, 'The shuttle is bent,' and retrieved a hammer. He continued ferrying in components and soon had nothing more to move, so went round to see what she was doing.

The shuttle screen was in place in its u-shaped seal along the top and down the sides while; with one hand against it, Anna hammered the bottom sill. Each blow was measured, exact as she worked her way along, bending the metal. Finally done, she dropped the hammer, put both hands against the bottom of the screen and shoved it up. He could see the chainglass actually flexing, then with a thump it went into the bottom seal.

'Now it's time,' she said.

The screen had gone in just in time to spot with droplets of rain. They went back around and climbed in the shuttle. Ben paused at the door to take in the surroundings. The passing thought that he should have gone round and said something at the graves came and went. The people in them were dead and decayed and humanity had long ago lost any belief in supernatural afterlives. And with the burial and the brief moments he had spent by the graves, he had long ago accepted their deaths. He pulled the door closed, fought the time-hardened seal until the latch clicked home, then went to join Anna in the cockpit.

She had put herself in the pilot's seat and he got a brief reminder of Grace sitting there. He went to the battery pack.

'Now?' he asked.

She nodded.

He clicked on the power and felt the brief drag of grav – not so intense now – then went and took the copilot's seat.

'Strap yourself in,' she instructed.

He grimaced, remembering why one had died and one had been so injured in the crash here, and pulled the safety harness across and engaged it, though with a struggle against corroded fixings.

'We don't know if that thruster turret will work yet,' he said.

She nodded. 'As we discussed – we don't have the power to expend on tests. If this doesn't work we'll need to bring all the solar panels out here.' She took hold of the joystick. Ben noted a few lights ignite in the panel – all amber warning lights – while two lower diagnostic screens shimmered, scrolling lists of warnings. She lifted the joystick.

The shuttle shuddered and under the floor behind the grav motor groaned. A clattering sound started up and he smelled a whiff of smoke. Then, with a jerk that shoved him down in his seat, the shuttle broke from the ground. The view ahead dropped away and the vehicle tilted to one side. It juddered again, doubtless tearing something from the earth, then tilted level and dropped as she lowered the joystick. It settled at about ten feet above the ground, lurching like a motor out of balance.

'Now,' she said, and eased the joystick forwards.

With a whumph the roof thruster ignited. The shuttle began drifting forwards, but also tilting nose-down to the ground. She picked up the almanac – plugged into the console with a skein of optics – and put it on her lap. Operating a virtual console on the screen, she righted the shuttle. It continued moving forwards, steadily accelerating. With a grating sound the thruster turret swivelled, the thruster still firing, turning them on the homeward course. Ben saw a path he had trudged into existence sliding underneath them faster and faster, winding them back towards his house. He forced himself to relax, unclamping his hands from the chair arms. He grinned.

Then after a moment he said, 'Damn.'

'Problem?' she asked.

It seemed so stupid, but, 'I forgot my wheelbarrow.'

Anna hauled the entire battery out of its compartment in the shuttle as Ben walked ahead and opened the door. As she came up behind him he ran for the house through the torrent, opened the house door and stepped inside shedding water. She didn't run, just walked fast and soon joined him. They re-installed the battery and, when he tried the light it came on bright for just a second, then went out. That accounted for the hard landing. He had thought mechanical problems by the thruster sounds, how long it took her to position the shuttle, then bringing it down hard on uneven ground rather than where intended. Lucky they had made it as far as they did.

'We will need much more power,' she said.

'To get up to the *Falcon*,' he agreed, then he studied her closely. She had helped him in every way as if his aims were hers. But were they really? It would be easy to think of her as an obedient servant of human kind, especially since she had been so accommodating, but he had to remember something else about Golem. It had been more than ten centuries since they had been obedient mechanisms. They were all unique and independent entities. They were not less than human beings and very often they were more. They experienced similar emotions, needs and wants to humans and, in some cases, could experience and feel things humans could not, without augmentation, feel.

'If that is what you want, of course,' he added.

She closed the battery cupboard and stood.

'What do you mean?'

'It has always been my aim to get out of here,' he said. 'I was marooned here and I dreamed of returning to civilization. You are helping me and I thank you for that – as you told me I would probably have been dead in another year or so without you. But what do you want? What are your aims?'

She looked at him with her head tilted to one side. Only now, as she did this, did he notice the scrub of blond hair on her scalp. Her own nanosuite had obviously been busy. She straightened up and abruptly walked over to the cupboard where he stored his podules finds. Looking inside she pulled out more of those eggs for synthetic skin, which had come out of the load of podules she had dug up, and along with some of the chrome rods, put them on the table.

'I don't know what I want,' she replied, beginning to strip off her envirosuit. 'I was part of something a very long time ago, but that is gone now. I am helping you until I decide what I want to do.'

'Well thank you,' he said, turning away feeling mildly embarrassed, not so much on seeing her disrobing but of his own visceral reaction to it.

'But a more pertinent question should be asked,' she said.

He turned back seeing her standing naked before him. Was it perverse that even with bare muscle around her waist and below her knees he still felt sexual attraction?

'What's that?'

'What do you want now?' She went over and sat in the chair.

She had a point. It had always been his aim to get off Afthonia and back to his life, but that life was gone. He had grown up on a high-tech world with parents and siblings, but by the time he was fifty had left them and that world to explore, seek adventure, find a direction. He had learned and uploaded many skills and much knowledge but still had no idea of where he was going. The job as a shuttle technician and surveyor of Afthonia had come up and he had taken it, but it had been a stop-gap while he considered what next. Now, he had no idea what had happened to the ship he had come here aboard, or the people. Perhaps they would find the *Falcon*, somehow get back to 'civilization'. Then what? Almost as if in response to that train of thought he abruptly stripped off his clothing and headed for the shower – he could think of nothing else to do.

By the time he was done he came out to find her still naked in a chair, bent over and working on her lower legs. Her torso was complete now and he studied the line of her back, also noting how her firm little breasts hung down, then shook himself and turned away to get dressed. Did Golem have sex? Too right they did. They were made to emulate human beings and had the same sensations in their skin and elsewhere and could, like with so much about them, even feel more. Her syntheskin and muscle had been installed with a fine network of nerves then connected up to her, but all the same, she could feel. He considered the new skin and muscle she had installed and was installing – her nanites had probably set about constructing new nerves in it, fining down and aligning muscle fibres, bringing her up to human standard and beyond. He dressed, told himself not to be a fool and walked over, pulled out the other chair and sat down.

'If I had thought it likely you would recover as you have,' he said. 'I would not have cut out so much to get to your internals.'

Without looking up she replied, 'It was necessary for you to get to that wiring. If you had not I would not have started up again.' She glanced up. 'Mostly it was finding those power plugs removed, though I still would not have started up without recharging.'

'I know... but I cut out your digestive system and fusion water supply.'

'Don't concern yourself. While I was working in the shuttle I found the materials I needed.'

He looked around, wondering what the hell she was talking about. She had them here? She could not possibly have installed anything at the shuttle because he would have seen – she would have had to have opened up her skin.

She looked up again, and obviously seeing his confusion said, 'I ate a variety of plastics and composites. My nano-machines are using them to rebuild my internals. I could also have directed them to rebuild my skin, but that would have taken time.'

He shrugged. 'We're not short of time.'

She gave him a look he could not interpret and returned to her work, folding up her right leg into a position no human could achieve to get to the sole of her foot. He looked at the foot and found his gaze wandering to between her legs, then abruptly stood up and got himself something to eat and drink. The food, drawing blood from the rest of his body, reminded him how long it had been since he slept and he went to his bed, and quickly fell asleep. Waking came with a raging hard-on. He recognised this for the good sign concerning his health that it was, but had to wait for it to subside before getting out of bed, since Anna was still in the house, working at something on the table. He got up and went to the toilet, washed and dressed then went over to see what she was doing.

'I've been thinking about power supply,' she said.

'And your conclusions?'

'We have a lot of work ahead of us getting the shuttle capable of leaving the atmosphere to hopefully find the *Falcon*. We will need to make some better tools. And I think we also need to still pure water.'

'Yes, for the thrusters?'

'No. We can run on just one thruster turret for our needs and grav planing. I can then alter the spare thruster fuel cells to make peroxide to run through the shuttle batteries to generate further power. That is also power we will need to run the new tools we will require.'

'I tried that and gave up – what you're talking about sounds like some meta-material method and we don't have what's required. I checked,' he said. He had considered making more peroxide to run through the shuttle batteries and even ventured into the chemistry. However, even though he'd managed to find a palladium sieve in the shuttle he could have used as catalyst and perhaps could have made some, he'd had severe doubts about the refining process and, finally, if he had got it wrong, he had stood a good chance of destroying the batteries.

She shook her head. 'But we do. We have programmable nanites that can make the required meta-materials. I can do this.'

'And that will give us enough power to run the shuttle into orbit?'

'And back down again if necessary.'

'It may well be necessary.' He still had his doubts.

She looked at him very directly. 'And then we get to the *Falcon*, if it is there, and a whole series of new challenges await us. And then...?'

She was harking back to the earlier question she had asked him. Then what? Maybe they could find the ship, if it was still up there, and get it running, depending on whatever had happened to keep it there. Maybe they could fly it out of here. After all that had happened since he found her he did not consider this impossible.

'I guess we'll get those challenges out of the way first, then we can decide,' he replied. But now he was beginning to think about options.

Anna immediately began working with the capacitor batteries while Ben stripped out the thruster water cells. He asked her if working with the batteries was a good idea now night was approaching, and had to accept she knew what she was doing when she said they would be back in place and charged by then.

Water cells and their support mechanisms left on her work surfaces – components laid out on a series of turtle-tree leaves – he unloaded the shuttle and in the same way he had dealt with the repairs on her, began stripping away the damage. Soon it became apparent to him what she meant about tools and the necessary power for them. The shuttle's hull was alloy, thankfully, and not composite, so much of the damage could be repaired in primitive ways. He could use heat to straighten out sections of hull and for that, well, he needed a furnace and a forge. After checking historical files in the almanac and consulting with Anna, he began collecting rocks and building what he needed. Then, in a concession to his needs, he took a long walk to collect his wheelbarrow.

At the shuttle crash site he collected items left scattered on the ground – thankfully none too large to go in the wheelbarrow – then took apart the make-shift screen salvaging all the optics and s-con he and Mickonsel had used to bind it together. The sun sat two hand-widths above the horizon as he walked back. Maybe thirty hours of daylight left. Anna had built something consisting of the batteries and water cells, and run a cable from this to plug into the house power supply through the wall. The stack looked factory made rather than put together out of unmatched components, and even when he inspected the power cable he could not see any joins. He left her to it and began to fetch more rocks.

With the sun a finger width above the horizon he felt incredibly weary but continued, knowing he would soon have time enough to sleep all he wanted. He finished his oven and began bringing barrow-loads of clay from near the spring to lather over its surface. The domed affair had its short chimney, required air holes he could block and another hole to which he intended to attach one of the shuttle ventilator fans, which of course would require power. Finally he left the clay to dry and turned to other matters.

They did not have suitable tech to make a deposition welder, but they could make an electric one. From a fusion drive nacelle he took a power convertor and with s-con fashioned leads. He was contemplating what to use for arc rods when he felt the first bite on the back of his hand.

'Innocular flies,' he told her.

'Go inside,' she instructed. 'I will turn on the power.'

He did so, closing the door behind him and then switching the light switch to on. The light was dead as he sat wearily at the table and waited. Finally he wondered why he was waiting, stripped off and got into bed. Sleep crashed on him like a falling wall.

It was night time, light coming on bright even as he woke, because she knew he had. As he surfaced, his body aching, he smelled cooking. Throughout the day he had not considered collecting more food, but it seemed that while he slept she had been decimating the local mantid population and finding further vegetation to eat. He headed for the shower, kind of envying her because at least she could do things out there in the dark.

'So our power supply is done?' he asked, coming to join her at the table.

'It is,' she replied. 'At this technological level you soon discover how necessary power is to make anything function. Like a welder.' She gestured to something she had been doing on the table. Lying on perfectly-fashioned racks made out of twigs were hundreds of rods, each with some coating drying on them. He studied what she had used on them and noted three of his jars of 'substances' from podules finds mixed up in a plate.

'Where did you get the rods?' he asked.

'From the seats. The alloy is right for the task – I just needed to straighten it out.'

He searched his mind, finally remembering a seat he had seen burned almost fifty years ago in a reclamation plant. The springs, he realised; yet surely they required heat to straighten them? He glanced at the welder sitting on the floor to one side. All he could think was she must have attached the pieces of spring between the leads and straightened them while they were glowing – further illustrating their need for a better power supply. He also felt almost appalled by the amount of work she had done while he had been sleeping.

'How long have I been asleep?'

'Eleven hours.'

'Fuck.'

'The changes your nanosuite is making require it and,' she conceded, 'you did work for a long time after the last time you slept.'

'Still, you shame me – I feel like I am not doing enough.'

She stood up and began clearing the table, placing the racks of rods over to one side of the room and putting away the other items. Apparently his comment had not been worth a response. He grimaced, again trying to keep it firm in his mind what she was, though all he saw was an attractive woman and an equal.

'Now you need food,' she said, giving him an almost matronly look.

Just then, out in the darkness, the Stalker whickered, and then huffed out a breath.

They both froze.

'And there it is,' he said.

She returned his gaze, then was abruptly in motion. She shot across the room, the floor boards splintering under her tread, grabbed up the machete and skidded to a halt by the door. He was glad of that because he thought she was going to go through the wood. Head tilted, listening, she opened the door as quietly as she could, and then leapt out into the night. Ben stared at the open door, dread coming and sitting on his chest. That door had never been open before when that thing was out there, but it was more than that. He could not lose her. Abruptly out of his seat, he went over and grabbed up the carbine and his torch, then stepped out after her. He considered closing the door behind as an innocular fly dropped onto his face, because he did not want them inside the house. But maybe he would have to flee back inside and close it quickly.

Moving out into the dark he turned on the torch, the beam probing out, picking up his kiln, the pile of shuttle parts and the shuttle itself. He listened, but could hear nothing. Moving further out, he considered calling, but rejected that as a silly idea. He swung the beam round, hearing a crunch to his right. Two eyes gleamed at him and his heart lurched before he saw Anna walking back from the direction of the spring.

'Fast,' she said. 'Very fast.'

'Did you get it?'

She peered off into the night. 'No, I did not. It was too fast for me.'

That just didn't seem to make sense because Golem could move very fast indeed – he had just seen a demonstration of that in the house.

'At least it ran away from you,' he conceded.

Looking back at him she said, 'Yes, and that is odd too – for a predator.' She stepped over and brushed a hand across his face, knocking away an innocular fly he had not known was there until it took off. 'Let's get inside.'

As they stepped inside and she closed the door, he decided it was time. 'You said you know of nothing like that thing out there, but when we were talking you mentioned tank grown monsters used in the war here...'

She went into the kitchen area again – all domesticity. 'It's been over a thousand solstan years. Those creatures were grown in tank because that was the only way they could be bred. Their biology was not very stable and any that survived the war would be long dead by now.'

He nodded. It sounded perfectly plausible, but again he felt there was something else she wasn't telling him.

'It's a mystery we may someday resolve.' She shrugged. 'For now we can be happy that it did run away from me. It perhaps sensed that I am very unsuitable prey. Quite likely it won't be back here.'

'Yes, let's hope so,' he said.

She brought a stew of meat and vegetables to the table and ladled it out filling two bowls, and sat with one in front of her. It seemed her nanites must have been busy enough to rebuild those parts he had removed while activating her. As he dipped in and began eating, it also occurred to him that being a tireless machine, with a large and powerful mind, boredom might be an issue. He had joked about Golem needing humans but now wondered if it wasn't so much of a joke after all.

After they ate she went outside for a long time. He heard occasional squeals and clatterings from her encounters with the night denizens, but none of that horrible whickering sound. She returned, bringing in sections of damaged shuttle hull he had managed to remove. He wanted to talk more about the stalker, but wondered if her apparent reticence was simply because the Stalker to her had no more importance than the mantids. Instead he put on his envirosuit with the visor down, and, the first time he tried the welder, spent some time blinking to recover his vision. The reactive visor did not operate as quickly as once before. Anna took over – her eyes not requiring the protection. Later she returned with sections of s-con and began putting them together using his glue to make unseen joins in the sheathing and creating a long cable. Feeling surplus to requirements he turned to the almanac and began researching things to do: how to seal the open thruster turret holes, the air supply, the possibility of putting another turret online since she had not used everything in her power supply, and anything else he could find.

She went outside again, this time carrying the welder, returning a moment later for the carbine.

Neal Asher

'Best thing we have for melting or heating some things,' she commented, and he knew it was reassurance.

When she went out again, the light of the welder flared through the cracks in the shutters. He stood there listening for a while but heard nothing untoward, then turned away when the light changed to red as she used the carbine for some task. Likely the arc flashes were enough to keep creatures that liked darkness well away. He had returned to his research when she came back for more rods – their coatings now dry.

'It doesn't need to be completely air tight,' he said.

'You are human, you need to breath,' she replied.

He gestured to the envirosuit he had discarded. 'It will be easier to repair that and connect it up to the shuttle air supply.' Before she could reply he continued, 'Yes, I know it's old and may leak, but in any case we won't need full air pressure in the shuttle itself.'

She nodded contemplatively, then said, 'Agreed. I doubt we can completely seal the shuttle anyway – we simply do not have the materials that can withstand vacuum.'

Thereafter she brought him items to repair each time she returned for rods – all of which she could have taken outside earlier. He could not help but think she had already considered all aspects of shuttle air supply, but not said anything. She was holding back on becoming dictatorial – allowing him to think of them himself. He turned his attention to his envirosuit, taking old worn parts for it he had stored in one of his numerous cupboards, and began making what repairs he could – sealing old holes with glued on patches made of seat material she brought for him.

They worked for hours and when Ben finally began to feel tired he checked the time and saw he had been awake for twenty hours. He ate again and retired to his bed, dropping immediately into dreamless slumber. When he next woke it was to find her sitting on his bed with a cup of coffee for him. Trying to hide that rather erect sign of good health he pulled himself upright and took it from her.

'I could get used to this,' he quipped.

She had stripped out of her envirosuit and wore one of his shirts. He supposed she must have cleaned herself and the suit. She might be a machine but she wasn't immune to dirt. Her hair was longer now and beginning to lose its spiky appearance.

'I'm not your personal servant,' she replied.

'No offence intended.'

'I'm glad to hear that.' She put a hand down on his hip, alarmingly close to his erection. 'I am a sentient creature with all the feelings a human has and more. But how do you perceive me? Am I just a machine do you?'

'No, not just a machine.' He gulped coffee, thoroughly aware that she was looking at him in a particular way. Her hand felt warm through the sheet, and that was having an effect on him.

Her expression became amused. 'Quite. In fact, now my supposed emulation is up to standard, I am finding I have needs I would like to fulfil. And I suspect, with the nanosuite doing its work, you are finding needs have awakened that were once dormant?'

No doubt about her intentions now and he didn't feel quite so embarrassed about his 'condition'. Looking at him very directly, she put her hand underneath the heat sheet on his bare thigh. He drank more coffee then put the cup down on the bedside table. As he moved back she slid her hand up and closed it around his cock.

'Yes, I see you are no longer dormant.'

'You could say that,' he managed, voice tight.

As she began moving her hand up and down, she reached in with the other and, with unhuman dexterity, undid her shirt buttons. She pushed the heat sheet aside, her hand still working, then shifted to sit astride his legs. Releasing his cock she took off the shirt and discarded that, then gripped it again. Giving him a warning look she said, 'Now don't you come too quickly. This is not all about you.'

'You have my –' he managed, choking off the promise as she leaned forwards and slid her mouth over his glans.

It felt utterly wonderful – that mouth was as wet and warm as that of any human woman and she seemed utterly expert with her tongue. He just enjoyed it, any thoughts about her being a machine, despite the amount of weight he felt on his legs, sliding out of his mind.

'My turn now,' she said, sliding back off his legs and opening her own wide.

He pulled himself towards her, kissed and chewed her nipples and worked down her stomach to her vagina. Everything was as wet and slippery as it should be and when she groaned it did not seem like emulation at all. He worked on her for some time, losing himself until she pushed him back then got astride him again. As she took him deep inside he fought not to come, and that became the complete focus of his mind as she began to gyrate on him. Finally he did, feeling he was completely emptying himself. He thought he had done well, until he realised his coffee was still warm.

He showered and found that not only was he no longer dormant, but his recovery time had itself recovered. She was sitting at the table by then, dressed in her envirosuit and preparing more food – dipping pieces of meat in some mixture of dry herbs and putting them to one side. He walked up behind kissed her on the neck and reached round to squeeze her breasts.

'The perfect housewife,' he said.

'I notice a tendency in you towards dangerous pursuits,' she replied.

'I think my sense of humour is returning, which may be a bad thing.'

'It's not been notably good thus far.' She pulled his hands from her breasts. 'And let's not get too ambitious – you haven't recovered your youth just yet.'

'Might my heart go pop?' He stepped round and sat in the other chair.

'It is still not quite as it should be. I thought sex worth the risk because of its therapeutic value.'

'That's thoughtful of you.'

She gave him an arch look. 'It's therapeutic value to both of us, though I don't think it's a good idea to work you too hard just yet.'

She cooked the food and it was delicious – better than anything he had cooked here, though that might have been because of the entrée. They worked again, her outside with the welder and him repairing those items small enough to be brought inside. She disappeared for a while and upon her return explained, 'I collected wood for the oven – we'll fire it up when we have daylight.' They made love, two more times before he needed to sleep again. It was, he thought, as the sky outside lightened and the innocular flies returned to their aestivation, the best night he had ever had on Afthonia. He ignored the paranoia that arose, about her maybe finding the perfect thing to distract him from the Stalker, and it faded.

Morning revealed the shuttle partially dismantled with pieces of the hull and superstructure stacked to one side. All of those, he saw, would need forging – they needed heating and bashing with his largest hammer. She had welded up most of the breaks, fixed back in place two further steering turrets, but only to seal those holes in the hull. One other turret lay to one side with all the parts required to put it back together. A large pile of dead logs sat beside his oven. He wondered if she had karate-chopped them into pieces.

He pointed at the pile of hull and other stuff from the shuttle. 'We'll need to slice the top off the oven to get heat to some of those. I hope it will be enough.'

'If not, we'll build another kiln,' she replied.

He nodded. He felt no urgency about getting the shuttle running at all. His life had taken a new turn into an unexpected and enjoyable area. Would it last? He was old enough to know that they had entered the initial stages of a romance and that later things might change.

They set to work.

Ben reassembled the second thruster turret while Anna worked inside the shuttle. He checked on her occasionally, mainly because he liked looking at her. She stripped down a lot of internal systems, was rerouting things, making repairs, honing down all the damage from the crash and filling in the holes in that system he had made over the years by taking things out of it. Some hours later she disappeared, hefting an axe he had made from hull metal, then returned with three large tree trunks. More firewood? No, because they were from living trees. She jammed them under the edge of the shuttle, set up logs from the wood pile as fulcrums and then turned to give him a meaningful look. Demonstrating her strength, inch by inch she raised the shuttle to expose the bottom on one side, while he jammed in logs to wedge it up, then finally she brought in further shorter tree trunks as props.

Underneath the damage was more severe. After waving him away she set to work removing the mangled landing skids, then cleaned and welded and patched. He meanwhile got a fire going in the oven, collected a ventilation fan she had put to one side from her work within the shuttle, then, using the power cable reaching to the house, set it to blasting air into the oven. He put his first component in – one of the hull struts – heated it to red heat, then bashed it straight using a log as an anvil. He next worked on a triangular section of hull, heating then beating flat tears so they could be welded.

The day progressed. Anna lowered the shuttle again, then lifted it from the other side. As they worked they talked, but not very much, since there seemed no need. They exchanged anecdotes and stories. He learned of her long past on a biotech world and how her actual expertise *was* biotech and she had been involved in developing the podules that had come in so useful to them. He told her of his family, long left behind, his travels through the ruins of the fallen Polity. They fell into a kind of rhythm, like people who had lived and worked together for a long time. He told himself this was all due to her accommodating him with a sensitivity that went beyond human senses, but at one point, when he mentioned a past dalliance, she was obviously not pleased and for a short time things turned frosty. He then remembered a Golem in a shipyard he had worked in, whose character grated and who had some friends and some firm enemies. No, her reaction showed something else entirely, and despite it being briefly unpleasant, he felt reassured.

'It's a shame about Afthonia,' she said at one point.

'What do you mean?'

'You have the podules and the other things that grow here. The weather is never any worse than the brief daytime rainfall and seasonal variation is small – on many other worlds the winters or the summers would have killed you quite soon.'

'But I was fortunate that the mantids and other creatures did not,' he pointed out. He then added, 'And the innocular flies.'

She shrugged. 'The like of mantids and other dangerous creatures can be found on most worlds. With the right equipment I could design and build methods of control, quite possibly using podule technology and some of this brute technology.' She waved a hand at their work.

'So where is the shame?' he asked, though he had an intimation of what she meant.

'That there is no population here. Afthonia could easily be returned to the paradise it once was, though,' and she smiled at him, 'without any foolish choices having to be made about the purity of biotech.'

'Yes, it certainly could.'

He looked back towards his house and imagined it being how he had once dreamed it could be: a couple of floors, balconies, constant power and water supply and so much besides. The dream had been a way to occupy his mind during the long nights and he had once made plans which even now still resided in the almanac. But that was before the constant sicknesses left him little more time than he needed to ensure survival. He then looked out onto the plain and imagined a city there, but then turned and positioned it up in the mountains. He put ships in the sky, bringing goods from a massive reach of star systems.

'Do you know what Afthonia means?' she abruptly asked.

'It's not something I've even thought about.'

She nodded. 'It's a word from an ancient Earth language. It means "plenty".'

'What business did they do here?' he asked.

'The products of podules which, cultivated grew to three times the size you see out there.' She pointed to the plain. 'The nanites were always in demand. Biotech of many different kinds. Here your compass is limited but many strange and useful things were grown and bred. We of course don't know what survived.'

'Give me some examples,' he said.

'Cactuses from which we tapped a variety of alcoholic drinks were popular. Meta-material membranes in many plants.' She pointed to the house. 'Your house stays warm throughout the night because of the turtle-tree leaves you used on the roof. They have nigh perfect insulating layers in them.' She gestured beyond into the mountains. 'You found edible funguses up there but also many you could not eat. You probably could not because they are the kind that gather and consolidate rare metals. While there are other plants that grow quantum processing gems in their seed pods.'

'I see,' and he did. 'This is not a place to leave behind.'

It took four days and four nights. Boiling and stilling extra water for the power supply had been one of the easiest tasks. In the latter part of the fifth day he walked out and gazed at the shuttle. It looked battered and some of the patches were ugly, but they had done the best they could.

'We can wait until we have a full day ahead of us,' he told Anna. He felt a decided lack of enthusiasm about the prospect and knew he was looking for further reasons for delay. He had enjoyed the last five days more than any other time he had spent on Afthonia and found himself drawing out certain tasks – being more pernickety than needed.

She gazed at him – her look unreadable – then shook her head. 'We have to at least try out what we have done.'

'I suppose…'

She dipped her head and strode past him. 'I'll get the power supply installed.'

'Okay, and I'll see to the panels,' he turned to look up at the roof.

They set about their tasks with grim resolution. As he climbed up onto the roof, Ben felt this was more about completing something rather than any wish for it to be completed and to move onto the next thing. He had also begun thinking about the danger. They had flown the shuttle once and then only ten or twenty feet off the ground, and now they aimed to take it into orbit. The thought of sitting inside it with its inefficiently maintained air pressure while wearing his leaky envirosuit made him sweat just a little. He would be risking his life, but not in any sense to save it, as he would have supposed before, but just to reach for a change he was not so sure he wanted.

He detached and took down the panels, leaning them against the house, aware that this was a job he could not have done alone a few weeks back. By the time he started carting them to the shuttle, Anna had moved the power supply inside, and was attaching it up. He began taking the panels up onto the roof and securing them. She came out of the shuttle at one point to watch him.

'I've been thinking,' she said.

'Careful – that's always dangerous,' he replied, glancing down at her.

She grimaced. 'I've been thinking that taking the shuttle straight up into orbit is a rather ambitious start. We should run some tests. Make a flight at low elevation then go higher when we're confident our repairs have worked.'

'That seems sensible.' He tried not to let the relief show in his voice, and returned to work with more enthusiasm.

But she wasn't done. 'We can take tools with us. You've denuded this area of mature podules and there may be other things to find.' She gestured to the shuttle. 'This is a lot more useful than your wheelbarrow.'

'I agree.' He nodded enthusiastically. 'With the things you've told me about – the other biotech that grows here – we could find many useful things.'

'And when we return to the house,' she added, 'we'll land nearer… so the cable reaches…'

'You are being very sensible today.' He grinned at her.

'Someone has to be.' She returned inside to continue her work.

With all the solar panels in place and connected as they were before, twenty years ago, he clambered down and went to collect tools. Bringing them inside, he observed the power supply bolted to the floor just behind the cockpit. All the cables and pipes were connected up and secured, and Anna was pouring in the pure water they had stilled throughout the last night. It reached the fill level and she put the container aside before carefully capping the tank.

She turned to him. 'Bring heat sheets too, and cooking items. We'll make this an outing. And anything else you can think of.'

He returned inside to collect those items and she followed him a few minutes later. It took a number of trips to ferry across what they felt they needed, and now, rather than this whole episode being a serious risky venture, it had turned into a potentially enjoyable adventure. Finally they were inside the shuttle and nothing remained but to secure their safety straps into newly oiled sockets and head out.

Anna no longer had the almanac plugged into the console, though they had brought it with many other tools – one of their contentions being that they needed all this stuff if the shuttle went wrong. She reached forwards and clicked down a manual switch and the console came on. Next working a touch screen she brought the grav engine online and this time there was no backwash at all. Ben listened, but all he could hear was the low hum of things working correctly. Taking hold of the joystick she lifted it and the shuttle rose smoothly from the ground until she brought it to a halt fifty feet above the house. Here she tried the steering, first feathering grav to make the vehicle slide through the air to one side then to the other.

'You got grav planing working,' he observed.

'Just a matter of programming.'

She similarly slid the shuttle forwards and then backwards. This was good, because it meant they could still get wherever they wanted to go even if the thrusters packed up, which was more likely with them having moving parts. She then used the thrusters to set the vehicle in a slow spin.

'So which direction?' she asked.

He pointed out towards the plain. 'That way. If we come down that should make things easier. Up in the mountains it gets a bit rugged.'

She used the thrusters to set them in motion, then switched over to grav planing. The low hiss of them passing through the air grew louder and louder. Ben was unsurprised – the repairs had not been helpful with aerodynamics. Underneath them the path he had made over frequent treks unravelled, frayed, and then disappeared. The plain unrolled ahead and recognising the vegetation down there he felt a surge of acquisitiveness seeing the intermingled dark green of food podules foliage and the red of the other kind. But to land now seemed far too soon.

They sped on and over to the right something rose out of the level landscape. It looked at first like a rocky mount, but as Anna swung the shuttle towards it he noticed a degree of regularity.

'Ruins,' she said a minute later.

He had seen the like before during surveys. They had landed at one mass and found little of interest but the empty coral and foamstone walls of homes and other buildings. He had wanted to explore more, but their remit had been to get a general overview and such ruins were scattered all over the planet.

'Do you see?' Anna pointed at the ground.

Here the podules foliage was dense, which was heartening, but then he saw what she meant. That foliage formed vague but even patterns. It seemed likely he was looking at where the things were originally grown.

'Shall we take a look?'

'Yes, why not? We can load up too and see how this operates with more weight inside.' Why he chose those particular words he wasn't sure, because it was not as if they needed to know how it would handle with extra weight – not for going into orbit.

She took the vehicle lower, and now Ben could see the straight lines of old irrigation or drainage ditches. She took them in closer to the ruins then slowly brought them down, finally landing just twenty feet from a standing coral wall and the maze of buildings beyond that. The shuttle crunched down into vegetation, grav steadily winding down, and she knocked off the power.

Ben unstrapped and headed in back, collecting up the carbine and then, because it was a long standing habit, his backpack and collection bags. Anna took the belt of bags from him and slung them over one shoulder, then took up the machete. He knew without talking that first they would explore the ruins, and he had no doubt they were the kind of place where night denizens would aestivate during the day. He opened the door to luxuriant dark red podule vegetation, stepped into it with his feet crunching down in a thick layer of old stalks. Looking at the thickness of the new stems he surmised that the ground below must be packed with podules butting up against each other – all older and more mature than anything he had dug up for many years.

'There's probably an artesian well here it might be possible to activate,' she said. 'But this far from the mountains means limited biotech growing in the area.'

'Limited vistas too,' Ben observed, and didn't feel inclined to question her observation.

Wading through the vegetation they came to the wall which he saw, drawing close, still stood because it was still alive. Occasional sparkles across the even pink and grey surface indicated air-feeding polyps feeding. Moving along it to a doorway, to the left of which a dead wall had collapsed, they went through. On the inside the slow advance of the wall showed by its fallen sheets of nacre – broken up and weathering into flakes. It had moved by about a foot in a thousand years.

'Must have got messy in their houses like this,' he commented.

'It was a way of keeping the inside walls fresh,' Anna replied. 'About once every three solstan years they peeled evenly to leave a clean nacre surface or, depending on certain additives they gave to the coral, inner walls of any colour or texture they chose.'

'And the houses would continuously be changing size and shape,' he noted.

'Only as much as they wanted,' she explained. 'This wall has been moving but a little tweak of the biology and it would stay exactly where it is.'

'I see.' Ben pushed his toe through the debris, then nearer to the inside of the wall lifted up a sheet of nacre three feet across. Surely he could find a use for something like this, perhaps even have it somewhere in his house simply for its beauty? He then eyed the wall itself. Since the stuff was still alive it would be a simple thing to chop some away and layer it on the exterior of his house. A spray of nutrients that he had no doubt Anna knew about, would set it into vigorous primary growth. All speculative stuff based on his previous needs and irrelevant should they get off Afthonia. He shrugged and rested the sheet against the wall by the doorway, certain they would come back this way. No reason not to take that with them.

They moved on through the ruins – through rooms choked with low growing weeds a bit like bubble grass but not as slippery, bright green vines overgrowing walls and piles of debris. Shoving away some of that with his boot, and the thick layer of plant debris underneath, revealed translucent slabs, then a pile of roof tiles that looked like huge fish scales. Amidst these were other remains of ceilings and roofs: broken ceramic pipes, lengths of petrified wood and triangular chunks of insulating foamstone. When he was building his house this place would have been a bonanza.

They continued. He found a water tank made of composite lying on one side of the room. Grabbing a protruding pipe he lifted up one end easily, then rapidly backed off when something scuttled about inside. Another room brought them to a still standing door. He ran his hand over the gnarled wooden surface.

'Tea oak,' Anna explained. 'It's very durable and was probably injected with special preservatives.'

'It's beautiful,' he said, thinking of his own wooden door and how long it had taken him to cut and join the wood even though then the atomic shear had still been working.

'Everything here was,' she replied. 'With so many of the necessities of life produced by biotech they had time to make everything as pleasing as possible.' She stepped forwards, grabbed a handle green with corrosion and tried to twist it. The thing shattered in her hand. As if angry, she gave the door a hard shove, further metal components breaking and the thing falling into the space beyond.

'But it became apparent,' she added, 'that having time on their hands was not such a good thing.' She stepped through.

'I note you refer to those who lived here as "them" as if you weren't one of them.'

Stepping out after her he saw they had now reached some sort of street. She halted and turned to gaze at him.

'I stopped feeling like I was one of them when they started arguing and then fighting about the most foolish things. I fought with one side because if the other side won that meant I would be shut down.'

'You would be killed, you mean,' he said.

'Yes.'

She was definitely angry – he could see it now. They walked along the street and when something crunched under his foot he stepped back and looked down. He recognised a human skull but the bone had been much decayed and was as frangible as egg shell. Seeing the brownish white powder much of it had decayed into he began noting that elsewhere. No large masses of it as if from whole skeletons, however. Picking up one whole but fragile rib bone he saw the scores of mantid mandibles on its surface.

'It's a sad place,' Anna commented.

Without even discussing the matter they turned round and headed back to the shuttle.

'Okay,' he said, as they waded back through the vegetation. 'Podules.'

She nodded curt agreement and they fetched tools. It soon became apparent that, as he had thought, the ground was packed with the things. Some were thin and rooted between others almost three feet across. Sweating in the sun, they freed up one of these and managed to lever and heave it out of the ground. Anna then picked the thing up and carried it into the shuttle. Ten huge podules later they moved across to dark green vegetation and uprooted five of the food bearing ones. As, again without discussing it because they both knew, they prepared for departure, he gazed at the wealth of podules. They had made just a small hole here and the things stretched for acres and acres.

'Where now?' she asked.

'Back towards the mountains maybe?'

'Other things to be found I should think. We'll keep away from the rugged terrain and look at an area away from the house.'

'Seems a plan.'

The flight parallel to the mountains revealed further ruins and then an old road for ground vehicles. Now it had been pointed out for him Ben could see the shape of old fields, drainage ditches and at one point what looked like the remains of a pumping station. He considered investigating the glint of solar panels and what other equipment might be useful there. It had been sitting there like that for a thousand years, but then, Anna had been sitting in the ground for as long. But what would be the point in investigating that place?

Their mood was sombre after the ruins and they flew for some time in silence. Below the landscape changed, becoming more arid and the drainage ditches fading out of existence. Vegetation turned to brown and beige and became steadily patchy. He could see tree-like growths but without leaves. Anna slowed the shuttle and pointed. 'There.'

'What is it?' he asked.

A lumpy blotch of something had come into view, swirled with colours. As she took the shuttle lower the patch began to resolve into fat barrel cacti, some seemingly stacked one upon another, all decorated with tubular flowers. Many sprouted pink, others in red, yellow, white and even blue.

'A picnic,' Anna said, bringing the shuttle down to land beside the patch.

'Are these the ones you mentioned?'

'They are indeed.'

They unstrapped and got out of the shuttle. Anna hoisted out a food bearing podule and put it on the sandy ground. Again without discussion – just knowing what they both wanted – they set up a small camp. They laid out the fibrous blanket from his bed, and plates, cups and eating utensils. He was about to set to work on the podule when she brought one of his bottle bamboo containers and a length of tube.

'Let's see what we've got.' She gestured towards the cacti. 'Bring the knife.'

He followed her over. 'Do we need Snooper?'

'Unlikely,' she replied. 'I can test whatever we find, but I doubt these plants will have changed much.' She paused for a second. 'Though admittedly I better check for isopropyl alcohol, or methanol – your nanosuite can handle them but better not to drink them in the first place.'

He remembered that at one time, when humanity was less rugged, those kinds of alcohol could, in excess, cause blindness.

Anna pointed. 'The ones with the pink flowers produce straight ethanol without flavourings. They usually got sold to companies that made their own drinks and when sold had built in obsolescence unlike those kept here. The flowers with other colours are more interesting.' She headed over to a single barrel cactus protruding red flowers and stooped down by it. 'The knife.' She held up a hand and he gave it to her.

He studied the cactus. Its skin was pale jade with sharp needle spines sticking out of ridges up its length. The flowers had bloomed out of the rounded dome of its top. Over to one side stood a cactus with yellow flowers and this had two sections. The lower one, with its domed top compressed by the section above, really did look like an ancient wooden barrel. He wondered if the shape had been deliberate. He turned back to Anna.

'You're tapping the barrel,' he said, remembering the ancient phrase from a virtuality he had once tried – one that had involved a 'tavern' and a great deal of 'quaffing'.

'I certainly am.'

Using the chainglass blade, she had cut a hole and even as fluid began to run out inserted the tube. It of course fitted perfectly. She ran the tube into the container for a short while, then, pinching the tube closed, picked up the container and took a sip before lowering it and letting the flow continue.

'All the ethyls – propanoate, isobutyrate, acetate,' she said. 'Oak lactone, the alcohols…B-damascenone.' She nodded. 'Heavy on the caramel flavouring but almost pefect.'

The liquid in the pot was as black as coffee and he caught a whiff of it as she pinched off the tube again, pulled it out and quickly inserted the plug of cactus she had cut out. It smelled familiar but precisely what it was escaped him.

'We'll give it a try shall we?'

He smiled and nodded. In the early years here he had tried making his own wine from things like large raspberries that grew in the mountains, and it had been good. He had enjoyed that brew for a number of years, but later it had started to give him a hangover and he did not have access to Aldetox. Progressively the hangovers had got worse and the next time the berries were available he had not bothered again.

They headed back over to the blanket and sat down. He took the knife and opened up the podule and just left it open – they could just grab what they wanted from this ready serving dish. Anna poured the drink into two cubs and handed him one. He took a careful sip and swallowed. The stuff was smooth and strong.

'Brandy?' he wondered.

She gave him a disappointed look. 'The genetics of the cactus contains some of that of cane sugar, some of vanilla and cocoa, and some of an oak tree.'

'That's my clue is it?'

'That's it.'

He sipped again, could feel it heating up his guts and remembered this pleasure in the days when inebriation was a nanosuite choice and hangovers could be dismissed with a nanosuite instruction or a pill.

'A bar on the sea front on Cansonia,' he said. 'They claimed the ancient cast iron anchor on the wall was an actual ancient Earth artefact. It might have been because they had a security drone watching the place, though a replica could have been centuries old and very valuable.' He lowered his cup. 'Rum. Dark navy rum.'

'You have scored ten points – you only have another fifty before you reach the prize!'

'I will endeavour to score.' He winked at her.

She winked back and sipped her drink. 'I last drank this precisely twelve hundred and sixty three solstan years ago.'

'That's not very precise,' Ben replied, cutting himself some cheese and meat.

'… and three months two days, four hours and thirty two minutes, presuming my internal clock is correct.'

She cut meat and cheese too, then opened a couple of 'paste' seeds to use as a dip. Ben began to feel the intoxication quite quickly, and he couldn't have been happier. He ate nuts too and seeing his cup was empty poured another shot. The container was nearly empty now too.

'I'm feeling quite a buzz,' Anna told him.

'As much as you want to feel?' he enquired, then wished he hadn't because it seemed somehow rude.

'I've set my emulation to match your likely capacity.' She seemed unconcerned. 'I'm using the alcohol as fuel at the moment, and storing it.' She picked up the container and drained the last of the rum, then swilled it out with water. 'Let's try another one.'

The next cactus she tapped – one with blue flowers – produced a clear liquid, glistening and nacreous like oil on water. He identified it at once as cips – or cool-ice psychedelic. It was usually served in two parts with the psychedelic component in the ice cubes. This cactus produced the whole drink, its chemistry subtly altered so upon freezing the ice cube component froze out before the rest.

'Twenty points!' she told him, but apparently he did not need to gain them all before receiving his prize, because a short while afterwards she pushed him down on the blanket and rode him like she needed to get somewhere fast, and did. He drank water afterwards, dried out and sucked dry, then fell asleep in the sunshine.

'How are you feeling?' she asked him when he woke.

He sat up carefully but, besides a raging thirst and a slight numbness telling him the booze had yet to completely dissipate from his system, he felt fine. He stood up and looked around, his gaze coming to rest on six bottle-bamboo containers now sporting caps made out of carved wood they had not had before.

'So what do we have here?' he asked.

She pointed to each in turn. 'Cips, rum, gin, ouzo, Clian bandy and a passable bourbon. They were always the most popular here hence the survival of these cacti, but they exported many others of which we might find surviving specimens.' She gestured at the sky. 'It would be nice to find some of the carbonated alcohol and non-alcoholic drink versions in this heat, but I suspect it is the alcohol content that has enabled the survival of these.'

'You're kidding. A beer cactus?'

'Many hundreds of varieties. They even had them growing company logos on their skins. Some versions even incorporated refrigeration.'

'You are kidding.'

'Am I?'

He drank more water and they made coffee using a stove plate he had brought from the house, and packed away their camp. He felt very good now, for this stop had been a perfect antidote to the ruins. Soon they were in the sky, desert rolling underneath them and further patches of what he dubbed 'booze cacti' becoming visible. Anna then turned the shuttle in towards the mountains.

'Let's take it higher,' she said.

'If you think that's okay...'

'I haven't had a single fault develop, but higher will push the grav engine and we might see something.'

'Okay.'

The shuttle began to rise and vistas opened out around them. They rose up through a layer of thin cloud into bright air, looking down and ahead at the mountains, some of which poked up through that layer.

'Oh,' said Anna, turning the shuttle and sliding on along a new course.

Ahead, leading up towards the mountains, he could see a line cut through the surface of the desert. As they followed this in, the greenery returned on low hills and the line became disrupted churned ground, heavily overgrown, slabs of rock and other items exposed. This had carved through the hills and terminated at what looked like some large old ruin on the side of a mountain. Perhaps the result of an earthquake, though he had not felt one here, or some devastation left by the war that had been fought here? As for the latter he had no idea. From what Anna had told him it had been a mostly biological thing without any of the kind of earth-shattering weapons like the Polity had once deployed.

'We won't need to go into orbit, I think,' she said.

He stared at her for a long moment, then turned to look back at what lay ahead. Of course, that line of torn ground was just a smaller version of the trench the shuttle had cut when it crashed.

'Did you know?' he asked, because it seemed more than coincidence that they had turned at that point.

'I didn't know, but I saw it long before you, which was why I came in this way.'

A hint of paranoia rose and then died. He believed her. The ruins at the terminus of the trench, now they were coming clearer, still bore the recognisable shape of a ship: the *Falcon*.

Anna landed the shuttle on a stretch of flat ground over to one side. The shape of the *Falcon* had been a long ovoid with a stretched-out turret along the top containing crew quarters and bridge, further cabins, holds and research areas below amidst the ship's other infrastructure. The back of the ovoid had the appearance of being sliced off where the throats of the fusion engine resided, while two nacelles that had protruded downwards to the fore had contained a twin-balance U-space drive. Now the thing had been severely torn up. The U-space nacelles lay far back in the trail of devastation along with chunks of hull and a net of beam-work torn out from the underside. The ship itself was bent to the curved shape of the mountain slope it had finally impacted against. It rested there as if deflated, overgrown with vines and with small trees growing amidst the debris strewn around it.

They climbed out of the shuttle with weapons and packs and gazed at the ruin.

'We should go prepared,' Anna said.

They returned inside the shuttle. Anna went to the power supply and, after disconnecting some leads and pipes, drew out one of the battery slabs, and then from their supplies snared requisite power leads. Ben collected tools he might need, though it struck him that the most useful would be the pry bar. Once they were both outside again he closed up the door on its seals. He wasn't sure why – a feeling that they were somehow unsafe. As they walked towards the ruined ship, he peered up at a young turtle-leaf tree, seeing a chunk of I-beam running through its trunk. Knowing how these trees grew, he surmised that it had not been penetrated by the beam but had grown up around it in the years since the crash.

'One moment.' Walking ahead, Anna stopped and reached back tapping her fingers against his chest. She dipped her head for a second, then turned to look at him.

'Fusion reactors do not do that unless a lot of safeties are overridden, well, at least in my time.'

'Thousands of safeties on them in even these primitive times,' he replied. 'What's the problem?'

'Fission products. Radiation. The shell and containment field must have been broken while it was still running. It would have spewed what was essentially a particle beam.'

'It would have had to have been deliberate,' he said numbly. 'So that's the end of our exploration?'

'No. It's dissipated and is low enough now for your suite to handle.'

As they trudged on Ben grimaced, wondering if this would be another unresolved mystery. Next, gazing up the slope of the hull, he did not feel disappointed, but the sight of the crashed ship did sadden him. They passed chunks of hull metal webbed with cooling pipes, optics and s-con wiring, standing like old monuments. Other things were scattered on the ground too: plasmel boxes, chunks of internal machinery, even a badly damaged nanoscope. Reaching the hull they walked along to where part of it had been torn away, vines hanging across the gap and darkness within.

'I never thought to bring a torch,' he said.

Anna gave him a superior look then took his rechargeable torch out of her pack and shone it inside. The beam revealed a hold space, the walls split and bulging crash foam like fungus, skeins of optics and s-con hanging down like the vines outside. They pushed through the vines and entered. Anna scanned around with the torch, picking out a stack of plasmel boxes still held to the floor by straps, and two large shipping containers that had slid into the left hand wall and dented it. Only now, looking at all this, did it truly impact on him that all their previous aims had come to nothing, and still disappointment failed to materialise.

'So we won't be leaving this world on this...' He looked at her. 'Will we?'

'I think this would take a bit more work,' she said dryly.

They moved further into the hold, towards a doorway at the back whose door hung off on one hinge. Twenty feet in, plant growth no longer matted the floor, but he began to see other items. Pieces of carapace lay everywhere, and amidst them he saw a carbine just like his own. He reached down and picked it up, then went to brush away the debris clinging to it. That's when he saw the bony fingers wrapped around the grip, one of them coiled in the guard over the firing button.

'I see,' he said, showing it to Anna. He wanted to take the weapon with him, because it could be made to work, but he put it down on the floor again. There would be so much here they could use and he could collect that weapon any time. And, even though he had no religious sensibilities at all, this somehow felt like desecration. It was, he knew, a feeling he would manage to get over.

'So what the hell happened here?' he wondered.

'I would say something similar to what happened to you,' Anna replied. 'This crash was hard and I doubt there were many survivors. The ship is open here and in other places.' She kicked at the carapace debris on the floor. 'Mantids.'

'But I survived them,' he said. 'They had more weapons and other resources...'

'We need to find the captain's log – I'm assuming such data stores are still hardened in this time?'

'Should be,' he agreed.

'That will maybe tell us what happened here on the planet, but more interesting to know would be why the ship ended up crashing in the first place.'

'Mutiny, probably,' he said. He could think of so many scenarios, in fact had already thought of many.

'There is something else to consider,' she said as they moved towards the door. 'It may well be that the U-space communicator is either still working or can be made to work.'

'I would have thought if that were the case, someone would have used it.'

'True, but it's worth bearing in mind.'

They moved through into a corridor, dark as pitch. Here, scattered about the door were perhaps the rest of the remains of the owner of that carbine. Ben picked up the skull and peered at the marks from mantid mandibles. He then put it down, gently, respectfully, when he spotted something else.

'Shine the torch over here,' he said, squatting.

She turned, blinded him for a moment with the beam, then brought that down onto the remains he squatted over. One side of a ribcage lay there still attached to a length of spine. He pointed.

'That wasn't mantids,' he said.

The ribs were blackened around a laser hole that had nearly cut one of them in half.

'So they fought,' said Anna. 'Why am I not surprised?'

He looked up. 'Your cynicism is showing.'

'Isn't it just?'

'Mantids will scavenge given the chance, just like any other predator.' He grimaced at the carapace scattered across the floor. 'I'm still not clear on what happened here, however,' He pointed at the carapace. 'If they came in to scavenge, then why so much carapace here? And I don't see any laser burns on them if they came in after surviving crew.'

They moved on, finding another corridor strewn with bones. Ben did not bother checking these for laser burns because there were enough on the corridor walls. Turning into another corridor and now recognising his location in the ship, he pointed.

'That makes no sense.'

There were no laser burns on the walls and no human remains here, yet mantid carapace had been piled against one wall.

'Perhaps they survived on mantid meat,' Anna suggested.

'Perhaps.' He gestured along the corridor. 'We go along here then up. We'll have to climb because I'm guessing the dropshaft isn't operating.'

The corridor dog-legged to the right, and then terminated against the opening into a dropshaft.

'Wait,' said Anna, pausing by the open door into another hold. 'In here.' She stepped inside and he followed, studying the contents of the hold as she shone the torch around.

Robots, painted with yellow and white stripes, were secured by straps along one wall. They were complicated, general purpose machines that ran on treads on most surfaces but could deploy spidery legs for rough terrain. Their tool arrays were folded up around their bodies and consisted of a wide variety of digging and cutting implements. Ben gazed at them and considered just how much easier his life would have been here if he could have deployed just one of them. Almost certainly their power supplies and sub-AI minds were still good, though the former would need to be charged up. It was something to think about for the future, now it seemed the future would be here.

'Look,' said Anna, shining the torch at something over the other side of the hold.

A great tangled mass lay there. For a moment he thought it a pile of cables and other junk a ship like this often acquired but, as they moved closer he began to discern the true shape of it: bones. At a glance they looked like human skeletons, but closer inspection revealed otherwise. The bones he could see were bulkier, the skulls crested with forward jutting jaws filled with lethal looking teeth. Most of the bones were under sheets of carapace with jutting spikes and sharp edges. He noted that the leg and arm bones were the same length. Here then was a creature that could probably both stand upright and run on all fours.

'Damn and fuck,' he said, looking to Anna. 'No tank-grown monsters?'

'No, none at all.'

He waved a hand at the mass. 'Then how do you explain this?'

'Descendants.'

'What?'

'It wasn't just the biology of this world that was altered for warfare, but people too.' She shook her head. 'These were on my side – vicious efficient killers. I got a scan at a distance on your Stalker but I wasn't sure. I told you about the dumb plague? Well, here are the descendants of its victims.' She squatted, reached in and pulled out a skull, then slammed it down on the floor breaking it open. Holding up one half she pointed inside. The thing had a series of bony compartments with spicules of bone growing across them – no place in there at all for anything like a human brain. 'Little more than animals now but retaining their weaponised characteristics. I imagine these wiped out the standard humans infected with the plague.'

Ben watched her as she put the skull down, almost regretfully.

'I felt there was something you weren't telling me,' he said.

'I didn't tell you because I just wasn't sure.' She shrugged. 'It's something I just didn't want to get into and... I didn't want to hunt that creature down until I knew.'

'Until you knew what?'

'I guessed it to be a descendant, but I wasn't sure about the mind. Perhaps I was trying to convince myself that people had survived. I hoped...' She shook her head. 'I should have known. If they had retained any human intelligence... if that Stalker had retained it then it would not have been hunting but digging up podules. If they had retained any intelligence this would have been a very different place.'

And there, he thought, a perfect example of the fact that Golem were not just machines – a whole gamut of complex emotions and impulses. He could not quite understand what she was feeling but did have some empathy for its effects on her.

'So what do you think happened here?' he gestured to the pile.

She stood up. 'They weren't stacked here like this. It looks to me like they gathered together – tied themselves in this knot – and I see no weapons burns. I think it likely that this is how they aestivated during the day, but their day here when they did this was their last one.'

Ben nodded. 'Radiation.'

'As I said, it is low now, but it would have been a lot higher at the beginning.' She pointed vaguely into the ship. 'Fusion reactors don't fail like that unless deliberately made to do so. It would have irradiated the ship in one burst and thereafter waned, but everything would have been toxic for some time. People here would have survived by dint of their nanosuites, though they would not have been in a good way. These creatures must have come in shortly after the crash, perhaps with some degree of human curiosity remaining, perhaps still running some war time programming, but certainly to hunt.' She shrugged. 'And, as you know, nanosuites are not heritable.'

'And now the whole scenario here has become even more complicated,' said Ben. 'We need to find the captain's log if we can, though I wonder if there are any entries after this crash.'

'Perhaps this is something we should leave for another day?' Anna asked.

'Why not now?'

'Perhaps you weren't paying attention to the position of the sun.' She smiled tentatively.

'Damn. How long?'

'Maybe two hours before the innocular flies, but they are not my main concern.' She gestured to the bones. 'The Stalker used to arrive at your house later in the night and whenever the mantid population was higher. It seems likely that this is where it aestivates during the day. And there may be others.'

'We'll take a look at the bridge – it shouldn't take long to reach there – then get out before nightfall. Agreed?'

'Agreed.'

They headed out to the dropshaft. Anna leaned into it and shone the torch up and down, then picked out the rungs running up the side. She clicked the torch off. He was about to suggest that wasn't such a good idea, but then his eyes adjusted to light penetrating from above – just enough to see the rungs by. Inside they climbed, Ben leading. The light steadily increased until he swung into a bright corridor with square chainglass ports running down the side and doors down the other. Crew quarters. Here lay the broken bones of what looked like two skeletons, scattered about a machine mounted on a circular grav sled. He inspected the large number of coiled power leads, the boxy quantum cascade units and the snout of the thing with its photon compression barrel.

'Industrial laser,' he said, again thinking how useful a tool this was. 'I wonder why it was up here.'

'Easy to speculate if we are considering mutiny,' Anna replied.

Pieces of carapace were scattered about the area, but when he picked up bone fragments and a cracked open skull he did not find the marks of mantids. All the large bones had been split open, probably to get at the marrow, which was something of which mantids were incapable. Doubtless the skull had been split open to access the lump of fatty matter inside. The fragments bore teeth marks and he did not need to speculate too much to guess from what.

'Seems the descendants came up here,' he said.

'Seems so,' said Anna tightly.

They moved along this corridor then round, finally turning at a junction through a long tubular corridor to a bulkhead door. He tried the locking handle then the manual wheel but had no luck. Stepping back, he studied cuts on the surface, before peering down at another device abandoned against the wall. Here lay an atomic shear, its cable plugged into a universal wall socket. Foolish, he felt, to try a shear on a door like this. It wasn't just hardened ceramal but layered with meta-materials that would rebind any narrow cuts and cracks. He supposed that's why they had decided to bring up the industrial laser.

'The bridge lies behind here,' he said. 'It's certainly locked and likely they damaged the mechanism when they first attempted to cut through.'

Anna stripped off her pack and put it on the floor with the torch on top, stepped forwards and gripped the locking handle.

'Are you sure about this?' he asked.

'They used the wrong approach – trying to cut through the door,' she said. 'They would have done better to bring a hydraulic lever of some kind. The door is very durable but the locking mechanism is plain ceramal and, to a limited extent, brittle.'

She struggled with the handle, then, bracing her legs apart, got both her hands on it. With a deep cracking thump it went down.

'It was damaged?' he asked.

'No, locked from the inside and corroded.'

Next she took hold of the wheel and, accompanied by similar sounds of things breaking, it turned. With a ripping sound the door lifted from its seal, but then just stuck there.

'Stand back,' Anna instructed.

She got her fingers in at the edge of the door as he stepped away. He thought her emulation pretty good, the way the muscles stood out on her arms, but knew they weren't doing the work. He saw the floor bowing underneath her feet, then with a crack something further broke in the door frame and it swung round on its hinges to crash into the wall.

The bridge was well lit too with the thick wrap-around chainglass screen set to transparency before the power went out. Consoles and screens with chairs before them ran around one wall. The other wall was screen painted and used to show cam pictures and other information about the ship but was now a nacreous grey. Two corpses lay on the floor, mummified and intact enough that Ben almost recognised them, almost. A third corpse sat in the captain's throne in the middle of the floor.

'Constance,' he said, recognising her long pale hair and the armoured envirosuit she always wore.

He walked over and peered into her empty eye sockets, then turned his attention to one arm of the throne. He pressed down a clip and hinged up a control panel revealing a line of data tabs.

'We have the telemetry and public log here,' he said. 'But I would be more interested in her private one, which should be in her cabin.' He turned. Anna had sat in one of the seats before a console – U-space control. 'Do you need the battery?'

She looked round. 'It should be possible to run a diagnostic without that,' she said, pulling up a sleeve then swiping a hand down her arm. Her skin split open to reveal glittery internals and she reached down to her pack to a take out a combined optic and power lead, and plugged it into her arm.

He walked over as she found the requisite port in the console and plugged in the other end, and stooped to take the battery slab and leads from her pack. The console powered up and a dim screen began to run code. She started working the controls as he headed back to the captain's throne. Power being limited he opened the other arm of the throne and took out a small tablet. He ran a power lead into that from the battery and it came on to show a charging bar. It surprised him to see that it still did have a charge. He put the tablet down then reached out a hand and patted Constance on the shoulder.

'Sorry about this, but time for you to move.'

'What?' said Anna, looking round, then, 'Oh,' as he hauled the corpse out of the throne and deposited it on the floor. How weirdly light she felt, he thought – a reminder that humans were essentially just bags of water complicated by some other chemicals. Brushing down the seat he turned and sat, picked up the tablet then made a selection from the other throne arm. Pulling one of the data tabs out, he inserted it into a socket in the side of the tablet and immediately on the screen got a long list of entries, with the first words spoken written out as text. He selected one on the basis of that text and pressed play.

The scene was the interior of the bridge with Constance sitting where he now sat. Off to one side he could just see two others sitting at consoles. Constance looked both worried and angry. She grimaced, then spoke.

'They were working against me almost from when this journey began, Alison, Kamarg and the others. They chose most of those aboard and they were all in on it, and the equipment manifest, and it was Alison who set the survey roster so my three main supporters were aboard when it went down. I don't know who sabotaged the shuttle...'

She shook her head and punched a button on the throne arm and the recording ended. He frowned and scrolled down the list. It was a long one and to run through it all would take many hours they did not have here. He would look at it when they got back to the house. Glancing round at Anna he saw that her hands were no longer moving and she was doubtless now making a mental inspection of the U-space communicator. He considered wandering off into the ship to find some useful items to take back with them, but then reconsidered. They had a lot to discuss concerning what they would do here. This ship contained a wealth of resources and perhaps his house – valued as it was – would not be the best place to be. Perhaps they should relocate here and, almost certainly, any further exploration and assessment would be better started with a new day.

He decided to pass the time while he waited for her to finish by setting the log to play at random, and from that perhaps get an overview, and know where he wanted to look. Setting random play he got Constance again, looking haggard, sipping from a water bottle. There was blood on her clothing, crusted below her nose and one of her eyes was bright red. Behind her and to the right he saw the corpses where they still lay now. When she was done with the water she looked up to speak, her voice hoarse.

'Kamarg told me when he was "negotiating" from the other side of that door. They'd spent ages scrubbing data stores of the location of Afthonia because they knew about the podules and what they contained, and knew that controlling them meant fortunes could be made. I was just the mug they used to get here...' She shook her head.

251

'I never understood the need for so many sub-AI digging machines with the materials to set up a base, nor the near half a hold full of expandable cargo boxes.' She put her hand up to her mouth for a second, looked startled then leaned over and vomited bloody water.

A brief recording selected next.

'They had no intention of letting any of those who weren't on their team walk away from this,' said Constance, then just turned away, and the recording ended.

Another brief recording, this one from earlier and obviously before the crash:

'They killed them. They killed them all.' She looked haunted, and then her face twisted with rage. 'And they have probably killed themselves and us too. What kind of idiot allows a fire fight with armour piercers around a fusion reactor?' She glanced round at the other two. Ben recognised them now but just could not remember their names. She continued, 'We've agreed. We can't U-jump out of here and the stored power won't last. We're taking the ship down. Judging by the present power levels…This may be my last entry here. In which case: goodbye.'

The next one was longer, she looked grey now.

'They didn't have time to get through the door. Through the ships cams that aren't busted I counted about eight of them, and then just five after that first night, and by the next day they were as sick as me. They started hauling out equipment to set up a camp when Kamarg started coughing blood. He came up here to try and speak to me, to get me to call for help. I told him to fuck off. The reactor failure had dosed them with enough radiation to kill a base format, but they could survive it. They would be very sick, though, and I doubted they would survive another night with the mantids…' She looked to one side. 'I was wrong about that.'

Ben stopped the random selection and flicked to the next recording.

'Kamarg was at the door again, begging for me to let him in, begging me to call for help. I can see the other two survivors in the hold, getting a heavy duty laser out of its case. I fucked them by turning the power off outside of here, but they have cable to run to laminar storage on the engineering deck. Could be they'll get through the door. They'll find an unpleasant surprise here if they do…'

Checking the time stamp he then saw a long break before the next recording. Constance looked even worse if that were possible.

'I saw three of them die. Maybe others. I can't tell. I saw someone or something else in the ship. Looked like a 'dapt of some kind – human but insect appearance. Heard someone screaming.'

Ben felt the skin on his back creeping and looked round to the door. Night had to be drawing in now. He glanced at Anna, but she was still rigid in her seat. He put it to random again. Random gave him: 'I'm pretty busted up and, with the radiation dose, I don't think my nanosuite is up to it. I'm aug linking and finding failures throughout. Thigh bones busted, pelvis and spine. Heavy organ damage. But it is keeping the pain down.'

Ben stopped it, feeling sick of what he was seeing. He looked to Anna again.

'We really ought to be getting out of here now,' he said.

She did not respond and he supposed she must still be deep in the programming. Putting the tablet aside he got up and walked over. Peering round at her face he saw her eyes had gone metallic again, but were also running rapidly changing cubic patterns. Next looking at the screen he watched the code, managing to work out some of what it was. It seemed to be stuck in a repeating cycle, though why that would be…

Cold fear washed through him and Constance's words replayed in his mind. She had said, *'Could be they'll get through the door. They'll find an unpleasant surprise here if they do…'* Kamarg, the leader of the expedition that had hired Constance and her crew to come to Afthonia had wanted in so as to access the underspace transmitter, which was precisely what Anna was doing right now. Without a second thought he reached down and jerked the dual function cable out of her arm. If he was wrong, maybe she would be annoyed with him but no harm would be done, if he was right…

She remained utterly still in her seat, the patterns in her eyes slowing. Some sort of virus? He reached out to shake her shoulder and a blinding light flashed and cracked, a shockwave took hold of him, compressing his chest and flinging him. For a second he was airborne then he crunched down on something, utterly dazed. Hauling himself upright he felt an object turning under his hand, glanced down through afterimages and saw a mummified face, the dry skin of the neck fractured. He had landed on the corpses. He scrabbled clear onto his hands and knees, blinking to try and clear his vision. Anna lay sprawled over to one side of her chair. The console had erupted, shards of composite peeled up like the rind of a podule.

'Anna?' No response.

He felt too shaky to get to his feet and the side of his face hurt. Reaching up to that he touched wetness and saw the blood on his hand. Probing his skin he found a long lump of something under his skin running from his cheek to up beside his nose and a ragged end protruding. A piece of his own skull? No, it had to be a lump of composite. Knowing now from long experience that this would hurt a lot more later, he tried to get a grip on that ragged end and pull the thing out. He couldn't, so crawled over to his pack where a fortunate addition had been a pair of pliers. With these he got a good grip on the shard and pulled fast and hard, and yelled, blood flooding down his cheek.

'Fuck you, Constance,' he said eventually.

Hand pressed against his face to try and stem the bleeding, he finally managed to get up and walk over to Anna. Her face looked burned and chunks of composite had stabbed into it, while the surfaces of the eyes were dulled and milky, but with none of that metallic look there now. He wanted to get hold of her and shake her, but that was a stupid thing to do with a human, and doubly so with a Golem. If she became conscious he would know about that at once.

He thought hard about what to do, trying to suppress his panic. He had to do something! The physical damage, if there was any beyond the surface, appeared minimal. The main attack had been from the U-com console – a virus put there by Constance. He could do nothing about that, in essence her internal systems would be fighting it just like the immune system of a human fought a biological virus. The best thing to do would be to simply wait, but he could not. He knew he was operating more on instinct than common sense when he collected up essential items of their gear and packed them in a backpack. He then took hold of her under the armpits and dragged her to the door. He had to get her home – that's all he thought.

Beyond the door he started panting, and when he looked down at the front of his envirosuit he saw blood there, and not that still dripping from his face but from inside. The blast had obviously injured him elsewhere, and it had certainly sapped his strength. He kept going, dragging her tens of yards each time then stopping to rest. As he reached the end of the corridor with windows along one side he looked out and could tell by the light that the sun was on its way down. He laughed at himself, wishing he had brought his wheelbarrow, and knew he must be a bit concussed. Then he looked ahead to the mouth of the dropshaft.

'Damn,' he said.

The shaft extended down at least forty feet into the hold area. He moved her to the edge and studied her eyes, but still nothing. She looked like the broken doll he had first found. Taking out the torch he shone it down below. He could simply drop her. Being Golem and very tough, the drop would probably cause very little beyond cosmetic damage. He couldn't do it. Though he knew he was being as foolish now as when moving her in the first place, he simply couldn't do it.

Leaning against the edge of the opening, he thought about trying to carry her down. Maybe in his condition upon first entering this ship he could have managed that, but right now the idea appalled him. He searched around for something to use. Then, looking along the corridor, realised Kamarg had provided. He went over to the industrial laser and shouldered the coil of cable. It appeared to be enough and, if it had been their intention to run it to the engineering deck, then it should be. Bringing it over to Anna, he dropped it on the floor, found one end and was about to tie it round her under her armpits, but had second thoughts and first threaded it through one of the rungs in the shaft before doing so. After securing her he tied the cable off, dragged her to the shaft and eased her in. Stupid to be so careful, but he could not help but treat her like a flesh-and-blood creature.

She swung into the shaft and hung there. Looping the cable about his body and getting a firm grip, he reached out and undid the slip knot he had made. Her sudden weight dragged him forwards so his face hit against the frame of the opening. He yelled and swore, then abruptly fell silent, sure he had just heard movement down below. Listening he heard nothing further. Maybe she had dislodged something and it had fallen…

He began lowering her and, as he did so, a burning sensation spread across his torso and something clicked painfully. Broken rib – he knew from experience. Gritting his teeth, he just continued, the pain steadily increasing. He began sweating, and then that started to turn cold on him. A glance over his shoulder told him why: the sun had been further down than he thought and now it was gone, and cold seemed to be oozing up from below.

At last the cable grew slack and he released it. Now hanging the carbine by its strap in front of him, he began to climb down, trying to take most of his weight on his legs because that hurt the least. At the bottom of the shaft he took out the torch and clicked it on, directing the beam at her face. Still no change. He hung the torch on his belt, still on, dreading the prospect of now dragging her out of the ship, but there seemed no other option. He used the chainglass knife to slice the cable high up and, gathering up that length, used it to haul her out of the dropshaft. And then, seemingly on cue, he heard something whickering nearby.

Cold ran through him. Dropping the cable he backed up against the wall by the shaft, grabbed up the torch and flashed it to his left, and then to his right. It was there, just forty feet away from him and, caught in the beam it opened its mouth and hissed at him. He stared. This was the clearest he had ever seen it. The skeletons and Anna's explanation gave it human origin but he could see little of that here. Segmented insect carapace, its body was long and its limbs too, but it had more than four of the latter. The major ones were kind of positioned like a human's, but were thin and as insect like as the other two protruding each side of its torso, which ended in scythe hooks. Its hands were similar: a small stubby thumb, two small fingers and one large forefinger also ending in a long scythe hook. Its eyes gleamed red in the torch light, but too close together, while on the outside of each was a subsidiary eye. The skull crest moved like the feathers on a cockatoo, but seemed to consist of blades. It hissed again, then flung itself towards him, almost seeming to go airborne with its limbs hitting walls and ceiling.

Ben abruptly understood that he had frozen up, that this wasn't a nightmare, it wasn't frightening sounds out in the night, but hard horrible reality heading straight at him. He scrabbled for the carbine, bemused about not having reached for it earlier, and dropped the torch while doing so. He raised the weapon and fired. The beam was blinding, lighting up the whole corridor in lurid red, and the creature much closer now. He hit one of its subsidiary limbs, the thing flaring and burning, and the shot tracked across it body. The creature shrieked and tumbled as the beam went out. Ben squatted, shifting the weapon so he held it by the grip with the butt under his arm, grabbed up the torch and shone it ahead. He was tempted to switch the weapon to continuous fire but knew that would soon deplete its battery. The creature was down on the floor and as he pinned it in the torch beam it emitted a combination of both shriek and hiss and rapidly retreated, disappearing into the hold where they had found the remains of its kin.

He found himself gasping for breath, but his torso no longer hurt. He glanced down once more at Anna, thinking about dragging her out, dragging her to the shuttle. Outside he would be in the open and this creature, or others could come at him from any direction and, anyway, this thing had plagued him for years. It was time to end this – one way or the other.

Ben advanced down the corridor, torch beam and weapon aimed at that entrance into the hold. He finally came up to the edge and listened. He could hear nothing. He thought about where it might be lurking. That pile of bones would be no hide so most likely somewhere between the robots. He abruptly stepped in and swung towards those robots, tracking the torch beam across and ready to fire. He could see nothing and he swung the beam back across in panic, then over to the pile of bones.

Movement – nearby – a wash of warm air like breath.

The horror of it froze his guts just before something slammed into his back to send him stumbling forwards, and then seemed to jerk him to a halt. He looked down in disbelief at the hooked claw protruding from under his collar bone and then, agonisingly, it began to lift him. How the hell had it got behind him? He then remembered a mistake he had made before when searching for the shuttle screen: flatlander thinking. He turned the carbine to point upwards even as he looked up to see his stalker clinging to the ceiling above the door, and fired, and fired again, and kept his finger on the firing button as it seemed the whole world fell on him.

Awareness came back in flashes. Had he been unconscious? He lay on his side with the creature on top of him and the damned thing was moving. Where was the carbine? He couldn't feel it in his grip and groping ahead of him he couldn't locate it. A light came on, throwing dark spidery shadows over him. His shoulder suddenly screamed at him and he screamed back as he felt a wrenching behind and heard a gristly crunch. Then the weight was off him.

'I think you got it,' said Anna.

He heaved himself up and looked to where she pointed the torch beam. The stalker was still smoking from where his shots had near cut it in half. He stared at it, then down at the claw still protruding below his collar bone. That crunching must have been her breaking the limb behind it.

'Best we remove that back home,' she said, reaching down and helping him to his feet. 'Pull it out now and you may bleed to death.'

They were grim words, but he abruptly felt unreasonably happy.

'Yeah, let's go home,' he replied.

While chatting to various readers on the social media I discovered something quite surprising. Many readers have been with me from or near the beginning – their usual introduction to my books being The Skinner *or* Gridlinked. *But now it seems that many dropped in quite late with* Dark Intelligence. *Whether early readers or late I often hear the same thing from them, 'Give me more Penny Royal!' Obviously there is something quite alluring about the black AI, mental casualty of the war between the Polity and the prador, and provider of 'transformations' that always come at a terrible price. Deals with the Devil. Penny Royal is perhaps an extreme version of the antihero, with its own particular morality, and a rather unique approach to its treatment of others and to how the universe should function. Here is the black AI again, in that time when it wasn't so cuddly.*

DR WHIP

The tough virus propagated faster than anything he had seen before, and even massive infusions of nanobots or drugs had not killed it. As Arabella went into her only hope – the zero-freezer – Doctor Whipple wondered again: *why am I alive?* He'd been caught in the lower hemisphere of Hercules Station when the AI went down and Master Alban ordered the full quarantine, and was now the only survivor here. He had tended people being eaten alive by the virus, been sprayed by their blood and other bodily fluids, and even been bitten by one victim as she fought for life, yet he remained uninfected.

He stepped forward and rested a hand against the freezer hatch as it closed. The machine began vitrifying Arabella's corpse and taking it down to close to absolute zero, before dispatching it to join thousands of others in storage. She had not been the last to die down here, but the last he had taken off life support. He still felt reluctant to let her go because the viral damage to her brain gave her little chance of resurrection. He remembered how they had planned to travel across the Polity together, maybe settle somewhere for a few decades and raise children... The future had been bright and open, and now it closed with a freezer door. Whipple swore and turned away, guiltily glad to be alive, even though he felt something had allowed him to live – something that had deliberately murdered thousands here.

It had all started with the arrival of that survey ship last month. An entity had been aboard; a thing that didn't show up on cams but still managed to leave a security team in bits before disappearing into the station. A subsequent security team found the four-person crew of the ship – naked dried-out husks of human beings – wound in a single knot and a forensic robot had needed to cut them into pieces to separate them. After that came the weird disappearances, followed by the horrifying reappearance of one of the same. Dr Whipple shuddered.

Iano Yulos had been working outside in a space suit, but when informed his shift had ended he failed to respond – just continued working. Paranoia already on the rise at that point, Alban decided, rather than send someone out to him, to usurp Yulos's suit motors. This he duly did and the man's suit returned him inside the station, only, when they opened his suit, they found no one inside. Internal station cam footage showed him getting into the suit. External cam footage, and his suit log, showed him outside working in it. Even the station AI could find no sign of data tampering. But he was gone.

Five days later he returned above the crowded station plaza in the lower hemisphere, naked, bloated and floating like a balloon even though grav plates tugged from below. He was kicking his legs and waving his arms and crying for help. This sight of course drew in an even bigger crowd before Security dispatched a crab drone to retrieve him. The moment the device gently closed its claws on him, he screamed in utter agony and burst. Offal and other bits of Yulos showered the crowd below, but medical staff did not learn until later that the shower had contained large quantities of the virus incubated in his body.

Dr Whipple headed out of the freezer room and paused at the caduceus engraved in the glass door to his ward to peer in at the rows of empty regrowth tanks. He then headed to his office. He would have liked to believe his particular affectation – the one to make him stand out from other qualifying doctors – had kept him alive. Most of them had internal nanosuites boosting their immune systems and constantly repairing cellular damage – some controlled and reprogrammed by fashionable sub AI tattoos. His Barnard suit – named after a pre Quiet War surgeon – ran a nanosuite it programmed before injecting from outside through microtubules. It constantly monitored him and modelled the function of his body. It did pretty much the same as the other augmentations but was older technology, unique, quirky, and appeared to be fashioned of snakeskin. However, the suit had given him no alerts nor had it intervened in any way. No, he felt sure he was alive because something had chosen him. On that night of his first sleep, after working for a hundred hours and knowing the stimulants weren't going to keep him going for much longer, it had visited him...

Sitting at his console, Whipple put a call through to Master Alban, but got no immediate response. Unsurprising, really, now the virus had penetrated the upper hemisphere. Alban also had no AI help since, just after Yulos's grotesque death, the station AI crashed – its crystal turned to dust. Alban was struggling to control the panic. He had already used troops to prevent a mob trying to get to the station docks – the protocol in this situation being that no one could leave until a forensic AI with its bio-crisis team had paid a visit. However, so soon after the end of the war, such AIs were still busy cleaning up the atrocious messes left by bioweapons of the alien prador enemy, and months had passed since Alban had requested one.

As he sat waiting, Whipple thought again about that sleep time visitor. He had been alone in bed while Arabella worked her shift. He had not known she would not sleep beside him again. A sound had propelled him to that state on the edge of REM sleep, in the territory where dream and nightmare incorporate reality. The nightmare had felt real, but his knowledge and experience, his rationality, denied it. Something in his bedroom had seemed to hone elements of the darkness to razor sharpness. It also tangled it with mercury worms yet he could see through it to his door, and to the cabinet alongside that. When he'd tried to focus on the substance of this presence, it had seemed to dissolve under his gaze.

It had whispered, too, that darkness, but no words had been clear. In response he gave his frustration and powerlessness in the face of the virus, of it killing all those around him. The darkness had found this interesting and focused on the heart of it. He had always wanted to be the best, but his ambition went further, and his choice of enhancement – the Barnard suit – reflected that. He wanted to be unique, iconic. Even as this had been occurring, he'd realised he was no longer sprawled on his bed, but hovered some way above it with his skin prickling as if being nipped at by thousands of gnats. It had all been too weird and his growing consciousness could not accept it. He'd suddenly fallen back to his bed, then jerked upright, completely awake. He would have next dismissed it all as a nightmare brought on by stress and stimulant overdose, were it not for his door being open, and it seeming as if cats had been sharpening their claws all the way across the soft coating on the floor.

'Alban is unavailable at present,' said a voice, catching at the last.

Whipple snapped back to the present, and gazed at the face on his screen. One of Alban's unnecessary PAs had spoken – Alban being the sort who liked to have plenty of human underlings, even having to generate pointless tasks to keep them busy. She was, Whipple could see, ill. Fractured capillaries webbed her pale skin, and blisters were just visible under her hairline. She would be dead within a few hours.

'There's no point me staying down here,' he said. 'Perhaps I can help up there?' He doubted he could save any lives, but he could give palliative care and, if he continued to survive, he could stick the last of them in a zero freezer.

She glanced to one side, then turned back. 'You're instructed to go to the axial drop-shaft, which is being opened for you now.'

'Good.' He nodded, cut the connection and stood up. Surveying his surroundings for a moment, he realised he had nothing to take. They had all the equipment he might need up there, along with access to the data he had gathered on the virus. And, in essence, his life had ended here when he closed that zero freezer door for the last time.

He headed out.

Once bubbling with life, the space station now felt haunted and sinister. Since the end of the war, it always had its streams of refugees, crews from Polity warships on patrol, teams on stopovers from clearing up the wartime mess, and its salvage crews and traders dealing in the rich strata of wartime wreckage out here. The population had waxed and waned, but had never been less than three thousand. Of course, the people were still here, in the zero freezers, in a refrigerated hold or, if lucky enough to have memplants, in a safe in medical, their bodies disposed of.

Whipple walked down the centre of a wide, deserted arcade, scattered with used analgesic patches, throwaway diagnosticers and drug vials. A couple of bars had been trashed, but the only movement he could see now was of a servitor drone, bumbling about the tables.

He noted a big chain pharmacist's had been looted, and paused to gaze at the caduceus etched into its window. Still the sight annoyed him. The winged staff with its two snakes entwined around it had become an icon of medical professions everywhere, but due to a mistake. This winged staff of Hermes was not the true medical symbol – that being the rod of Asclepius with its single snake. He had pointed this out to Alban and his people, noting that those who had named their station Hercules should know this. As a result, Station Medical had lost the wings but, in what almost felt like a snub, retained the extra snake.

Even as he studied the old image on the pharmacy window he felt a presence, almost like a shadow falling over him. He saw the servitor drone quickly dart out of sight as if terrified. Perhaps it sensed that other too.

'What do you want?' he asked.

Sensing, in some manner he could not fathom, objects sharpening themselves in darkness, he moved on. Hellish amusement arose, somehow related to his distraction with the caduceus, and he quickened his pace. Finally reaching the dropshaft, he palmed the control panel. He stepped inside and the irised gravity field took hold of him to waft him upwards. It felt like escape, yet he knew it was not.

They grabbed him the moment he stepped out on the upper level – station police clad in combat armour. They weren't gentle and stabbed the tranquiliser implant into his neck without anaesthesia, using a plain steel needle. Next, they slammed him down on a grav-sled and towed him to the upper level hospital where sampling and testing equipment awaited. He tried to tell them he had already done this, but no one listened. Then they tried to take off his Barnard suit.

'What the hell?' said one of the three medical techs. 'What the hell is this?'

He couldn't reply. He felt guilty, ashamed, just couldn't talk about it. However, now that someone else had seen, a lock seemed to come off in his mind and he could at least think about what had happened. He had wanted a shower after that night, wanted to feel clean before returning to the fray, only, he hadn't been able to take off his suit. It had bonded to his flesh, seemed a snakeskin formation of it, as if he had become an ophidapt. He then remembered something else. He had grabbed quick snacks while working, drunk copious amounts of coffee, yet, when was the last time he had felt the need to use a toilet?

'Take your samples from his exposed skin,' said someone brusquely. 'We need to talk to him.'

While a body scanner slowly traversed on its rails above him, the med techs took blood samples from his carotids, snipped off some of his hair, and took biopsies out of his face and hands. When they finished, two troops hauled him to his feet and dragged him off to a cell where they strapped him down in a chair. One air-blast injection dispelled the tranquiliser, and other drugs had him babbling freely while a cap monitored his brain. As it went on and on, he thought those who questioned him must be on rotation, but later realised that the new questioners were replacements for those who had died. He demanded to see Alban, learned he was dead. Eventually they tried an interrogation aug, but it died on his head and fell off like a dry scab.

Time derailed. More drugs ensued, then the beatings. He could hear pulse-rifle fire beyond his cell, screams and a composite moaning of terror. The half-mad guard with skin peeling from the backs of his hands came. The man used a ceramal combat knife on Whipple's face and demanded the truth and, after being told it, used the knife to gauge out his right eye and demanded it again. Whipple sat screaming and begging before losing the other eye. In dark agony, he heard a gunshot.

Time passed.

'It's you again,' he sobbed as the darkness all around began sharpening itself.

His straps fell away and a presence lifted and cradled him. Agony returned to his eye-sockets but he could not scream, could not move at all. He sensed terrible madness and for a moment understood what he was: a product of that madness, art.

Sight returned – afterimages of that caduceus in the pharmacy window first, like a taunt – and he found himself lying on a composite floor scored with a thousand knives. He stood up and walked out, stepping over corpses, caught a glimpse of his reflection in a window in a shopping arcade, found a mirror and speculated on how he could see with empty eye sockets, then noted the glint of something golden deep inside. Afterwards, he stole some sunglasses from another shop. He could feel it inside him: the division and transformation. He ate and he drank but never needed to open his suit, found it impossible to do so, and in acquiring a sense of touch it now seemed to *be* his skin. He then set to work, powering up a grav-sled with attached autohandler. It took him weeks to transport every corpse he could find to a zero freezer, but still the place filled with the stench of decay from spilled blood and pieces that weren't worth salvaging. The gold in his eye sockets expanded, giving him golden snakes' eyes. He retained the sunglasses. A few days after loading the last corpse he had his first shedding. His skin and his suit blistered, felt tight and finally split, and he peeled away a layer as thick as a finger to reveal exactly the same underneath.

At length he realised that he was truly alone – that his night visitor was no longer aboard the station. He wondered when rescue would arrive and, when it did not, he checked the docks. Here he found an ECS hospital ship full of corpses, dismembered Golem androids and the glittering remains and dead remote bots of what he supposed must have been a forensic AI. He knew at once, and with little logic, that this had been the point. The deaths aboard the station had just been a way of luring this entity here so the other thing aboard the station could... What? Perhaps gain something, learn something, or test itself in some way? He knew then that he couldn't stay and wait for whoever or whatever came afterwards. He had become part of the visitor, a product of the visitor – Polity AIs would never trust him and never be done with him. They would never let him go. He stole a ship and fled from the Polity, and found himself in a place just being named: the Graveyard.

Dr Whip gazed at the thing lying on the floor of his cabin, flipped it up with the toe of his boot and caught it in his right hand. He gazed at a rubbery deflated version of his own face and a seemingly exact copy of his Barnard suit, then wadded the whole mess together and tossed it over in the corner where, after a brief hesitation at the mouth of its hole, a cleanbot came out, seized it and dragged it inside. No point keeping this latest shedding of his outer skin. He did not need to run meticulous scans of it, because he knew what he would find. The skin would be precisely twenty-three grams heavier. He would learn nothing new from its intricate layering and mix of his own genes with those of a terran cobra. The nanoskin underlying these, which had produced the exact copy of the Barnard suit incorporated into his new skin, would reveal nothing more. He also knew that he would have grown a little taller, a little paler, and that the awful changes occurring inside him would have progressed a little further.

He turned to the full-length mirror in his cabin wall. The layered tech of his Barnard suit had been shaped like the musculature of an athlete, but on his tall thin frame gave him the appearance of a particularly ectomorphic high jumper. However, the suit covered a body that wasn't quite the right shape and didn't move quite as it should. He considered, yet again, how he seemed to consist of braided together worms, and smiled coldly. It wasn't a nice smile. His teeth sat translucent and spiky in a long pale face rendered all the more sinister by snake eyes. He turned and picked up his sunglasses from the bed, and put them on.

'Was it the suit, Penny Royal?' he asked.

During the war, some AIs had gone black, and the one called Penny Royal was the blackest of them all. Hercules space station had been just one of the places it had attacked, and what it had done there just one of its many atrocities. Now, fifty years after Dr Whip had departed the place, the station was still under investigation. A horde of forensic AIs were still meticulously scanning and taking the place apart. Dr Whip had been right, apparently. The AIs surmised that the black AI had done what it had done to lure in the forensic AI he had seen destroyed there. No one knew why. Those AIs had also managed to divine that one station resident had been the particular focus of Penny Royal, and had survived, though much changed, and escaped. And they wanted to talk to him very badly.

Dr Whip had his own theory about why he had survived. By now, he had the full story of Penny Royal's 'transformations'. He had met the contract killer whose weapons the AI had melded with his body, and the singer whose vocal range became immense, while her head became that of a bird, with a birdbrain inside too. He had seen one seeker of immortality frozen in a diamond and one seeker after God who, when taken out of induced coma, could only stare at the sky and scream. In every case, something unique about them had interested the AI, and influenced its transformation of them. And so it was with Whip, though he did not recollect asking for change. The Barnard suit had been a rarity in the Polity back then, and was rarer now. He felt sure that it had stimulated the black AI's insane curiosity and that, in some twisted warp of its mind, it had decided the suit must be preserved and so made it a permanent part of him. But the other changes? They baffled him. They bounced most forms of scan and he could not fully understand them, though they were drastic and terrible.

'I will ask you,' said the doctor, then turned and headed for the door.

The small vessel he stole from the space station had belonged to Alban. In the ensuing years, the doctor had made changes, converting luxury apartments into a large laboratory and, when it became known that Polity AIs were hunting him, he acquired a prador second-child ship mind and dumped its previous querulous AI. He walked along the corridor to the bridge, feeling an odd shift all around him as his ship dropped out of underspace, perfectly on time. He ensconced himself in the single chair there, reached out and tapped a button, then sat back as armoured shutters drew back from the wide chainglass window to reveal his next destination, his next place of employment.

For Dr Whip the acquisition of the wealth to buy his research tools and other equipment, and to run this ship, had ceased to be a problem within just the first few years of him entering the Graveyard. This buffer zone, between the Polity and the Prador Kingdom, had quickly become the preferred destination for scum from both realms, and even scum required doctors.

And Dr Whip was a very good doctor indeed.

He knew, with utter clarity, that before Penny Royal had changed him he had been brilliant, and with memcrystal installed in his skull had managed to load a vast repository of medical and related scientific knowledge. The only problem with this had been his mental access to it, sorting it in his organic brain and encompassing a wide variety of disciplines. But Penny Royal had done something there too. He now *remembered* all that data and all the skills, for Penny Royal had completely incorporated them in his mind, and he remembered them with the eidetic precision of an AI. Dr Whip frowned, he also remembered other places like the one lying before him, and wondered if he truly would find here what he had long been seeking.

Earth forces had hollowed out the asteroid during the war to take some kind of watch station. Snyder Clamp and his lackeys now occupied it. The man had become wealthy in the Polity by dint of his clothing and accessories brand becoming fashionable to the runcible culture and thus across many worlds. He had become incredibly wealthy because, unlike many designers, he had been able to maintain his position as doyen of that culture over many years. Unfortunately, the wealth had disconnected him from reality, specifically the reality that AI law applied evenly and without favour to all and, if you committed murder, no amount of money could buy you out from under a death sentence. However, wealth, and contacts, had enabled Clamp to run, here to the Graveyard. Now, apparently, he had a bit of a problem. He was dying and, like so many, didn't really want to.

'Doctor on call,' said a voice.

Dr Whip transferred his gaze to one of the three screens below the chainglass window to see a woman gazing at him. He felt something lurch inside him at the sight of her.

'Arabella,' he said, before he could stop himself.

She tilted her head and grinned in precisely the same manner as Arabella once had, then said, 'Nice name, but it's not mine. I'm Susan.' Then her smile quickly faded as if it had found itself in alien territory.

'Of course you are, my dear,' said Whip, quickly re-establishing self-control. And of course she wasn't the woman he had loved, for Arabella was still in that zero freezer in Hercules Station, until the AIs found a way to resurrect her virus-eaten and freeze-damaged brain.

'We've shunted instructions to your ship mind and you're clear to come in now,' said Susan, all business and seriousness, and something else, fear? 'Will you need any help carrying equipment from your ship?'

'Not initially,' replied the doctor.

'Okay, I'll take you straight in to see Snyder.'

Dr Whip noted how her face became grimmer when she mentioned her employer. Was she sad that he was dying? Somehow, he didn't think that the case and, more than anything, he wanted to see her smile again.

The small space dock looked like the balcony to a cliff dwelling. Two autohandlers for vacuum unloading of any cargo were parked to the rear and an airlock tube extruded across the tiled surface to the edge. His ship mind brought his vessel to that edge where it stuck with gecko pads, and the tube closed in to engage with a thump. Dr Whip, meanwhile, headed for the airlock.

She waited for him at the far end of the airlock tube, where the second door opened into the asteroid dwelling. She stood exactly the same height, wore her blond hair in the same cut and had a similar fashion sense to Arabella, which had always been to sling on brightly coloured items of clothing at random and somehow get it right. She even had a touch of glitter on her eyelids. Dr Whip suddenly realised he wasn't breathing, and so started again. He was being foolish.

Arabella's beauty was of a kind anyone could possess: a catalogue number and a fast autodoc procedure with nil recovery time. In the Polity, people changed their faces and their bodies as often as women in antiquity changed their nail varnish. Everything else here – the clothing and the glitter – could be related to how those who chose certain body shapes and faces, generally had the same tastes elsewhere.

She looked him up and down, her expression haunted, then said, 'This way.'

Until that moment, so focused on her had he been, Dr Whip hadn't noticed the security and its bizarre dress. As he stepped after her, two men quickly moved in behind him. He glanced round at them. Physically they were the typical hoodlum's enforcers out here in the Graveyard. Their boosting had resulted in muscle so thick on their reinforced bones they looked incapable of turning their heads or raising their arms above shoulder level. Their thighs rubbed together as they walked with a leaden tread, while their dress was something else besides. They wore black leather harnesses covered with spiky silver studs, their genitals filled pendulous red leather pouches. On their right hips they each carried large antiquated projectile guns, while on their left hips they carried shock sticks. Black leather masks covered their faces, with pink lenses in the eyeholes.

'Interesting attire,' said Dr Whip.

Susan glanced at him and nodded mutely then, as if searching for words she dared not utter, nodded to an item in the corridor ahead. 'Part of the decor.'

The woman in the body cage was dead – Dr Whip sensed this immediately. She had been tortured to death, doubtless dying from an internal bleed when someone had shoved into her stomach one of the numerous serrated spikes now protruding from her body.

The asteroid home was an anteroom of Hell.

As he progressed, screams and cries of ecstasy punctuated the thumping music that seemed the throb of the asteroid's heart. Open double doors revealed a red-lit room filled with naked people in a tangled orgy, more body cages, and more torture. Dr Whip saw a woman in some kind of tank, apparently drowning while a man in breather gear fucked her. He paused for a moment and found himself counting perversions, just before one of the heavies straight-armed him in the back and sent him stumbling into Susan, who had been just about to enter this room. For anyone else, for anyone normal, that shove would have resulted in cracked ribs. Dr Whip glanced back, read the puzzlement in the heavy's pose and moved on in, suddenly feeling tired and peeved, his insides writhing and tugging against each other as if, like a breaking battleship towing cable, they wanted to fly catastrophically apart.

'Perhaps you shouldn't have come?' Susan whispered into his ear.

Yes, it was looking increasingly like that.

Snyder Clamp was as grotesque as his surroundings. He did not need to be so hugely fat or display such diseases on his skin, for even the Graveyard had the medical technology to deal with those. He sat ensconced in a huge ornate throne up on a dais at the centre of the room. A rotating table stood beside him, laden with delicacies. He reached out and speared a large beetle with a two-pronged wooden fork, inserted it into his mouth, and crunched. Dr Whip felt his peevishness transform to contempt as he stepped over writhing bodies. Was this then Snyder Clamp's wonderful fashion sense in action? The diorama here anyone could find in a cheap VR fantasy. Or had Clamp been elegantly *retro* in the silly world of the Polity runcible culture?

'Dr Whip,' Clamp shouted over the din, spitting out pieces of black carapace as he did so. 'You have come to examine me.' He waved a dismissive hand – a beringed one of course – and the music stopped. Much of the activity all around quickly ceased, though some weren't capable of stopping, just like the two in the tank. And some sounds didn't stop, because he heard sobbing, and groans of agony.

'Where are all these people from?' Dr Whip enquired, coming to stand before Clamp, and placing his bag on the ground at his feet.

'They followed me,' said Clamp, 'they are nothing without me.'

'And you kill them?' Dr Whip focused his attention on the corpse of a man nailed to one wall.

'Sometimes – if that's what they want.' The man peered at him with reddened eyes. 'So, Dr Whip. I like your name.'

Just the words were confirmation, and Whip felt a weird division cleaving his thoughts and trying to separate him physically into two parts. He folded his arms across his chest, apparently confident, but in this small fashion trying to hold himself together. Now, on the mental plain he began processing data exponentially as a product of that mental division; dual processing, the two halves of his mind feeding off each other, synergy. He became suddenly larger than his surroundings and knew that his name had been the reason Clamp had summoned him here, for the man was a collector of perversions. But Dr Whip's analysis did not stop there.

The compass of his vision widened and Clamp became transparent to him. He gazed down into the man's cells and noted the changes Clamp had deliberately wrought: the shutdown of life-maintaining nanotechnology so he could suffer numerous STDs, the syphilis eating his brain, the deliberate physiological imbalances resulting in obesity... and then deeper still. The man's mind was falling apart. Now integrating what he found there with earlier research data on the man, Whip saw that Clamp had been a relatively normal businessman until his success, whereupon he became insecure, unable to believe in that success and perpetually having to challenge it. The perversity of his second line in clothing and accessories – a perversity deliberately made to test his own vaunted brilliance – had led to more success, whereupon he had set his course. Perversity led to obscenity and thence to murder as art, and now to deliberate self-destruction. However, Clamp certainly wasn't dying, not yet. Dr Whip reached out through U-space into the man's body with implements that had been no part of him fifty years ago, and which had grown in him. He began reprogramming Clamp's nanosuite to set certain things in motion.

'I have examined you,' Dr Whip intoned.

Clamp had shrunk back into his throne and gaped at him in puzzlement – his damaged brain unable to decide whether it was hallucinating. The girl had moved back and now squatted down by one wall. At Clamp's emergency summons through a control set in the arm of his throne, more security guards ran into the room, while those already here began drawing back. For it had happened again: something of Whip's transformation within had shown itself, and that always badly frightened people. He surveyed those entering the room, weapons drawn, checked the two behind him, but all feared to approach him. He looked down on them, of course, because he grew as much as half a metre on these occasions.

'I can give you the cure you want,' said Dr Whip, 'which is death.'

271

Clamp, through syphilitic befuddlement, managed to regain some composure.

'What about your Hippocratic Oath, where's that?' he asked.

'The same place the Polity AIs put their three laws of robotics,' said Dr Whip. 'Or I can,' he continued, 'cure you of wanting to die.'

'Enough of this,' said Clamp, now sitting upright. He beckoned in his guards. 'Take him out of my sight for now – we will continue this later.'

The guards began to close in just as Dr Whip unfolded his arms, held out one hand and snapped his fingers, the sound dry and unnaturally loud in the room. One of the guards went down as if the doctor had cut his strings. All theatre, because with something else entirely Dr Whip reached out to press this nerve nexus or that, to squeeze this or that gland or constrict various arteries. He snapped again and the rest of the guards fell. He snapped a third time, the pulse spreading out, all the people but he and Clamp slumping into unconsciousness. The constant background din faded and stillness settled.

Dr Whip strode across the room, meanwhile surveying the asteroid population on many different levels. Upon reaching the tank, he put his fist through the side, shattering armoured glass. The water inside rushed out, spilling the two bodies on the floor. He turned over the woman and rested a pale hand between her breasts, tweaking certain nerves and muscles. Her chest contracted to eject a stream of water, and she coughed and hacked as he turned her on her side, then she began breathing evenly.

'Now, to the matter of payment,' he said, as he stood up.

'Payment?' Clamp repeated, staring in disbelief at the prostrate forms all around him. He had begun to think more clearly now, and the befuddlement had gone from his expression. His internal nanomachines were getting back to work, issuing emergency drug packages and now beginning to make repairs inside his brain, rapidly wiping out the ills he had allowed himself to suffer. Clamp now possessed enough comprehension of his surroundings to know fear.

'I was informed that in return for my services I would be given the location of Penny Royal's planetoid,' Whip replied. 'I want that payment now, before I complete my work.'

'Complete –'

'I'll get it for you,' said a voice from one side.

Whip turned to gaze at Susan. He must have made some unconscious decision to leave her out, for how else had she not joined the prostrate forms all around her? He gazed at her harder, found her to be entirely human – too easily human, too generic. She would bear closer inspection, but later.

'It?' he enquired.

'The object in which the changing coordinates of Penny Royal's wanderer planetoid are recorded,' she replied.

He nodded once, gravely. 'I will of course need to check it.' As she swiftly exited the room, he turned back to Clamp.

'Your mind is clearing now,' he said, 'but still you have the problem you had before, which is a mental one and nothing to do with the physical ills you have allowed yourself to suffer. I always find, on these occasions, that self-knowledge is the cure.'

Somewhere inside this man, there might have been an earlier Clamp, a version undistorted by perversion but, as Dr Whip had discovered on other occasions, those versions were often amoral and when exposed to the sins of their older selves reacted with indifference. The key, he found, was empathy. It was the cure Clamp required but, whether or not he could survive it, was moot.

Dr Whip made the man the utter focus of his divided mind, again probing deep inside him on a cellular level. Even now, he did not fully understand the toolkit Penny Royal had provided. He used radiations across the emitted spectrum, and he reached through U-space with complex force-field technology. He read the pattern of Clamp's mind, the mechanisms of thought and action, the governors of behaviour and the building blocks of morality, and from the patterns of neural firings read the man's thoughts and traced out the shape of his internal being. In moments like this, Dr Whip knew he functioned at the level of a forensic AI, and utilised the tools such beings carried about inside their bodies. In moments, he began plotting the solution to Clamp: instructions to his internal nanomachines to issue certain neuro-chemicals, targeted electro-magnetic pulses to seize synaptic firings and make the whole fall into a new pattern, along with the deliberate destruction of certain neural structures. Initiating these changes, Dr Whip strode forwards, reached out with one pale hand as Clamp shrank back, and touched the palm of that hand to the man's forehead. Clamp shuddered as if electrocuted, then slumped. Dr Whip stood back.

Enough.

Now the time had come for him to pull back from the precipice. He reached up to pass a numb hand over his forehead, feeling the line of division there, leading up into his scalp, then down his nose to his chin, splitting his lips, which even now were bloody. He touched inside his mouth and felt it there, then gazed down at his Barnard suit, seeing the line, the indentation, spiralling round his torso to his groin. The division was not only mental but physical, as if the stress of using his powers to their fullest extent might split him in two but, as yet, he had not gone so far.

He fought to pull his mind back together and, as he did so, felt himself contracting, shrinking. The world became duller as he closed other eyes and felt himself locking back together. The indentations began to fade but never went away completely; always the process had *advanced.*

'What have you done to him?'

Dr Whip turned, all at once coming back to himself. 'I've cured him.'

She smiled a smile that wasn't Arabella's but her own, and not bad for all that.

'But not perhaps the cure he wanted,' she suggested.

'Perhaps not,' he replied, now focusing on the object she grasped as she approached. She held out the fossilised spiral shell of an ammonite formed of some hard black rock inlaid with the fool's gold of iron pyrites.

'The coordinates are recorded in one of the pyrite crystals,' she said. 'There is a microport for access at the centre of the spiral.'

He would have to take it back to his ship to check, he decided, and began heading there. She fell in beside him and they walked out to the airlock in companionable silence until she said, 'Take me with you. Take me away from here.'

'It will change here,' he said. 'Clamp will not be able to continue as he did before even if he is able to continue at all.' He paused contemplatively to listen to groans and curses issuing from a room over to one side. 'His grip on these people will fail, at which point they will either leave or turn on him. It's over.'

'Nevertheless,' she said.

Just then, a raw scream issued from behind as Clamp regained consciousness. He now had an empathic understanding of all his previous actions, and resultant guilt. Another scream followed, and thereafter they continued with machinelike regularity. Dr Whip, meanwhile, gazed at Susan with more than just his eyes. The guise of humanity had slid away like old skin revealing something bright.

'He never knew,' he said.

'He never knew what?' she asked innocently.

'That you are as unhuman as I.'

'No, he didn't.' She smiled sadly. 'Nor did he know that the cures you sometimes provide are like the gifts of a certain black AI.'

That froze him. He knew this about himself but rarely acknowledged it. Yes, he healed even those who turned against him, but often his healing became a curse. Penny Royal had made him in its own image.

'You still haven't answered my question,' she said

He nodded once solemnly. 'Yes, you can come.'

He could not run from the Polity forever so might as well allow one of its representatives to accompany him. It didn't matter. He liked her form and its associations and even she could not change his course now.

He weighed the fossil in his hand, and turned towards the airlock.

He could gaze at and into Susan with a clarity and precision beyond human and, on these occasions, equated his abilities to that of a haiman – one of those people who had taken augmentation to the cyborg limit beyond which flesh fails. This level still lay some way below what he had attained while looking into Snyder Clamp and altering him, yet he felt that he might need the next level, because there was something about Susan.

He could trace with utter precision the curves and angles of her ceramal skeleton, he could measure the torques of her joint motors and read their design codes, map her artificial nervous system and gaze somewhat into the processes of the AI crystal residing in her chest, but this was not the entirety of her, for something else lay underneath. She was Golem, yes, but her metal bones contained a marrow of further AI crystal, nanotech packed her body, some of which formed nodes scattered throughout whose complexity he could not plumb, and which occasionally emitted energy signatures indicative of U-space processes, just like the U-space transmitter inside her skull, and just like the tech inside him.

'So where are we going now?' she asked, as she watched him plug a hair-thin optic into the microport of the ammonite fossil.

'Do you need to ask?' he wondered.

As his ship detached from the dock inside Clamp's hollow asteroid, he cast his vision back into that place. The occupants were beginning to wake from their long nightmare, now the core of the madness no longer fed them. Snyder Clamp had ceased to scream and sat on the floor at the foot of his throne, one of those antique pistols resting in his lap. Three times, thus far, he had placed the barrel of the weapon in his mouth, tasted metal death, and three times removed it. Dr Whip sensed that the man did not have the courage to kill himself and would try to make some form of restitution, and in the end that would drive him back to the Polity.

'It's a deeper question than one about your travel plans, Aster,' said Susan.

He gazed at her, Clamp fading from his compass as his ship accelerated under fusion drive out from the asteroid. She sat in the high chair he usually occupied while working in here.

'No one has called me that in a long while,' he observed.

'Aster Whipple,' she said, 'but shortly after you arrived in the Graveyard you dispensed with your forename and insisted on shortening your surname. Why did you do that?'

The pyrite crystal inside the ammonite fossil began spilling its data. Dr Whip studied a screen, noting the course of Penny Royal's home, the wanderer planetoid, mapped out for the next two thousand years. With his extraordinary vision, he gazed into the ammonite itself. There he found chunks of code like fragments of memcordings, time-crystal loops, strange and nightmarish images. He withdrew, because he had what he wanted now.

'I will answer that question when you tell me why you bear the appearance of a woman I loved,' he said.

'Surely that's obvious?'

Dr Whip nodded gravely. 'So that I would say "yes" when you asked to accompany me.' He paused for a moment then continued, 'Did you insert yourself in Clamp's retinue after he transmitted his request for my services?'

'Of course not.'

Again he nodded. 'You inserted yourself there beforehand and persuaded him to ask for me. Did he possess this?' Dr Whip gestured towards the fossil, then continued before Susan could reply, 'He didn't – you brought it with you. Why did you choose him?'

'Because once in his presence I knew you would be unable to resist him.'

'And?'

'And then I could obtain a better view of what you are becoming.'

'And what is that?'

'The utter apex of your profession, a healer without parallel, and a physical though mistaken representation of that same profession.'

Just then, his ship mind sent them on course towards the coordinates he had given it and, with a wrench that seemed to distort the bedrock of the universe, they dropped into U-space.

'Who are you?' Dr Whip asked.

'You know part of me very well,' Susan replied. 'And you found the remains of the rest.'

'Explain,' Dr Whip instructed.

Trying to resurrect someone who had died from a flesh-eating virus that delighted in dining on nerve tissue, and who had then been flash frozen and thus received more damage in that process, was an immense and arguably pointless task. Only fragments of the original mind could be extracted from the cerebral mush and to weave them into a coherent whole might result in a viable human being, but it would not be the one who had died. Only three people had thus been recovered from Hercules Station, and two were those who had entered the zero freezer before the virus had reached their brains. The third was a special case.

Susan Epsilon 02 had her personal motive for pushing for the resurrection of this individual. Earth Central had employed her to investigate Penny Royal's atrocity aboard that station because of it. Her previous iteration had been the AI originally sent, along with the Polity medical team, to investigate the incident. Susan Epsilon 01 had been the forensic AI Penny Royal had torn apart and whose pieces Dr Whipple had found.

Susan had taken the body of Arabella Cotisian from a zero freezer and set to work measuring and coding her wrecked mind even down to the quantum states of the atoms forming it. She put together perhaps ten per cent of the original human being, then set about weaving the rest. Research was required. Every scrap of data pertaining to Cotisian went into the weave: her journals, her network profiles, all recorded data from the time she had an aug and until she had it removed, second- and third-hand knowledge of her, family history, genetics, medical history – everything. Of course this could not all be simply lumped together with the expectation of a complete human being resulting. Susan had to translate it and fit it into the skeletal mind she was moulding. She had to make decisions about what to discard and what to retain. Human memory, with its inaccuracy and distorting effects, she had to account for. The task was immense, even for a forensic AI, and when the observer forensic AIs realised this task had engulfed the one performing it, the process was too advanced to stop.

'Arabella is now an integral part of me,' said Susan. 'As I maintain her so she maintains me. We are mental Siamese twins permanently locked together. To separate us would result in one of us dying. We, or rather I, decided to accept the meld, for we have work to do, and a mission to complete.'

Dr Whip knew with absolute certainty the truth of this story, because Susan had used more than just words to convey it, had in fact taken him into the lengthy processes involved. He felt both humbled and disappointed – the first because the complexity of what Susan had done was so utterly impressive, the second because having seen it, up close, and come to know the mind of the woman he had loved so intimately, he could no longer love her. She had become to him the product of nature and nurture; a complex but wholly predestined biological machine. She was data.

'One hour,' he said.

It had taken five days for him to obtain the whole story and now they were just one hour away from arriving at the coordinates from within that fossil. It seemed obvious Susan deliberately edited said story to use up the time their journey would take. Had she, obviously knowing things about him that he did not know, deliberately limited the time he had to ask questions?

'Did you love me?' he asked accepting that the amalgamated being before him was partly the woman he had loved.

'No, I did not,' she replied, 'but I love you now.'

Just one question and one answer left him mute until they surfaced from U-space within sensor range of the wanderer planetoid – home of the black AI Penny Royal.

A prador dreadnought hung out there in vacuum. It resembled the rounded carapace of a terran crab, fashioned of brassy metal, its guts ripped out and strewn across a hundred thousand miles. Focusing on some of the debris, Whip saw creatures like some mix of wolf spiders and fiddler crabs, but large and armoured. These were prador first-children and second-children, but showed no signs of life.

'I wonder what happened,' Dr Whip said, speaking at last.

Susan had, annoyingly, taken the only seat on the bridge, and sat with her knees clutched to her chest like some shivering waif.

'It's not just humans who have their dealings with Penny Royal, Aster, but the prador too.' Susan paused, and Dr Whip sensed the energy signatures of her internal nanotech ramping up. 'A deal turned sour and arrogant prador coming here to exact vengeance on the entity they had tried to cheat. That planetoid contains some serious weaponry, and it is best not to go there without invitation.'

She waved a hand at the console, and a new image resolved in the laminate of the chainglass screen. Now they gazed upon the planetoid itself, cold and dead and no more sinister than a trillion others of its kind strewn across the galaxy.

She turned to gaze at him. 'And we won't be receiving an invitation.'

Now he reached out, groping, searching through the strata of the universe, locally, across debris and the whispers of dying computing to a hot intense point where strange machines seemed to be twisting reality. The mechanisms of the planetoid were there, as active and dangerous as a fleet of battleships. They contained intelligence, of a kind, but as adjuncts to a centre – layers of computing about an absent core.

'Penny Royal isn't home,' he stated, disappointment hanging inside him like a lead hook.

'No, it isn't,' Susan agreed.

Dr Whip stepped back and leant his weight against one of the side consoles, certainly disappointed yet, somehow, relieved.

'You've been chasing rumour, following up on sightings, talking to those who have had personal encounters and always, it seems, Penny Royal has stayed beyond your grasp,' said Susan. 'Could it be that in your heart the search is all, and that you don't want to find that AI?'

'Nonsense,' said Dr Whip, suddenly intensely uncomfortable.

'So why is it that you haven't decided what you will do when you finally stand before Penny Royal?' Her chair swung round seemingly of its own accord to face him. 'You have healed people, your steady transformation making you increasingly adept at doing so, yet vaguely you search for the AI that wrought its changes in you and vaguely have some expectation of that encounter.'

'It would be pointless to ask how you know my mind so well,' said Dr Whip.

'I have examined it very closely, which is why I love you.' She blinked at him, slowly. 'So what will you do?'

'It isn't human love,' Dr Whip procrastinated.

'How could it be? Do you see any humans here?'

'Admittedly not.'

'What are you going to do, Aster?'

Under the intensity of her gaze, the vague need in him for some resolution, some explanation, something from Penny Royal, clarified in his mind. Of course, it should have been obvious to him right from the beginning – the perfect story arc and conclusion. He knew precisely where he fitted now, and knew precisely what he would do.

'I am going to heal Penny Royal,' he stated.

'Then it's time.'

Without any orders from Dr Whip, his ship dropped into U-space, coordinates set, destination as inevitable as fate.

The world was hot, an oven of a place where humans survived only at the poles, and even then spent most of their lives in hotsuits or inside insulated houses. Susan stood out amidst them, clad in her usual colourful attire, with the addition of sunglasses, seemingly enjoying the sunshine and a winter temperature in the low sixties. But the looks she received weren't because as a Golem the temperature was irrelevant to her, but because Golem were generally loyal to the Polity the people here did not trust.

Dr Whip thought the street looked like something transplanted from a Mediterranean preserve, only the houses weren't white-washed but built of reflective white and highly insulating foamstone. The vines growing up over pergolas were genetically adapted bougainvillea, and an alien plant sporting blue leaves and nodular black peppercorns favoured in some cuisines, but only after the chemical treatments rendered their lethal poisons inert. Meanwhile the gardens, with their stunning arrays of colour, were protected by shimmershields.

'Do they all know, or just the ruling families?' Dr Whip asked, gesturing to the people thronging the street.

'They have all been warned in a general broadcast,' Susan replied, 'and the AIs in the ships above have offered assistance should they require it. However, it seems Penny Royal's interest is in the ruins at the equator, so is no immediate *physical* threat to them.'

'I would have expected the Polity to do something, despite the situation here.'

Susan shook her head. 'My kind take matters of jurisdiction very seriously. They have offered to land at the equator to seize Penny Royal, but that is precisely where the people here don't want them.'

'Because of the ruins.'

'Because of the ruins,' Susan agreed.

It was an odd situation, Dr Whip felt. Though the people of this world lived at the poles, the source of their wealth lay at the equator, scattered across a flat island sitting at the centre of a boiling ocean. One of the three known but extinct alien races had once lived here – the Jain. Apparently, evidence existed proving they had moved this world in the process of transforming it to their preferred environment, which was hot, wet, and with an atmospheric pressure twice that of Earth's. On that island, the locals had found Jain tech artefacts that commanded fortunes in the Polity, because they were dangerous and because the AIs did not want them to fall into the wrong hands. Trade was good here and fortunes being made, however, the people felt sure that the AIs intended to subsume their world into the Polity and take control of the equatorial excavations. In fact, the ruling family already believed that Penny Royal's presence here was some sort of ruse towards that end.

'Here we are,' said Susan, as they turned a corner into another street. This led straight down to a harbour, the cluttered scene of loading docks and huge barges, cranes, jet foils and grav rafts seeming to shrink into insignificance before the wide hot vermillion ocean below the pink sky.

'That?' As they walked down, Dr Whip pointed towards a huge grav-raft settled on the waves, where armed personnel in brown hotsuits incorporating dish-like helmets were loading equipment.

'Indeed.'

Of course, the inhabitants could not simply ignore the presence of a rogue AI at their excavations and, while they did not want Polity intervention, they had to do something. The ruling family was dispatching a military force along with some serious firepower to oust Penny Royal. Dr Whip felt a degree of pity for them, remembering that gutted prador dreadnought out by the black AI's planetoid. Meanwhile, after some negotiation, the rulers here had allowed Polity observers to accompany this mission. Susan and Dr Whip were those observers.

As they drew closer to the dock a woman approached them, trailing two subordinates. She was clad in a chameleoncloth hotsuit made distinct from those the others wore by blue armbands, epaulets and, rather than one of those dish helmets, which rather reminded Dr Whip of the kind of headwear worn during World War I on Earth, a flat peaked cap incorporated into her suit. On her breast, she also had a patch of chameleoncloth rolled and clipped back to reveal a small display of what appeared to be military decorations.

'MC Severax,' she said brusquely as she came to stand before them, gloved hands on her hips. 'You're the Polity observers.'

'Pleased to meet you,' said Susan, holding out an ignored hand.

Mission Commander Severax gazed at each of them in turn, then said, 'Neither of you is human.'

'That is so.' Susan lowered her hand.

'Our agreement specified two observers and only one of them could be an artificial intelligence,' said Severax.

'My intelligence is not artificial,' said Dr Whip.

'But you don't require a hotsuit.'

'My body has undergone certain —'

'MC Severax,' Susan interrupted, 'allow me to introduce Dr Whip.'

Whip felt glad not to have to continue with his explanation. Severax meanwhile fell silent and stared at him intently, her hands now down at her sides and her mouth falling open. He probed her gently and realised she had just received some kind of shock. He sensed excitement in her, whereupon she abruptly closed her mouth and raised a gloved hand to gesture at the vessel behind.

'You can wait for me in the wheelhouse,' she said. 'We'll be done loading in half an hour.' She turned abruptly and marched off, her two subordinates casting glances behind as they followed her.

'You underestimate your own fame, Doctor,' said Susan, leading the way to one of the gangplanks stretching from the dock to the grav-raft. 'There aren't many people this close to the Graveyard who don't know who you are and, of those military personnel who know you, there aren't any who would not be glad to have you along on a mission.'

'Really?'

'Really, and especially a mission like this one, which even MC Severax realises is very unlikely to succeed and will very likely result in heavy casualties.'

'Why then are they going?' he asked as they walked along the deck of the raft towards the fore.

'It's a gesture,' Susan replied. 'They have to assert their authority here and make some response to Penny Royal, even if that response is likely to fail.'

'Stupid.'

'Yes.'

Serpents swam in the boiling water, long glassy things with paddle limbs like swan feathers and heads out of Chinese dragon fantasies. A large shoal of them accompanied the small armada for a little while on the way out, then mostly seemed to lose interest. Some remained, however, and these Dr Whip probed and studied. Their insides were fascinating and, obviously, a modification from some form evolved for colder waters. Were these too a product of the Jain? No, searching his massive data store Dr Whip came up with the answer. They were an import a mere forty years old from a similarly hot world within the Polity where geneticists had patched them together from the Terran DNA of seahorses and the alien code of a native creature of that world.

'So what's the plan?' asked Susan.

MC Severax stood in a steering lectern, her hand down on a palm control. She glanced at Susan and seemed disinclined to reply, but when the Whip turned to face her, she did.

'We've transmitted first requests and then demands to Penny Royal that it leave our world. We sent these in every way we could. We even sent a sub-AI drone,' she replied.

'What happened to it?' asked Whip quickly, leaving Susan's next question stillborn.

'It came back,' said Severax. 'It was no longer sub-AI and it screamed as it dismantled itself in the Senate.'

'The plan?' Susan pushed.

Severax glanced at her in irritation. 'We fired a missile too – five kiloton warhead.'

'And that came back?' Susan asked.

'It flew straight into the Senate building and settled on the senate floor.' She shook her head angrily. 'The area has been evacuated – no one dares touch the damned thing.'

Whip's attention strayed to the other vessels accompanying this big grav-raft. He could feel the multiple lives inside and counted just over a thousand heavily-armed troops. Other vessels contained mosquito autoguns but, surprisingly, not much in the way of large ordnance.

'No further missiles to be fired,' he stated.

'No,' said Severax.

'Because they might be sent back armed this time?'

Severax stiffened. 'There's that, and Penny Royal's present location. The AI was out on the sifting plain when we fired the first missile. It's now in the ruins.'

Whip sensed her resentment. She was a military commander already hamstrung before going into battle.

'We go in by land,' she continued. 'Then we blow the shit out of Penny Royal.' She turned to Susan. 'That's the plan.'

Had their vessels been conventional boats and not grav-craft, landfall would have been a problem, Dr Whip saw. The coastline was a stone wave – a five-metre high cliff made concave by the attrition of the sea and rounded elsewhere by erosion. As they approached, the grav-barge heaved underneath them and rose out of the sea to bring more of the landscape ahead into view. A flat plain of rock and orange dirt lay beyond the shore – that mentioned sifting plain – but only for a mile or so for it ended against a forest. The trees, like massive asparagus sprouts, stood widely spaced. Very quickly, the armada reached this, then it slowed and all its vessels began to drop to the ground.

'Why not go over the top of those trees?' Dr Whip asked as they disembarked.

'Nowhere to land on the other side,' replied Severax. She gestured towards the forest. 'The ruins are in the middle of this lot.'

'An attack from the air, then?' he suggested.

'No, our tacticians feel that the systems of our transports will be too easy for Penny Royal to seize control of.'

Whip glanced at Susan, who shook her head. Implicit in that statement was the simple reality that the black AI could probably seize control of any computer system these people possessed. They were going up against it poorly armed, poorly prepared and with unreliable technology. This gesture warfare would be costly for those now disembarking from the surrounding craft. As Severax stepped down from her podium and headed for the exit he plodded along behind her, remembering the last time he'd been in a similar situation. It had been a fight between two salvage organisations inside an old prador ground base. They had been inside what they were fighting for, so did not use highly destructive weapons, and the gunplay had devolved into hand-to-hand combat. Whip, employed by one side, had helped who he could, but many died before he could reach them.

'How many of your people have memplants?' he asked.

Severax glanced round at him as her staff approached. She reached up and touched a small red patch on her hotsuit on her left shoulder.

'About half,' she said.

Whip nodded and then placed his doctor's bag on the ground as a row of chrome-shiny mosquito guns marched past him. He opened it and gazed at the contents for a moment, shook his head then allowed his senses to range. In a moment, he picked up the memplants many of the soldiers contained. If these were badly injured, he would merely shut down their consciousness so they did not suffer. The others, however, would be a big problem. Yes, he could deal with many injuries, but they were not his major hurdle, because here that was the heat. The moment a projectile or energy weapons hit any of these people, their hotsuits would be open, thus exposing them to oven temperatures.

Whip pressed a tab in the bag and watched a small console fold out, then, with a sour smile, pressed the tab again and watched it fold back. He had not needed to program the thing manually in twenty years. Next, he reached into the bag's system with his mind and selected what he required. The microbots he chose sported numerous spider-like spinnerets and where generally used on victims of fire – quickly knitting a temporary layer of artificial skin over burns. Just a few tweaks resulted in a tougher more heat-resistant skin. He set the bots to multiplying in two spray containers then took them out of the bag.

'Here,' he said, tossing one to Susan.

She had been facing away, but snapped round and caught the thing with ease.

'They do have suit repair kits,' she said.

'I know, but some of the damage might be extensive.'

MC Severax now moved off with her command staff, but others were approaching. Their hotsuits were brown like the rest, but also bore light blue stripes. He recognised a badge on the right breast of each of these: a caduceus, but again the wrong one. Dr Whip felt a flash of annoyance, then shivered – the hint of some knowledge just evading his grasp.

'Dr Volger,' said an individual stepping out from this new group. 'It's a pleasure to meet you.' He held out a gloved hand.

Dr Whip stood up and shook that hand.

'They're moving in now,' said Susan.

Whip looked over and saw this was indeed the case. Mosquito autoguns had formed a line and strode into the trees, the scattered troops moving in behind. After these floated ordnance-loaded grav-sleds the medics would no doubt later utilize for casualties.

'You'll be joining us I hope?' Volger asked, gesturing to the rest of the medics.

'I presume you'll be spreading out amidst the troops,' said Whip.

'Of course,' said Volger, irritated, worried. That Whip would stay with a group of medics had not really been the man's question.

'I'll do what I can,' said Whip.

He squatted down again, closed his bag and took it up. Without a backward glance, he strode towards the troops, now reaching out to them with his extraordinary senses. The greatest concentration of those without memplants advanced on the right wing, so he headed there. Soon he walked amidst them, troops glancing at him, some smiling, others just frightened. He moved on, aware of Susan falling in to one side of him and one of the medics on his other side.

'Do you feel it?' Susan asked.

Ranging out further, his body seeming to uncoil and certainly growing taller, he touched the minds and bodies of lizard gibbons in the trees, gelid flatworms and burrowing hot-form mole rats. Beyond a certain point, it seemed the whole forest had slid into some abyss. The minds of the creatures there were not functioning right; their behaviour twisted into shapes they could not hope to survive. Seething giggling madness lay in the abyss, but with the eyes of the animals Whip saw through the metaphorical darkness and through the forest in glassy overlay to the ruins.

And to Penny Royal.

Trees were stunted and gnarled about the ruins – a grid of low walls laid out in conjoined triangles. Upturned slabs and snapped-off twisted spires were scattered amidst these. A translucent brown substance formed the walls and slabs, all their edges sharp and un-eroded despite having sat here for millions of years. The spires were metallic – like marcasite. At the centre a black flower had sprouted. It rose on a stem of twisted silver threads spreading petals like black sword blades. It was swaying slightly as if in some unfelt breeze and, on a level beyond hearing, Whip sensed a strange singing.

From his studies of the rogue AI, Whip knew this to be just one of the many forms it could take. Those black crystalline blades could reshape themselves at the nanoscopic level to become shorter, longer, spikes or rods. The silver threads could thin down to invisibility and spread like cobwebs through the air. The whole thing could separate and turn itself into a swarm entity.

Stepping among the trees now, Whip studied a nearby soldier. Clad in a brown hotsuit, the man lugged a pack with dangling feed-lines to his weapon. Whip recognised a coilgun powered by a U-charger in the pack, ammunition also fed from there. He was big, muscular and almost certainly boosted. A number of men armed likewise were scattered along the line, but most of the rest were conventional soldiers sporting pulse rifles or squat missile launchers. Ahead, the mosquitos carefully picked their way between the trees, alert for any attack. Whip wondered what their programming might be – how they would recognise the enemy.

A hundred metres into the trees and Whip sensed a change ahead. Penny Royal had stopped singing. Gazing through multiple eyes and his U-space extended sensorium, Whip saw that the AI had stopped swaying too, and now its blade petals shifted as if in agitation. The thrum of pulse-gun fire impinged and Whip dropped down into a squat, all his senses now local. Over to the left a trooper flew backwards in a cloud of blood spray, smoke and pieces of his own body and equipment.

'What the hell?' said the medic.

'Get down!' Whip instructed.

Too late. Pulse gun hits snatched the man from his feet and tumbled him backwards. He hit the ground and bounced with one side of his chest and one arm ripped away. He shuddered for just a second and then lay still, but for the smoke and steam rising from his body. Whip ignored him – he was already dead and possessed a memplant. Over to their right the soldier with the coilgun opened fire and something silvery exploded ahead with the sound of shattering glass.

'It's taken control of the mosquitos,' said Susan, from where she squatted down behind one of the trees. 'I'll see what I can do.' Her eyes had gone glassy – the pupils no longer visible – and her skin had turned metallic. Whip briefly scanned her, recognizing the power surge through her bones. She was going full AI to combat Penny Royal in the territory of the mosquito gun's computing. He knew, with utter certainty, she would fail.

He left her and moved on as gunfire and explosions erupted all around him. The air filled with smoke, steam and screams. Splinters of wood rained down, mixed with the twisted shrapnel from broken machines. Gobbets of flesh too. Noting a splash of blood on a tree, he tracked its course down to a body lying half-covered in the churned ground. While scanning deeply, he dragged the man out. The man screamed, and Whip just reached in and switched of his consciousness. Steam gusted from a ripped-open suit, and blood welled from holes stitched down his side. Heart undamaged, lungs and liver holed, a kidney turned to mush. The wounds looked as if blades had made them. A military nanosuite worked to preserve the man's life by staunching the bleeding, but not fast enough. Whip pulled two sprays from his doctor's bag, first covering the wounds with surgical glue, then spraying on the hotsuit material spray – the bots swiftly knitting both his skin and his suit closed. Whip meanwhile connected to the man's nanosuite and adjusted it outside its usual parameters, cybernetic clotting agents flooding the blood, briefly enough to stop the bleeding, then back into parameters. Clots in places other than the wounds would result in tissue necrosis, but that would not kill him as fast as bleeding out would.

Whip stood and moved on, felt something slam into his upper arm and dodged round behind a tree. He tracked an object behind him and saw a black blade swing round through the air, hover for a moment as if inspecting him, then flash away. Others passed overhead – a shoal of obsidian fish. Penny Royal had taken on one of its many forms – that of a swarm robot – and had moved out to face its attackers. Almost without thinking, he flexed muscles in impossible ways to draw his wound closed. His Barnard suit material then closed over it too, and, in a moment, the damaged tissue drained away. Did Penny Royal recognise him? Almost certainly. Did it think him a threat? No it did not, but nor did it think the soldiers here a threat either, for it was just playing its bloody games with them. Whip grimaced and glanced over at a nearby trooper, it seemed from some height. The man stared up at him in terror, then just turned and ran. This was good – it was what they should all do.

Two people down now: one whose leg below the knee was burned ruin, one pulse-shot through the heart. The first victim's hotsuit had reacted by closing a tourniquet above the knee, but still he writhed in pain as the exposed flesh below steamed. Whip touched his forehead and switched off his mind. As the man slumped, Whip turned to the woman. Her chest smouldered and bled, so Whip sprayed the glue then reached in with force-field fingers drawn fine and thin, hot-pinched arteries closed, plugged veins, then drew tubing from his bag. He then penetrated the nanosuites of each victim in preparation to align their immune responses, as he plugged into her carotids and into the arteries in the man's legs, sealing split suit behind. He paused, seeing something odd about the suites: they were already functioning outside of their usual parameters. This required examination, but first the two lives here. He adjusted immune systems so that neither would eject the other. Now her brain would remain functional bathed in his blood. She would lose much of her body but she would survive.

Squatting by the two, he next went deep and felt a further wrench of his body uncoiling and his mind dividing. Examining the suites from two different perspectives, he bounced scenarios between his two halves – synergistic computing. He saw that nanomachines were interfering with their bodies' thermostats and gathering about certain neural nexuses in their brains. Was this military, to kill their fear? No, the alterations would make them feel hot and claustrophobic, irrationally fearful and impulsive. He knew what was being done and who was doing it, especially when he tried to change the programming and slid off it as if off an icy rock and, even as he stood, he heard shrieking all around.

'MC Severax, withdraw your troops or they will die,' he said, his penetration of military coms not requiring the coms unit she had provided.

'What the hell?' she exclaimed.

He was in her in a moment, feeling her struggling to tear open her hotsuit. Others were doing the same. He had no time for explanations and the time for that retreat had run out. His steady work through the surrounding victims had been like a warm up. His examination of what Penny Royal had done to their nanosuites had raised him to a state way above that he had reached with Snyder Clamp, and he reached out with all his power, and knocked out a thousand human minds. All around him, throughout the forest, the soldiers dropped like unstrung puppets. Whip next moved from victim to victim, closing suits, spraying new material. And it seemed, as he darted fast between the trees, Whip was weaving in towards the largest victim of all. Bent over a woman who had lost half her face, moulding a reactive dressing there while adjusting her nanosuite to kill the cerebral swelling in a brain partially parboiled, he looked up as smoke cleared and saw he had drawn close to the centre, and that Penny Royal had returned. Now was his time.

Stepping over the glassy remains of walls over five million years old, he moved towards the AI. Incidentally, he reached out to remaining victims scattered about the battlefield, reading their injuries through their nanosuites, ignoring them if they were memplanted, adjusting and optimising the rest, healing them even as a great shoal of black spines swirled like a bait ball ahead of him, then abruptly aligned and faced towards him.

'You made me for this,' he said aloud.

He sensed agreement, and then he sensed a tentative probing behind him and began to relinquish his hold on the fallen soldiers.

'I have them,' said Susan.

She was at his back, taking the load. In overview he saw her controlling robots and bringing them in to collect up the casualties, and now she too was moving from victim to victim to do what she could to help them. He knew he could do more, but he also understood that to prevent more victims like those around him he needed to heal what lay ahead. He rounded a charred tree – just a blackened spike of wood surprisingly upright in this ruination. As he released the soldiers, he felt his touch winding back in like tentacles and his power concentrating. He stood a metre taller now and thin, so thin. Glancing down at his body, he saw the changes there more pronounced. The musculature of an ectomorphic high jumper twisted into a strange thick braid. Releasing the last soldier, his power peaked and now he reached forward with all of himself, into the AI.

At once Whip found a mind shattered into pieces at war with each other. He touched one and found himself rolled in a wave of hostility, malevolence and hatred. The force of it in his mind translated into a pulse of hardfield energy in the air, slamming him back against the burned tree. Three spines shot towards him, stabbing into his body and nailing him to the tree, but there was no pain. As the madness of that mind fragment grabbed him, he had little thought to spare for self-examination, but enough to see that the spines had pinned him through the lines of division deepening in his body.

Finally, he managed to free himself from the hating part of the AI's mind even as he absorbed its source in the past. Penny Royal had been a destroyer AI gifted with emotions and empathy and ordered to murder. He saw the ship poised over Polity military forces on the surface of a world. He saw them burning in particle beam fire, he saw the CTD explosions turning them into radioactive ash. He felt the AI appalled but unable to disobey its orders, and was appalled himself as he slid to another fragment of its mind. Here he found rationality and understanding, but the immensity of it terrified him. He tried to focus just on the memories. The prador enemy surrounded the eight thousand troops and, in this case, their death was preferable to capture. How could that be? He grabbed another fragment and tried to meld the two together, to heal the wound. Crazy laughter echoed. Dropping straight into his mind were the memories of a man, caught by the prador, a thrall unit installed in his skull without anaesthetic, and the horror of his ensuing life. This is what would have happened to the troops. And this wasn't just amusing; it was hilarious.

The complete disparity in fact, the cognitive dissonance tried to cast him out. He realised he needed to encompass all the fragments before him, and, for this, he needed greater synergy. He expanded himself, and widened the break in his dividing mind as he reached out to every fragment, each one greater than a multitude of human minds. Agony coursed through him from head to foot, while he heard an awful tearing sound – his very being pulling apart. His natural vision had blurred into two. He tilted his head to look down at himself and felt just half of his head tilting. The bright green and red scales of his Barnard suit gleamed as the coils of his body parted. One of his boots fell to the ground, which seemed further away now, and his foot extended into a tail. He could not see the other because it lay out of sight behind the tree yet, he knew, that with the other half of his head he could turn there to see it. Instead, he pulled further apart and gazed into his own eyes. They were golden with slot pupils. He possessed two of them on each half of his head – the new ones revealed in the split on either side. His half mouth swung round, the heads reforming and equalizing.

The heads of snakes.

Synergy.

Half to half gazing into his own eyes; mind to mind ramping up the power reaching out to the fragmented mind, now swirling around him, a shoal of black blades. Behind he could feel Susan, a weak cup around his consciousness, trying to catch him. And in Penny Royal the amusement grew in some fragments and gained ascendancy. He understood that his own division reflected in microcosm what had happened to the AI. He peered into his divided self to see how he could reunite it, and saw that he could not, nor could he heal the thing swirling around him.

I have failed, he thought.

You did not, came the multiply echoing reply.

292

He had always wanted to be the best, and *iconic*, and he had sensed right from the beginning that Penny Royal had moulded him to that end but, as ever with gifts from that AI, to a poisonous and grotesquely artistic end.

The shoal swarmed out before him, satisfied with its work here. All the blades and spines slammed together into a great black sea urchin form even as something massive appeared in the sky above, casting them in shadow. Penny Royal disappeared with a deep thump as air rushed in to occupy the space it had occupied. Impossibly, it had jumped through U-space from the surface of a world. Whip now focused his doubled and intense vision upon the woman who moved round to look up at him. He studied Susan's being with such ease. As a combination of forensic AI and the remains of a human being, she was so much less complicated than the thing he had just faced. He saw that he could separate them, if he so wished, if he had any purpose in doing so.

'We hoped you were the mechanism Penny Royal created to heal itself,' she said.

He tried to reply, but only hissed.

'But again, as with so many others, you are just the product of a grotesque sense of humour and an utter disregard for suffering. I'm sorry Aster. I'm so sorry.'

Why was she sorry? He possessed a superior medical mind divided into two, with the halves synergistically reflecting each other, ramping up their power, their competence, their ability. Hadn't he always wanted to be the best? He next looked through her mind and through her eyes, at himself, admiring the two snakes into which he had divided, now coiled about the charred tree and facing each other head to head. Was it not appropriate that his form of a Caduceus reflected his excellence?

Until this morning the provisional title of this was 'Hooder Segment' but I knew it wasn't right. Reading parts of it again a little switch in my brain clicked down to give me the title and in retrospect it seems obvious. Here marks a return of Jonas Clyde – the guy who discovered that hooders are 'devolved' biomech war machines created by the alien race the atheter. And, of course, with him present hooders also need to be on the scene too. In this I also take a look at something I've been dealing with in a few stories: the ennui barrier. Eternal life is great except, late in the second century, those living it can become immensely bored and embark on some risky pursuits. Mostly, these result in the individuals concerned killing themselves, but sometimes the result can be catastrophic…

RAISING MOLOCH

Trying to find some reaction to it, Jonas Clyde studied the inside of the apartment. Hints of emotion arose and he acknowledged how it felt both strange and also like coming home to be allotted the same rooms in the research base as he had used decades ago, but he felt no inclination to take the AI's unsubtle lure. Hoisting his pack's strap onto one shoulder he headed out. He would not be staying. The event that had summoned him across the light years to Masada was one he felt he could not miss, just as a matter of form, but once it was over nothing could keep him here. He walked down a corridor – the bubblemetal worn down by the passage of many feet – then out through a chainglass door onto the first level balcony ringing the central dome. Cheller stood waiting for him, staring out through the quarter glass covering the balcony and keeping the breathable air inside. The dark aubergine sky of morning still displayed the glassy sculpture of a vast nebula, while Calypse – the nearby gas giant – sat on the horizon all pastel shades swathed in cloud, bright on one side in the light of the unseen sun.

'You're ready?' Cheller turned.

Over the years, Cheller the Golem had managed to lose all those tells Jonas usually detected. This was probably because twenty-five years ago Jonas had told him about them – up to and including the possibility that humans might even be able to detect the absence of pheromones in the air around him. Cheller had black hair shading to grey, wore a slightly mucky envirosuit, had a scar on his cheek and a slight sheen of sweat on apparently sun-tanned skin. Jonas grimaced, thinking that maybe the Golem had overdone things a bit when he detected a whiff of body odour.

'I'm ready,' Jonas replied and followed as Cheller led off towards the stair. They both pulled on breather masks that simply added the required level of oxygen – the first through appearance and the second through need. Pressure differential being minimal, just a single door opened to the stair and they headed down to the courtyard of the inner ring. Here, sitting on foamstone slabs bordered by flute grass sprouts, sat a grav platform – a simple circular vehicle ten feet across with a steering lectern at the centre and a variety of equipment bolted to the rails or in storage lockers below them.

'So we get a platform today,' said Jonas as they walked across to it.

During his years here such had been the number of researchers it had always been a constant battle over the tagreb's transport. Jonas had often found himself heading out on an aerofan or on a long journey in an ATV, that was until he spent some of his own money and bought a platform.

'It's yours,' Cheller replied.

Jonas peered more closely. It looked like the platform he had bought and left here when he departed, but now old, with new rails and equipment. He put a finger up to the Chimetech augmentation behind his ear and turned it on with a touch. Third-eye vision gave him thousands of screen options and virtuality if he so chose, but with an inner mental touch he found the link to the platform and confirmed it was his.

'Another not so subtle attempt to make me feel welcome,' he said.

As they reached the platform and Cheller opened the gate, the Golem enquired, 'Will you be staying?'

'The reasons I left haven't really changed, have they?' He reached up and touched his aug, turning it off. He didn't want access to the informational world to interfere with his experience of this place after so long away. Perhaps being here could make him feel something… real.

'Those being?'

'Well, Shardel, having made no further inroads into The Gabble, is no longer here and is unlikely to return…'

He remembered her frustration in trying to understand the nonsense language – if it could even be called a language – spoken by the gabbleducks of this world. The creatures – duck-billed things bearing some resemblance to a by-blow of a giant caterpillar and a bear, but with rather too many legs, had proven to be the devolved descendants of one of the ancient and arguably extinct ancient races – the atheter. Here on Masada, which had been identified with certainty as their home world, they lived like animals. But like mynah birds they spoke the phonetics and words of the Anglic of the inhabitants but jumbled up and without real meaning. Shardel, like millions of linguists across the Polity, had tried to find some meaning in it but ultimately her frustration drove her away. She had been his lover.

'Shardel's presence or otherwise is not the reason you left,' said Cheller as they climbed onto the platform. 'You stayed here for a further four years after she went.'

'I had learned all I could about the hooders. It was time to move on.'

'I disagree.' Cheller moved over to the lectern and punched a control. The platform vibrated through Jonas's feet. 'There is still a great deal we can learn from them.'

Jonas felt a flash of annoyance, immediately followed by gratitude for the emotion. This was old ground and an old argument. His instinct was not to run with it, but the frustration that had driven him away rose up again. And any emotion being a rarity with him nowadays, he exercised it.

'I studied hooders for ten years. I detailed everything about their physiognomy, genetics and habits, and even tracked down the evolutionary changes they had undergone over the two million years since they were… decommissioned.' He considered saying more, but the frustrated anger guttered out like flame starved of oxygen.

'There is still more to do,' said Cheller, trying to probe the wound.

The platform rose up into the air and Jonas looked back at the tagreb. At the centre sat one dome while four more sat on the 'petals' of the thing that had folded out when it first landed. Foamstone had been injected underneath to protect the research station from the depredations of tricones in the muddy soil of Masada; that had been extended and now other buildings clustered around it. He wasn't sure why, since personnel numbers were now way down from what they had been in his day. The thing gleamed with lights in the twilight – a small constellation in the darkness of this world.

They slid over the bushy growths of spring flute grasses, paths crushed down by ATVs from the tagreb. A moment later they passed over the outside fence and he watched a proton cannon, on one of the guard towers, briefly track their progress.

'I studied hooders,' Jonas continued, trying to feed the flame. 'I found out that they, like the atheter, were devolved – deliberately devolved. They were once biomech war machines the atheter used, but were taken back to being animals with their one kink, which is to destroy completely the remains of a gabbleduck should it die – such did the atheter loath themselves. It was mine, and Shardel's, discoveries that led to the accepted theory that the atheter committed a weird kind of racial suicide.'

'All true,' Cheller agreed.

'I completely elucidated those parts of the hooder genome that are artefacts – remaining components of their war machine past, like that producing their armour, that producing their feeding apparatus, the superconductivity, the remnants of structure made to take grown devices.' He felt the comforting warmth of anger and looked at Cheller carefully, but knew he would not read anything there the Golem did not want him to read. 'It was me who also discovered the quantum storage crystals in that genome that might well contain their original genomic schematics.'

'Original is a rather debatable term.'

Distraction, but Jonas continued to push. 'Ah, you're talking about the theory that they were supposedly natural organisms before they were turned into biomechs. I suppose I should not have used the term "devolved". They were converted to animals to fit into the ecology here. That they were devolved to some original animal form is moot.'

'But still worthy of study.' Cheller looked round.

'Yes, still worthy of study, but not by me.' Emotion began sighing out of him.

'Because the AIs won't let you study those quantum crystals or the data they contain?'

'Precisely.'

In the end it was that. Being one of the Polity's leading taxonomists he had been given freedom to study whatever he wanted on Masada. He had chosen the hooders and done his job to the best of his abilities. He remembered the excitement of it all – the steady sketching out of a picture of the past. He remembered that excitement peaking when he discovered the quantum storage crystals in the genome, and his disappointment when he chose a new direction for his research and made requests for new analytical equipment to delve into those crystals, and the tagreb AI simply said no.

'Dangerous technology,' said Cheller. 'The AIs wanted to assess it first.'

'Yes, because humans like me are infants who must not be allowed dangerous toys.'

Cheller nodded and remained silent. Colour had begun to leach into the world and then the sun broke over the horizon with a mauve flash. Jonas could now see the rainbow colours of the flute grass flowers. A light wind sent the grasses rippling but Jonas only caught a hint of a mournful wail. Towards the end of the Masadan year the grasses would shed those flowered side shoots that presently gave them their bushy appearance and the central stems would dry. Holes, from the side shoots into those hollow stems, would have them singing the tunes from which their name had arisen. Now there was no music.

'But neither Shardel's absence nor your being unable to study all you want are why you won't stay,' said Cheller.

Jonas shrugged. 'You know I have reached a certain age.'

'One hundred and seventy two years,' Cheller agreed. 'Ennui.'

Jonas had never thought it would happen to him. His life was too interesting and he had enough to study in the universe for a thousand years, but it seemed he was not as unique as he thought. Ennui, or the ennui barrier, was a life stage many Polity citizens had to go through: a time when they had seen everything, when all patterns matched those from before, when life became simply too boring, emotional responses arid, and when the desperate search for novelty, for the new, began. Many didn't get through that barrier because their search often led to lethal pursuits as in desperation they put aside everything, including sensible risk aversion.

'So tell me about the hooder,' he said abruptly, uncomfortable with this subject.

'Of course you know that they normally take prey every couple of weeks. Their activity is tracked so I soon noticed this one feeding voraciously and paid closer attention to it,' said Cheller, as if the previous conversation had not taken place. 'It was taking prey every day and when I put a scanning drone on it I detected massive internal changes – it was packing resources separately into each of its segments. When it lost its first leg I sent you that message.'

'Exactly as predicted.'

'Exactly as *you* predicted.'

'Quite,' said Jonas, pretty sure this was all part of the buttering up process. 'And how do things stand now?'

'I did send you imagery,' Cheller noted.

Yes, the Golem did – regularly updated. But Jonas wanted to talk about this hooder now rather than try to elicit a response in himself to previous bitterness. Even so, he raised his hand to his aug, hesitated then lowered it. Not yet.

Cheller quickly continued when Jonas did not reply. 'The creature has lost further legs and is beginning to undergo division. It ceased hunting yesterday and, judging by the internal changes, it won't be much longer.'

Jonas nodded and surveyed his surroundings. Over to the right the mountains reared in a pinkish haze while in the flute grasses to his left he could see a heroyne striding along looking for mud snakes. Below, muddy channels cut through the grasses, still quite wet and gleaming like spilled mercury. Peering ahead he awaited his first sight of the hooder, since it wasn't that far from the tagreb. Instead he first saw a derrick standing in the grasses.

'I had a couple of locals transport that out with aerofans yesterday evening when it became apparent the creature wasn't going anywhere,' said Cheller. 'I don't know how long we'll have to wait...'

Of course: the platform had a limited power supply and they could not hang in the air for longer than half a day.

As they drew closer to the derrick, Jonas spotted the long and slightly coiled dark form in the grasses. He felt a brief stab of excitement at his first actual sight of one of the creatures after so long, but as ever it waned. The thing was about two hundred feet long, its body only slightly slimmer than the monorail train he had travelled on a few days previously. It bore some resemblance to the spine of a terran vertebrate but with centipede legs protruding. Cheller brought the platform in over the derrick, which lay only a hundred feet from the creature, then hesitated.

Those legs shifted and, in doing so, revealed some missing while others fell away even as Jonas watched. Its front end – a spoon-shaped armoured head cupping the ground and resembling the body of a horseshoe crab – jerked to one side and then rose up. Fifty feet in the air it still faced away from them, but then it turned to reveal the nightmarish underside. Here rows of limbs like glass sickles pulsed in rhythmic waves either side of the upright slot of its mouth. Vertical rows of red eyes on both sides of the mouth and in from its feeding utensils, shone from within its shadowed cowl. Cheller had been right not to land the platform just yet. But then, as if the effort had been too much, the hood dropped down again. The creature writhed briefly as if in pain, then slumped. Cheller landed the platform with a clunk.

'The signs of division are much more noticeable now,' said Jonas.

He found comfort in being analytical – the machine of his mind just running and its engine action drowning out the reality of his condition. He concentrated on the creature. The hooders he had seen in the wild, though they resembled animal spines, had a smooth continuity. The body segments of this one now had gaps revealing yellowish flesh and they were leaking clear fluid. The thing in fact more resembled the drowned corpse of the one Jonas had studied to come to his conclusions. He stepped over to a device attached to the rail, quickly familiarising himself again with the controls. The wide front disc of the scanner used lased EMR across the spectrum and picked up radiations bounced back by various materials, and by ultra and infrasound pulses the lasers generated within the body. He turned on the screen, expecting little detail because hooder bodies were notoriously opaque to this kind of scan, and, just as before, that was the case.

'Some overall loosening of structure,' he commented.

'I can give you a lot more detail than that,' said Cheller.

Jonas looked round at him.

The Golem continued, 'This is such a rare occurrence – the first we've seen since the Polity took over here – so we could not let it go unrecorded.'

'How?' Jonas asked.

'We've been sinking scanners in the ground wherever it located itself and have attached a five-thousand pinhead array to its body.'

Jonas could not really object to that so nodded and turned on his aug again. Inner vision presented the double link to him. One was for the scanning and the other to include Cheller if he so wished. He initiated both and took control of the scan data, putting an overlay on the hooder

The scanning sketched out detail with options on depth and opacity. He linked it to blink control and secondary focus. The hooder shimmered briefly then its armour seemed to dissolve to reveal the internal organism he had become so familiar with. All was still in motion, however, so that was novel.

'I should have used this twenty years ago,' he said.

'Quite,' said Cheller.

The image he was now seeing and could manipulate worked in conjunction with the tagreb AI and his aug. When he had come here he decided on as little AI assistance as possible because he found that twisted his perspective, and he had wanted to get down and dirty in his examinations of the creatures, not sit in his room auging all the time.

He began looking for the differences. They weren't hard to find.

'See here,'He pointed with a virtual finger, highlighting rings of nodes in each segment.

'Nutrient storage,' Cheller replied. 'Take a look at segment one.'

Jonas did so, zeroing in on the segment just behind the creature's spoon head. Here the nodes were much smaller and ran a network of tubes in towards the centre into which they were draining. There, just visible, lay a spiral. He tried to focus in closer, managed to see some segmentation in the spiral but little else.

'One of the babies,' he said.

Hooder biology was odd. The creatures were incredibly long-lived, energy efficient and rugged, but even though they had been biomechs in their past they were animals now and subject to the usual rules. They did die though infrequently. Drowning was one way – if they got caught in the ferocious tides on the North coast – like the one Jonas had examined. One had apparently died of disease while Jonas had been away – its body overloaded with a wide variety of viruses and local microbes that finally brought it to collapse. These were rare occurrences, however, and the main cause of hooder deaths, since people had come to this world, had been them. Death being a factor, reproduction became a necessity for survival of the species. Jonas had found that they did possess organs for sexual reproduction but that had simply never been seen. Data from the pre-Polity inhabitants – the vicious theocracy that had ruled this world – indicated that the things broke into segments with new hooders growing inside each. These segments then sank into the mud of Masada out of which, after an indeterminate time, new young hooders arose. That seemed utterly apposite for 'devolved' war machine biomechs: the sowing of the dragon's teeth.

And now at last they were seeing that happen.

'Forming from the head end first,' said Cheller, 'though I'm not sure what that indicates.'

Jonas pulled back for a moment because the hooder had started moving again. It shed more of its legs and now some chunks of outer carapace. He dived back into the scan and saw the line of division. The thing would shed all its legs and the thick protrusions of carapace to leave an inner perfectly smooth and rounded segment – rather like a thick coin. He focused in closer to examine this and noted further nodes forming just inside that inner surface. He tried to zero in on these but scan lost coherence.

'Can we redirect for close focus on one of those?' he asked, mentally indicating one of the nodes. 'Then after that on that head-end zygote?' He posed it as a question but knew the AI could manage this.

'Easily done,' said Cheller.

A square framed just one of the nodes and within it the image began to clear, meanwhile the rest of the hooder turned into a blur. Jonas now examined a tangled mass of fibres within the node, pores leading to the surface and a venous system leading in to where the zygote was to grow. He analysed detail and hypothesised. Again this was something he had expected.

'Rather like the microfibers of a certain nasty alien technology,' he opined.

'All advanced technologies that glean materials from their environment have something similar, as do plants with roots and funguses with their mycelia.'

Jonas grunted agreement, studied the object for a little while longer until it went out of focus – the AI now transferring that to the spiral in the segment at the front end.

'So the segments sink into the mud and put out roots or mycelia to collect nutrient for the new hooder's growth, just as I predicted.'

'Just as you extrapolated from the genetics,' said Cheller, perhaps to quell his arrogance.

Jonas turned to the Golem, 'Yes, I extrapolated from the genome *some* form of nutrient gathering whose nature remained obscure. I'll give you an extrapolation right now too: the source of the code for building this nutrient gathering is not in the genome per se, but in those quantum storage crystals.'

Cheller blinked, doubtless getting something over the link from the tagreb AI.

Jonas continued, 'I've no doubt that this is an artefact from the specialised environment hooders were grown in, and perhaps partially constructed in, when they were biomechs.' The bitterness came back then: 'It's precisely because of stuff like this that I wanted to see the data in those quantum crystals – why I wanted to study them. Every facet of the hooder that I nailed as being related to that biomech past is, as such, in open-ended genetics. Yes, the armour is there in the genome, as are many others of those facets, but ready to become something more.'

'Yes, we understand that,' said Cheller.

Jonas noted the 'we' and that this meant the tagreb AI must me fully in the circuit – occupying the Golem's mind.

'Let's look at that zygote.' He turned away, focused. The zygote was simply a segmented worm wound in a spiral with little inside it that he could resolve. He pulled back and looked to the other segments, but none of them had the spirals inside them. Yet it was evident now that the creature had begun to break apart. He examined the thing further, looking for new linkages between segments but found none. He reckoned overall control ran from the creature's mind and the link was simply its nervous system.

'Schematic test,' he said.

'Pardon?'

He flicked a finger at the coiled zygote. 'It wouldn't surprise me if that simply dies and breaks down with the rest of the creature. In living organisms you don't see this so much but of course you see it in factory production: the first test piece of a new run of some component to see if it is turning out as expected.'

'I don't follow,' said Cheller. Jonas knew the Golem did but just wanted him to elaborate and elucidate.

'Another artefact from their biomech past,' he said. 'It's created one of its young to see if everything is functional and if, over time, any errors have developed in the schematic or, rather, it's finding mutations and removing them, or has probably removed them.'

'I see,' said Cheller.

They both turned back towards the hooder. The changes were accelerating now and with the gaps widening between segments its length had grown by twenty or so feet. It tried to move again – rolling as it writhed – and scrubbed off the remainder of its legs and more of its carapace against the ground. Jonas also noticed glinting objects in the grasses near its front end, focused in and saw it had begun to lose its eating apparatus too. They continued watching over the ensuing hour – neither saying much. Jonas felt his own inclination to talk because he was witnessing something unique, but also aware that the thing felt pain, and it almost seemed rude to keep talking. Finally he moved closer to the rail of the platform and looked down at the framework of the derrick.

'All quite inevitable now,' said Cheller.

Jonas nodded. 'It is indeed.' Grasping the rail he vaulted over, got his feet on the cross struts of the derrick and began to make his way down. Glancing up, he saw Cheller looking down at him. The Golem said nothing because, of course, warnings were redundant and Cheller knew precisely what was happening.

Jonas dropped into flute grass reaching over his head, multi-coloured buds all around him, and pushed through to where it lay crushed down. He moved out, feeling the sense of danger and relishing it, then some disappointment with a thump on the ground behind. He glanced round to see Cheller pushing out after him. The Golem would not let the hooder kill him and that in turn killed some of the frisson. He moved in closer, smelling something both putrid and spicy, picked up a leg and inspected it before moving closer. The hooder abruptly shifted and scrubbed itself against the ground again – outer carapace peeling away and lying scattered all around it like debris from an explosion. Jonas kicked one of them over, saw black prawn-like creatures already feeding.

The hooder, but for a few remaining patches of carapace, looked like a stretched out coin tube. Between each segment 'coin' the flesh was shrinking, spilling fluids as it did so. He moved even closer, then took a step back when one of these joins near the rear just a few segments in from the tail, broke with a wet snapping sound, remaining flesh retreating into the relevant segments. Jonas saw the pain of this when the hooder's front end reared in response. He felt Cheller's hand on his arm but no intent to drag him away just yet. The front end came up high as if reaching for something in the sky, then a series of those sounds ensued. The hooded head, with that test segment behind, snapped off and fell. Other segments behind snapped away too as the rest of it fell. Its impact with the ground transmitted a shock through the soft surface below Jonas' feet, and all along its length the rest of the segments separated. He wondered if the original beast was actually dead now, or if, its brain having been a neural snake stretching the length of its body, some kind of mental continuity ensued.

'What happens now?' he asked, glancing back towards the derrick then beyond towards the tagreb. He saw platforms and aerofans rising into the sky over there.

'We collect all extraneous remains but none of the viable segments,' Cheller replied. 'Each of those will have scanning gear attached so we can watch their growth in the ground.'

'Interesting work for someone,' said Jonas. What he had felt for a moment there had begun to fade. How prosaic, he thought, to be behaving utterly as expected and seeking out danger. Now, he waited for Cheller's and the tagreb AI's final pitch, certain he would refuse and not just because of what he wasn't allowed to study.

'It will be necessary to analyse the quantum crystal data in conjunction with this,' said Cheller. 'Anyone who commits to this will have to agree on limited publication and, otherwise, proscription on the data he can share.'

Jonas stared at him. 'But, nevertheless, that person gets to see the data?'

'Nevertheless,' Cheller agreed.

Jonas abruptly realised he wasn't quite so far gone as he thought.

'Looks like I may be staying, then,' he said.

*

Jonas felt a boiling anger inside, but also a crazy joy that he could feel such anger. The period of emotions dying had now moved into a new phase, as if they were thrashing about in their attempt to stay alive. Sometimes they surged in him, like this, other times he simply felt dead. He ran with the anger, turning over the apparent reasons for it. Evidently he was not to be trusted, even with the data excised from his mind – relevant portions of his memory edited out. The injunction not to leave the Polity had seemed almost irrelevant. Hell, he had so many alien environments to explore and so many life forms to examine within its borders, he hadn't really taken it seriously, that was until he did actually try to book passage into this semi-borderland.

He'd researched the place a great deal before coming here. It was well known that, when the alien prador usurped their king and made a truce with the human Polity to end a devastating war, both sides agreed on a border area between their two realms. Because it encompassed ruins of that war it came to be called the Graveyard, and it also came to be a home for the dispossessed from both realms – usually of the criminal kind. Less well known was that the edges of the Graveyard are not clearly delimited and on the Polity side there are areas of space neither Graveyard nor Polity. These are places where illegality in the main border is tempered by Polity AIs, but where they do not and cannot hold full sway for fear of infringing the truce. They're halfway realms – neither one thing nor the other. And so it was with Moloch Three occupying one of these zones.

At a mere fifteen miles long the war factory was one of the smaller of its kind, and one of the oldest. It was Polity territory and it was not. It being a war factory the prador did not like it being in that *maybe* border territory but, with its engines war-damaged and its AI somnolent they did not push the point. In fact, they found it quite useful. This practically lawless realm right on the edge of the Polity, with inhabited areas wound through its structure like fungal growths throughout a rotting log, had its prador areas. Other prador – supposedly having fled the kingdom – could go there. And no doubt some of them were spies keeping a careful eye on their old enemies. It was also, Jonas realised, the kind of place where a person could be hunted down and killed without anyone knowing.

And that was a rush.

He paused, leaning against one wall, gasping for breath. Peering down at his leg he noted his internal doctor nanosuite had stopped the bleeding, and took a patch from his belt to slap it on the envirosuit tear. The slug had just clipped his calf, cutting a groove through the skin and muscle. He'd filled it with healer gel and the nanosuite had taken away the sting. It didn't slow him and in reality he'd got off surprisingly unscathed considering who was after him. He tried coms again but just got a fizzing from his aug. They'd used some other kind of weapon against him in the construction bay when Olsen's men threw him out of the airlock – terrified when he told them who was on their tail because of him. Some kind of EMP with a viral content took down his aug. But right at the moment that was the least of his problems because though the envirosuit had saved his life in vacuum, it had begun to run out of air. Yes, pressure surrounded him now, but the nitrogen-argon mix used in some sections of Moloch Three was deliberately free of corrosive but life-giving oxygen.

Shrugging his pack up higher, and re-tightening the straps, he moved on. He didn't really understand why it had come to this. Down on Masada there had been rules about the life forms on the world, but they mainly concerned not getting killed by them. All sorts of concerns had arrived there even while he was studying hooder growth to sample the local wildlife. Ares Combine had taken tricones – molluscs that could grind their way through rock – and modified them for a mining operation on another world. The black prawn-like creatures that acted as the morticians of that world had been adapted for recycling elsewhere, while some of the animals and plants were appearing in collections, parks and private gardens all across the Polity. So why were they so serious about him, and that damned injunction, when all he knew about hooders was in the public domain?

Unless they knew?

Emotion rose again at that thought – the sense of danger, of risk, of being bad, but the fear he wanted to feel remained muted. He reached up to touch his scalp but his fingers bounced off his head covering. With too brief annoyance he lowered his hand and looked around.

The walls of the large square corridor here were dented and scarred. The size of it told him it must be an access for manufactured war drones and this gave his some vague idea where he must be. He moved on, gecko soles sticking him to what he deemed the floor. Vaguely remembering the map he had loaded to his now inaccessible aug, he felt sure this corridor must be one of those that ran between construction bays. He reckoned on being two bays down from Porrit Town – a small city built on one of the bay walls.

He moved fast along the corridor to where it elbowed right. A human-sized bulkhead door lay ahead of him and he tried the handle. It opened easily which told him he must be near an inhabited area. Glancing back he saw no sign of his pursuit. He knew he'd lost them by running deep into the old war factory because, by shutting down his aug, they now only had infrared scanning to find him, and his suit cut most of that. Beyond the door he entered a smaller corridor and turned right as motion-sensor light squares ignited in the ceiling. Breaking into a steady jog, he came athwart a long window overlooking a manufactory. The machines were motionless of course but, even after so much time, they still gleamed.

Cleaning and maintenance robots crawled amidst them, as he had learned they did amidst much of the machinery of this station. Also, though the AI of Moloch Three had become somnolent, robots responded to any attempt at salvage with hostility. Some of the machinery and infrastructure of the war factory had been stripped out, sold or repurposed, but the danger in doing this now outweighed the gains. However, the people living here did have free access to the systems and manufacturing of this station just so long as they did not try to remove them. They had access to power, water, air, recycling and hydroponics too. Some said this was because the AI was one of the dispossessed that felt it had no purpose when the war ended. It allowed people here just as someone might give a person the keys to a car he is abandoning for a time – to run it for a while to ensure everything still worked. The speculation was that the AI had merely gone into somnolence to await the recommencement of the war.

Beyond the window a series of doors punctuated the corridor. Jonas checked beside each until finding one with a map screen beside it. He touched the thing, half expecting nothing, but it came on showing a local map of the war factory and his position within it. He had just a couple of miles to go before reaching Porrit Town, and now other concerns, though not really worries. He might have lost his pursuers but sure as shit they would head to the town knowing that was the only place he could go. He needed to send a message – Ganzen would know what to do.

Right and left, then through an airlock door out onto a gantry, his envirosuit puffing up around him in vacuum. He paused here, staring into the vastness of the construction bay. Down on what could nominally be called the floor lay four skeletons of attack ships – ribcage structures marking out shapes like giant squids, each a quarter of a mile long. Above these, occupying most of the bay, hung a partially completed dreadnought. According to what he remembered of his history upload, before people came to occupy this ship it had no name. because that was usually imparted by the installed AI. The residents of Porrit Town had called it *Brueghel's Fist*, but he could not remember why now. The thing did sort of have a knotted appearance like a fist made of grey, yellow and black alloys and composites two miles across. It hung in place with gantries and crane extended structorbots all around it, while leading to the bay wall were numerous bridges. Many people lived in that ship but, since the water, power, air and other facilities within were supplied at cost by Ganzen Combine, most lived in the town.

Porrit Town sat against the left-hand wall under a series of three geodesics – the masses of interlinked buildings there almost touching that roof of chainglass hexagons, tunnels and enclosed bridges spearing through it to reach the *Fist*. Ganzen would have people in the town and should be able to send any over fast. He just needed to talk to him.

Jonas walked the gantry to the left wall then turned in towards the town, standing at ninety degrees to his perspective. Ahead, a square frame about the gantry had been painted with hazard stripes and, as he drew closer, the pull of grav twisted his perception. Leading through the square the gantry twisted to the wall in which grav plates had been set. He followed the twist easily, the town turning until level with his perception, and walked towards the entry arch.

Loading...

The word flashed briefly to his inner perception. It meant his aug was coming back online, but it also meant the two pursuers would be able to locate him. He hurried towards the arch but before even arriving there a text page in his aug appeared to his inner vision.

>Stay where you are and we'll come collect you.

He stared at the words and then tried speaking to see if the to-text conversion was working. 'Fuck off,' he said succinctly and the words appeared.

>Understandably you have concerns.

'You fucking well shot me,' he replied, but with no heat in his words.

>It was a shot intended to disable.

'Oh, that's all right then.'

>You agreed not to leave the Polity and you have done precisely that.

'And this is so serious I have Polity agents on my tail taking shots at me?'

>This is a Beta Level injunction, which means we make every effort we can to take you back, but if that is impossible, another option remains.

He felt a thrill of fear but then it immediately turned to delight in rebellion – a brief wave of emotion that quickly foamed out of his mind. When he received the first message from this individual he had been half inclined to obey the instruction not to board the trade ship heading here to Moloch Three. But he then felt delight in rebelling at such tight control of his travel plans.

Before his last return to Masada, all worlds he had ventured to began to fit into variations of many he had already seen, as did the people on them and the life forms he studied. The excitement of discovery he had felt exploring hooder biology with Shardel had been lacking. In fact, excitement about anything much at all seemed to be lacking. After his last visit to the world of the hooders and gabbleducks he had travelled just a bit more and studied further alien life forms, but the ennui allowed it to be no more than repetition. Until he received that message from Ganzen.

Reaching the gate, Jonas paused and looked around. Unless they had been trying some subterfuge it seemed likely the two agents were outside of the town and some way behind him, else they could simply have waited on the other side of this gate for him. He walked up to the outer door, fisted the panel and it thumped up on seals and swung open. As he stepped inside more of his aug functions came online and he was able to sort through addresses. Voice to text still the only option open to him, he selected one and spoke while the airlock pressurised.

'Ganzen, I'm coming in through the factory side gate into Porrit Town. It seems that even though all my studies are now in the public domain the Polity objects to me coming here. I have two agents on my tail. Some help would be good.'

He received no response as the airlock reached the required pressure and opened its inner door. A street lay ahead with shops, bars and restaurants on either side, stairwells leading up to further gantry streets above, all weaving through the wide mix of buildings here. He touched a control on his collar, both his visor and hood softened as they withdrew air from their foam structure and the suit sucked them back into its neck ring. The smell of barbecued food hit him at once. Ridiculously, despite his danger, he suddenly found more interest in a nearby stall selling meat and vegetables on skewers. He began to walk towards this when the reply came.

>Head for Gantry Six – the Hoffstader.

'They screwed my aug and I have no map available at the moment.'

>Take the nearest stair up to Six – it's marked – then head in towards the middle of the dome you're in.

'Okay.'

Jonas swerved right to the nearest spiral stair and began climbing. As he did so he looked back towards the entrance airlock and through the geodesic panes on one side saw two bulky forms heading towards the airlock from the outside. He speeded up, his hunger forgotten, passed access to 'Level Two' then the others in quick succession. Reaching the access to Gantry Six he peered back down and saw the two figures now in through the airlock. They wore heavy suits someway between an envirosuit and a full spacesuit, with helmets that concertinaed back and visors that rolled up to the fore. A man and a woman stood there, the latter looking up directly at him. Of course they might not be human at all but Golem. He stepped out onto the wide gantry and hurried along it. Halfway, a couple of hundred yards ahead, he could see one of the bridging tunnels running across to the *Fist*, with people walking along it horizontal to him. Just before this the sign for the Hoffstader blinked from pink to green – the bar or restaurant itself a series of circular platforms arranged like those of a 3D chess set. He hurried towards it.

'Jonas Clyde!' The shout came from behind. The two had moved very fast because they were now up on the same gantry as him. He suspected either enhancements or that they were indeed Golem. Glancing back, he saw weapons drawn. There were people around him so surely they would not shoot? After only a second's thought he dismissed the idea. If they were agents they would select the right ammo for the circumstances and shoot it very accurately.

>Last chance.

The text appeared to his inner vision.

Would they really kill him? Did he want to die? Just for a second he considered raising his arms and turning back, but intransigence arose and he just kept walking.

>Okay.

Something smacked into his upper legs sending him stumbling forwards. He looked down in disbelief at the blood, open flesh and protruding shattered bone just before his leg gave way and he collapsed.

'Stay on the ground,' said a voice nearby.

He glimpsed a mercenary type in combat gear, other similar figures stepping into view. Pulse gun fire stitched through the air. Something exploded nearby and he saw the gantry erupt, flinging up a sculpture of metal shards. He rolled, seeing flashes and explosions towards the other end of the gantry, one figure going over the side and another, flecked with burning points, falling back into the stairwell.

'Okay, we got you,' said someone.

A hand closed on his envirosuit and hauled him up. A glance along the gantry revealed scattered bodies – some emitting tails of smoke – and that was his first intimation that he had recently made some very stupid decisions. But he groped through emptiness trying to care about that. When the armoured man hauled him up and slung him over one shoulder, the pain hit like a hammer. Consciousness fled.

Consciousness slid in and out, gave him a glimpse from the bridge tunnel and then others of corridors. It fled completely when the rescuer carrying him ungently dropped him down into a surgical chair. Then later it returned with an absence of pain, and paralysis from his waist down. Jonas lay seeing only the feed from his aug – numerous messages and potential links to make. Too confusing. He reached up and pressed a finger against it, shutting it down. Now his immediate surroundings came into focus. He found himself in an aseptic room all white and chrome surfaces, familiar Polity instruments, and a nightmare stooped over his leg.

Surgical robots never looked very nice and very often bore the appearance of large chromed insects. This thing was something else besides. Yes it had some of the appearance of an insect but also some of the form of a human being. It crouched on metal legs like those of a skeletal Golem android but sheathed in bare white muscle. He could see a ceramal pelvis, spine and rib bones similarly clad. A vaguely human arm protruded from the shoulder nearest him – the white anatomically correct hand resting on the chair arm nearest him. The other arm steadied the thing with its other hand pressed down against the floor. Everything else was at huge variance. Numerous arms terminating in clamps and hooks protruded from the torso and these had immobilised his leg. The head was coiled over this. The back of it consisted of armoured plates. He could just see movement underneath and feel the transmission of movement through his body. He could also hear the sounds: the sizzle of a surgical laser, the hum of a cellwelder and the whickering of printer heads. Something about that head really bothered him, until he realised it seemed a copy of a hooder's head but extended half the length again relative to its width.

Perhaps now aware that he was conscious, all the movement and the sounds stopped. The robot, or whatever it was, abruptly reared back and raised its head. First he saw his leg, opened out like an anatomy display, bloodless and with the bone back in place with printer ridges sealing the breaks. Then he focused on the head. It was packed with surgical cutlery similar in appearance to that of a hooder, but consisting of shiny metal and grey composite and terminating in surgical instruments no hooder possessed. It had a slot mouth too, and the rows of eyes, but like canary yellow tourmalines. The sight of the thing seemed to confirm an earlier thought about bad decisions. What did it tell him about this place when they made a surgical robot look like this? But the speculation had no emotional weight for it seemed he was just noticing things and slotting them into place, like an inventory.

The thing dipped down again and continued its work. While it fixed him up a door opened and a grim-looking woman with cropped grey hair and wearing a doctor's coat wheeled in a pressure feed. He tried to think of something to say to her, to ask her, as she used a shunt gun on the side of his neck to put in a port, then attached a tube no doubt conveying artificial blood and other fluids.

'How many were hurt out there?' he finally managed, trying to care.

She stared at him like he was an idiot, then said, 'The Polity agents killed five civilians. Durk sent my staff over there to help the wounded – eight of them.'

Durk Ganzen.

He stared back at her, because that had not been what he had seen at all. Yes, one of the Polity agents had shot him in the leg, but it had been the return fire that had brought down those civilians. He felt the pedantic need to object – to defend the Polity – but still on a wholly intellectual level knew this the wrong thing to do.

'I guess I was lucky,' he said.

'Yes, you were,' she replied dismissively, and, having completed her chore, quickly departed.

The tugging from the robot increased and now he heard only a cellwelder at work. Finally it stopped and shifted back to look at him again with those rows of tourmaline eyes. Perhaps because he had spent so long studying hooders and knowing their inclinations, he felt its look to be a sinister inspection, which oddly amused him.

After a moment it took its hand away from the chair arm and reached up towards his face, fingers spread. All of this told him that no way was he dealing with a simple surgical robot here. It then closed that hand into a fist for a moment, before standing up. It loomed well over seven feet tall, but seemed somehow incomplete – just a collection of parts. Leaning in, it now brought its nightmarish visage close to his. He could see his blood and small pieces of flesh and bone caught on its surgical cutlery but, even as he watched, it began folding these inside its head then back out again, cleaning them. Only when feeling abruptly returned did he realise it had reached down behind his back to detach a neural blocker. He gasped – his leg a sore aching mass that felt twice the size he could actually see. The robot retreated to the other side of the room, and ducked down to squat below a long work surface. From there it simply watched him. He wondered if it was capable of human communication.

'Thank you – good job,' he said.

The robot hissed at him.

He turned away, deciding not to continue the conversation, and next contemplated getting out of the chair when the door opened again. In came one of those he had seen on Gantry Six. The man looked boosted, wore an armoured combat suit that looked none too clean, sported handguns at both hips with other items – probably ammo and power supplies – around his belt and a pulse rifle across his back. His face was wide and thick-featured below ginger hair. A web of scars showed bone white against the ruddy skin of one cheek.

'So the good doctor has put you together again,' he said, seemingly bored. 'You can walk?'

'Doctor?' Jonas asked, glancing at the robot.

'Ganzen calls him Dr Giggles,' said the man. 'The name doesn't really make him anymore attractive and most here get any surgical work done in Porrit Town.'

Jonas nodded. The casualties out on Gantry Six, the form of this robot and now its name all indicated that yes, he had been foolish to come here.

'To answer your question,' he said, 'I've yet to try.'

'It's either that or over my shoulder again.'

So this was the one who had carried him here. Jonas eased himself forward, getting his good leg to the ground then carefully pushing himself upright. A rush of dizziness had him slumping and a meaty hand closed about his upper arm to support him. He got the other foot down and put some weight on it. His upper leg felt half dead and otherwise painful but he found that he could move. He should be fine. The bone repairs would likely be stronger than the bone itself while the muscle would just need a few hours of binding. Reaching up to his neck he felt the tube and looked across to the suspended pressure bottle. The indicator showed it had emptied its contents into him so he pulled the tube out of his neck, the port snapping closed. He walked a few steps then nodded to the man, who released him.

'I'm to show you to your room.'

'What's your name?' Jonas asked.

'Hoskins,' the man replied, stepping out through the door.

'Thank you for rescuing me,' Jonas replied – the gratitude being rote.

Out in the corridor Hoskins shrugged then led the way, Jonas struggling to keep up. He wondered what he might ask the man that would not arouse suspicions about his keenness of otherwise to be here, but did not feel well enough to manage subterfuge so simply studied his surroundings.

This corridor told him little because it seemed a pretty standard ship interior with a soft blue floor, cleanbot burrows at the base of the wall, plain doors and panel lighting above. But then Hoskins took a turn and he found himself in a different area. Here the floor was decorated with the patterns generated by bacterial growth in a tough gel. The lights above were brighter and needed because dark green ivy spread along the walls. This was space station stuff: the plants and the bacteria acting as oxygenators and air cleaners that fed off the detritus produced by all human bodies. He passed a series of circular windows giving him a view into other growth areas that looked too chaotic to be hydroponics. Finally Hoskins brought him to a door that slid aside when he punched the plate beside it.

'You've got an hour to sort yourself out, then I take you to Ganzen,' the man said, then moved off.

The defences here were obvious. Lights ran down the ceiling to the end of the corridor, while in between them hung large ellipsoids. These were security drones, while in the walls the heads of weapons turrets protruded – ready to be extruded all the way to deploy their lethal hardware. At the end guards stood either side of a large armoured door above which a heavy autogun sat in a recess. And these were just the visible security – probably much else besides filled the surrounding area.

'It's been what, three years since you were on Masada?' Ganzen enquired.

Jonas studied the man. Ganzen, it seemed, liked the mercenary style of those of his employees Jonas had seen out on Gantry Six. He had long black hair tied back in a bun, a cropped beard and wore Polity desert combat gear, including the armour and weapons. No such clothing had been provided for Jonas. After showering, getting something to eat and drink from a fabricator then searching his room, he had found casual clothing. None of it suited him so he cleaned and repaired his envirosuit. He wanted to keep it on because it would be necessary when he got out of here.

He next transferred his gaze to the Siberian tiger, for it seemed Ganzen liked his pets. The creature paced at the man's side like a loyal dog. It probably was completely loyal and probably possessed more in the way of intelligence than usual for such beasts. Its skull jutted up higher than nature designed and to its rear sat a heart-shaped lump of polished metal. Someone had fooled with its genetics, operated on it and installed an augmentation.

'Yes, three years,' Jonas replied distractedly, thinking about his recent hurried tour of Ganzen's animal collection and sight of the other tiger. It was a Bengal tiger and, as far as he had seen, had no alterations to it. A high window had given a view into its pen, which lay two hundred feet across. A stream ran through this, ending in a deep pool to one side. Trees and bushes grew from the imported soil while a rock formation on the other side of the pen from the pool provided a cave in which it could secrete itself. Above, it had been provided with a sky effect ceiling then running fluffy clouds. All had looked good. The creature had been given better accommodation than most humans had when not on the surface of a world, though Jonas would have preferred it to be running free in a reserve somewhere, or perhaps in one of those mixed environments where predators had simply been altered so as not to attack humans. The whole setup had in fact looked little different from something one might see in the Polity, that was, to the inexperienced eye. The problem was the debris.

The tiger had recently fed and the remains of its last meal had yet to be removed, doubtless by the quadruped robot Jonas saw gecko stuck to one wall and cleaning it with a spinning brush. Or, perhaps, only easily identifiable remains had been removed. The tiger had eaten flesh and proceeded to gnaw on a bone, other bones scattered nearby. Without his training, knowledge and experience, Jonas would not have given the scene a second glance. However, in his profession, he had learned much about the anatomy of many creatures, including humans. The tiger had been gnawing on a human femur while a tibia and fibula lay nearby. Other chunks lying scattered in the area he had identified as parts of a human pelvis.

'Hopefully you haven't forgotten much of what you learned there.'

Jonas came back to the conversation with a brief stab of panic from dying emotional substrata and reached up instinctively to touch his scalp. As with the agents who had been pursuing him he wondered how much Ganzen knew, and whether he knew more than Jonas would have liked.

'I've forgotten nothing at all,' he replied. It wasn't really a lie because having memories edited out wasn't really forgetting. Anyway, no one beyond a few AIs and tagreb staff knew about that procedure.

'Good. But of course I want something beyond just what anyone can download.'

Jonas nodded. 'Most of my research is in the public domain now, but you should be aware that published research is just a summation, just some conclusions. It does not include everything that led to them, nor the expertise involved.'

'We will see,' said Ganzen, as they reached the door.

Jonas glanced at the guards. They didn't look comfortable and he rather suspected they were here just for display, just for him to see. The door separated and ground open, revealing thick armour with cooling layers and other inlaid tech. Really, guards here would little complement the security already in place.

'Here we are.' Ganzen gestured to the wide chamber within.

The room entire was circular but a chainglass screen ran across the middle dividing it. On this side the place had been neatly laid out with all the equipment Jonas might need. Work surfaces sported nanoscopes, nanofactories, matter printers, fabricators and a wide variety of analytical gear. Up in the ceiling hung spiderbots, hoists and other stuff. Cylinders of basic chem and matter printer formulations stood arrayed to one side. Ganzen led Jonas up to the chainglass screen and thumped a fist against it.

'This was probably the most expensive item here,' the man said. 'It's laminated with clear sapphire and chain-diamond threads. Even if hit with a decoder this will remain intact enough to stop a tank.'

'The walls?' Jonas enquired.

'Ceramal and adapative armour – kind of stuff the hull of a Polity dreadnought is made from.'

Jonas nodded, looked up at the spider bots and scanning heads in the ceiling of the space beyond, then focused on the single item on the floor. A large crate sat there – plasmel and held shut with braided monofilament bands.

'I'd like to go in and see it opened,' he said.

Ganzen showed surprise. His tiger looked up at him and thrashed its tail. This brought home to Jonas that there must be some sort of link there.

'Is that a good idea?'

Jonas waved a hand at the case. 'It's completely inert now and will remain so until provided with the correct environment. There is no danger yet.'

'Very well – you are the expert after all.'

Ganzen glanced at the tiger. It ducked as if given a slap on the nose, then wandered over and flopped down underneath a nearby work surface. Ganzen headed to a door one side of the screen, pressed a palm against a palm reader and stepped back. The door hummed and came out of its frame like a bung out of a bottle, then swung aside on heavy hinges driven by thick rams – at least a foot of solid ceramal armour. A short airlock lay within but when they stepped in Ganzen did not close the door behind – just opened the equally thick door ahead.

As they entered the sealed room Jonas scanned around. He noted holes running along the base of the wall and others higher up. They had to be for atmosphere and other environmental controls – the ones along the bottom for injecting the required ground substrate. He needed to learn all this, he thought, then just froze for a second, not really knowing what to do, until logic kicked in dictatorially. No, logically what he really needed to do was work here until an opportunity presented, then get the hell out just as fast as he could. He reached up and rubbed his face – outward expression of the conflict he felt inside. It seemed evident now what Ganzen was. He ran an organisation that obviously edged far enough into criminality for it to be better located outside the Polity. He had an overweening interest in nasty pets and it was evident he used them for nasty purposes. But… the opportunity here…

'You should be able to link in,' said the man, watching Jonas carefully.

Jonas hadn't used his aug since shutting it down when the surgical robot had been working on him. He felt reluctant to reactivate the thing since the Polity agents had used it to trace him. That was irrelevant now since, if they had survived, they knew precisely where he was. He reached up and pressed a finger against it, turning it back on.

Multiple screens and controls opened to his inner perception. In an instant he saw the coded feed locking him from contact with the overall AI net. The *Fist* had its own informational network cut off from that. Also numerous other coded links became available to him locally. Ganzen tapped a finger against his own aug and nodded. A message had just arrived from him and Jonas opened it, getting the code for those local links and inputting it. In semi-virtuality the laboratory around him opened to him. He now had access to all its equipment and functional control over it.

'So, open your present,' said Ganzen.

Jonas nodded and looked up to the ceiling. He targeted a spiderbot and accessed its system bringing up a sub-AI menu. A nod brought it down from the ceiling on a thread of umbilicals to land beside the crate. He chose a simple unwrapping procedure from the menu and plugged in a telefactoring option stored in his own aug, and, feeling he had gained a number of limbs, moved the spiderbot forwards. It scanned the package then reached out with one limb terminating in shearfield scissors and snipped the straps, pulling them aside and discarding them. Next it ran a vibro-blade around the join in the box and pushed up the top half to reveal shaped foam packing. Jonas had it probe gently, slitting some packing and pulling at other stuff. It all came away easily to reveal the object within, which, with four of its limbs he had the robot grasp and lift out. With the flick of a limb it sent the box skittering across the floor, then lowered the object and released it.

Jonas waved a hand, dispatching the robot back to the ceiling. He walked over, abruptly enjoying the sensation of his heart thumping with both excitement and guilt. The thing was a large brownish grey lump with the shape of a thick coin, edges rounded, three feet across and two feet thick, faces and edges dished inwards. He reached down and pressed a hand against its surface. It felt cold and inert but he knew the potential here, for this was a breeding segment of a hooder.

'You removed the transponder and other tracers I presume?' he asked.

'Two imbedded tracers and a scattering of micro scanners.'

Jonas looked up. As far as he knew there had only been one hooder that had an array of micro scanners put on it. There had been no others the Polity had seen go through that process and all those prior to that had been buried in the Masadan mud. He returned his attention to the thing. The segment was smaller than it had been on the hooder but that followed his extrapolation of what would happen when a segment was produced in the spring. It consolidated and lost moisture, compacted and grew dense so that when the ground softened again at the end of the summer its density would take it down. A gestation period would then ensue.

'It might be dead,' he said. 'If it had micro scanner on it this is one of those I saw three years ago.' He added no more, astounded by the lie, since hooder segments could sit inactive in Masadan soil for decades before gestation.

'That is for you to find out.' Ganzen stood with his head dipped, fingers up against his aug. After a moment he looked up. 'I'll leave you here to familiarise yourself with the equipment, and expect a report on any progress you make.' He tapped his aug again, indicating how he expected the report. 'I meanwhile have matters to attend to.'

Jonas considered things that should be his concern, if that wasn't to get out of this place as fast as he could.

'My money?' he asked.

'Your first payment is in your account.' Ganzen headed to the door.

'Not something I can check,' Jonas replied.

Ganzen paused on the way out. 'I'll give you access to the Polity net when I'm satisfied my money is being well spent.' He departed.

Jonas returned his attention to the segment, his internal conflict now arising again. He had thought that Ganzen Combine wanted data on hooder biology – something it could sell. Even that, he now realised, was not a great idea, there being stuff here that the Polity had edited from his own mind. He now felt that Ganzen himself simply wanted another cruel toy – another pet. In its way that was better on the larger scale of things, but it would be utterly horrific and agonising for any of the man's victims. He should go. He knew on an intellectual level he needed to leave this place. But also he really needed to examine this segment... But then, even if he did find a way to leave, surely Ganzen would get someone to bring the creature inside this thing into the world? He would stay, for now. If he left he would have no control on events and some fool would be here in his position... Jonas grimaced, wondering who the fool might be.

Numerous high intensity scans finally, when stitched together, gave a clear image of the inside of the segment. The spiral of the hooder body had formed, nutrient stores were depleted and the nodules containing those root-like growths had expanded and now only lay under a thin skin at the surface. He wondered how long the thing had been off Masada. He had not asked Ganzen about that and felt he should. He suspected it must have been taken from that world years ago and this accounted for its dehydration. Quite possibly various concerns had been trading it between each other for some years. Was it now beyond recovery? He considered how he could present the data, garnered to say this was the case, and thus rendering his employment here redundant. He also considered how Ganzen might react and shelved the idea.

Now again lowering another spiderbot, he had it approach the segment. Meanwhile a previous bot was in place, its limbs terminating in scanner heads poised over a particular area of the surface. The second bot inserted a limb between scanning heads in readiness. Jonas was about to initiate the program then paused and looked up. He got out of his seat before the array of screens and controls that gave him more data and ways to control it than just his aug and walked over to the big bung door. He pressed a hand against the touchplate, wondering if it was keyed to him, and both inner and outer door drew closed. He expected little reaction from the segment at this point, but best to be sure. Young hooders moved fast and fed voraciously to achieve their pre-adult size of about twenty feet long and three feet thick.

Back at his seat he sent his instructions. The second bot sprayed the surface of the segment with a nutrient gel of his own design – based on what would be found in the soil of Masada. He focused on the scan returns as it went on. For some minutes nothing happened at all, and then the node of 'roots' shifted as if uncomfortable, before settling. It seemed a confirmation. He had already picked up on numerous sensory pores over the surface of the thing and supposed some factor here prevented initiation unless the segment was completely buried with nutrients accessible to every root. Or perhaps some other factor? This led on to speculations about the exact makeup of those nutrients. Hooder segments dropped down deep so the soil around them would have a different constituency from that at the surface. He accessed his aug-stored data on Masadan soil chemistry, noted its paucity and wished for access to the Polity AI net. He then thought about how that might not be a good idea because, with a hooder segment missing and agents following him here, he guessed some AI might have sketched out the scenario. He sat back.

Anger momentarily swirled in his chest. Damned AIs. They had allowed him to study the data on the quantum storage in the hooder genome but not allowed him to remember it, so why the hell should he be concerned about them? Again he felt that stab of panic thinking that maybe they *did* know… He closed his eyes, abruptly stood up and began pacing. His intellect would give him no rest because he knew his thinking wasn't right. Those surges of emotion were indicators of someone going into ennui. He knew that his old self would get out of here fast – would not have come here in the first place – but his new self felt the attraction of risk and novelty and, if he stayed here long enough, would win the battle.

'Ganzen wants you.'

He looked up. The mercenary character Hoskins must have entered quietly, for he was now sitting on a box beside the open door.

'How long have you been here?' Jonas asked.

'About ten minutes. He told me not to interrupt you if you were in the middle of something.' Hoskins stood and walked across the lab. He peered in through the window at the hooder segment, then back round at Jonas. 'You know what he wants that for, don't you?'

'Biotech research,' said Jonas, not believing it for a moment.

Hoskins smiled without humour. 'Do you know what Ganzen Combine does?'

'As far as I can gather a bit of everything – they buy and sell a great deal.'

'You got that right, but seem to be ignoring the direction of that trade.' Hoskins shook his head. 'They buy in the Polity and sell into the Graveyard. So what do you reckon their customers are like?'

Jonas understood at once, but quelled any reaction. 'You're a mercenary, aren't you?'

'Yup. Ex ECS.'

'Does the direction of trade here concern you?'

'Not really.'

'And so it is with me. I get a chance to work with something I have a great deal of interest in and I get to walk away with a large payment.'

Hoskins snorted and gestured to the door. 'Let's go.'

As he followed the man Jonas understood the reaction. If a live hooder as a pet was Ganzen's aim then yes he had a chance of walking away from this. However, if the man's aim was to produce hooders to sell into the Graveyard, then he knew that, from Ganzen's point of view, his work would never be done.

Hoskins led him through the *Fist* and finally into what looked like an empty shuttle bay. Here a number of people were gathered – most of them with the same look as Hoskins. He didn't spot Ganzen for a moment but he did see the tiger, so knew he was near. Hoskins caught his arm and pulled him through the crowd, which parted around them to reveal a man lying on the floor. Jonas thought for a moment this must be one of the agents that had chased him, but the man wore stylish strap-weave trousers, a blouse-like shirt in ever-white and extremely pointed mirror boots. It struck Jonas as unlikely that a Polity agent here would shed combat clothing for this attire.

'Apparently he knows nothing about them,' said Ganzen at his shoulder.

Jonas looked round. 'I'm sorry, but I've no idea what you're talking about.'

Ganzen peered down at the man, then stepped in and drove a boot into his guts, seemingly just as a matter of form, then turned back to Jonas. 'You've been around so I'm guessing you know about places like this sitting on the border with the Polity on one side and prador on the other. Both sides let places like this exist so they can put their operatives in them.'

'Yes, I understand that.'

'Some of their operatives can be a bit inept and everyone knows who they are. Skerr the prador, supposedly having fled the kingdom during the usurpation, is their well-known operative. Heathic here is the Polity one.'

'You asked him about the two that came after me?'

'I did, but he says he knows nothing.' Ganzen looked round at the crowd. 'Move back,' he instructed.

Jonas noted that mercenaries weren't the only ones here since others were in more conventional attire. He saw the female doctor from before, peering grimly down at the bound man before moving off. He returned his attention to this Heathic. The man had a bloody mouth but showed little else in the way of damage. He knew in an instant that none of this was about getting information, else Heathic would have been in much worse condition than this. Ganzen stooped down, drawing a combat knife from his boot, flipped Heathic over and cut the bonds about his wrists and ankles before stepping back. The man struggled to his feet, rubbing his wrists.

'Polity agents killed many people here,' said Ganzen. 'Recompense must be made.'

Jonas felt slightly sick and couldn't help feeling some guilt about what he was sure would happen next. Heathic stood there looking forlorn for a second, then it was as if a switch clicked over in his mind. He abruptly threw himself towards Ganzen but the tiger, moving fast and smooth for something so huge, hit him in mid-air. Two swipes of its claws sent him sprawling with his shirt ripped open and rapidly darkening with blood. He tried to get up to run but it came in and clawed him again, opening the back of his thigh. Then it lunged forwards to close its jaws on the back of his neck and shook him. They all heard the vertebrae crunching and breaking. It then moved off, dragging its kill with it to the other side of the hold.

Jonas had expected something like this, but still the reality of it shocked him. Ganzen had just grabbed someone to deliver a lesson – just plain ugly murder. There would be no police, Polity monitors or agents to come in and drag Ganzen off for trial or otherwise dispense justice, and none of them here to protect Jonas. His malfunctioning mind had walked him into a situation he would struggle to extract himself from. The spectators filtered away leaving only Ganzen, Hoskins and Jonas. Ganzen was watching him, a slight smile on his face.

'So how are things going with the segment?' he finally asked.

Jonas stared back at him, acknowledged what he had just seen with a brief nod, then said, 'It still shows signs of life. Once I sink it in the required substrate things should proceed well, though I can give you no timeline.'

Ganzen nodded. 'Take a break for now, then get back to it when you're ready. Hoskins will show you our facilities.'

Jonas turned to follow Hoskins out, hearing the tiger tearing and crunching.

Jonas sat on the edge of his bed and, trying to get his mind in order, weighed pros and cons. He was entering ennui or perhaps already in it, the condition not being clearly defined. He had reached a point where interest and emotion outweighed his life. He was seeking novelty like all the others and that novelty might end up killing him. However, over the last week he had felt more alive than he had for years. So what should he do?

Ganzen was obviously a nasty character who probably had some terrible purpose for a hooder. The killing of that man with a tiger perfectly illustrated that. The right thing to do would be to undermine Ganzen, maybe kill the segment, or simply escape and report what was happening here. But attempting either of them would likely lead to his death. He shook his head. Despite many ideas to the contrary, being without emotion did not necessarily lead to pristine logic. He closed his eyes, tried again to put things in order. What did he want?

That was difficult from his present perspective but he could get to the bones of it. He wanted to survive ennui and return to gaining pleasure from existence. Yeah, fine, but that did not make his future actions any clearer. Perhaps it would be better to think about what he would have done, before ennui, and in the unlikely event he would have ended up in a situation like this. The thought gave him discomfort, but at least that made him feel alive and he pursued things to a logical conclusion. Despite ennui he was still a moral creature and knew that his past self would not have countenanced his work being used by the likes of Ganzen. However, despite being a moral creature, he had never been prepared to sacrifice his life to that end. He would have calculated risks and gains and tried to ensure his own survival while screwing up Ganzen's plans. This was a delicate scale to balance considering the present state of his mind. What to do?

Jonas woke with utter calm, his aug muttering to his mind and pages of text constantly scrolling for his inner vision. He had set it to refreshing his knowledge of hooders while he slept and he dreamed of their biology, always waking up with new insights and remembered detail. He even now had some hint of what he had known and now didn't know –

those memories excised from his mind. Upon thoughts of this he often reached up to touch his scalp – just feeling the slight lump under his hair. Thankfully Ganzen knew nothing of the mem-tab made of bone he had inserted there three years ago.

As was his custom he then turned off the aug replay, climbed out of bed and headed straight for the shower. After cleaning himself and inserting a tooth-cleaning bot in his mouth he dressed in an insulated body suit that allowed access for urine collection and the anal catheter of his envirosuit, and then put that on. He had cleaned it last night and replaced the cartridges storing unrecycled products of his bowels and bladder, as had become his custom too. Hoskins had been curious about him constantly wearing the suit. It allowed him to continue working without interruption, Jonas told him, and he needed it now he had filled the segment enclosure with the air of Masada.

Once dressed, he ate a breakfast of porridge and coffee from his fabricator, meanwhile accessing the data stream from his laboratory. The tanks were filled and ready to run the gel fluid into the chamber containing the hooder segment. He had engineered it so that it remained transparent despite being loaded with the nutrients of deep Masadan soil. The additional nanites he had made were in and propagating, and today it would be time to open the spigot. He had seen increased activity within the segment since adding the new atmosphere, which told him it was ready for this. Finishing his food he sat back, contemplating what he was about to do, his thinking now as clear as that gel would be.

Next, he headed out of the apartment and, as he had done for over a week now, he went for his morning constitutional. He had the free run of the *Fist*, and his laboratory with all its manufacturing capability, had provided. He walked his usual route – he'd told Hoskins it helped him relax. Hoskins had been doubtful but when it became evident Jonas was walking in those areas of the ship that did not lie near the exit tunnels, had ceased following him.

Soon he entered that part of the ship unoccupied by Ganzen staff. And finally he reached the airlock. Stupid of them, he felt, not to have taken his envirosuit away. Stupid also to think that the central lock-down on these airlocks would be enough, or that watching through the cams here a suitable precaution. He quickly took the vibro-knife and decoder out of his pocket – the former taken from the lab and the latter put together by one of his micro-factories from schematics stored in his aug. He ran the knife around the edge of the simple keypad lock and pulled it off, detached the optic feed then plugged in the one from the decoder and initiated it. The inner door thumped off its seals and the manual locking wheel spun. Pulling the door open he stepped inside, disappointed that he felt no excitement at all – that what he was doing now just seemed a natural progression from before.

He closed the inner door manually, closed up his hood and visor, then hit emergency evacuation and felt his suit inflate as the air went straight outside. The outer door opened easily and he pulled himself out onto the hull of the *Fist*. He had already decided that Porrit Town was not the place to go, but Moloch Three had many such areas scattered throughout – all with their space docks and departing ships. Engaging gecko function he walked round to an area he had already selected, looked up from his perspective, squatted, disengaged gecko and jumped.

Jonas sailed out from the ship toward the bay wall. He looked back at the *Fist* and then Porrit Town as it came into view and almost felt disappointment that his escape had been so easy. In mid-air he turned over and re-engaged gecko function as he headed for the bay wall. As he drew closer he saw that what had apparently been a clear area between the bases of two structor towers – the long umbilicals from their tops stretching to giant multi-limbed robots attached to the hull of the *Fist* – was in fact patchy. He saw holes through the bay wall where massive sheets of bubblemetal or composite had been removed from an underlying framework. Closer still and he saw his course would take him straight through one of these. No matter. This would take him closer to his destination – to those materials conveyors leading to an internal factory and then to the next bay.

Movement over to one side.

He turned to look and saw a shape heading towards him fast on a vapour trail. Had Ganzen fired a missile at him? The shape grew clearer and he soon saw an armoured man – the vapour being output from suit thrusters. The man raised some kind of weapon and fired as his course took him behind Jonas. He felt something hit and next found himself tumbling through vacuum wrapped in the sticky strands of an arrest net. Just seconds later the impact of a hard surface drove the wind from his lungs. He didn't bounce away, however, because the sticky net stuck to that too. He lay there gasping as Hoskins floated in, carefully adjusting his course with air-blast thrusters and landed. As he gasped for air and noted pain probably from broken ribs, Jonas tried to care about his failure, but couldn't.

Hoskins hadn't said much after dragging him back through the airlock, just deactivated the sticky net then ordered him to remove his envirosuit. When Jonas was tardy in doing so Hoskins hit him, hard in the stomach, and he found that pain still worked as a motivator despite his fucked emotions. He undressed, struggling because the ribs in his back hurt badly and his shoulder too, which seemed to be stiffening up. He did manage to walk, but wincing all the way as Hoskins brought him naked here to this chair.

'I guessed you would try,' said Ganzen, 'but I wasn't really sure. The behaviour of someone entering ennui is not completely predictable.'

Jonas looked past him, expecting to see the tiger, and felt a brief frisson at the thought of that, but it quickly faded. He next looked aside, slowly because his neck was stiffening up too. The robot Dr Giggles still crouched under the bench where it had gone after finishing its surgery on him that first time. Probably Ganzen would have it repair his ribs, since the injury would interfere with his work. He would be glad of that at least because the pain in his back and shoulder had only grown worse. He sat there feeling cold, but none of fear he should be feeling, just a hint of chagrin about being captured.

'Of course I had to try,' he said. 'You soon made it plain how stupid I had been in coming here. Perhaps you should consider *your* stupidity in so quickly demonstrating your violent and vicious nature. But then I guess for people like you it's almost obligatory.'

Ganzen tilted his head, smiling nastily. 'It gets the job done.'

Jonas looked away from him, bored with the exchange.

'I also guessed you would try something with the hooder segment,' Ganzen continued.

Jonas turned back. 'I don't know what you mean.'

'The hooder segment requires a substrate that contains the nutrients of deep Masadan soil – see I've been keeping up with your reports.' Ganzen moved closer and leaned over him, face to close. 'You designed a transparent gel that contained all those nutrients, all set up to flow in automatically this morning.'

330

Jonas acknowledged that with a shrug. 'Yes, that was today's job.'

'So why the nanites?'

'Oh I see,' said Jonas, next continuing with the lie he had earlier prepared should questions be asked about the nature of the gel when he was making it. 'They're essential to weave the fibrous matter the segment also feeds on. Without them it would be necessary to get soil directly from Masada.'

Ganzen snorted and stepped away. 'How unfortunate for you that you are not the only expert here. Caster worked it out fairly quickly.'

'Caster?'

'I've had another expert watching you constantly – she knows enough to recognise when you're doing something you shouldn't be doing. She analysed the nanite and found that yes it will generate fibres out of the substrate, but highly loaded with radicals that would make them poisonous to the forming creature.'

Jonas focused, managed to find some fragment of passion. 'Do you think I would willingly allow someone like you to have a hooder? Do you think I would then help you breed the things?'

'I guess not.' Ganzen turned away. 'You haven't had suitable motivation yet.'

Jonas just stared at him.

The grey haired woman arrived pushing a drip feed again, put a port in Jonas's chest and plugged in two tubes – one there and one in the port still in his neck. Ganzen walked back to the wall and leaned against it, watching. Jonas pushed against the straps holding him in place but he wasn't boosted and had no other physical augmentations so desisted. The woman leaned over and undid the two straps about his torso but, leaving the others in place, tightened straps about his biceps before picking up a remote from the side of the surgical chair and stepping back to operate it. The chair shifted, bringing him to an upright sitting position. He winced in pain from his back, then wished he had more self-control. Another shift behind, and he felt a section of the back of the chair drop away, leaving the pieces to the sides with the biceps straps. She moved behind him and brought in a scanning head. His back felt hot and sensitive now as she operated it.

'You have a broken scapula, three cracked vertebrae and one broken, and four broken ribs,' she told him. 'I'm surprised you managed to walk here.'

Ganzen pushed himself away from the wall. 'Thanks Margaret, that'll be all.'

She moved to head out but paused at the door. 'You sure he's worth the trouble, Durk? I would have thought a trip through the airlock without his suit a better option.'

Ganzen nodded. 'He's the expert I require.'

She shrugged and departed.

Ganzen walked over and tapped a finger against the drip feed. 'This provides all the fluids you require, but also a cocktail of neurochem and stimulant drugs. I can assure you that you won't die, though you will wish to, nor will you lose consciousness.'

The sound of soft mechanical movement drew Jonas's attention as Ganzen moved over to one side to grab a chair. He carried the chair over and put it down on the floor ahead and sat astride it. Dr Giggles, meanwhile, was out from under the bench and standing. The thing walked over, stooped and looked closely at Jonas with those tourmaline eyes in that nightmare face, then moved round behind him.

At the first stab of pain Jonas yelled, more in disbelief than anything else. As the cutting continued he shrieked. The unbelievable agony of the robot peeling skin from his back brought rhythmic groans and the utter irrelevance of emptied bowel and bladder. Eternity passed in that room, the robot cell-welding his bitten-through tongue a later subtext. As it ended and some coherent thought returned, Jonas knew he would now do anything Ganzen told him to do.

The main aftermath lasted two days. The aug loading clicked over switches in his brain while the drug 'factor stuck to his ribcage fed him neurochem and other drugs to quell the psychological damage. The terror and the phantom pains dropped to a manageable level and finally Jonas became capable of coherent thought. And then Ganzen put him back to work with just the one warning:

'Imagine what it will feel like to be flayed alive,' he said. 'And then to have the doctor put all your skin back on, only to take it off again, and again.'

In his laboratory Jonas dumped the gel he had made into recycling, then made another precisely to the nutrient specifications of deep Masadan soil and without the additional nanites. As he finished this work he received a message notification in his aug. At first he thought it might be someone from outside trying to contact him and felt a terror of opening it and this somehow deserving punishment. He then realised he wasn't thinking clearly because the *Fist* network was enclosed, and opened it. The message was text only and this again rolled out the terror because that was how one of the agents who had pursued him had communicated.

>That nutrient profile is the closest you'll get in a gel substrate.

'Who is this?' he asked.

>Caster. I'm sorry for what happened to you.

'The closest I'll get?' he asked.

>Masadan soil is complicated.

The subsequent sudden surge of terror at this observation, and that the gel might not work left him coiled up on the floor where Hoskins found him. Another day of drugs and aug loadings and he was functional again, even the fear that he might not have the intellectual capacity for this work now, faded. He became robotic, but did everything he could to ensure that the hooder would be born – fear still rolling in the under-strata of his mind. He answered the questions arriving in his aug from this Caster woman in precise detail and then with elaborations and explanations as fear that she might not understand arose. After her previous comment about what had happened to him in that room he tried to engage further with her, but she simply ignored anything that did not relate to work. And the hooder grew.

The segment now sat in gel three feet deep. He implanted pinhead scanners all around it and watched the internal changes. Just a few hours after the gel had solidified the nodes at the surface of the segment burst and spread fibrous roots throughout it. These and other changes to the constituency of the gel soon rendered it opaque about the segment and translucent beyond it, however, relaying scan data to his aug he set it up so he could look at and into the thing as he had that hooder breaking apart on the Masadan surface three years ago. After two weeks the infant hooder began to expand, more clearly showing its carapace divisions, and the hints of legs appeared, while a terminal segment spread as it turned into a hood. Also at the end of that time Jonas noted less of that shadowy fear and that the drug 'factor did not need to be topped up so often with its base fluids, and felt happy about that. It was a strange and rare emotion for him.

Anger returned next when Hoskins told him to stay in his room while Caster assessed his progress in the lab. He allowed the feeling to roll through him and inspected it from a safe intellectual distance, knowing he could never allow it to govern his actions because that room and Dr Giggles waited. Then, thinking about what Caster would see in there – about the growing hooder – he felt excitement and the weary opening eye of pride. And he wondered at Ganzen's radical cure for ennui, for it seemed he had come out the other side.

'Come with me,' said Hoskins, later on in the day.

Jonas hadn't even noticed the man come into the room. He felt a smile awakening in his face and suppressed it, knowing its source had much to do with Stockholm syndrome. He swung his legs off the bed and pulled on his slippers – now of course wearing only the clothing they provided.

Hoskins led him through the *Fist* towards the hull on the Porrit Town side. The corridors here were more salubrious with floors of thick carpet moss and alcoves made to take sculptures. In passing he glanced at a leaping tiger, paused at a very realistic skinless man and eventually came to hooders rendered in something like obsidian, coiled on pedestals either side of what looked like double real-wood doors. Hoskins opened the doors.

'I've brought him.'

'Send him in,' Ganzen replied.

Hoskins stepped out again and gestured him in, closing the doors behind him. The apartment was wide and luxurious, a sofa pit in the centre, wood furnishings scattered around, paintings hung on the walls and a collection of smaller sculptures scattered around. On the far side a wide bubble screen gave a view across to Porrit Town and Ganzen sat there on one side of a table laid out for dinner. He gestured to the seat opposite him.

Jonas walked over, resenting this display. Ganzen had tortured him and now he must sit down to dinner with the man and be polite – any other option was unconscionable. He took a breath while stepping up onto the raised floor on which the table stood, stepped to the chair and there paused to look out. Something was happening in Porrit Town. He could see crowds by the space dock at the end, others heading out of various exits into Moloch Three, and sparkles and flashes he felt sure must be gunfire.

'What's happening over there?' he asked, and sat.

Ganzen poured him a glass of red wine before answering. Jonas stared at the drink, frightened he might lose his fragmentary self-control with alcohol inside him.

'Porrit Town was first simply extra accommodation for Ganzen Combine staff and warehousing for goods brought in,' said Ganzen. 'Over time it grew as any human community does. The problem with that is it has brought in those who are not loyal to the Combine and do not have its best interest at heart.'

'Like Polity agents.' Jonas took up the wine and sipped. It was very good.

'Yes, like them, and spies for other concerns. I could not find the two agents who came after you and this has compelled me to do something I have been contemplating for some time. I am clearing the town.'

'You can do that?' Jonas asked.

'Quite simply there is no one to stop me.' Ganzen smiled. 'I cancelled all their rental agreements, since I own all the property there and told all those not in my employ to leave. Some are reluctant as you can see.'

Jonas had nothing more to say about that, though the small frightening idea of another escape attempt involving hiding in that town and trying to contact those agents receded.

'Time to eat now,' said the man, looking past Jonas.

Jonas glanced round and felt any appetite he might have had collapsing. Dr Giggles had come out of a nearby kitchen carrying some joint of meat on a large salver, with other dishes clasped in its multitude of hands.

Emotions rose and fell in Jonas now as they did for any normal person. Coming out of the other side of constant fear he felt his mind reasserting and knew that others would label that his arrogance. His emotions settled over time as he assessed what had been done to him, and out of this rose a simple motivation: utter cold hatred of Ganzen and his combine.

Now he gazed upon a perfectly formed hooder coiled in the segment. About the exterior of the thing the root system had begun to degrade and he estimated that the creature would break free in about ten days. When it did so it would be about ten feet long and the width of his thigh. He contemplated what next.

When the hooder broke free it would be hungry. Fabricators were already programmed to produce flesh, bone and venous systems that matched the genome and nutrient profile of Masadan grazers. A problem might then arise concerning feeding stimulation since he knew of no hooder that would feed on dead meat. Now, using screens, control panel and aug, he set about designing skeletal robots to carry that meat and hoped these would be enough. A fact that had him putting a lot of effort into this was that Ganzen might decide on some other form of mobile meat for the creature, though Jonas would argue that the nutrients from Masadan life were necessary at this stage of its development.

As he worked he thought further. He would never be free of this place. However, as he fed it, the hooder would grow to adulthood and then Ganzen would be pushing him to get it to segment. He knew there was a way but that this work could continue for years. He also knew that others could find this way because, in his previous research, he had discovered the creature's biological clock and seen how it could be altered. It might be that Ganzen knew this, perhaps from Caster, and would consider him no longer worth the effort. The moment this creature was born he would become dispensable. Failure, or even Ganzen's boredom with him, now would be punished terminally and he was certain as to how, because the man would soon have a new toy out of that segment.

Jonas sighed and sat back. He had made no attempts to escape or to sabotage what was being done here out of the terror of Dr Giggles and that room. But memory of pain necessarily grew dim and now he began to realise that inaction had ceased to be an option. He had to do something. As he leaned forwards again to continue designing the carrier robots he reached up and touched his scalp. A possibility was there, under the skin, highly dangerous and likely to get him killed. He needed to find out.

Jonas manufactured a chainglass knife to his specifications, then used it to whittle a chunk of hooder under-carapace he had printed so as to run comparisons with the growing beast. He did this while running biological models he necessarily handed over to ship computing, or during other times when at a loose end. The block of material began its transformation into a human skull. He was oddly pleased with this – muscle memory taking over from when he had learned this skill over a hundred years ago.

On the next day of beginning this, he slipped both nascent skull and knife into his pocket when it was time for him to return to his apartment. Usually he saw no one no his walk back to his apartment. When he found Hoskins waiting for him just outside the door, he showed surprise.

'Hand over the knife,' the man said, almost gently.

Of course, though the knife would be ineffective against the armoured mercenaries here, he could use it as a method of escape, though he doubted he would manage to bleed out before the cams and other scanners in his apartment alerted someone. Even if he cut his throat death would not come quickly enough for him to be unrecoverable in the manipulators of Dr Giggles. He took out both skull and knife, and weighing the skull in one hand, passed the knife over with the other.

'I wasn't going to do anything stupid with it,' he said.

'So you say,' Hoskins replied. 'We meanwhile have a military autodoc on standby in your apartment – it's been there from the start.'

'Your concern for my wellbeing is touching,' he replied, and walked off.

In his apartment he went through his usual routine of washing and eating, then sat on his bed weighing the carved skull in his hand, trying to ignore the cam up there in the ceiling. He went to bed, negligently shoving the skull under his pillow. With the lights out he meditated, bringing his body down to a state of complete relaxation – aware that they would be monitoring him in others ways too. He did nothing that night – just drifted into sleep.

In darkness on the second night he again calmed himself with meditation. After an hour or so he carefully reached under the pillow and, by feel, searched the surface of the skull. The piece of chainglass, blunt on the outside but atomically sharp in the inside, pulled out easily. He had manufactured the knife in two pieces – one made to break off when he pushed one side of the knife into the sculpture. He lay there for a moment, then climbed out of bed to go to the toilet. While sitting there, as if reaching up to scratch his scalp, he made a quick slit along the edge of the small lump and pressed. The memtab slipped out easily and he pushed it between his fingers while dropping the piece of chainglass down the toilet, then quickly got a finger up to the cut. Pressing, he held it there for a while, then took it away. For a scalp wound there was hardly any blood, but that was down to the speed of his nanosuite. He went to wash his hands, incidentally cleaning the blood off the memtab, and returned to bed.

In all this he had managed to maintain his meditative calm. In the bed he just lay still for a while wondering if anyone would come. When it became apparent his actions had alerted no one, he reached up and pushed the memtab into the slot at the base of his aug and memories, he had excised but in a moment of rebellion had managed to copy, once again became available to him.

'It was a complete war machine – completely grown as such from its genome and the final stages input through it from the quantum processing,' said Cheller.

Jonas had to agree as he studied and modelled the masses of data from the quantum crystals. The hooders they now saw were just empty mobile vessels capable of procreation. Blurred boundaries between life and not-life made him think of the old label Von Neumann machines, but they were just animals now.

'The atheter effectively broke the link to stop the data feeding across rather than excise it,' he said, trying to keep his voice level as he modelled from some of the data how fusion nodes would grow. 'Those features I picked up on related to their biomech past are just foundational structure from the genome waiting to take the rest.'

And so it was with Jonas' memories. The memtab supplied content to fill holes in his mind and easily transformed from data accessible in his aug to actual memory. But there would not have been enough room in the memtab for all the data in those quantum crystals – just his perception of it. Certainly he now knew things Polity AIs would probably consider dangerous, like how to grow fusion nodes and how a living creature could generate hardfields, but the totality escaped him. The vastly complex integration of it all he could not grasp and he was only just getting a handle on some link between hardfield technology and U-space – neither of which were his area of expertise – when the work came to a natural conclusion. This had become territory for AI to work out, and probably one of those introverted AIs that lost track of outside reality. However, for his purposes now he knew enough.

Jonas walked back to the laboratory thinking on the things he had learned. The missing link was the one between genome and those quantum crystals. There was the necessity, after all, in converting quantum information into chemical code. While studying this data that had been forbidden to him, he had put it together. The quantum crystals were already imbedded in the genome and that genome produced more crystals to which the data were recopied. In his mind he ran through all those genetic switches that needed to be clicked over to have the genome growing its new overlaid strands which then translated something akin to protein replication, which would then build the hooder its inner mechanisms and expand its ganglion to control them. A virus could flick over those switches – a Masadan one of course – and he knew how he could make it.

Once back in the lab he turned his attention to the food they intended to fabricate for the beast. He had designed simple composite and metal skeletons comprised of ribcage, legs neck and skull with superconducting threads running through them to various points on their surfaces. Within the ribcage the cell printers would print proto-organs and on the outside on the limbs neck and head muscle, a venous system and skin. The whole then ran on simple electricity, there not being much in the way of a nervous system.

'These need to be more complicated,' he told Caster – by text since she had still not actually deigned to speak to him yet.

>*Why?*

'The hooder sensorium runs across the EMR spectrum and it will be able to see inside them. I do not want it to decide they're not edible.'

>*Then you must improve them.*

'I will. Perhaps you can assist? Perhaps you know something about Masadan wildlife beyond hooders?'

>*I will observe.*

Once again his attempt to engage with her had been kicked into the long grass. He knew nothing about the woman, but it seemed, after one lapse to say she was sorry for what happened to him, she was deliberately keeping her distance.

Jonas returned to his design. He had the grazer genetics all perfectly mapped out and bioreactors ready to make anything he wanted. He also had detailed schematics of the body of an adult. First he focused on that skeleton, making a copy of the first design and setting to work on that. He erased the superconducting wires, sat thinking for a moment, then erased the whole thing. Instead he made a copy of an actual skeleton and began simplifying it for some things he had in mind. Next he turned to the genome again, which he had input into one of a series of bioreactors in the structure surrounding the lab and set to manufacturing this creature's equivalent of stem cells to feed into the other reactors. Already these were making muscle, fat, blood and other cell lines. The process took time – in each reactor running conversion routines to give those cells specificity. He now had cells for nerves, gristle, lungs, eyes and more besides, including bone since he might as well make the skeleton out of that, and began using more and more ship's computing. The cells thereby produced would then go into printer matrix holding tanks ready for production. In reality, he did not think all these were needed – he just wanted complications in which to lose some very small items.

As the process continued he took up his chainglass knife and skull and began carving again, muscle memory taking over so the actual application of thought remained small. He breathed evenly and enforced a calm meditative state while focusing inwardly on aug processing. Here he began designing a virus. Putting the genetic changes he wanted to make into a base format design program he soon saw that what he needed would require somewhat more than the simplicity of a virus. He expanded parameters, gradually producing something that also incorporated much of the support structure of a bacterium but one with a carbon meta-material shell, because this microbe would have to survive hooder digestion.

During all this he kept pausing to tweak the design of his grazer substitute. The thing now looked a lot more like an animal and functioned with a rudimentary nervous system powered by an equally rudimentary ganglion. He wondered, the thing having now risen from some vague definition of not-life to life, if it would be capable of suffering. He then tweaked the design further so damage reporting, in the form of pain, did not exist. After three hours he finally sat back, that other design of what could only be described as a collection of viruses in a transport mechanism, reached completion. Now fear arose again, because this thing was complicated and he wondered if he could get it past Caster.

Jonas sighed out a breath. Up until now, in doing this design work in his aug, he had done nothing Caster or Ganzen could detect, but he needed to get his viral mechanism into the grazers before manufacture. To do that, he needed to input this data into one of those bioreactors. He switched over to another menu in his aug and began to check the EMR around him. He soon compiled a long list of connections extending from the visible spectrum through to long wave radio. These were all the device links scattered throughout this ship. Just the likes of Hoskins would have many in his suit functions, connecting him to weapons. Aug and other enhancement connections were also there, links between discrete computing – in the end a whole ecology of EMR. He began sorting, first deleting all quantum entangled links then the otherwise coded ones because he wasn't an AI and had no chance of breaking into them. Those remaining he began opening and examining. Further fear and excitement now returned when, as he had expected, he found that wireless transmission to the bioreactors had not been shut down. Whoever had set them up for Ganzen had set them up with optic connections to the computing here, but left wireless available and uncoded.

The muscle. He identified the bioreactor turning stem cells into muscle cells after he linked and pinged it for a report. He went through further reactors, finally tracking down the one producing the basic stem cells. He could insert the virus carrier here. Now he had to decide if he dared to do this, and whether or not Caster would see it.

'You won't tell me much about yourself,' he said – voice turning to text for her.

She didn't reply so he tried again.

'There's no danger in conversation surely?' he asked.

>*There is always danger here.*

'You are under as much threat as me?'

Again she paused for a long time then answered >*Yes.*

Jonas nodded then looked around the lab. It seemed to have distorted and appeared oddly bright. He recognised the moment of unreality as one of those symptoms of anxiety – as if it had escaped chemical suppression. Partly in dream he began sending data to the bioreactor, only after he had begun to do so knowing there was no going back now.

'Did he put you in that room?'

>*Yes I have met Dr Giggles.*

'Why did you come here in the first place?' he asked. Yes, curiosity was driving him, but he was also being manipulative. If he could keep her distracted she was less likely to notice what he was doing and, once the process was installed in the reactor, she would be unlikely to notice it unless she asked it for a report. He opined that if she did not see him altering its program she would not check.

>*Ganzen paid me for some work. I was curious.*

'Hooder related?' he asked.

'Hooder related yes, but I did not know that at first,' she replied, this time using voice. 'I came to install the laboratory you are in. I did not realise he was also interested in my knowledge of hooders, which I acquired while working in the tagreb on Masada.'

'Oh I see... when were you there?'

'Four years during that period you were not there.'

'So what happened?' The loading completed and, there being no reports of possible problems, he initiated the new work in the bioreactor.

'I finished installing most of the lab, also the external paraphernalia like the manufactories and printers, and those bioreactors...'

Dread came and punched Jonas in the gut. He bowed over clutching his hands to his torso for it was a physical thing. Why had she so specifically mentioned the bioreactors?

'Then what happened?' he managed to ask.

'He gave me design parameters for the enclosure, asked me for my input and told me what it was for. I told him I would have nothing to do with it and that I was leaving.'

'He did not let you leave.'

'No, he took me to see Dr Giggles.'

'Then I'm sorry,' said Jonas.

'Perhaps he will let us leave when we are done.' Her tone was leaden – she did not believe that at all.

'Perhaps.'

'Anyway,' she continued. 'It's good to see the work is progressing so well. Your new design for the grazers should work very well, very well indeed.'

He assumed everything they said to each other was checked over by some other member of Ganzen's staff, so she had to be careful and he had to be careful. He supposed she had reached a conclusion similar to his: that they had to do something to get out of this place, even at the risk of them ending up dead. For he knew now, with utter certainty, that she had seen that he had done something and, though she could not know what it was, fatalistically agreed with it.

Inside the segment the young hooder began moving. He watched it coiling out and shifting around leaving a channel behind it, and realised it was eating out the stuff all around it. Finally it moved to the skin of the thing and chewed its way through. He half expected it to now push its way to the surface of the gel, but instead it began working its way around that skin, eating that up too. It was certainly voracious.

'Absolutely fascinating creatures,' said Caster.

After getting the bioreactor to make his viruses and their transport mechanism, he had returned to his room with dread sitting on his shoulders and nibbling his ear, but there had come no knock on his door, and Hoskins had not dragged him off for another visit with Dr Giggles. Over the ensuing days he and Caster had continued their conversation while he was in the lab. They discussed the work at the tagreb, Masada, taxonomy, but there were limitations on what they could say. Her hints had been broad enough to confirm that she knew he had done something, so much so in fact, that he had broadly hinted that maybe talk about the bioreactors and grazers was something they should avoid. He really hoped nothing they had said had raised suspicion. She got the hint. But in the end he knew she could not actually know what he had done, because she had no more access to the quantum data stored in crystals in the hooder genome than he was supposed to have had. He decided he must try to find a way to tell her.

'Fascinating, yes, but empty shells in some respects,' he said.

'What do you mean?'

'You are aware of my theory that they are deliberately devolved war machines – biomechs. Just like the gabbleducks they were taken back retrograde steps to be, or be returned to being, mere animals.'

'Of course I am aware of that. You're famous for it and that's why Ganzen wanted you.'

'Well, when I say "empty shells" what I mean is I sometimes think of them like the shell of a war drone before the weapons are installed. Or perhaps a better analogy would be an attack ship after it's been decommissioned and converted for civilian use.'

'I guess so,' she said dubiously.

Jonas continued, 'Hooders are very rugged efficient dangerous killers. It is perhaps frightening to imagine what they were like when they *were* war machines.'

'Yes, frightening,' she said, utterly toneless.

Jonas felt he had said quite enough on that subject. He suspected she understood now.

'Well that's very interesting,' said Ganzen, entering the laboratory just twenty minutes later.

Jonas looked round at him. He came in with his tiger at his side, Hoskins and four other mercenary types walking with them.

'What's interesting?'

Ganzen tapped his aug. 'Your earlier conversation with Caster.' He looked towards the enclosure. 'I wonder if they can be trained and rigged up with weapons.'

Jonas felt some of the tightness relax in his chest. That Ganzen had said this meant he had no idea what Jonas had done, and what would occur after the hooder ate its first ersatz grazer. Then again, Jonas too had little idea of what would occur after that first meal.

'I have no idea how one could be trained.'

Ganzen just gave a brief nod, then said, 'It's soon to show itself, I understand?'

Jonas climbed out of his chair. His apparent x-ray vision showed him that the hooder had nearly eaten away the remains of the segment. Standing up, he worked some controls on the console.

'Isn't it too soon for that?' Caster enquired, her voice coming over the lab PA.

Ganzen looked around at him sharply. The tiger thrashed its tail and Hoskins and the rest had hands straying towards weapons. Jonas grimaced. That was Caster reassuring Ganzen that she was watching him closely as instructed.

'No, it's not too soon,' he replied. 'The molecular chains will take some time to collapse and the system will take further time to extract all the water released.'

'What did you do?' Ganzen asked.

Jonas glanced at him. 'I injected a decoding molecule for the gel. It will begin collapsing down to a rubbery amalgam just a few inches thick while the enclosure draws off all its water. It's just an environmental change. I'm not sure about a hooder's atmospheric requirements at this stage of life but assume they must push for the surface quickly, since they do have a vulnerability in that they can drown, though of course that process is different for them – Masada lacking much oxygen in its atmosphere. I certainly don't want that to happen.'

'No, you do not,' said Ganzen. He looked back at the enclosure. 'Hooders with particle weapons – imagine that.'

'That might be why they're interested,' said Hoskins.

'Hooders with Gatling cannons,' said one of the others.

Jonas looked at them as if he did not understand, but that last comment had been the giveaway.

Ganzen explained, 'I have buyers interested and one of those is Skerr – a prador father-captain resident here. You may recollect me telling you about him. He's supposedly a prador that fled the kingdom because of the usurpation but is actually an agent of the new king.'

Jonas nodded mutely. The idea of the prador getting their claws on hooders was not appealing. And with what he now knew from the quantum data it became even less so. He felt a momentary surge of panic, thinking that in what he had done he might well have provided this erstwhile enemy of the human race with a formidable weapon.

'And this is why,' Ganzen continued, 'I want you to get onto working out how to drive this creature to segment. We need to go into production.'

Jonas pointed towards the enclosure. Throughout this exchange the hooder had finished with its birth segment and begun pushing towards the surface. 'It will need to be a lot larger before it can segment,' he said, just as the front of the hooder's hood broke the surface.

The hood came up with its back towards them and, at this stage, looking like the ribbed back of a sea louse. Jonas noted colouration here he had not expected and which his scanning of it, mostly structural with colour filled in from record, had not revealed. The thing was bright red with blue mottling – its colour closely resembling that of a terran giant centipede. Legs rippling down its sides, it came higher, then abruptly twisted its hood round towards them. He now saw the rows of sickle limbs and other appendages. Its rows of eyes were orange. Abruptly it shot out of the gel and, writhing like a snake and kicking up chunks of that gel with its feet, it shot towards them.

'Motherfucker!' said one of the mercenaries, stepping back.

It came on fast, looking as if it was going to hammer straight into the chainglass window, but at the last it looped up and brought its hood to touch the glass. There it paused for a moment, its sickle limbs grinding against the surface, before it crawled up the glass, writhed along it to one side, and then began to explore the rest of the enclosure. Jonas could not help but feel it had seen prey and gone towards it, assessed the barrier as impenetrable, and was now looking for another way to get to them.

'Impressive,' said Ganzen. 'Feed it one of the grazer constructs.'

Jonas nodded and bent to his console again. Four of his ersatz grazers were lined up to the feeding window, body temperature high enough to maintain their facsimile of life but low enough to keep them immobile. He shifted one of them forwards into the tube throat and microwaved it, bringing it up to temperature. Its image appeared on a screen, shifting weakly, then a plunger drove it up into the 'breech' of the feeding tube, closing a thick armour block behind it.

'Now,' he said, stabbing a control.

Up in the wall of the enclosure a plug of armour thumped out then swung aside on hydraulics. In the breech another plunger pushed the creature out and it fell to the gel surface. The hooder meanwhile had frozen, hood up high. Above, the armour plug swung back and closed. Below, the grazer lay on its back limbs moving weakly. The thing was the size of a large dog and apparently possessed four limbs, though its forelimbs consisted of two sets of limbs partially melded together. In the real animal these could separate, but not in this case. Its body was bulbous behind a wide triple-keeled chest, while the head, on the end of a long neck, bore some resemblance to that of a cow, but with a longer mouth and too many eyes.

Still the hooder did nothing, and Jonas contemplated what it might mean for him if it failed to feed. But then, the prior warming finally getting things moving, the grazer followed the program loaded to its simple ganglion. It writhed for a moment then rolled over, coming up on its limbs. It began to move forwards, pausing every now and again to dip its head to the gel as if feeding – the jaws moving as if it were chewing, Jonas felt had been good addition.

The hooder shot forwards seeming almost not to touch the gel surface as it did so. At the last it whipped round hitting the grazer from the side, tipping it over and pushing it down. Usually hooders were slow meticulous eaters and that was part of the horror of them. This creature's hood went into the grazer like a milling wheel. Greenish yellow blood sprayed out along with gobbets of flesh. The grazer kept moving while this was happening, even when the hooder had eaten away half of its flesh, for the thing did not die as easily as its real kin.

'Motherfucker,' repeated one of the mercenaries – Jonas wasn't sure if it was the same one.

'It's good that you selected this kind of grazer,' said Jonas, trying to keep his voice level. 'It's not the kind that has the poisonous black fats inside, therefore the hooder can feed more quickly.'

'I'm surprised anything poisons them,' Ganzen replied.

Jonas glanced at him, but said nothing. It was nice to learn that the man's knowledge of hooders was limited. Hooders killed grazers containing black fats very slowly. Initially the reason for this was theorised to be because when such a grazer died the poisons in its black fats passed into the rest of its body and would poison the hooder. Jonas' understanding of the hooder physiognomy and genetics had effectively dismissed that. The poisons in the black fats would have little effect on such a creature. It ate them that way out of preference, though whether that preference was for the taste of flesh without poisons or for the pleasure of slowly eating a living prey, was debateable.

After twenty minutes the hooder was finished. Jonas noted that while it had dismembered its prey and stripped out all the soft matter it had left the bones intact. An adult tended to chop up the bones too, eat a great many of them and discard only pieces. He supposed this must be because the young hooder's eating apparatus had yet to attain its tool-like hardness and sharpness. Now the thing began searching around the area picking up stray pieces of flesh and even hoovering up spilled grazer blood.

'Feed it another one,' said Ganzen, his expression predatory.

Jonas nodded and got another grazer on the move in the feeding system. He increased the microwave dose this time and gave it longer in the breech for its facsimile life to establish. And he wondered how long it would be before Ganzen decided to offer the creature other, more entertaining, food.

The hooder easily finished off the four grazers and now the machines around the laboratory were making more. As he lay on his bed Jonas briefly thought about how he would delete the viral mechanism from the bioreactor and scrub the file. Thereafter, as the hooder changed, there would be no evidence that he had done anything.

He then contemplated the beast itself. When they put the second grazer in the thing was halfway up the wall to the feeding hatch as it came through. By the third one it went into the hatch as it opened and Jonas had to stop the thing closing on it. It explored in there for a moment, then dragged the grazer out, dropped with it to the shrinking gel surface and there fed on it. After it had fed it came up to the window again to briefly grind against the glass before then working around the edges. The damned thing was trying to find a way out and in an intelligent manner. He did not know if that was 'normal' behaviour because of course nothing like this had ever been done before. After it again went through the hatch to first explore then drag out the fourth grazer, it dropped to the floor and fed more slowly. This time it began taking apart the bones and eating them. It then turned to the bones of its previous prey and set to work on them too. This was certainly not the expected behaviour of an adult, because they never returned to remains. But how could he know what to expect here? There had been rumours of hooders being taken into illegal zoos but he had no detail on that and did not know how they behaved in captivity. And again, he had no idea about the behaviour of the juvenile form.

Jonas grimaced. He wished he knew more but he simply did not. This was expected but he wished he could distinguish between 'normal' juvenile hooder behaviour and that of one making a transition into something else. Now, almost certainly, the mechanisms had spread their viral load and the creature's code was being rewritten. Was its apparent intelligence a result of that? He could not know.

He now considered all the implications of what he had done. He had been fatalistic when he came to the decision to disrupt what

Ganzen was doing here in the way he had chosen. His feeling had been to smash it all up, hope for some opening so he could escape, but at least cause a great deal of disruption if he was to die. This felt right; this felt better than simply making further doomed to fail escape attempts likely resulting in him being tortured. If he ended up as lunch for a hooder, Dr Giggles would not be putting him back together again for the nightmare to continue. But would the hooder behave as he supposed?

When he had started this he had felt that the creature evident aggression, being weaponised, would result in extreme mayhem. Now he wondered. Intelligence was part of the package – part of those genetic changes – and an alien intelligence too. Maybe it would simply grow to its altered form of adulthood as a biomech war machine and simply await instructions. He might well have provided Ganzen with something that would be even more profitable. He closed his eyes on these doubts, intensely worried about all he could not predict. No, he had to go back to the aggression idea and stay there, and hope. Of course one hope had to be that when the hooder finally did something, he could put as much distance between himself and it as quickly as possible.

'Are you awake?' Caster's words rang in his ears, mildly distorted and via his aug so could not be heard by any of the equipment watching him in his room.

He jerked as if slapped. He had not expected this at all and certainly there seemed something odd about it. He doubted Ganzen allowed communication outside of lab time. He pulled up menus to his inner vision and studied them. Something seemed out of kilter in his aug: optic reception seemed to be off, distorted, like he was seeing things through thick greenish glass. Then, despite this, he saw Caster had used another comlink and he simply had not allowed it, that meant Caster had hacked his aug – an exercise supposedly all but impossible but for by an AI.

'Yes, I'm awake,' he replied, speaking only in his head.

'I've hacked you, aug to aug.'

'And it seems caused some disruption in my aug.'

'What?'

'Optics aren't working properly.'

'That shouldn't happen,' she replied. *Whatever*, he thought, and waited to hear what else she had to say.

Finally, after a long pause she said, 'Nobody can listen in unless you're stupid enough to speak out loud.'

'I'm not that stupid,' he replied. He paused, reviewing his earlier thought about AI and paranoia arising. 'I'm also not so stupid as to think you capable of hacking an aug.'

Another long pause ensued, then she spoke again, 'I guess you think Ganzen has suspicions, has copied my voice and is now trying to get something out of you.'

'Not that there's anything to get,' he replied.

'No? Really?' He could almost hear the gears of her mind grinding, which made him think that this really was her. But he could not concede that. If he was wrong then he had no doubt Dr Giggles would be next.

'Okay,' she continued. 'You set one of the bioreactors to making viruses and a carrier shell to get them through the hooder's digestion and into its body. From things you said previously I'm pretty sure they are to make genetic changes related to the creature's biomech past. And that's as far as I've got.'

Jonas just lay there feeling scared. This could be Ganzen speaking to him or maybe this was Caster and her link was not as secure as she hoped. But, as he thought this, he realised there was nothing he could do. In either case he would be fucked. He had to just go with it and not overthink.

'You're right,' he said. 'The virus is making genetic changes that will result in the hooder turning into its ancestral form of a biomech – a war machine.'

'Damn and fuck,' she replied, and he noted awe in her voice. 'But how is that possible? Where does the data come from?'

He decided at this point to take a half-measure. This could still be Ganzen or the man could be listening in and, at least, it would be better for him not to know about the quantum storage crystals.

'It's all there in the genome,' he said briefly. 'Just blocked.'

She snorted, then said, 'It really is me speaking to you and there is no way anything less than an AI can penetrate the coding of this link. Ganzen has no AIs – they would not approve of what he does.'

Jonas allowed himself a wry smile. He always found the faith some people had in AIs touching, and naïve. But she was probably right in this case. To be honest, if Ganzen had a rogue AI working for him it would have seen what Jonas had done; in fact, with such an entity, the man would have had no need of Jonas at all. He decided to tell her.

'Quantum crystals in the genome. The viruses merely reattach the link between the two,' he told her.

'So what does that mean for us?'

'I am hoping an opportunity to escape, though it may well be an opportunity just to die.' He grimaced, thinking maybe he should not have added that last. She might get scared enough of the hooder to end up confessing to Ganzen. 'I'm pretty sure the hooder will attempt to escape and will have the means to do so. And when it does I'm also sure it will be aggressive and highly destructive.'

'I tried to kill myself three times,' she said. 'I'm with you.'

'We'll need to do what we can to prepare.'

'I'll be able to get envirosuits,' she said, 'if I'm sure that the hooder is breaking out.'

'I'll need to be able to recognise you.'

She sent a picture: a waif-like woman clad in blue overalls with cropped silver hair and big eyes with thick eye-shadow around them, or genetically darkened skin there. He noted points to her ears, pronounced canines, long fingers and something almost predatory in her stance. He reckoned she must be some sort of 'dapt but had no idea what kind. He took a picture of himself out of a file in his aug and sent it to her.

'That wasn't really necessary,' she said. 'I know what you look like.'

'Okay.'

'Is there any requirement for those viruses now?' she asked.

'No, they will either have done their work or failed.'

'I'll erase them from the bioreactor, and their record.'

'We'll talk again,' he told her, uncomfortable with how long this had gone on. 'I need to sleep now.'

'Night,' she replied, and cut the link.

Jonas turned off his aug and lay there worrying, still half expecting Hoskins to crash into his room. After a little while he turned the aug back on again and saw that the optical effect remained and briefly, up to the right of his internal visual field, an effect like that of a kaleidoscope appeared, shifted for a while and disappeared. It seemed that despite her claim otherwise, her hack had caused some damage. Or was it Ganzen trying to penetrate his com? Cold sweat then arrived with a return of the shakes. At some point he carried his anxiety down into dreams about running an endless corridor with a hooder after him. Far far too ominous he felt, when he finally woke.

The hooder grew and grew, occasionally shedding just pieces of its carapace, but then eating those. It hardly seemed to excrete and when it starting eating the rubbery layer into which the gel had transformed, Jonas suspected there must be something missing from its diet. Inside the thing he could see changes at variance from the anatomy of hooders on Masada, along with concentrations of metals and other odd materials. He turned his attention to the food supply, determined to try something.

Returning to his files he found the early design of the skeleton for the grazer – this one made out of composite and metals. He matched it to the present skeleton he was using then began making changes. All were subtle but matched in quantity the materials profile in the hooder. Also, because he knew more about what the thing might grow in its body, he added other elements and compounds.

'Why are you doing this?' asked Caster – as was her duty to ask. He had now switched her communication over to the intercom. Because his aug still did not seem to be working right he had shut down many functions and had it running a diagnostic.

'I intend to try something experimental but very unlikely to harm the hooder.' They had agreed on his use of 'experimental' as a secret signal during night-time conversations he had increasingly curtailed – his aug malfunction giving him a headache. 'Experimental' meant he was doing something he felt necessary for the new hooder – for the growth of the biomech war machine. They were in dangerous territory now in regard to that too. They had also agreed that she should point out some of the changes in the thing as slightly aberrant, but no more, and hoped that Ganzen did not know what a hooder should look like inside, or simply would not bother to check at this stage.

Jonas quickly finalised his early iteration of food source and set the manufactories and printers to making just one, which he shot through the feeding tube. The hooder had ceased trying to explore that now and didn't search around its enclosure as much as it had before. It spent long periods in stillness as if concentrating on the changes within. The grazer came through and dropped to the floor, flipped upright much faster than the other version, then ran across the enclosure straight into the far wall. Though it ran on muscle and was covered with skin it did not really look like a living thing, nor move like one.

After hitting the wall it paused for a moment, turned round like the robot it was and ran back. The hooder, having raised itself to observe, shot forwards and knocked it over halfway across, but then pulled back. The grazer robot flipped upright and ran in a new direction, this time hitting the viewing window, falling over again, then running again. The hooder flipped it again, then again. At one point it used its tail to flip the thing over too. Jonas watched all this and could not help but feel that it was playing, and somewhat amused by the robot's antics. At last it pinned the grazer down using one leg to hold it while raising its hood above the thing. It was inspecting it, he was sure it was inspecting it. It then dipped abruptly and began to feed. Again it ate fast, shredding its prey in moments and ingesting it, then hoovering up the fragments. Jonas felt satisfied. It had been hungry for those things it was lacking, found them and responded.

When it had completely finished its meal the hooder came up to the glass and inspected him for a long moment. He felt his skin prickling and recognised the sensation of active scan. Checking his equipment he saw that yes, it had used radiations close to what he used on it. It caused no alerts because his own scans produced a lot of this EMR but he really hoped it would not do the same when Ganzen or any of the others were in here. As it finished and turned away, the prickling of his skin continued, but down his back. Was it checking him out as potential prey and a source of the nutrients it needed, or curious about the one feeding it? He began making more of the earlier iteration of robot grazer and feeding them in. By the end of his day the hooder had visibly grown – half again its original length and now the thickness of his torso.

'Soon,' he told Caster that evening, as they talked, but again curtailed their conversation because the diagnostic and reboot had not rid his aug of its problems.

Ten days, thought Jonas.

Ganzen, sometimes with his men and sometimes alone had visited four times. On every occasion Jonas had been on edge, half expecting the hooder to scan them. He had his excuses in place, having upgraded a scanner on the far side of the room so he could explain away the scan as having come from that. Yet it seemed to show no interest in them, while it had scanned him four more times.

In that time the hooder had continued to grow. The structures within its body had become much more defined and harder to ignore by anyone who inspected them and Caster had, by agreement, ceased to comment on them. They did at least have an organic appearance – they were not like the components of some early machine – but then so it was with most Polity robots now. When Ganzen arrived again, this time with Hoskins and two others dragging along some other individual between them, Jonas thought on inevitability.

'Now it's time to see some real action,' Ganzen said.

Jonas stared at him, then at the woman they had brought. For a horrible moment he had thought she was Caster, felt relief when he saw the dark hair and ripped envirosuit, then guilt because he felt relieved.

'What do you mean?' he asked.

Ganzen just stared at him for a moment then said, 'You know exactly what I mean.'

Jonas began to get up out of his seat, but Hoskins was soon beside him pressing a hand hard down on his shoulder. The woman, slumped between the other two men, looked up. She had been beaten – one eye swollen and her mouth bloody. She looked a bit out of it as she studied her surrounding, then her gaze fixed on the window and what lay beyond it.

'Oh Christ no,' she said, then began to struggle. 'Ganzen, please no.'

Ganzen walked over to the heavy outer door beside the window and palmed the control there. The plug door lifted out then swung aside as the two dragged the woman forwards.

'Ganzen! No! I can work for you! I can get things from them!'

One of the men cuffed her, then looked guiltily towards Ganzen, who gave him a stern look. Jonas felt sick. They had obviously been instructed not to beat her senseless because he wanted her conscious for what was to ensue. They shoved her into the space between doors, but she wasn't going easily and kept throwing herself out again.

'Fuck it,' said Ganzen. 'Atres, stick her.'

The mercenary presumably of that name took a shock stick out of his belt and this time when they forced her into the space he jabbed her with it. The thing contacted with a crackle and left her shuddering on the floor. Ganzen set the door closing but apparently the shock had not quite been enough. She tried to get out again. Jonas saw her hand as she ridiculously tried to stop the door closing, her shouting turning to a scream as the door thumped home with a sickening crunch. As it locked into place a mess of blood and mashed flesh squeezed out at one point of the rim and dropped to the floor.

Ganzen worked the control again, this time opening the inner door. He turned away as that door began to open, obviously annoyed, and moved round to look through the window. The hooder was up like a cobra about to strike, its hood directed towards that opening door. It abruptly dipped and shot over, its head end disappearing out of sight behind the door and wall on that side. The woman started screaming in sheer raw terror, then the hooder moved abruptly and Jonas saw her sail through the air, arms and legs wind-milling, to land in the centre of the enclosure. Only when she shouldered into the rubbery surface and scrabbled up again did Jonas see the blood squirting from where her right arm had been crushed away below the centre of her forearm. Terror still drove her, for she scrambled for the other side of the enclosure as far away from the hooder as she could get. There she sat making a horrible keening sound.

'What's it fucking doing?' said Ganzen.

'It's trying to find a way out,' Jonas replied.

The sound of the creature scrabbling in the door opening came over the sound system, but also through that door. It sounded like someone taking power tools to stone. Abruptly Jonas felt his skin prickling and knew that the thing was scanning the doorway, but fortunately no one else seemed to notice. Perhaps other physical effects, like excitement and perhaps abhorrence, were overriding it. But then something happened that there was no way of hiding. A loud thump resounded and a wave of pinkish light escaped the doorway within the enclosure. Jonas froze for a second, then glanced to the exit from the laboratory.

'What the hell?' said Ganzen.

Jonas thought fast. Maybe the thing would get through that door, though he suspected the technology growing within its body had not reached sufficient maturity. If it got through he would run, now

Hoskins had moved away from him to try and see more of what the hooder was doing. If it did not he needed an explanation.

'You fucking let her in there with a weapon!' he exclaimed, all anger and offence as he stood up, though he stood up so as to more quickly get to the exit from here.

Ganzen looked round and stared at him, then transferred his attention to the two that had brought the woman in here.

'We scanned her and physically searched her,' said Atres. 'No way she had anything on her.'

The hooder now backed out of the doorway. Ganzen stepped forwards and hit the control again, closing that inner door. Jonas nodded confirmation to himself. Whatever the hooder had used it wasn't yet strong enough to break the creature out. He moved round his consoles and closer to the window.

'You could have damaged it,' he said, still apparently angry, but less so now. 'But they are tough creatures and it seems okay.'

Ganzen gestured to his consoles. 'Go back and check.'

Jonas nodded, all serious, and headed back. But he did not like the suspicion in Hoskins' expression as the man watched him. He sat down and called up scanning images of the hooder in motion. They were current, but he and Caster had created a filter program so they showed nothing of the new growths inside it. Then he looked up into the enclosure.

The woman still crouched, bleeding out onto the floor. She was whimpering now, her eyes wide as she stared at the approaching hooder. Jonas felt a clench in his guts as he recognised something there: that utter disbelief in what was happening to one, even while it was happening. But surely, her in an envirosuit and being a totally different prey to everything thus far provided, the hooder would kill and ingest her quickly?

It rose up before her, then came down on her as she raised her arms to defend herself, then up again with her dangling, like a cat with a mouse. With her legs kicking and her screams sounding hollow in that hood, it turned her to the centre of the floor, and dropped her. She hit the ground on her back, turned over and tried to crawl away. The hood came down again. It didn't cover her completely like and adult hood – her arms legs and head lay clear. She screamed in utter agony and thrashed for at least two minutes.

'Motherfucker,' said the mercenary who was not Atres.

Jonas looked at him, and then at them all. There was no sympathy there, no empathy. They were watching with horrible fascination and relish. He turned back as the tone of the screaming changed. The hood had come up again and she was crawling again, all the skin and muscle of her back stripped away to the bone. Watching her contemplatively, it waited until she neared the wall, came down and took her up again. This time it worked on her in mid-air, before dropping her. Jonas gaped in horror. I had stripped her skull down to the bone and she was still alive. And it had left her eyes. She crawled, slower now, and then like a cat tired of the game it came down on her and really went to work. Her screaming stopped a few minutes later and thereafter they just heard the sounds of feeding.

In utter silence now they all watched as it stripped her down, cutting up the pieces and feeding them into its vertical maw. It even ate her clothing and started hoovering up the blood and fragments that had escaped it. Finally Gazen turned away from the window. He appeared replete, satisfied, his eyes half closed with closely remembered pleasure.

'Harsh indeed,' said Hoskins.

'I don't like spies,' said Ganzen. He sighed, turned to Jonas. 'Check the creature has not been harmed and do whatever needs doing to keep it healthy.' He headed for the exit, the others falling in beside them.

As Jonas watched them go he noted that Ganzen, like the previous two times he had visited, no longer had his tiger with him. Perhaps he no longer considered it such an exciting pet now he had something to replace it? Jonas shook himself, feeling numb, aware that his 'factor had been pumping more drugs into him. He stood up from the console and stared at the hooder. A species of disappointment had risen in him. He had hoped for something other than the horrible lengthy death it had given. Turning to the door he reached down and detached the drug 'factor and pocketed it. He was done for the day.

The shakes and the vomiting hit him in the night long after he finished his latest conversation with Caster – mostly because he simply did not want to talk, not because of the increasing malfunction of his aug. She had seen it all too, and he wondered if she had a 'factor pumping calming chemicals into her all the while. Never thought to ask.

357

After his second round of vomiting and the feeling of just sheer awfulness, he contemplated putting the 'factor back on. He then thought again about that woman in the enclosure and knew that he had to have his mind at the best it could be, and for that he needed to be free of the thing. Justifiable paranoia was also involved because he would be unsurprised if the factor did not have some kind of tracer in it, and some way of knocking him out. Sleep finally took him again and when he woke in the morning it was to a deep depression, even so, after washing and eating he found that beginning to dissipate. His own body was fighting it as was his own nanosuite because it too balanced neurochem, just with more subtlety than the 'factor.

When he returned to the lab the hooder was waiting by the glass, observing him. He nodded to it, as if to a work associate, then went to his console to check unfiltered scans and set the feeding routine running again. The creature seemed to have returned to being voracious and he could not help thinking that it killed the woman the way it had because she was capable of suffering. This led him to thoughts on its form – how perfectly designed it was to extract every last dreg of agony from a victim – and that perhaps the Atheter who had made its kind had been cruel.

Alternating grazers and adding elements to those with composite and metal skeletons, he soon ascertained that the hooder's internal and external growth had accelerated. It seemed the woman had provided something it had desperately needed, which he tried not to think was pain. Later, when it began to leave parts of its prey scattered about its enclosure, he stopped feeding it and stood up from his consoles to head over to the window. The creature came up to its side of the window too to watch him. He went up to it, face to face, and stared back. Its eyes had turned from orange to red and its carapace was turning obsidian black like those on Masada, though with odd streaks of white here and there. He then turned away and walked over to the outer door through which they had put the woman, and opened it.

'What are you doing?' asked Caster – direct into his aug this time, the words slinging shards like broken glass across his inner vision.

'Checking something,' he answered offhand.

The door thumped and then oozed out, a thin film of blood, flesh and bone peeling away and hanging there till he brushed it away. Glancing across, he saw that the hooder was now out of sight – almost certainly on the outside of the inner door to its enclosure. As the door on his side swung open he inspected first its inner face then the space within. Both looked burned, and with a weird white frosting over that. Here and there patches of holes had been drilled into ceramal – an impossible task for most living creatures. A hemisphere of ceramal lay on the floor. He stared at it, then reached out and touched the burned material of the nearest surface. It felt odd and he prodded it. The stuff crunched and his finger went in up to the first joint. When he pulled it out flakes fell to the floor.

The realisation hit him as he pressed a foot down on one of those flakes, turning it to granular dust. He considered how he had been feeding it all morning, when he should have been as far away as possible. Time had run out. If the thing could do this it was all but free and he should wait no longer for some undefined point in the future when it supposedly reached its full adolescent size. He stepped back and hit the control, watched the door swing back into place and lock down with a rusty crunching. As he stepped away again the hooder shot back into sight, moving fast, violently. It came up to the glass and hammered against it, and this seemed to reflect in his aug with internal vision of menus disappearing in a kaleidoscope flash of migraine optics. He could not help but feel it had expected him to let it out, and was now angry that he had not. It retreated then and ran a couple of circuits of the enclosure, while Jonas moved around the lab, collecting up two items he had made and just left amidst the other tools he had scattered around the area. Into the end of the cylinder he inserted a chainglass knife handle first and locked it down, before sliding the cylinder into his sleeve.

Surely now…

Doubts came and sat on his shoulder. He gazed back at the hooder as it came up against the glass again, felt intense scan once more and stepped back. The hooder did not hammer this time, just moved the underside of its hood close to the glass. A thump resounded and the whole window turned white. A moment later a whitened inner lamination of chainglass fell to dust. The thing had just decoded it. He walked backwards to the exit, horrible fascination slowing his steps. Now that wave of pink fire spread across the glass from its hood, and another lamination turned blue then crazed into hexagonal fragments. Another lamination, probably sapphire.

'We go now,' he said to Caster, then turned and ran for the door from his lab.

'Really,' she replied. 'You think?'

Jonas jerked the door open and stepped out, straight into the path of Hoskins.

'What the hell is going on?' Hoskins asked, gazing at him with almost tired contempt. The man had looked at him like this many times before. He was their pet scientist who had been sufficiently subdued into obedience. He wasn't an ex-ECS soldier now working as a mercenary. Jonas walked straight at him, dropping the cylinder out of his sleeve into his hand and drove the sharp end into his face – the chainglass blade going straight into Hoskins' eye. The impact initiated the charge in the in the cylinder and the thing crackled in the man's face spitting out smoke. When Jonas pulled it out Hoskins dropped bonelessly to the floor. Jonas stepped over him and ran, the cylinder whining up to charge again. This had been something he and Caster had discussed. What the likes of Hoskins tended to neglect, was that you didn't get to live for a hundred and seventy years without learning something of violence.

As he rounded a turning at the end of the corridor a great crash resounded from the lab. He glanced back as a wall of energy, like glowing pink fog, burst out of the corridor leading to the lab. It hit the wall and spread down towards him, but more diffuse now. He turned and ran, but not fast enough. A sizzling meniscus swept over him, picking him up off the floor with his legs kicking in the air. It transmitted a shock through his body, as if every bone in it had been hit with a hammer, then discarded him. He scrabbled on the floor trying to get his limbs working as debris and smoke exploded into the corridor behind, got to his feet and staggered on, gradually regaining control. The utter certainty that the hooder had broken free and was now behind him, gave him the edge he needed and he ran again.

Following a route he had rehearsed in his mind many times before, he ran faster than he had thought himself capable. Yes, he was terrified of what lay behind him, but also shivering with a weird excitement. However, every time he had taken this route in his mind he hadn't thought too much about the contingencies. He had reached Caster and thereafter they had followed through their escape plan. In none of those imaginings had he run straight into four heavily-armed mercenaries. He skidded to a halt as they raised their weapons and moved forwards.

'We have to… we have to –' he began, wanting to get them running too.

One of them stepped right up to him, grabbed him and slammed him against the wall, armoured hand round his neck like a docking clamp. One of the other three reached up to touch a control at his collar.

'We've got him,' he said, and then tilted his head to listen for a moment before turning to Jonas. 'What happened?'

The adrenaline must have gone straight to his brain, because he had excuses and explanations he had rehearsed with Caster clear in his mind.

'The hooder broke out,' he said tightly, struggling to get the words past that clamping hand. 'I think that woman Ganzen fed it…'

The man held up a finger, silencing him and listened some more. Jonas meanwhile opened the link in his aug to Caster, allowing her to hear what he was hearing and see what he was seeing.

Jonas?'

He didn't reply – too busy marshalling his thoughts.

'Explain what you mean about the woman,' said the mercenary, as the one holding Jonas relaxed his grip a little. Meanwhile the other two moved past and then broke into a trot down the corridor.

'She had some kind of weapon that blew up – Ganzen knows about that. I think it must have damaged the enclosure. The inside of the door is all burned and it must have affected the glass because the hooder broke it down.'

Again some listening, then a nod. 'Chard, take him to a holding cell.' The man moved after the other two. 'Then we might need some help. We're to drive it back to the lab and keep it there till Ganzen gets a crew down.'

'Keep it there?' asked Chard.

'Apparently – too valuable to kill.' He moved off.

As the man rounded a corner after the others Chard jerked Jonas away from the wall and shoved him stumbling along the corridor.

'Your name is Chard?' Jonas asked.

'Yes.'

'Your friends are going to have some problems.'

'No shit.'

Talk for talk's sake while he slowed and allowed the guy to get closer. He dropped the cylinder into his hand, deliberately stumbled so Chard came closer, then turned and stabbed for his face. But Chard moved too quickly. The flat of his hand came up and hit Jonas' forearm a numbing blow. The cylinder left his hand and hit the wall, discharging there with a flash and gust of oily smoke before dropping to the floor with a clatter that released the knife. They both looked at it, then at each other. Jonas felt the horror of realisation tighten his guts. No lie could cover this. He had tried to take the man out and now it would be obvious to him, and to Ganzen, that this was all some kind of escape attempt. Jonas saw that room in his mind, and saw Dr Giggles coming out from underneath his bench. Chard drew a weapon from his belt and pointed it, and Jonas recognised a pepper pot stun gun.

'Walk ahead of me and don't try anything stupid again,' said Chard. 'In this suit it's no more trouble for me to carry you than have you walk.'

Jonas moved ahead, the shakes starting to hit him again. He simply could not end up in that room again, yet he could see no way clear. He just hoped Caster was on the move – that she could get away without him. He walked carefully, hands held out to his sides, as he frantically tried to think of some way to escape, because unconscious there would be no chance. Just then a hollow boom resounded and the whole of the *Fist* shuddered. Jonas staggered to one side and heard the familiar slapping sound of the stunner firing. Narcotic beads hissed along one wall of the corridor. He stepped away from there, turning, hands held up.

'The fuck was that?' Chard wondered.

He obviously hadn't meant to fire the weapon by the way he was looking at it.

'I've no idea,' Jonas replied.

Chard touched his collar, listened, and as he did so the look he gave Jonas was not pleasant at all.

'The fucking thing is weaponised, and they found what was left of Hoskins.' He listened some more, then nodded. 'You are so going to be having a lot of giggle time.'

Jonas stared at him and didn't know how to respond. If the man had been pointing a weapon that could kill him he would have attacked.

362

But if he attacked now he suspected the next place he would wake up would be in a surgical chair.

'*I'm coming for you,*' said Caster. The words were clear but with dazzling internal visual effects. He felt certain her hack had damaged his aug, and that had now been exacerbated by something the hooder had used – perhaps some scan radiation to ascertain how to break that chainglass window. Irrelevant now, really. He ached for the idea of rescue, but his self-esteem won out.

'*Do not come for me,*' he told her. '*Just get out like we planned.*'

'Keep moving,' said Chard.

Jonas turned and continued along the corridor, turned right when told, then left.

'Door on your right,' said Chard.

Jonas turned to it as the man came up beside him, pressing the nose of the stunner into his neck as he palmed the control. Locks clicked and he pushed it open.

'Inside.'

Just a plain blank cell – its only furnishing being a single toilet and water spigot in one corner. He supposed they only provided that because they did not want to clear up any mess. Chard gave him a shove as he entered and he stumbled to the middle of the room and turned.

'This will all be over before you wake up,' the mercenary told him.

Jonas raised his hands and was about to protest. The cloud of beads, loaded with neurotoxin hit him in the chest. He staggered back into the wall, felt the wind knocked out of him and numbness spreading, tried to throw himself back upright at Chard, but just slapped a hand weakly against the floor. Then the lights went out.

Bright light surrounded Jonas and, after just a moment of confusion, terror surged as he felt sure he would find himself in that other room, sitting in the surgical chair. He didn't want to open his eyes to bring himself into that scene and just lay there feeling sick, with his body aching. But then, aware that he was physically in the wrong position to be in a surgical chair, he opened his eyes.

He was on his side on the floor, with his back against the wall. The cell was incredibly bright – the whole ceiling emitting an almost sunlight glow. He guessed they added sleep deprivation to whatever else they did to people they kept here. Painfully easing upright he sat there trying to nail down something that had felt wrong here since the moment he woke up. Then he realised he felt as if he were in some moving vehicle. The cell kept shifting, jerking, and when he put his hand against the floor he felt a constant vibration. Some other mechanism to keep inmates from sleeping?

He climbed to his feet – he needed to get mobile to take any opportunity for escape presented, and he needed to have a close look at that door, because perhaps he could break out? He needed to do *something*. He used the toilet then drank from the water spigot. The water had a chemical slightly salty taste and he puzzled at it for a moment before abruptly vomiting in the toilet. Certainly they wanted to make things uncomfortable for the prisoners. He walked, trying to get the numb stiffness out of his limbs. The light waned and he lay on the floor again, started to drift into sleep, then came out of it abruptly, heart thudding, when a loud clattering sounded behind one wall and the lights came up again. He realised some cell program had initiated in here from when he woke. He paced again, felt thirst growing, and then tiredness again almost certainly a result of the stunner. He tried his aug and found not only the kaleidoscope lights but the network of the *Fist* slow and disrupted, though he could see that Caster had tried to contact him a couple of times. He tried her, but received no reply. One more time the weariness took him down to the floor, but this time the door opening woke him.

'Get up,' said Chard.

The man looked harried. His armour shed grey ash as he stepped in and a molten scar ran down one leg. He drew that stunner again.

'Get the fuck up. He wants you.'

Jonas swung round into a sitting position. He saw no reason now to avoid being stunned if Chard intended to take him to Doctor Giggles – that would at least delay the inevitable. Chard took a step towards him, and he abruptly reconsidered. He'd just seen two people in Ganzen overalls run past the door and now he could smell smoke. Something was certainly happening out there and this meant more chances to escape. He stood and walked slowly forwards, then through the door as Chard backed out ahead of him. The man then gestured along the corridor with his weapon.

Definitely something was happening. The shaking and the odd jerking of the ship he could feel even more out here. A layer of smoke swirled along the ceiling and, as he walked, he could feel grav plates fluctuating under his feet. At one point the lights went out, but Chard was on him in a moment with the weapon pressed into his back until they came on again. They reached a junction and Jonas stopped, because a group of people was crowding along the corridor – Ganzen staff in distinctive overalls or lab jackets, execs in businesswear. Once they were past he stepped out, damning himself for not diving in amongst them because maybe he could have got away then.

'What's going on?' he asked.

'Like you don't fucking know,' said Chard.

Jonas halted and turned towards him. 'Actually, I don't.'

'I told you to keep damned well moving!'

Chard stepped towards him, pulling back the weapon ready to hit him. He stepped back. 'Look, I really don't know!' But he did, and the idea sent a shiver down his spine.

'Get ready to drop to the floor,' Caster told him in an explosion of broken emeralds.

Jonas shook his head. Her speaking to him now felt like too much input. She wasn't making any sense. Why did she say that?

'Drop now!'

Conscious thought being merely a surface to the subconscious, the latter took over. Jonas dropped without knowing why until he hit the floor and pulse rifle fire flashed in the corridor like a transformer short circuit. He rolled to one side and looked up to see Chard staggering backwards and knew that only the assist of his suit was keeping him upright. The top right quarter of the man's skull was gone, with the remainder of his brain hanging out and steaming. The man took another step then went over with a crash.

'Bloody hell,' said Jonas.

'Come on!' Caster ran up carrying a pulse rifle. She was clad in an envirosuit and had another one slung over her shoulder. Jonas stood up, trying to get his mind back into motion.

'That was a hell of a shot,' he said.

'We talked about this,' she replied, and held out the envirosuit to him.

They had, even before his recent encounter with Hoskins. He had discovered she was old like him and they had talked about how, them being 'scientists', some seemed to discount their skill set – old standard lifetimes of skills.

'I told you to run,' he said, stupidly feeling miffed because she had not done what he said nor acknowledged his sacrifice.

'Come on, we have to go,' she told him as he looked at the suit. 'You don't have time to put it on now.'

Jonas began thinking clearly again. He could not afford any more moments of bafflement and he could not afford any more slip ups. Abruptly turning away he went over to Chard and relieved the man of his main weapon – a stubby laser carbine – energy canisters, and a sidearm pulse gun. He did not bother with the stunner because he very much doubted he would choose unconsciousness as an option for anyone they encountered. Weighing the weapons he felt a sudden lightness in himself. Now, no matter what happened, he would not end up back in that room with Dr Giggles. He would put the barrel of the pulse gun in his mouth first.

They ran on, Caster leading. Intermittent map display in his aug got him their location and that she was taking them back to the route already planned. A huge crash shifted the *Fist* again and sent Caster down on her face. As he pulled her to her feet the shaking of the structure became a shuddering, and now he could hear stuttering and electrical hissing, cracks and booms of weapons' fire. They staggered into a room as the ship jerked violently yet again. This was someone's apartment – hastily abandoned. Jonas quickly shed his clothing while heading over into a kitchen area, found a drinks fridge and downed a carton of some fruit-coconut concoction, then began pulling on the envirosuit, catheters engaging, the thing powering up. It was better than his old version – he felt the tightening of assist ready to kick in, for the thing had a sliding layer meta-material structure.

'How did you get the pulse rifle?' he asked.

'I'd planned on getting it all along,' she replied. 'I will not be captured again.'

Her thought was much his own.

'You never told me,' he said, but it wasn't an accusation. He perfectly understood her need to keep this option to herself – her fear of telling him and him perhaps blurting this news while receiving the attentions of Dr Giggles. She simply shrugged.

'What's happening out there?' he asked.

'The hooder is happening.' She shook her head. 'Data are difficult at the moment, but I have never seen something wreck things so fast, besides some major weapon. Ganzen tried to contain it – I don't think many of his men made it out alive.'

Jonas nodded, then looked at her. 'It is a major weapon.'

She acknowledged that with a sharp impatient nod.

With the pulse gun shoved in his belt, he checked the operation of the laser carbine, thankful to find it wasn't code locked to its owner. He then took out the pulse gun and checked that wasn't either. They opened the door again, to immediately pull back coughing and quickly close up their suit hoods and visors. The smoke in the corridor was flowing quickly in one direction, which could mean atmosphere breach. Jonas peered through it the way they had been heading, puzzling over something that did not look right there. Then the smoke cleared and he saw that the floor walls and ceiling of the corridor just ended.

'What the hell?' An icon came up in his visor – comlink to one other suit – and he blinked at it to open it. 'What the hell is this?' he added.

Caster moved forwards and he followed her to where the grav had gone out in the floor. Beyond, a great hollow had been carved out in the heart of the ship, all the structure compressed into tangled junk piles. Looking up at a sloping surface above, he tapped Caster's shoulder and pointed. One of the armoured mercenaries had been opened up and spread in an even mandala across that surface, his armour neatly divided up with the rest of his body, blood painted in arcs and spirals that matched across a centre point like a Rorschach blot. Then, over on the far side of this hollow, a mound of wreckage shifted and the hooder came up through it. Larger now and completely bone white, the thing swung its body in a circle cutting the wreckage into a funnel shape. Jonas now remembered something he had heard on Masada about a legendary albino hooder – one that made sculptures out of the bones of its prey. He had always thought the story apocryphal.

'Come on!' Caster shouted. 'We'll find another way!'

Such had been his fascination he had not seen her head off. He turned to run after her then paused as the hooder swung its hood towards him. A brief instant of something passed and that reflected in internal vision – an unfolding mandala of crystal lights. Recognition? Then the thing fountained out of its hole, hooped up and over and slammed down again, ripples of some energy running down its body, ahead of it wreckage swirling and turning molten as it dived in and disappeared.

They kept running, took a route around that wrecked area, and headed for the airlock they had chosen. Grav stuttered and went out and thereafter they began propelling themselves along slapping feet and hands against anything available. They passed over an area where a hole had been punched through one wall, tearing up the floor, then through the other. Peering in each direction, Jonas saw it curving off through the ship. They passed two more of these, each going through the corridor from different angles and he visualised the vessel as a worm-eaten apple. Further along they found the tiger.

'What the hell?' wondered Caster.

Hell indeed, Jonas thought. Perhaps, as with that woman, the animal had contained some trace element the hooder had needed, because most of it was gone. The skin lay stuck to the floor with blood, spread out like a rug. The teeth had been neatly placed in an arc ahead of the head skin, while the claws lay in similar arcs just beyond the skin of each limb. What made the hooder leave the remains of its prey like this? He looked towards the hole down through the ceiling, noting there had been no exit hole, noted the pulse fire scars along the walls. Had the hooder taken Ganzen?

They moved on and, though the ship continued to shudder, the sounds of weapons' fire receded behind them. Jonas realised they were approaching their destination when they entered a corridor with square chainglass ports running down one side. These gave the illusion of being able to look directly out into vacuum, but he knew that fibre optics through the ship's armour provided the image.

'Damn,' he said.

'We'll have to get to one of the escape pods,' said Caster.

The port showed no sign of the construction bay in which the *Fist* had resided, just a sparse star field. Some of that movement they had felt earlier must have been the ship undocking and heading away from

Moloch Three. This made no sense. The structures linking it to Porrit Town had looked solid and permanent, while the clamps and robot infrastructure about the vessel had not moved in an age.

'Why would Ganzen do this?' he wondered as he followed her.

'I can think of no reason,' she replied.

He considered what that might imply then, after struggling to call up aug menus, felt a lack of surprise to see that though the ship's internal network still functioned, the blocking was down. Supposing his busted aug could manage it, he should now be able link to the network of Moloch Three, which in turn linked to the Polity – if Ganzen had not actually shut down the transceivers for that purpose. Labouring to open links he found the feeds spotty and slow, disappearing in migraine lights, but he could get through. Then someone got through to him.

>*So you certainly stirred things up here.*

He caught hold of Caster's shoulder, pointed to his aug and included her.

'You're one of the Polity agents who were chasing me?' he asked, so she knew.

>*Well spotted. Twenty points.*

'Why are you talking to me now?'

>*We've been throwing messages at all aboard the* Fist *for the last six hours, but only now has Ganzen's blocking gone down. I felt beholden to contact you, and warn you.*

'Warn me about what?'

>*You have less than an hour to get off that ship, maybe not even that much time.*

'What?'

>*Well, it seems that having an alien biomech war machine activate within its station was enough to wake up the Moloch Three AI. And it's woken up tetchy. It ejected the ship you are aboard, incidentally tearing up half of Porrit town in the process, and now intends to neutralise the threat with a CTD imploder. It's obviously quite anxious, or peeved about the situation, since it appears to have loaded a gigaton warhead.*

'How far are we from the station?' Caster interjected.

>*Who's this... ah, Caster Neamuller. You're eighty miles out. The AI will hit you at a hundred miles even though that'll cause some damage here, and may hit you earlier if that thing you have aboard looks to be getting out of the ship.*

'We only have envirosuits,' she said.

>*Doesn't really matter what you're wearing. You need to get clear in an ejection pod as it seems most of the surviving Ganzen staff are doing.*

Caster caught hold of his shoulder and gestured ahead. 'I've got it mapped.'

Jonas tried to access the station map but got nowhere. Meanwhile it seemed the Polity agent had no more to say.

They threw themselves onward, breaking the gecko stick of their boots, grabbing and propelling themselves forwards using rungs on the corridor walls provided for just this purpose. Back in towards the centre of the ship through another corridor brought them to a drop shaft, a fire burning down at one end. They went up it in the opposite direction, tracked along another corridor to another of the exterior ones. Along here, bulkhead doors interspersed the square ports. Beside each door a red light glared, which indicated what they could see through the ports: that the escape pods here were all gone. Jonas swore.

'Try the network again,' he said. 'My aug is screwed.'

She gave him a puzzled look then frowned in concentration.

'Patchy now, but I'm getting a link to Moloch Three,' she said. More frowning then, 'Time series program giving me release of the escape pods. Yeah, got it. I know where there are some left.'

'Then let's go.'

'Someone's following us,' she said, indicating with a nod the corridor behind him.

Jonas looked back. Smoke misted the long curve of the corridor here and many of the lights had dropped to a dull red glow. But peering through this he could see a figure coming fast, frog leaping from wall to wall. He felt a sinking sensation – that looked like someone in power armour and though they had their weapons he could not see how they stood a chance. They propelled themselves on.

'In!' Caster shouted, gesturing to the next turning, and they went through towards another drop shaft and hurled themselves into that. Intermittent grav from below began to tug them down so they grabbed the ladder up the side.

'Up,' she said, and they climbed fast – the grav effect feeling less than a quarter terran normal. As Caster went through an exit he looked down. Coming fast up the shaft the figure did not look like a human bulked out by power armour, and something was wrong about the shape of its head. It then passed one of the lights set in the side of the shaft and he got a much clearer look. Dr Giggles was coming after them.

'Oh hell,' said Caster.

They swung into the new corridor – grav at about a half – and ran. Ganzen must be abandoning the ship, he realised, but had first sent Chard to get him, and now Chard had failed he had sent the Doctor. Predictably the man wanted revenge against Jonas who had, effectively, destroyed the heart of Ganzen Combine. As they ran a curve away from the shaft exit, he kept looking back, seeing the robot still pursuing. How had he mistaken that for an armoured man? Too many limbs and it moved more like a spider. He brought up his carbine.

'We go up from here then across,' she said, and made an attempt to send him a map which he managed to get the gist of before it shattered like a safety screen.

'You realise we're probably heading towards Ganzen,' he said. 'He'll be at the remaining escape pods.'

She caught his shoulder, them both coming to a stumbling halt. 'We're going nowhere,' she said.

His focus had been back towards Giggles – just an awareness of wreckage and a fire burning ahead. He looked properly. The hooder was coming out of a hole in the wall, its hood up and facing them, steadily focused on him, he felt, as the coils of its body oozed out behind, filling up the corridor.

His mind, frantic in speculation wound down to the horrible conclusion: Giggles coming in from behind and now the hooder ahead. They were dead, and it seemed the only choices remaining were how they died. He reached up and touched the control on his collar, the visor rolling down to the neck ring, the helmet softening then doing the same at the back. Hot vapour in the air tightened his lungs and had him wheezing in a moment. Caster had also shed her head covering and inverted her pulse rifle, lodging it under her chin. He turned away, not wanting to see her kill herself, drew his pulse gun and brought it to the same position. Could he do this? Or would he, like so many before, keep delaying until too late? He gripped the gun tightly, terrified of it being knocked out of his hand, but then the scrabbling sound of Dr Giggles approaching behind initiated a wave of sick anger.

Jonas abruptly holstered the pulse gun and turned, raising the carbine. Giggles came down the corridor fast, bouncing from wall to wall. It was the nature of the hooder to do the things it did and it was here through no fault of its own. He knew that Giggles was much the same – just made and programmed to be what it was – but he could not dismiss the anger. He feared and detested the robot, yet felt an illogical kinship with the more fearsome creature behind.

'Fuck you! Just fuck you!' he shouted, and opened fire. A moment later pulse rifle fire punctuated the air along with the air-searing half-seen beam of his weapon.

Their fire intersected on the Doctor, but the thing was moving too fast for them to hit it for long. He saw a surgical limb flaring and spraying metal droplets, a leg burning and white muscle turning black and peeling, but the robot did not slow. Then something slammed him aside into the corridor wall, a large insect limb hit his chest and the hooder was coming past. On the other side of it Caster fell against the other wall, looking bewildered. A moment later the creature's tail section passed over his legs. Looking along the corridor he saw the thing knock Giggles down from the wall and, like someone trying to catch a spider in a cupped hand, the hooder bringing its hood down on the robot. But Giggles shot free, bounced against the wall again, then up to cling to the ceiling. Hooder and robot faced each other, hood to hood, then the robot, who must have had some survival instinct programmed in, began scuttling away along the ceiling.

Jonas had his hand around the grip of his pulse gun, his carbine in his other hand. His mind felt slow for he couldn't decide which weapon to use on himself. A thump ran through the wall behind him and a vague pink meniscus passed down the corridor, raising sparks from his envirosuit. The main wave he saw went the other way to sweep over the robot and bring it crashing to the floor. Then the hooder was on it, nearly covering the struggling thing.

'Time to go?' suggested Caster.

They got up and ran.

Again grav was out when they took the next drop shaft. Lighting flickered for a while then flipped over to emergency power saving. Jonas suspected a reactor had gone down, but even though the spectrum of the lighting had taken on a blue tint it was more than bright enough – the light panels did not draw a great deal of power and would be amply supplied by subsidiary generation from meta-material convertors throughout the ship. Light enough to die by.

Why was he now so utterly sure the hooder had taken its time over Dr Giggles because the robot had been so interesting? And now why, with that curiosity resolved, did he feel so utterly sure it was coming after them? That they, or rather he, had become its intense focus?

'Hopefully it's found something or someone else to occupy itself back there,' said Caster, revealing that she felt nothing of what he felt. This seemed to key into his mind and crack open something that should have been obvious but which, on some unconscious level, he had been denying. As they exited the drop shaft and towed themselves through further corridors – it now rare for them to find anywhere grav still operated – he concentrated on his aug feed. His inner vision opened up with kaleidoscope and fractal patterns filling everything. He mentally pushed, groping for deeper connection he could usually obtain through menu selections – for voice, data input feeding into his brain, for virtuality. Then it hit him and he lost control of his limbs, slamming into a wall and drifting limply through the air.

Hadn't the supposed malfunction of his aug started directly after the hooder ate its first meal that initiated the changes within it? Hadn't this malfunction increased when he had supposed it had expected him to let it out of its enclosure? When it was angry? He found himself in a glittering space, distorted imagery falling past him, data like the untranslated feed from an AI directly into his brain. Pain burned in his forehead and he lost perception of his self. And there with him he felt the mental presence of something utterly alien. He tried to understand something he could in no way get a grip on. He felt some vast and callous darkness pulling him apart and on some level knew he was screaming.

– *haitus* –

Jonas came back to himself, flat against a surface, his visor open and Caster pinning him there. He could smell vomit and saw the remains of his last meal drifting away like some airborne amoeba. Gradually he got control of his shaking and managed a nod as she held something up in front of his face: his aug, unplugged from his skull.

'It had to be that,' she said. 'Ganzen must have put in a virus or something.'

She pushed away from him as he got his limbs under control and floated from the wall. He held out his hand and she gave him the aug, which he put in a pocket of his suit.

'No, not Ganzen,' he said.

'Well what then?'

'The hooder. Right from the start it initiated some connection – probably something automatic. Maybe it assumed I was one of its atheter creators.' He glanced back the way they had come. 'Let's keep going – maybe it can't find me now.'

They moved on. Jonas was glad of the lack of grav here because he wasn't sure if his legs could have supported him. Gradually strength returned and they were travelling quickly again when they began to find the bodies.

'What's been happening here?' Caster wondered.

'Ganzen,' Jonas replied.

Three bodies were floating in the corridor just ahead. He had noted that two wore Ganzen Combine overalls and one was clad in businesswear. All had been burned either by pulse gun fire or laser. They moved on, pushing the corpses aside, entered a new corridor and found more of the same.

'Why has he been killing his own people?' Caster asked, then answered her own question. 'Probably concerned about the number of escape pods or they were just in the way.' She paused speculatively, then added, 'None of his mercenaries here.'

They kept moving, Caster counting down the corridors at each intersection.

'Here,' she pointed ahead.

At the end of this corridor, crossed by one of those hooder burrows, lay another of those running around just inside ship's armour. Here Caster's very intermittent link back to Moloch Three had told her escape pods were still in place. But when they crossed to the nearest port and looked out they could see none, and red lights glowed all the way down the corridor.

'Can you get an update from Moloch Three?' he asked.

'Mine seems to be malfunctioning too,' she replied. 'Weird fractal patterns. But I still have some data streams.' She dipped her head and closed her eyes, then after a moment raised it. 'Every escape pod is gone.' Her eyes looked glazed as she concentrated on the information.

'Seems they were leaving intermittently until twenty minutes ago, then every remaining one detached. Wait a minute…' She grimaced. 'No, there's one pod left.'

'Ganzen,' said Jonas. 'We're going to be walking into a trap.'

It seemed obvious. Ganzen had aug access to the ship's network, spotty and malfunctioning as it was. He also probably had a link to Giggles, prior to the hooder attacking that robot. He knew where they were and where they were heading. He knew they needed a pod to escape this ship and had sent all but his own out into vacuum so they had no choice but to go there if they wanted to live. Caster nodded at him, asking no questions, she too had worked all this out.

'A pod can fit quite a few people,' she said.

'And he'll certainly have those people with him,' he replied.

'Not normal working stiffs – mercenaries in power armour.'

'We don't stand a chance.'

'We don't have a choice.'

They moved on. Almost certainly there would be a fight, Jonas thought. He would die in that fight rather than let Ganzen capture him. They moved inward again, up a length of dropshaft then back along another corridor linking to one of the hull corridors. Jonas caught hold of Caster's arm as she moved ahead of him, held a finger to his lips and then crept forwards to peer around the edge. An armoured figure squatted facing him in the corridor. Two other figures were coming behind, and fast. He jerked back as narcotic beads shattered near his face and on the wall to his left. He urgently waved Caster back and they retreated, but that same armoured figure slammed into the wall where his bead shot had hit, denting it, then threw himself towards them. Jonas opened fire with his carbine held in one hand, hit the control to close his visor and hood, then drew his sidearm too. A bead blast hit him square in the chest sending him staggering back just as Caster opened fire. Another bead blast hit her too but by then he realised the beads did not penetrate their envirosuits.

The mercenary crashed into him, groping for his weapon as he burned into the man's stomach armour. He rolled with it, thinking to shove the man into the drop shaft, but then realising the stupidity of that now grav was out. Caster came in close, shooting the man in the back, but she got too close when he backhanded her and sent her crashing into the wall. A hand closed on Jonas's neck – a choke hold –

and he knew he could not burn through that armour fast enough. He would be unconscious in a moment or this one's comrades would be here in a moment. Then, on the edge of unconsciousness, he saw a human hand, skinless, the muscles white, reach round the man's visor. The visor turned white then collapsed –chainglass decoded – and the hand went inside and immediately turned bloody. The grip on his neck slackened and he kicked away to the sound of screaming. Now he saw Dr Giggles, hand deep inside, the man kicking and flailing then growing limp and discarded in a slew of blood, minced flesh and shattered bone sketched across the air.

The two others crowded in at the end of the corridor and bead blasts swept the bloody debris from the air. Jonas felt impact after impact on his suit as Caster grabbed his arm and propelled them both towards the drop shaft. He had time to glance back and see Giggles bounce off the wall and slam into the approaching figures – a weird shrieking sound penetrating. In the shaft he got control of his limbs again, realised that despite what had happened he had at least retained his sidearm. Caster, he saw, had lost her pulse rifle. They started to go down but in dim lights below saw another figure enter the shaft, so climbed quickly. A figure appeared above and bead blasts hissed through the air.

'Here!' Caster moved down past him, pulled a lever freeing a hatch to a maintenance bot tunnel. She still had access to the station map – or at least he hoped so.

'What the hell just happened?' he asked as they scrambled through the tunnel.

'I have no fucking idea,' she replied.

They exited into another shaft and went up. He didn't need a map to tell him that the next corridor took them to the one the mercenaries had come along. A body tumbling past, its armour torn up like a descaled fish, confirmed this. Weapons fire flashed in the escape pod corridor and looking round the corner they saw Giggles up against the ceiling wrapped around another mercenary and steadily tearing away armour. They started to go in the other direction, but two more mercenaries came stepping towards them on gecko stick. As they fled down the only tunnel available Jonas grimaced at their previous thought about fighting to the pod or dying in the process. Actually coming face to face with people in power armour had a stimulating effect. They passed a turning, but then another figure appeared ahead and they backed up and took it. More turnings, more figures appearing.

'This is directed,' Caster gasped. 'We're being herded.'

'We'll try for an airlock,' Jonas said. 'Maybe we can get clear in time. Maybe there someone out there...'

Caster just gave him a blank look.

Figures behind again, side routes blocked, and then they came out, sailing over a railed gangway into a small chamber packed all around with tangled machinery. Some kind of nexus – maybe something to do with the engines or other ship machines. Even as they sailed out to catch one of the looped skeins of optics, Jonas realised they had arrived precisely where someone wanted them to arrive. Caster jerked backwards from him, shuddering through the air with electric discharges crawling over her suit. He reached for his sidearm and was just searching for someone to shoot when the second shot hit him. As he shuddered and jerked through the air he saw Ganzen, propelling himself up from another gangway, and then the rest of his mercenaries coming in.

He and Caster drifted through the air. Whatever he had hit them with left them weak as if beaten, but had not rendered them unconscious. With a suit steering jet Ganzen slowed to hover before him then moved in close, pulling the sidearm from his hand and tucking it in his belt.

'So what did you do to Dr Giggles?'

The question sounded utterly reasonable, but the vicious anger written in Ganzen's expression overrode that. Jonas coughed, tried to get his voice working.

'No... thing,' he finally managed.

'So you did it.' He had turned his attention to Caster. 'You will tell me the hack you used or things will start to get really bad for you.'

'Like they aren't going to anyway.'

Jonas understood Giggles must still be operating, but even if the robot was he could not see it going up against the hardware in this chamber and surviving.

'There is that,' said Ganzen. He jetted closer, grabbing Caster's suit then slicing something down the front, splitting it open. She managed a weak yell and beads of blood floated through the air. He then reached over and snared Jonas, who now saw the short vibro-blade. He felt the hot slice of it down his front but, by the length of the blade knew this had not been to kill, merely to open their suits. Pushing back, Ganzen pulled a bead blast stun gun from his belt. Jonas began trying to force some movement into his limbs. He managed to reach up and press the control to open his visor and hood.

'What do you want with us now?' he asked, just to say anything, just to delay the man from using that weapon.

'What do you think I want?' said Ganzen. 'You've fucked my operation here. The world of pain you are going to enter when we're away from here is going to be legendary. I may let you die. In a few years.'

Jonas groped in the pocket of his envirosuit. Ganzen was watching him closely so he didn't try to hide what he was doing. He simply took out his aug, raised it to the socket in his skull and plugged it in.

'Those agents on Moloch Three aren't going to help you,' the man said.

The lights crashed on in his skull – the fractals forever folding into each other. He pushed for connection and the broken crystal patterns seem to explode out of his skull into his surroundings. Maybe he was calling his own death, maybe not, but he was definitely calling. The patterns shifted, bringing the mercenaries and Ganzen into relief, highlighted. He just thought about their situation here, about dying and pain and what lay in store for them, packing as much detail into the narrative as possible, hoping for something to get through. He felt sure of an acknowledgement, and a weird hissing delight in purpose. The patterns folded again and retreated into his mind – a whirling core.

'No, they won't help me,' he said to Ganzen. 'But maybe something will.'

'The fuck,' said Ganzen. He looked around. A keening teeth-aching vibration had started up and everything seemed to distort. Light flashed and one of the mercenaries simply exploded as a lightning-bright beam stabbed through him, straight across the chamber to nail another one of them. The thing then cut across, slicing through machinery in a fog of vaporised metal, chopped another in half, then flickered out. Angle of firing difficult, Jonas understood, as the patterns ground their way into his mind. A moment later the pink wall of energy slammed in from the side. Hurled mercenaries and debris across the chamber, picked up

Ganzen, Jonas and Caster too and flattened them against the far wall. Then the hooder exploded into view.

Those of the mercenaries that could, opened fire on it, but their shots just disappeared into a shimmering surface passing down its length. Jonas felt its playfulness as it coiled, smacked its tail into one of them and smeared him across twenty feet of wall. It reached down and grabbed another in its hood, peeled him as if he was being run through a lathe, then discarded him skinless and screaming.

You are cruel, Jonas thought.

Seemingly in response to that, the bright beam stabbed out once, twice and turned two more to burning fragments. Then Ganzen was on him, pulse gun jammed up under his chin.

'Stop it! Make it stop!'

The beam flickered and flashed again and the last of those in the chamber who had not managed to flee became drifting clouds of burning debris.

'I'll burn your fucking face off!'

Jonas hiccupped a laugh, then found it difficult to stop. The man pressed closer to him as the hood rose up before them, as if proximity might save him. Jonas felt the trigger go down and just didn't really care, but nothing happened. The gun tumbled away and Ganzen pulled the vibro-knife, blade extending, then he just jerked away from Jonas, drifting back towards that hood, kicking and stabbing at the air. The hooder closed its sickle limbs around him and took him down.

'We're too… late,' said Caster.

He looked over at her. She pushed herself away from the wall, reached up and opened her visor and helmet. Dark circles round her eyes and blood on her lips.

'The hooder… the energies it used. Moloch Three has fired that missile,' she told him.

Jonas pushed away too and caught hold of her arm. He looked down at the hooder where it had pinned Ganzen, the man kicking and screaming as the thing did what hooders did. It had responded to him calling it cruel and now he felt sure it was responding to his feelings about Ganzen, and killing the man slowly.

'Send detail on that to my aug,' he said.

She blinked and he certainly felt something arrive, though it dissolved in the swirling patterns in his mind before he could grasp it. He didn't know if it would do them any good, but he had to try.

The hooder abruptly jerked up, sending Ganzen tumbling across the chamber. He was making a horrible gobbling sound. The thing had stripped him down – his ribs and the musculature of his face exposed, a thread of intestine trailing him. The creature swung up towards them and Jonas wondered if, time being limited, it intended to give them their portion of pain. He felt a force grab him and tow him out into the centre of the chamber with Caster beside him. The hood of the creature came up close to them and that force pushed them together, even rearranged their limbs so they were wrapped around each other. Then its body coiled in all around them, enclosing them in a sphere consisting of segments and legs and the underside of its hood facing in, only a few feet away from them. He saw through gaps between the coils of its body, but as through distorting glass for some kind of energy field shimmered there. He could still see Ganzen kicking weakly through the air, then everything whited out. A moment later came a wrench, light glaring in so brightly he could feel it burning his face. He turned away, the wrench becoming a deep twist he felt in his bones, and at last recognised as a sensation he had felt many times before when a space ship dropped into U-space. The glare waned and he looked out again and saw that somehow they were surfing a wave of fire and debris out into vacuum. Then they slid beyond it and now he could see Moloch Three in the distance and the huge explosion nearby. The ball of fire expanded outwards, filled with chunks of debris and molten materials, then it stuttered to a halt and collapsed back, growing ever brighter as it collapsed down the intense gravity slope the imploder had created. The bright point then exploded again – a fusion blast expanding another ball of fire, but this one consisting only of disassociated atoms and hard radiation.

'And that's the *Fist* gone,' said Caster.

Her face was close to his, he felt her breath on his cheek.

'And now what?' he wondered, unable to feel much emotion now, overloaded.

The hooder began to uncoil around them and his apparent lack of care quickly faded. Though it had contained air around them, vacuum lay beyond and Ganzen had split open both of their envirosuits. In his mind the patterns kept shifting as if the thing was talking to him, but the language meant nothing. Abruptly the loosening sphere rolled, bringing an object into view: a simple bullet shape, thrusters burning at the back and that went out even as he saw them. The hooder descended towards it and thumped against its side, rolled around to bring and airlock into view between its coils.

'I'm struggling to believe this,' said Caster, as the force holding them together came off and they pushed apart.

She kicked against the hooder's body to send her to the airlock and worked the touch panel. A moment later Jonas followed her. He caught hold of the back of her suit as she opened the outer door. From there he looked back into the underside of the creature's hood, at those columns of red eyes and in his mind the patterns shifted, then began folding back into each other and winking out. Perhaps he was anthropomorphising the feeling of disappointment coming through and the feeling that its attention was turning away from him, reaching out elsewhere, searching.

He followed Caster into the airlock. They pulled the door closed and sealed it. His ears popped as pressure came up to standard. They pulled close together to peer through the narrow chainglass window as the hooder rolled away from the escape pod and uncoiled further. It straightened up then writhed across vacuum as if its feet had some purchase on nothing, waves of light ran down its body and it seemed to stretch out to infinity, walking across space, then disappeared in a pink flash.

'Where has it gone?' Caster asked.

Without a doubt Jonas replied, 'In search of its real masters. It won't find them.'

They turned to the inner door where she worked the controls. It would be crowded in the pod, but the journey back to Moloch Three was short. There, he had no doubt, the Polity agents would grab the both of them. They would face lengthy interrogations about these events, and probably some kind of punishment.

But they were alive, so there was that.

Also from NewCon Press

London Centric – Edited by Ian Whates

Future Tales of London. **Neal Asher, Mike Carey, Geoff Ryman, Aliette de Bodard, Dave Hutchinson, Aliya Whiteley, Stewart Hotston** and more. Militant A.I.s, virtual realities, augmented realities and alternative realities; a city where murderers stalk the streets, where drug lords rule from the shadows, and where large sections of the population are locked in time stasis, but where tea is still sipped in cafés on the corner and the past still resonates with the future...

Ivory's Story – Eugen Bacon

In the streets of Sydney a killer stalks the night, slaughtering and mutilating innocents. The victims seem unconnected, yet Investigating Officer Ivory Tembo is convinced the killings are sar from random. The case soon leads Ivory into places she never imagined. In order to stop the killings and save the life of the man she loves, she must reach deep into her past, uncover secrets of her heritage, break a demon's curse, and somehow unify two worlds.

Dark Harvest – Cat Sparks

Award-winning author Cat Sparks writes science fiction with a distinct Australian flavour – stories steeped in the desperate anarchy of Mad Max futures, redolent with scorching sun and the harshness of desert sands, but her narratives reach deeper than that. In her tales of ordinary people adapting to post-apocalyptic futures, she casts a light on what it means to be human; the good and the bad, the noble and the shameful.

Frequencies of Existence – Andrew Hook

Andrew Hook sees the world through a different lens. He takes often mundane things and coaxes the reader to find strangeness, beauty, and horror in their form; he colours the world in surreal shades and leads the reader down discomforting paths where nothing is quite as it should be. *Frequencies of Existence* features twenty-four of his finest stories, including four that are original to this collection.

www.newconpress.co.uk

CPSIA information can be obtained
at www.ICGtesting.com
Printed in the USA
BVHW071358231220
596343BV00001B/6